ATRAVESAR
To Go Through This

C.E. Ostra

Amapolaris Press

This is a work of fiction. Names, characters, places and incidents either are products of the author's imagination or are used fictitiously. Any resemblance to actual events or locales or persons, living or dead, is entirely coincidental.

ISBN 978-0-9895477-4-1

Typeset by Amapolaris Press
Cover design by J.K. McGann

Printed in the United States of America

If we treat people as they are, we make them worse.
If we treat people as they ought to be, we help
them become what they are capable of becoming.

- Johann Wolfgang Von Goethe

Give yourself a try.

- The 1975

▭► Prologue ◄▭

At the edge of a copse of cottonwoods, a lanky young man leans against a sturdy brown trunk, gazing gloomily out over ripe rows of corn and squash. August heat blankets the river valley; clouds sail by under a turquoise dome of sky, skimming the ridge of dun hills along the river. But in the shadow of the trees he shivers. An ache ghosts his bones and there's a twinge of queasiness in his gut, a constant hum of discomfort that drains even this idyllic scene of color and joy.

Mara's cut his dosage down, to *nada*.

He takes a deep drag off his smoke and shuffles restlessly, ducking down a head of dark, unruly, white-shot hair to pluck at a loose thread on the tunic he wears over patched pants. Irritably, he snaps it free.

How she expects me to heal when I feel like shit –

For well over a year he's been tending to the needs of

everyone in the camp: from toothaches to snake bites, broken bones to flu to parasites. Not to mention all the time spent transfiguring food and water supplies. For a while he was the sole option for all prana-related needs.

At this point though, more people can handle the basics on their own. Out among the stalks and vines several figures glide, pausing here and there to apply hands-on pranaic energy to keep the crops free from any taint of old world contamination. This is the same kind of transfiguration that he was taught to do as a child in the ranchos, and he's been busy passing the knowledge on to anyone who wants to learn. A few have even shown some real healing talent. True, it's not the near-miraculous ability that Lang possesses.

But it's enough that she could cut me a break.

He exhales a cloud, throat constricting.

For months he'd been doing fine on an eighth of a dropper a day, just enough to smooth out the worst of the edges. He thought they'd finally reached a permanent accommodation. He's not a mess, not at all, nowhere near where he was a year ago. But last week Mara had made it very clear; the ultimate goal wasn't to reach some kind of stasis, it was to wean him off entirely.

And so she had.

Red-faced, he'd begged her to leave it be. There was no reason for him to have to be one hundred percent Class E-free. He was fine, he was stable.

It was no use.

'You'll adjust,' she'd said, lips a tight line.

But it's been a week now and there's no sign of that happening.

ATRAVESAR – TO GO THROUGH THIS

Although the CERS sickness was short-lived and relatively mild due to how little he'd been taking before she cut him off, a general malaise lingers – one that all the transing in the world can't seem to touch. He's been skulking around the camp like a kicked dog, smoking through his stock of dried hemp and looking for any distraction. Yesterday he even tried to get drunk, though the one bottle of cider hadn't gone very far. He'd drunk it as fast as he could, but despite his best efforts his feet had remained firmly, maddeningly on Earth.

Unlike some people, he thinks, before tamping that line of thought back down.

Like fusing, Celan is another subject he's been trying very hard to avoid. Because it's been seventeen months (and six days) since she left, and eighteen months was how long she said she'd be gone – off on a quest to join up with some kind of council of galactic elders. Sometimes it doesn't even seem real. Like he imagined the whole thing. That's what Mara's always thought, and sometimes in Lang's darkest moments he's scared she might be right.

So thank Madre for Brophy. Because he was there when Celan left, another witness who saw the whole thing – the Plejarans, the ship – and he's never wavered in his belief for a second.

'She'll be back,' his friend keeps saying, 'don't worry.'

But he does. Constantly. So even a tiny fuse would go a long way towards soothing some of that stress.

Instead, I get this shit.

Sighing, he stubs out the last of the smoke and straightens, trying to stretch some of the tightness out of his back.

"Hey, güey!"

Lang turns to see a tall, broad-shouldered form tramping through the bosque – faded blue braids bobbing above a rugged, yet affable face; Brophy is about the only person he could actually deal with right now.

"Astral lesson?" Brophy says.

"Not in the mood."

"Venga ya. Don't be like that. It'll get better."

"Like you know."

"You know I do."

"No," Lang says. "You don't. You had some miracle cure, remember? Life flashed before your eyes? 'Boom! No más Class E?' You never had to deal with this…torture."

"Now you're just being dramatic."

"No," Lang says. "I'm not."

A beat passes.

"Mira," Brophy says. "I'm sorry, OK? I know she's being a little harsh."

"A little? Serio? And it's not like I'm the only one! I don't see her cutting Sig off."

"Sig's got Zeeb. She's not gonna get between that."

"Yeah," Lang says dryly. "I know."

Brophy dips his head, runs a hand over his braids. "You want me to talk to her?"

Lang grimaces. That's all he needs – to look like he's lobbying Mara's man behind her back. That kind of thing's not going to win him any favors.

"Never mind," he mutters.

But if Brophy really feels bad…

"You think maybe you could, y'know, *lend* me a transfer? Not permanently," he adds, "just once in a while. Zeeb has all those extras everyone turned in. He's never gonna notice." He risks a quick, hopeful glance at his friend's face.

"Can't," Brophy says. "You know that. I'm sorry," he appends, noting Lang's dismay.

Lang sighs. "I know. It's not your fault. I know she has a point. Or had one anyway, in the beginning. I mean, you almost died. And it was all my fault."

"Not really. We were all pretty fucked up for a while there."

This last is true enough. When they first set up camp here – a small crowd of former denizens of Transway in the first flush of exile from the environs of the city of Albakirk – everyone had gone kind of crazy. Zeeb and his former crew were well-organized and showed up in a small flotilla of rollers loaded with food, clothing, and kitchen sink's worth of other salvaged necessities, including multiple cases of booze poached from wherever they could find it.

Those were strange days. Lang wasn't drinking much (except for that one night he doesn't like to think about) but he more than made up for it with fusing. For him, that time is like a walking dream. Up until the moment that Brophy fell off a roof and broke his back, lying there in terrible pain and possibly dying until the others ferreted Lang out from one of his hidey holes and gave him a hefty dose of Class D to get him on his feet. He'd managed to heal Brophy, but not with much time to spare.

And Mara's never going to let him forget it.

"You know I was drunk off my ass up on that roof," Brophy says.

"Yeah, I guess."

"And things are different now." He gestures at the figures

in the fields.

"True," Lang says. "But if anything had happened to you –"

A bolt of pain shoots through him at the thought, so deep he winces.

"But nothing did," Brophy says. "And no matter what your condition's been you've still helped a lot of people. Remember those hornets? That giant nest? That was around the same time. They almost swarmed us until you transed 'em back in. Think you gave those fuckers a contact high."

Lang finally cracks a grin.

"Hey," his friend says. "Forget the astral. Let's go for a swim instead."

Lang swallows hard. Shivery as he is, the water always feels good. Sometimes he forgets about the things that make him feel better, other than the fuse.

"Sure," he says, lamely adding, "race you."

Brophy laughs, then they turn and trot off down the dusty path towards the best swimming spot on the river.

1

"OOOuuuuhhhOOOH."
"OOOOOOOOOOOOOOOzzzzBVBVBahh."
"OOOuuuuhhhOOOH."

Celan Mairs sighs, twisting the quantum band round and round on her finger as the coven of WDM,K*DU wibbles on about the rogue planet currently approaching theirs somewhere in the Scutum-Centaurus Arm of the Milky Way. She's not sure 'wibble' is the right word for their particular ululations, but it was the first that came to mind. 'Coven,' however, fits perfectly – the shell-like protrusions that protect the soft meat of their eel-like heads are shaped exactly like the witches' hats in an old world picture book she'd loved as a kid.

She's sure that they use a different word to define a group of themselves, but if there's one thing she's learned over the past seventeen months it is that transentience is not an exact science. It's a far trickier business than it first seemed back when she was chatting on a mesa with Chan, Ness, and Ree.

"OOOOOOOOOOOOOOzzzzBVBVBahh."

She bites her lip, trying to will herself into the state of relaxed concentration necessary for understanding. It was so much easier with the Plejarans, who, due to their physiological and linguistic similarities to Madrens, turned out to be the beings that it was naturally easiest for her communicate with. It's far simpler to transentiate actual words spoken by recognizable mouths than howls, hums, chemical signatures, or waving tentacles that may not even be obvious attempts to communicate. Bur she hasn't seen Chan, Ness, and Ree in over a year now. The triune had been sent off on some kind of mission shortly after bringing her to the K'Shiran Convention. They're due back soon to facilitate her return to Terra Madre (aka Earth, a name that was already officially on record as referring to a moon in the Cllii system), but that's not going to leave a lot of time for them to work with her on actually getting the damn thing to *work*. She twists the band again, in increasing frustration, and shuffles impatiently under her desk.

She can do simple things with it – activate the Suster, create new holos, or upload information about her species and homeworld into the Convention's formidable infobanks – but as far as any kind of suitably impressive demonstration is concerned she's dead in the water. And no one else seems to be able (or willing) to help. It is true that quantum bands are a tricky business as well – the methodology and degree of energy manipulation required to make one function vary as widely from species to species as the appendages to which they are attached. But surely someone could assist her.

It can do more; she knows it can – maybe not clean the entire Earth in one swoop, or power a rocket to Mars, but more than she's been shown how to do so far. What are they waiting for? Is she really about to head home with nothing to show for all of this?

"Madren Celanmairs?" The querulous chirp resolves into the sound of her formal address, and Celan starts out of her ruminations to see the holo of Ech'unu Wehoo peering at her owlishly; a literal description, as the being's big round eyes, feathered face, and tiny tufted ears cause him to more than resemble that particular Madren bird. These features, combined with his humanoid body, lend him the look of some ancient old-world hieroglyphic come to life.

"Yes?" she replies, tentative. It's been ages since anyone has called on her in one of these discussions. She's gotten used to just keeping her head down and doing whatever minor tasks they throw her way. But Wehoo is famous for putting those Convention members who he deems not to be paying the appropriate amount of attention on the spot.

Another chirp. "What is your advice on the matter?"

"Well…" she says, frantically calling up some specs via the knowledge implant all Convention members receive upon arrival. Privately, she finds it more than a little creepy, like a second brain in her head. She'd be far more comfortable with a trusty server in her hand, but at the moment fast recall is crucial. Maybe not fast enough, though; especially when one *hasn't* been paying attention.

Celan clears her throat, stalling for time as she refreshes her memory. The Convention is once again deep into a discussion of possible solutions to the plight of the WDM,K*DU, a transentient (though not very technologically savvy), RCN (as in radially symmetrical, carbon-based, nitrogen-breathing) species inhabiting a moon of the fourth world out from a K class star in a seven-world system. Actually two moons if you count the one inhabited by the VDM,K*DI. But VDM,K*DI are not transentient and the WDM,K*DU regard them with a sort of noblesse oblige as an animal version of their own species, even though the physical differences between the two are almost nonexistent (at least as far as Celan can tell – she's never met a VDM,K*DI, but she's seen images).

The WDM,K*DU moon, the name of which, when verbalized, sonically resembles a cross between a coyote howl and a dying engine (Celan thinks of it as Aroooodzz) is tidally locked to a gas giant that it orbits once every sixteen Madren days at a speed of 7.890 km/s. That orbital period is what the WDM,K*DU call a day. Their year, which consists of the orbit of the gas giant and its attendant moons around the K class star, is roughly equivalent to fifteen Madren ones; and their life expectancy is one hundred of these years. So although the rogue planet is still five hundred years out in Madren time, it's only a few decades to them. Thus, a fairly urgent problem.

The first option in this kind of situation is to try to change the trajectory of the rogue without sending it toward any other inhabited system. A difficult process, but one that's preferable to relocation; there is a prohibition against resettling a species in any system containing conscious life that is not yet transentient, and thus unable to consent to receiving new neighbors (and also, if sufficiently technologically advanced, highly likely to attack any 'alien invaders'). And even without these complications, finding a suitable match to an imperiled species' native planet is close to impossible. Planetforming and genetic engineering can go a long way toward aligning a species with a new environment but there are other factors that present more serious challenges. Wholesale resettlement is always a last resort unless the match is one-in-a-million.

Celan had learned all of this soon after her arrival at the Convention, when she'd offered the WDM,K*DU one of the moons of Jupiter in a splashy gesture of goodwill. Out of nearly eighty she figured they were bound to find something. But even the closest match, Ganymede (tidally locked, magnetic field, subsurface ocean), had the problem that its rotational period around Jupiter would shorten the WDM,K*DU days by half. This, along with the faster orbital speed, was shown in simulations to cause severe mental decompensation over time. A lot can be done with planetforming, but it's impossible to change orbit and rotation without the risk of serious unintended consequences for the system as a whole. So Ganymede was relegated to a kind of Plan D – "if all else fails" status.

She had felt a little insulted by this at the time. And now, with Wehoo fully glowering at her she feels more than a little stupid too. Her palms dampen and she swallows, but only within the privacy of her Dyson cell. Her holo in the Convention hall remains the picture of calm even as she's starting to wish she could drop down a wormhole and disappear.

Wormhole...disappear...that's it!

The main problem with the rogue is that its large size and density have made its trajectory extremely difficult to alter more than a few degrees. And the WDM,K*DU's system is spread out enough to be effected by its gravitational pull unless it is removed from the area entirely.

She clears her throat again, but from a place of introducing of an idea instead as a stalling tactic. "What about a wormhole?"

Wehoo cocks his head, seeming to not have heard right. Celan tries again, smoothing out her speech into a kind of sing-song; not real singing like Cyrinda and Taegh used to do, but a kind of recitative that she's found helpful in facilitating other species' understanding of the apparently very staccato nature of Madren communication.

"I mean, there must be a wormhole near the WDM,K*DU system or the Convention wouldn't have been able to transport them here."

Wormholes, the tentacle-like filaments woven throughout the galaxy, are how the convention members manage to keep one foot in their system's current time even as they meet in a particular space that is operating in another. Many of them move in predictable cycles and can be used to help facilitate the movements of large objects, such as spacecraft.

"Yes," Wehoo allows. "But there is only one that has a stable cycle."

"But you only need one, right?" Celan says, sitting up straighter. "That's how it works – we map the cycles and use them to jump from hole to hole until we come out where and when we want. Like ocean currents. Well," she amends, "for those of us that have oceans."

Her view of the Convention hall draws back to reveal a mélange of various holoform sensory appendages now solely focused on her.

She swallows reflexively and continues. "So why not knock the rogue down that stable wormhole, wait for it on the other side, and then knock it down another stable one? Like a pinball – keep it in play until we find a hole that comes out in the middle of nowhere where it's not going to bother anyone."

She's not quite sure the visual analogy will translate, but at least some of the gathered beings seem to find the idea intriguing. There are scattered signs of acknowledgment.

"That is quite...creative, Madren Celanmairs," Wehoo says. He still looks stern but those words from him are high praise; the Ech'unu are not known for their sarcasm.

"We will need to examine this possibility further," he continues. "Would you be content to serve as director of this inquiry?"

Celan beams. Since the Ganymede study, she's had nothing but the paltriest of roles to play in any formal inquiries. And even her role in Ganymede was just a formality, a nod to the fact that she was the system representative. Finally, she'll get to do something important.

"Claro," she says.

The rest of the meeting passes in a blur of planning, subcommittee forming, and delegation. By the time Celan turns off her holo and takes a breath her brain is running a million miles an hour. But it feels good. It's been a while since she's felt so involved; kind of like how it used to be back in the day, with her old pod in Albakirk when they were trying to solve a particularly knotty problem.

She marvels once again at just how many worlds away from that whole life she is now as she stands and stretches, waving her band at the Sustenancer and ordering up a thick, algal-protein-infused strawberry-flavored shake. The Suster works with her band to provide her with complex nourishment and can replicate almost any food she can think of, but of late her tastes have been simple. When the shake appears in the window, Celan picks it up and carries it over to a porthole, taking in the starry vista as she sips, musing:

Shariah, Bryan, Bev…wonder what they're all up to now? Probably deep in En training. They'd never believe all this in a million years.

She has a sudden pang to see them again. To see them and explain. To tell them what really happened. That she didn't try to destroy Albakirk; that she and Lang had actually saved them. But more than that, she just wants to talk to somebody *human*. Because as happy as she is about her wormhole idea and finally getting to direct an inquiry, it all feels kind of empty without anyone to share it with. This whole adventure isn't quite what she thought it'd be like based on the old world novels and screeners she grew up with – no hanging out at the space station bar sharing gargleblasters and lively interpersonal drama.

Because only species of similar physiology, like Madrens and Plejarans, can spend long periods of time in each other's physical space. The biofilm protects against any swapping of infectious organisms (though most viruses and bacteria are adapted to their host systems only and are unlikely to do someone from an off-world ecosystem any harm), but that's the least of the issues. It's no simple matter to have a species adapted to 9.807 m/s^2 of gravity, an approximate 80/20 atmospheric mix of nitrogen to oxygen, and an average temperature of 16 C mix with one that mostly breathes argon, lives at 19.807 m/s^2 gravity, and thinks -50 C is a balmy day. That is why most cross-species congregating only happens in holoform.

It was different when Chan, Ness, and Ree were here. They'd introduced her around, brought her to social events (mostly holoform but occasionally real); there are endless options on the main station – lectures, demonstrations, and cultural exchanges. When the Plejarans had first left, she'd been happy to continue to take advantage of these (there's nothing quite like an Orofuchan ballet). But at some point, it all started to blur together into what felt like some long, strange dream. Plenty of species were pleasant to chat and spend occasional time with, but there was no one with whom she really felt a connection.

But space is supposed to be lonely; that's what all the old songs say. And it won't be long now. She'll be home soon and once everyone finds out where she's been and what she's been doing they'll all want to talk to her. She'll have so much interaction she'll probably be ready to hole up and hide again within a week.

Meanwhile, there are certain consolations.

Celan tips back the last of the shake and returns its empty container to the Suster, then flops into a large, overstuffed recliner. Tucking her legs up, she slips a hand into the pocket of her soft, fleecy, sleepwear-like pants and draws out the small, cool vial tucked inside.

She waves the band to set a countdown in her chamber – three minutes to zero-G. It'll hit right about the same time the fuse does and last a good half-hour before gravity gradually returns to baseline and sets her gently back on solid ground...or chair, or floor, or bed as the case may be.

She doesn't do this particular trick very often (the fuse is *medicine*), but after her success with the inquiry she feels she's earned a treat.

The mix she's got in the transfer right now is a 10:1 ratio of Class E to D. Enough E to maximize the calm, euphoric effect combined with just enough D to compensate for the lowered heart rate due to the effects of E in zero-G.

She unscrews the cap and draws some pearly fluid up into the dropper.

At this point, she's got it down to a science.

2

"No need for the third degree, my dear. Really. There's nothing going on." The woman across the table grins, trying for winsomeness and, in Mara Brees' opinion, failing miserably.

They've been back and forth on this issue for months and she's sick of it; Maddy knows how she feels and this putana crap needs to stop. Ahora. Her opinion's not going to change.

But some people never learn.

"Claro," Mara says briskly. "That's why Alex and Leo were at each other's throats the other night –"

"Oh, it wasn't that bad. Just a silly little spat. A misunderstanding. We worked it all out."

"I'm sure."

Maddy purses her plush lips into a moue. "You know how it is – people get a little liquor in them, get their hackles up –"

11

"Oh I do. Créame. Which is why I don't want to be giving them shit to fight over. Everyone's got what they need here – food, shelter. They don't need to be fighting over who's ass is whose. There's no reason to start all that Transway shit again."

"'That Transway shit', as you so charmingly refer to it, is just as necessary a human function as eating and sleeping. It provides an outlet for energy that might otherwise be directed unproductively."

"People can direct their energy wherever they feel like it. Whenever they want. Wherever. For free. No one's stopping them." Mara raps knuckles against the top of the wooden picnic table for emphasis, inhaling the aroma of sautéed onion wafting from the kitchen at the back of the empty dining hall. "People want to fuck? They fuck," she continues. "They don't need some special place to do it in. Or some special ass on reserve."

But Maddy is shaking her head, with that maddening air of condescension that irks Mara nearly as much as her high-toned speech. "That can cause a lot of problems," the woman says, one slim hand smoothing her grey-blonde, pinned-up braids. "People intoxicated. Not knowing what they're consenting to. With my girls, back on Transway, there was never a question."

I'll bet.

"Everyone clean and over eighteen," Mara says, parroting the well-worn Maddy's motto with more than a dollop of sarcasm. "We know."

Dark eyes narrow. "Well, you're lucky enough to have a partner, Mara. So maybe you don't remember what it's like to

12

be frustrated."

Mara's stomach sours, thinking on the last time she and Brophy…honestly, she can't even begin to recall. But she's been busy. Running a whole camp is a lot bigger responsibility than running a wayvern kitchen. Sometimes she's up all night thinking, planning, getting shit done. She doesn't have time for a lot of nonsense.

Plus, Brophy's been spending so much time with –

"Please," she says, neatly chopping off that last line of thought. "People aren't running around *assaulting* each other. They don't need professionals to help keep them in line. And what are the girls even getting out of it anyway? It's not like the old days when they got to sit their fancy little asses around and eat cake while the rest of us actually worked for a living."

"If you think it's not work maybe it *has* been a while."

Mara takes a deep breath, refusing to rise to the bait. "Like I said – they're not even getting anything out of it besides… what? Some chores done? A few small favors?"

Her opponent blinks, the picture of innocence. "I don't know what you're talking about. Like I said, nothing's going on. As you so astutely said, if people want to fuck, they fuck. I don't see what you or I can do about it."

"Bullshit!" Mara says, slapping a palm on the table. "You're running those girls, Maddy. You know it and I know it. And if you want your people to stay in this camp it needs to stop. Because I make the rules here. And I say this is not Transway. No más funtime. This is survival."

Her trump card; no one's going to survive for very long outside the camp without anyone to trans the water and fix their booboos. And Maddy has no healers. The one girl she had with any of that kind of talent, Willa, has been firmly under Mara's thumb ever since she hooked up with Taryn, former Tosh's bartender and one of Mara's oldest friends. Maddy let Willa slip through her fingers.

Big mistake.

And she knows it. The woman is silent for a few beats, appraising Mara coolly. "Rules," she finally says. "Yes. You're good at those, aren't you?"

"Have to be."

"Transfers all locked down…"

Mara's eyes roll skyward, then dart around the barn-like room, calculating. In a few hours the long tables will be full of people eating and drinking. All two hundred and forty seven of them. There'll be food to serve and dishes to wash after. Tables to wipe. Floors to sweep. Stuff to compost. Of course, she won't be doing it all herself. But she has to supervise.

So.

"Are you going anywhere with this, Maddy? I've got *work* to do."

"Just saying, not everyone seems too happy with the rules these days."

"Like who? Lang?" Mara waves a hand, dismissive. "He always gets bitchy after a cut. He'll be fine."

"Really?"

"And because of the *rules* he's a hundred percent clean now. Down to nada."

"How nice for him."

"Yeah," Mara says, getting to her feet to indicate that this discussion is over. "It is."

"Hope it stays that way. For his sake, of course. Poor thing.

You know how desperate Class Es can get."

Something in Maddy's tone prickles the back of Mara's neck. "It better," she says. "Because if I find out anyone's got a transfer hidden somewhere – "

"You'll what? Destierra them?" A throaty chuckle. "Careful with that. They might end up taking your best healer with them."

"Lang's not going anywhere."

"Maybe not," Maddy concedes. She rises, buxom form a full head taller, and eyes Mara slyly. "Maybe he's got something else keeping him happy these days. Something bigger than a transfer."

She chuckles again, and Mara's stomach drops. She knows what Maddy's insinuating. There've been subtle signs for a while now – the way Brophy looks at him; all the time they spend together. She'd hoped she was just being paranoid, because as far as she knows Lang's only ever been interested in girls. But that can change, and Brophy *is* very attractive. And if others are noticing too…

"Well," she says, in a voice like cracked ice. "I guess we'll see about that."

"Yes," Maddy replies as she strides to the exit. "We certainly shall."

TRAMPING BACK TOWARDS CAMP WITH the sun warm on his shoulders and damp hair cooling his neck Lang feels almost relaxed for the first time since his last fuse. The river path skirts the foot of a large hump of juniper-tufted hill before opening back out onto cropland; water burbles placidly on his left while on his right, Brophy chatters on, recounting

15

some ribald tale involving one of Maddy's girls and two of the more lascivious males. Lang doesn't really care about any of it, but he chuckles occasionally to let Brophy know he's paying attention.

After Lang's people (the former tenants and friends of Alamora and Casa del Oso and the staff of Tosh's wayvern), Maddy's group of former brothel workers is the second-largest contingent in what they've dubbed Camp Rinconada – a stretch of the Rio Grande gorge flanked by remnants of farms and orchards that had been taken back by nature after the collapse of the old world. But there remained good bones of many structures, some still semi-intact even after a century and a half of neglect, and various materials lying around to repurpose. Sometimes, it's almost like he's back home in the ranchos, though in some ways this is even better. It had been a relief to them all, even to those who'd spent their whole lives on Transway, to find such a well-favored spot.

But it's a lot of work. Everything – from water and soil to any foodstuffs caught or picked or foraged – has to be transfigured. Crops have to be irrigated, hand-pollinated, and protected from harm (rain, while helpful for growth, can also spread pollution so every storm requires hours of prana application afterwards). At least they *can* grow, though. If they hadn't, and if Mara hadn't saved all those seeds –

Lang shudders.

It's wilder up here than in the ranchos though. They've come across some strange creatures – mutant, misshapen – two-headed rattlers, overlarge spiders. Not to mention the gnarly nests of stinging insects. The elders had generations to cull such things back home, but here they still lurk. And the weather can pull some tricks as well. Last summer they nearly lost half the corn to a flash flood.

In general though, other than missing his family (now that they're a hundred miles away instead of a short hike) he's fine with where he's landed. Or he would be, if Celan were here.

And if Mara would cut him a break.

A muscle twinges between his shoulder blades and he shrugs, twisting around to try and keep it from tightening up again. Brophy's advised him to try to talk to Mara when she's in a good mood, and although that seems to be an increasingly rare occurrence these days he's willing to try; his friend had promised to let him know when it was a good time.

A hammer rings out, followed by a shout. Their path has turned away from the river and into a clutch of buildings composed of a haphazard mix of adobe, stone, new wood, and old metal, many still in various states of construction or renovation. He and Brophy approach the back of the big, barn-like dining hall, and are rounding the outside corner when a furious figure appears, scowling beneath faded pink bangs.

Mara. And this is obviously not a good time.

"Hey," Brophy says. "Que pas' querida?"

"You!" she thunders.

"What?" he says. "What'd I do?"

"Wasting time with *him*." She points accusingly at Lang. "What were you doing? Fusing?"

"Claro que no," Brophy says soothingly.

Loud as she is there's a catch to her voice like she's holding back tears.

"We went swimming," Lang says, dumbfounded. Mara's

not the teary-eyed type. "See?" He dips his head down for verification. "Our hair's still wet."

"Oh, I'm sure," she says, crossing arms in front of her chest and looking back and forth between them. "I'm sure it was great. I'm sure it was fucking amazing!"

"Uh, what – " Lang starts, but Brophy cuts him off, seeming to understand something he doesn't. "Nothing happened Mara," he says. "It's not like that. You know I love you."

"Right," she says. "Looks like I don't know shit these days."

And with that she turns and stalks off to the kitchen's side door, slamming it behind her.

Lang gapes in confusion. "What, does she think we're in *love* now? Maybe I'm not the one that needs to quit fusing."

"She's just freaked out," Brophy mutters. "It'll blow over."

"But why would she think that?"

Brophy is silent for a moment, scratching at the stubble on his chin. Gold-brown eyes flick over Lang's face like filtered sunlight on a forest floor. Then: "Back in the Fused Up! days before me and Mara got together I used to go with guys and girls too."

"Oh," Lang says. "But it's not like; you don't cheat on her – "

"No!"

"Then why is she so pissed off?"

"Because of Sig."

"What?" Lang reaches for the smoke pouch at his hip and quickly rolls one. "What happened with Sig?" He's definitely sensed some kind of weirdness amongst those three in the past but never had the nerve to ask what it was about. He strikes his flint and takes a long drag.

Brophy sighs. "When you were back in the ranchos that

year me and Sig started hanging out a lot. It was mostly a fusing thing; he was like the only one left. You were off being good and Raf was…"

He trails off and Lang shuffles uncomfortably. They don't talk about Raf very much. Sometimes Lang secretly pretends that his cousin's not really dead, that Raf is back in the ranchos with the family, happy and healthy. Sometimes he almost even believes it. He knows it's fucked up though, so he keeps it to himself.

"Anyway," Brophy continues, "Sig used to joke around about us being the perfect couple or whatever. At first Mara didn't care but then she started getting mad. And then he kind of made a play – "

"For you."

A nod. "But nothing happened. Sig's not my type."

"OK. But then why is she freaking out about me? She knows I love Celan. And I don't go around saying shit like that, even as a joke."

Brophy shrugs. "No sé, güey. She's just been real edgy lately. Like control freak out-of-control."

"Yeah," Lang says dryly. "I know."

A beat passes.

"So maybe you better go talk to her."

"Yeah," Brophy says. He starts off in the direction Mara went but halts after a few steps and turns, looking almost sheepish. "You're not mad, are you?"

"No," Lang says. "Claro que. Just do us all a favor and go talk her down."

Brophy grins. "Thanks."

"Yeah," Lang says, watching him go. He takes another long

drag and exhales, thoughtful. Because truth be told, there have been a few occasions when he's gotten a more-than-friendly vibe from his friend. But he never gave it much thought; as long as he's known them it's been Brophy-and-Mara. Period.

Just because he might be into guys, doesn't mean he's into your dumb ass. Then: *Cállate, stupid brain!*

Shaking his head, Lang takes a last puff, grinds the maize wrapper into the dust with the toe of his boot, and scuffs across the central plaza toward the healer's hut – a compact adobe structure topped with a slanted tin roof and set in a grove a few lengths back from the main bustle. His head is starting to pound and he just wants to lie down for a few hours. Fervently, he wishes he had some whiskey to help knock him out. Of course, a fuse would be even better. No chance of that now Mara thinks he's trying to steal her man.

He shakes his head. It would be funny if it wasn't so ridiculous, and if she didn't seem so upset. But maybe something else is bothering her. Maybe she was already upset and seeing them together set her off. Maybe Brophy will talk her down and everything will be fine.

He's still ruminating as he reaches the front door of the hut, which is slightly ajar and emitting ominous sounds of distress. His heart sinks; someone must be sick or hurt.

A glance through the cracked front window reveals his two healer-apprentices flanking a weeping woman seated on a bench, twisted and massively swollen foot propped on the chair in front of her. Sturdy, red-haired Taryn is attempting to minister to it, but every time her hands get anywhere near the injury the woman wails anew and she draws away. Wispy little Willa is trying to relax the patient, rubbing her back and speaking softly, but it doesn't seem to be doing much good. From the hideous angle of the injured foot, it looks like some kind of compound ankle fracture. No wonder they're having trouble.

Lang grimaces.

This is really going to take it out of him and he's running on fumes as it is. Not that it's his own energy he'll use to heal her; he'll call on the Universal prana for that. He's merely a channel. But the more sick, tired, and miserable he is the rougher the edges of that channel will be – each a barb for pain to catch on, for bits of the badness he's extracting to get stuck in him instead of being released into the ether. A bit of Class E would work wonders to remove those stubborn chunks. Without it he's in for a rough night.

He sighs as a small, unbidden, voice in his head says, 'Bet you would have learned to do it the right way if you hadn't quit 'scuela.'

Lang shuts his eyes tight as the rest of the litany of self-loathing commences: If he'd stayed at Pranascuela and listened to the elders. If he'd followed the Precepts; if he'd taken the blue robe; if he wasn't such an idiot. *If, if, if* – but there's no point in dwelling on what can't be fixed.

When he lifts his lids it's to find three faces bright with relief staring hopefully at him. So he arranges his features into the most reassuring expression he can muster and yanks open the door.

MARA BANGS A PAN DOWN on the kitchen stove a just little harder than necessary and right on cue Jaslene's baby Isaac starts to wail.

21

Someone shut that little shit up, she thinks, forcibly resisting the urge to slam it another half dozen times for good measure. But Jaslene reads Mara's tension immediately and scoots over to the basket on the table to take Isaac out into the hall.

Mara exhales. She likes kids well enough and Jaslene's is usually tolerable. Right now, however, her head is pounding, and a wave of exhaustion nearly knocks her off her feet. She needs a hit of D; and she's earned it. She was up half the night last night with Zeeb, Jae, and Alex trying to work out the logistics of a new irrigation system for next year's growing season. The one they have is functional enough but not perfect, especially since every drop has to be transed as well as delivered to the right spot.

Massive pain in the ass, but it has to be done. Keeping almost two hundred fifty people in two meals a day is no simple trick.

She takes a quick look around – Alex's broad back is turned, peeling potatoes, while skinny Effie stirs the pot of stew Jaslene abandoned, eyes carefully lowered – so Mara slips a hand into her pocket and palms the vial, heading for the solar-powered walk-in evaporative cooler. She needs to grab some stuff out of there anyway.

A blast of cold air hits her as she tugs open the door, welcome after the sweltering fug of the stoves, and the bang of Class D to her hip (she's never quite gotten the hang of transing burns and long sleeves are not practical in the kitchen in summertime) has the same effect – cooling the molten rage into something more abstract and manageable.

Mara licks her lips and crouches, reaching into the dank lower bins to pick some mushrooms, using her apron as a collection basket. The same water circulating through the cooler condenses down here to help feed them, and is also used to keep other perishables chilled. Before this room was rigged up, most of their rations were either cooked immediately or dried and reconstituted, so it's really opened up a lot of new menu options. All thanks to Brophy's skill with mechanics.

She sighs. Of course he'd come after her. And of course he'd kissed and hugged her and apologized profusely, swearing up and down that there was nothing between him and Lang and there never would be. But no matter what Brophy does or doesn't do about it that shine is there plain as day on his face. She could see it when they came around the corner – and see Lang doing his best Mr. Adorable and encouraging it.

That's how he plans to get around her. Brophy as good as admitted it when she'd informed him that if Lang was flirting with him the only thing he really wanted to get his hands on was a transfer: Her man had laughed, saying 'he already asked' and that he wasn't going to give him any and that Lang well knew it.

Pinche Class E prettyboy.

Mara grits her teeth and stands, apron clenched in one fist as she rummages through the bins on the upper shelves.

It's not worth it. *He's* not worth it.

'Not one minute's worry,' as her nana used to say about those deemed beneath her concern.

But she can't help it: Why do people keep falling for him like this?

Jaslene she could understand – back in the day the girl had nothing else going for her. Just a pudgy piece of Transway trash. No one else was interested; not Rafael, who had his pick of every litter, none of the Alamora guys or the del Oso crew. But she could be good fun, and so they let her hang around until the perfect mark showed up – Rafael's gangly cousin, fresh out of the ranchos and green as grass. Not much to look at at the time but he was in with the right crowd, helping out Zeeb so he had some chits, and he'd taken to fusing so thoroughly and immediately that Jaslene knew he wasn't going anywhere. She'd wanted in – a roof over her head, a permanent bed – and Lang had been her ticket.

Mara could respect that.

Even Celan Mairs, whether as part of a tech plot or as a fuser looking for someone to share her habit with (or a little of both), had had a reason for hooking up with him.

But Brophy? It makes her sick. Even if he wasn't her man it would.

Because Langton Shays is the *worst* – the kind of punk-ass bitch who whines about how much it huuurts and expects everyone to help him and save him because of his wonderful special specialness. Minus the healing shit he's as useless as they come.

He's the reason they're all in this mess to begin with!

Though it's not like Mara really misses Transway much. Even if their exile was totally his fault (which is debatable) it hasn't necessarily been a bad thing. It's given them a chance to start over. Do things right.

And it's not like she hates Class Es either. But with Brophy and his friends back in the day it was different. The techs and their tests, the rampant spread of fusing and its attendant hopelessness, all had caused a lot of their generation to grow up hard. Mara herself had been raised by her mother's mother, who passed when she was only fourteen. After that she was mostly on her own. Tio Nalo hooked her up with a job washing dishes at Eli's, but then drank himself to death within a couple years. Tio Mario was more stable; he was with Zeeb's mother, Lavinia, and they were getting by fine until some tech testing he'd done caught up with him. Mara had ended up moving in and supporting them all until Zeeb came of age and started raking in the transferon-trade chits.

And Brophy'd had it even worse. His mother, a popular server at Arlo's, was stabbed to death in front of him when he was just eight years old. He'd escaped the same fate by jumping out a window and running for help on a broken ankle. The Arlo's crew found the murderer and dealt with him (the man's body never was found) but Brophy had been left with no one, so they'd let him sleep in the storage room and do odd jobs until he was old enough to fend for himself.

Everyone who grew up on Transway had a story like that, or knew someone who did, so it was no surprise when people fell into fusing and some had a hard time getting out. (Or didn't, like Tomás). But Brophy she'd stuck by, even during his messiest days, because she loved him and could see his worth. He wasn't afraid of hard work and she knew he'd come correct in the end.

And she was right.

She always knew about people, and so she knows this damn well about Mr. Shays – healer or no, at the end of the day he's just another loser who'll do anything for another fucking fuse. Sure, he'd had a hard time with Rafael; they were all sad to see Raf go. She'd cried too! But that one hard death didn't give him a free pass to act tragic for the rest of his life, especially not around those who'd endured so much worse.

And it especially doesn't give him the right to play kissy-face with my man.

Releasing a few fistfuls of green onions into her apron-basket, Mara stands in front of the fan and lets the cool air wash over her until she can think of Lang's face without wanting to scream. It takes a few minutes, but when she pushes open the door into the kitchen everything, inside and out, is under control. Even baby Isaac is gurgling happily in his basket as Jaslene stirs the stew and Effie helps Alex peel potatoes. Mara moves to the chopping block, dumping out the produce and grabbing the biggest knife she can find. The first thwack of it against the wood is the sound of satisfaction itself.

Next bullshit Lang tries, it'll be his head on here.

3

"Shariah!"

Bryan's voice echoes faintly from somewhere across the plaza as the girl being addressed glances up from her server, tosses white-blonde hair over one sharp shoulder, and hurriedly looks down again. Boyfriend or no, she does not want him invading her quiet corner, and dragging his gang of idiots with him.

Chronies are the worst, she thinks.

It would be better by far if they kept their conspiracy theories to themselves and didn't embarrass friends and family by obsessively circling the plaza and making calculations on the angle of the sun, loudly insisting that the calendar is somehow off by three days and has been for at least a year. Everyone knows tech timekeeping is precise to the attosecond. But because some stupid crystals didn't shine in some stupid fountain on some stupid day they insist that the whole Chron system has been compromised.

Completely ridiculous. Shariah shakes her head; doesn't he care how silly he looks? Doesn't he want to be a Lead MechEn someday?

But then she sneaks a peek at him out of the corner of her eye and sighs. Tall and buff with that thatch of sandy hair, blue eyes, smooth dark skin – all perfectly styled. And the way he kisses, among other things. A thrill runs through her and she smiles despite herself.

How could Lana have ever turned that down?

A quick wince, and she adjusts her lissome form on the sleek, white bench like she's working out a kink from an old injury. The name still hurts.

But it's a bond she shares with Bryan, strong enough (when combined with the other things) to override even incipient Chronieness; both had been close friends of the infamous Lana Timanti. Daughter of Lead SocEn Theodore Timanti, Lana had been the target of an elaborate expro plot to destroy Albakirk. Led astray by Lang Shays, an evil fuser who warped her mind with transferson and made her do his bidding, she'd attempted to knock everyone out and give the expros full access to the city.

Shariah shudders.

It's not something she and Bryan discuss often, but every once in a while, late at night, curled up in bed in his cozy single bunk the questions come: 'How could she – ?', 'Why would she – ?' and 'Was there anything we could have done?' Because not one of Lana's former podmates – not she or Bryan, nor Kirk or Bev, nor Lucas – ever saw it coming.

'How could she hate us so much?' Shariah's sobbed more than once against Bryan's chest. 'She was my best friend. How could she hate *me*?'

But they both try not to dwell. Lana is dead, bones in the desert, and so is that evil fuser and with him the rest of Transway. Due to Shariah's mother's cleverness and courage they're safe now, and no expro will ever get within a hundred miles of the city again.

And those transers in the ranchos better watch out too, she thinks grimly. *If any of them come anywhere near here we'll* —

"Hey." Bryan's voice again, shockingly close. Shariah looks up with a start. Mercifully, the gang of idiots has dispersed and he's alone. "Want to go to caf? I'm starving."

"Sure," she says, flicking her server screen closed and getting to her feet.

Bryan drapes a warm, faintly citrus-scented arm across her shoulders as they join the blue- and tan-uniformed throngs crisscrossing the immaculate plaza. A fine spray of mist rises from a fountain fringed with manicured foliage as, many lofty stories above their heads, the interior of a grand, translucent-paned pyramid blazes gold in the noontime sun.

Shariah tips her head back, admiring it, and hoping Bryan keeps any spurious new angles to himself. Or at least gets them out of his system over lunch. That's what she'll do: As much as it pains her, she'll ask him for any updates and smile and nod for half an hour. Then he'll be all talked out on the subject. Because tonight they're having drinks with a new couple, Malcolm and Zoe from her SocEn program, and she wants things to go as smoothly (and sanely) as possible.

She grins, anticipating their visit to one of the cute little holoshops that sprout like flowers around the edges of Main plaza every evening. A product of pure imagination, Albakirk's

Lead SocEns had approved this new form of entertainment shortly after the razing of Transway as a replacement for the social outlets that the district used to offer. The shops appear at 17:00 and vanish by 23:30 – perfectly engineered facsimiles that reproduce all of the color and cheer of Transway without its general air of unwholesomeness.

The shops are staffed with real, live SocTechs, who take turns dressing up like the servers in the old wayverns and serving drinks and snacks (sourced from the caf) to their fellows. It's nothing they're required to do, just a lark, and therefore a hugely popular activity. Totally undignified, of course, for En trainees like Shariah and Bryan. But it's just as well; Shariah doesn't think she'd enjoy serving anyone, even as a goof. She does enjoy visiting the shops, however, as do most people her age. Tonight they'll play some of the delightful old-world 'board' games that are all the rage at the moment and she'll direct conversation to the Mars landing, another of Bryan's favorite subjects.

That should keep his Chronie in the closet.

Satisfied, Shariah circles an arm around Bryan's waist and gives him a squeeze. As long as the stupid thing *stays* in the closet it ought to be a really nice night.

"THEY'RE FULLY RECOVERED NOW THOUGH, right? And no one else has been ill? You'll all be ready for docking day? And what about Gil and Morrison – have they been doing their landing simulations? Phobos' orbit is no joke."

Tall and trim in a slate-blue uniform, Theodore Timanti paces through the three-minute communication delay in front of the giant screen in the command center. He runs a hand over his neatly-trimmed beard and moustache as his mind races with last-minute orders and double and triple checks, trying to outguess every possible worst-case scenario.

It's been over two decades since the horrible day when the Luna Sigma, pride of Albakirk and his parents' crowning achievement, had lifted off in a blaze of glory only to have its hull breached by a piece of old-world space junk before it even left Earth's orbit. Everyone aboard, including both of them, had died instantly.

So far though, no such calamities have plagued the Mars-bound crew aboard the Passerine. The trip has proceeded with almost insane smoothness. But of course it couldn't last; Andrea Johnson Chavez and John Nakai, two of the nine members of the crew, have apparently just suffered some kind of mystery illness, possibly HZE radiation-related. And only a week out from their destination – the Nido, the bot-built orbital station currently positioned between the Martian moons Deimos and Phobos. The crew will dock there for a few days before six of them continue on to plant the first boots on the surface of the red planet in a century and a half.

The plan is for three to stay on the Nido at all times, rotating every few months with the others living and working in the bot-built habitats on the surface. That way, everyone can limit their radiation exposure. They'd kept the trip as short as possible for that same purpose and they'd gotten extremely lucky with the timing. Between the current close planetary positioning (only 81 million miles!) and the recent advancements in fueling, three months to Mars was completely feasible. But it will be another two years before such a short trip is possible again.

So everyone needs to stay healthy.

"Yes, Theodore," the reassuring voice of Nigel Gallegos snaps him to attention as his colleague's serene, grey-eyed countenance unfreezes on the screen. "Don't worry. They're both fine now. Everything is in place. And Aubrey and Mo have been doing nothing *but* simulations. We have to tear them away. Matthew's been at them too, as backup."

That's a relief; Nigel knows what he's talking about. Though all crew members were extensively cross-trained in the various disciplines prior to departure, he is a MedEn first and foremost. If he says all is well then it undoubtedly is.

Theodore blows out a breath. "Did Ellin get the habitat feed back online?" he asks. "If not, we can hook you up to ours. There'll be a bit of a delay but at least you'll have eyes. I can assure you though, the greenhouse is looking good. The harvesters have a whole cooler full of potatoes and parsnips. And there'll be fresh food too when you get there – lettuce, tomatoes, cucumber. Oh, and one of the water tanks was damaged during the last big dust storm – Tank BA-13, but the bots have repaired it now."

Theodore stops transmitting, pauses again for the delay. At this point, they've perfected the art of paragraph-at-a-time conversation. Of course, they could type messages instead but it is psychologically reassuring to use spoken-word, face-to-face communication in these circumstances. Everything they say is automatically transcribed in the recs.

"Mr. Timanti?" a soft voice from within the command room says, and he turns to find the pert face of Beverly Callahan, flanked by her mentor, Marshall Yazzie, nervously regarding him. Yazzie is the MedEn for the next Mars crew, currently in preparation mode here on Earth. Callahan, still an En trainee, is slated to be part of the third.

It's rare and brave for a junior team member to interject during a live transmission, and, in acknowledgement of this, Callahan dips a head of red-gold curls deferentially before continuing, "Aren't the habitats better at mitigating HZE-exposure than the Nido? At least on the surface we've managed to build some more atmosphere. And the underground portions are thickly shielded."

She bites her lower lip. "So I wouldn't Mr. Nakai be better off trading places with one of the crew going planetside?"

Nakai, along with Ellin and Feeley, is slated to be part of the first orbital group on the Nido. Despite his illness, no one in the crew has suggested any substitutions.

"That's a solid idea," Theodore says, giving her what he hopes is an encouraging smile and extending it out to the rest of the team ringing the screen. "I will mention it to Nigel. But I will also abide by whatever decision the crew makes. They're the ones who know the situation best."

"Of course." Callahan visibly exhales as Yazzie pats her on the back, job-well-done style.

There's a respectful murmur among the others before the screen jumps to life again.

"Affirmative, yes. Eyes back on the prize," Nigel says. "Our AgEn is happy. I'm looking forward to a salad myself after three months of freeze-dried gunk. Hopefully the bots can whip us up a nice vinaigrette – "

This sparks a few titters from the group in the command center.

" – and good to know about the water tank. We'll take a

careful look at it when we get down there. Anything else?"

Theodore relays Callahan's suggestion and signs off.

Nigel acknowledges and follows suit.

And that's it for the final weekly in-flight update. The next time they speak it will be docking day. The Earth team members mill around jabbering excitedly; Theodore watches them, eyeing Callahan with a pang of envy.

How proud her parents must be!

The bitter aftertaste of his own daughter's catastrophic flameout still lingers, though enough time has passed that almost no one side-eyes *him* anymore. Thank Madre for the Mars mission; it's given them something else to associate him with, something successful – though in a perfect world he'd be on the Passerine instead of here in the command center. But if he can't be there personally he's glad that Nigel is, almost in his stead.

His server chimes then and Theodore fishes it out of his breast pocket, sitting down in a high-backed chair and swiveling himself out of view of the room. He glances at the screen.

Miller. Ugh. What does she want now?

He re-pockets it without bothering to check and leans back, knitting fingers over his middle as he contemplates:

In a perfect world many things would be different – Lana would be here, happy and healthy, pacing Shariah through the SocEn program, maybe even sharing a first independent bunk, as unpartnered friends often do.

Or maybe not. Maybe Lana would have a boyfriend. A suitable one, someone intelligent and kind. Not like –

His jaw clenches, then his fists. He can still barely stand to think about that piece-of-shit expro she threw it all away for: A man she 'loved' so much that she refused to recognize how he was destroying her. She was never *really* in love with the piece of shit in the first place, just out of her mind on transferon and under a terrible spell. But surely Lang Shays has been dead long enough that the spell has been broken. Maybe Lana's had a chance to reconsider. Maybe she's had enough of the dirt and hunger and ignorance of the ranchos (because that's where he's sure she's still holed up) to want some semblance of a life back. Maybe she's desperate to contact him but has no way to do so.

This is the reason that he's here in the command center, instead of out on the Passerine.

Theodore takes a deep breath; maybe it's time for another visit. It's been a while, nearly a year, since he's been to see Lana's people at Rancho Pescados. When she disappeared after the Destierra it was the first place he'd looked. Garbed as a Transway refugee to avoid suspicion he'd gone out there and leaned on them hard. Cajoled and threatened but never got anywhere. Radio silence.

Until, eventually, his trips had started to look suspicious from a tech point of view and he'd had to suspend them indefinitely. It made sense to have eyes on the ranchos when Transway was first shut down and there was a temporary influx of refugees, but once those were accounted for he couldn't keep justifying the visits. He kept an eye on the occasional drone shots of the smattering of refugee camps outside the hundred-mile perimeter, but those hadn't turned up anything either.

And why would Lana bother with one of those rat holes? Aside from her 'love' she didn't seem to have known any other expros. Shays was the one who groomed her and he's dust in the wind. True, his body was never found, but diseased as he was there's no way he could have survived the elements for very long. He probably got eaten by something nasty, or fell off a cliff. Maybe even offed himself on purpose when he got too sick to function.

So wouldn't the surviving expros blame her for his demise? And for the failure of their sabotage attempt? Maybe they even think she foiled the plan on purpose.

The ranchos, on the other hand, are where she grew up. They're familiar. Lana has family there. And as far as dirt and hunger goes they're a million times better than some ragged camp that probably won't last another winter. Plus, the ranchos are populous enough (and immune enough to drone surveillance) that she could easily hide in plain sight, refusing to be found unless she wanted to be.

But she's had time to cool off now, to come to her senses. To want to come home.

Though she can't return to Albakirk. As far as everyone in the city is concerned she's dead, and a miscreant to boot. But she could still have a good life in Winnipeg. He has contacts up there, people who could take her in and keep it quiet. He could visit, and when his term as Lead SocEn is up, move there and help her have some semblance of a normal life.

First, though, he has to *find* her. So maybe he can drum up some reason for a trip out to the ranchos this week – one that will get him back on track with that goal and also give him something else to think about besides the many, many things that could go wrong on the Passerine between now and docking day.

And who knows? he thinks, as he swivels back around to

face his colleagues in the command center. *Maybe this time I'll be in luck.*

"MO ~ OM?" SHARIAH CALLS, WHOOSHING OPEN the door to her parents' bunk. Technically it's still hers too, though these days she spends the majority of nights in Bryan's miniscule single. He'd moved out of his parents' bunk here in Main almost immediately upon being PostEd, a move which, due to his very junior status, should have banished him to a single somewhere in the outer rim. But he's only one plaza over, in Kiva. Shariah's sure her mother had something to do with this minor miracle, and with the fact that Bryan's room has a real window instead of just a holoflat on the wall. Usually, she enjoys staying there.

But not tonight. Not after how badly he just embarrassed her.

"Mo ~ om?" she says again, tramping through the kitchenette and down the darkened hall toward a rectangle of yellow light at the far end: the living space, a luxury afforded only to Leads and their families.

He just doesn't get it.

If you want to be a Lead people have to take you seriously. Everything counts. You have to use your trainee years to establish a good, solid reputation, not waste time acting like some fringy freak.

She pauses in the doorway in case her mother is busy and needs a minute. She doesn't want to interrupt important business. But Ariana Balor looks up from the screen on her sleek, silver desk and smiles, crisp blue eyes crinkling in the corners.

"Daughter dear," she says, red hair ablaze against the

night-black bank of windows. One corner of her mouth turns up wryly. "To what do I owe the honor?"

Shariah heaves a sigh.

"It's Bryan," she says. "He just doesn't understand – "

And, after coming in and flopping down on one of the squashy beige sofas, she launches into a blow-by-blow account of the failed evening. Things had started off well, all of them playing games and laughing, Shariah humbly mentioning how thrilled she was for her good friend Bev, who'd scored such a coup during the transmission session with the Passerine this afternoon.

That had impressed them alright. She can still picture Zoe's jaw-dropped awe.

So she'd been flushed with borrowed success, until Malcolm made a crack about Chronies and instead of just letting it go (the necessity of which she'd tried to impress via a swift kick under the table) Bryan had had the temerity to argue the point, outing himself as one of them in the process.

Things got awkward fast after that. Enough so that Malcolm and Zoe had made their excuses and left early, leaving Shariah and Bryan to a blistering argument from which she's not sure their relationship will recover.

As her rant winds down, she looks up, expecting to find commiseration in her mother's eyes. Instead, there's an odd wariness.

"What," her mother says, "is a Chronie? And why haven't I heard about this before?"

"I don't know," Shariah says, a bit sulky at being denied full and immediate sympathy. "It's not a big deal – just a few weirdo Mechs. I just had the bad luck to get involved with one of them."

"But what exactly do they believe?"

"They think the *calendar's* off."

Her mother's jaw clenches like her patience is being sorely tried. "Yes," she says carefully, "but why?"

"Because of the stupid fountain!" Shariah says, pained to have to describe this in detail after all the trouble it's caused. "The Mechs who built the first original pyramid way back when put some kind of 'Easter egg' in it. Once a year on the summer solstice the light shines through at the exact right angle and it lights up some secret crystal in the fountain and makes, like, a pretty design. It's ridiculous, but they wait for it every year. Like a bunch of goony transers."

"So?" her mother prompts.

"*So*," she says testily. "It didn't happen. Or it did, but on the wrong day. Like, last year it didn't happen and no one could figure out why. So this year they had someone stationed there 24/7 starting a week before the solstice and they saw it happen, but not on Ord 172 when it should've. It happened on Ord 169.

"So that's why," she finishes.

Her mother's lips tighten. "I see."

"Told you it was dumb. And I've told Bryan a million times that there's some rational explanation. Maybe someone moved their stupid crystal as a joke."

At this last, Ariana Balor visibly relaxes. "Yes," she murmurs. "That's probably what happened. A practical joke. Preying on the gullible."

"I know," Shariah says. "That's what I keep telling him. But he says that's impossible."

"Nothing's impossible, especially when it involves this level of foolishness," Ariana says, rising from her seat and walking over to the sofa, where she settles down next to her daughter.

Finally, Shariah thinks.

"It will all work out," she says, with a reassuring pat. "You'll see. Men can sometimes be stubborn in their beliefs."

"Did Dad ever do anything like this?"

"No, your father's always been very level-headed. But as a Lead SocEn I've had to deal with all manner of testosterone-fueled nonsense over the years."

"Like Mr. Timanti? And Martinez?"

Her mother chuckles. "Exactly. But that all worked out for the best, didn't it? Martinez is gone and Theodore's come around nicely. Doing some very impressive work these days." She gives her daughter's shoulder a squeeze. "So you'll see – either Bryan will get over this silly delusion and you'll get back together or he won't, and you'll find someone with a stronger character. Someone who's not so easily led."

"I know," Shariah sighs. "I just really thought he was the one. But then again," she adds bitterly, "I thought Lana Timanti was my best friend."

At that, Ariana takes her daughter's chin in hand and tilts her face up, boring a steady, ice-blue gaze into Shariah's dark eyes. "Do not *ever* blame yourself for that," she says. "Or for whatever idiocies those around you fall into. What Lana did was a result of her own weak-mindedness. She was transfusing, and it made her completely insane. You, my dear, suffer from no such failings. You are perfect. True, you have been sorely tested by the faults of others, but it's only served to make you stronger. If Bryan is weak-minded too then you're far better off knowing that now. You want someone as smart and strong as you are or you'll never be happy."

"But – " Shariah starts.

"You are the best this city has to offer," her mother says, with a force that brooks no argument. "And you deserve nothing but the best in return."

Shariah sniffs back a few more tears before managing a smile. Then a cheerful whistling draws her attention to the hall door.

"And how're my best girls this evening?" comes a pleasant tenor. Both she and her mother brighten instantly as Nathan Balor appears on the threshold, warm brown eyes taking them in like they are the most welcome sight in the world.

"Dad!" Shariah jumps up and rushes to him, all misery at bay. "I missed you."

He laughs as he embraces her. "I've been right here."

"Yeah, I know. But I was spending so much time with…" she trails off, turning to give her mother an arch grimace.

"Ah," he says, looking back and forth between them. "So I take it that the romance with young Mr. Patten is at an end?"

"Yeah," Shariah says, not without some regret. She rests her head against her father's broad, comforting shoulder, and breathes in the clean reassuring scent of him. "I guess it actually is."

4

Heart pounding, Celan starts awake, tendrils of the awful dream still wrapped around her throat. She'd been screaming (whether out loud or only in the dream she's not sure) because in it she'd returned to Terra Madre to find that the Plejarans had lied and that eighteen months here equaled eighteen hundred years there and everyone she'd ever known and loved (and hated too) was long dead and gone. And there were no other humans left in their place either; her beloved blue marble was a crumbling, gray ruin.

Alone.

She shudders.

Forever.

She presses a hand against her chest, willing herself to breathe deep as she sits up and stares into the swirling sleep mode pattern of her holo.

Nothing like that is going to happen. She's going to go home and everyone's going to be there and everything's going to be fine.

But even if the awful dream scenario doesn't play out, the more research she does about planet-killing galactic phenomena the more horrifying possibilities her mind conjures up – so many things can go wrong it's a wonder any transentient species has managed to survive, let alone build some kind of federation. Rogue planets, exploding stars, black holes, unstable worm holes, asteroids: There are a lot of ways to die in the 'Verse. Lots of ways to wipe out a whole system.

All of which has made her increasingly determined to find a solution to the WDM,K*DU's problem. Foreign as they may be on a personal level, in the larger scheme of things their dilemma is eminently relatable. 'Don't let our home get destroyed,' doesn't need much translation.

Celan blinks, rubs her eyes, and checks the time.

Terra Madre!

No wonder she fell asleep; she'd been up for almost thirty-six Madren hours working with a contingent of WDM,K*DU and some Orofuchans and X'z'x'z – all of whom are used to much longer days. Her marathon research session was only a few measly hours to them. Her holo probably shut down mid-sentence.

She confirms: There it sits in the meeting space, staring stupidly. Everyone else is still working away; a X'z'x'z holoform waves purple tentacles to emphasize a point while a coterie of palm-sized, winged Orofuchans debates whether slipping a rogue planet past an inhabited but non-transient system violates any prohibitions as long as it's only there for a 'minute' and doesn't do any damage.

Better find out how long their minutes are first, Celan thinks, with a jaw-cracking yawn.

She's about to dive back in but thinks better of it and gets to her feet, stretching and groaning. Her nap had lasted all of an hour but her whole spine feels compressed. She's going to need some exercise to work out the kinks and more sleep to really bring her A-game to the table. The others know that she has a very different temporal rhythm than they do, but it's still kind of embarrassing. Next to some of the more time-protracted species she often feels like a mayfly.

Which reminds her, she should dial up a simulation to-night – something pleasant, a forest stream maybe. It's been a while since she's seen anything other than stars and the smooth, silver-grey walls of her chamber. The capsules that members of each species reside in (Dyson cells as Celan likes to think of them) are customized for each species' physiol-ogy – things like gravity, radiation tolerance, solar exposure and rotation, nutrition, and chronological cycles are all taken into consideration. Normally, the interior of Celan's capsule resembles her old bedroom in Albakirk, but she can simulate other Madren environments if she'd like to enjoy an evening stroll through a meadow or a mountain vista.

But it's just not the same.

Wistful, she walks to the window and presses her nose against the glass, watching the orange dwarf star 60QR slowly sink from site as her cell enters the night-faced portion of its rotation. The capsule system is safe, but solitary – like an old world screener she once saw about a boy who lived in a bubble and couldn't ever touch anyone or go outside.

It would be different if 60QR had a planet that she could spend time on unencapsulated. It has several, but all are cold, distant, and environmentally unsuitable for a Madren. She has been down to the surface of the fourth plant, Xela, several times, but if you've seen one lake of hydrocarbons, in her opinion, you've seen them all. For some species though, Xela is practically a beach resort.

Must be nice.

Even worse, the system is over 90 light years from home, not the measly four she thought she'd be travelling back when Chan said the K'Shiran Convention was currently located 'not far from Alpha Centauri.' Turns what he meant was 'not far by ascension and declination' (60QR is a star in the Madren constellation of Centaurus) rather than 'not far in light years'. In his attempt to see things though Madren eyes he'd merely confused the issue.

She grimaces, wishing she could set her feet on the solid soil of something, even if it's not her home turf. The last (and only) time she'd gotten to do that was a month after her arrival, when Chan, Ness, and Ree took her on a two-week trip to Va'anak, a world of briny oceans and islands in a system nearly 160 light years from Terra Madre. But despite its being even further away from home, Va'anak had felt much more familiar than the 60QR system.

Celan had had to be thoroughly biofilmed before setting foot on the surface, but that wasn't a barrier to sensation. The warm blanket of sun and cool kiss of spray as they flitted from island to island in the glider-like contraptions the Va'anaki use in lieu of boats (their islands being steep and rocky and their seas full of large, toothsome creatures) were worth a thousand holo simulations.

Each inhabited island had a glider landing pad at its peak,

and from there each burnished, pearlescent city spiraled down the outer wall of rock to the most coveted sections closest to the water. Like Plejarans and Madrens, the Va'anakai were BCOs (bilaterally symmetric, carbon-based, oxygen-breathers), but they were half the size of Madrens and of a semi-marine vintage that retained retractable webbing in hands and feet and the ability to breathe both air and water. They were also fantastic hosts, with dwellings and gliders that could hold visitors of many shapes and sizes, as well as underwater observatories that offered views of fantastic aquatic life-forms.

Celan tips her face up, closing her eyes and sighing as she recalls the bracing freshness of the breeze through the suite of rooms she'd shared with the Plejarans during their stay. Between the salty-sweet scent of the air and the fact that the planet's gravity was slightly less than that of home she'd felt buoyant enough to privately conclude that the atmosphere must be at least five percent transferon. She'd laughed, and then immediately wished someone were there to share the joke.

A certain someone.

In her first flush of introduction to the Convention she'd been far too busy to spend much time pining for Lang, but the trip to Va'anak had caused her to miss him viscerally. She knew he would like it there; could picture him standing beside her, looking out over the soughing sea and the fuschia sunset.

Maybe we could go back there together sometime.

She wriggles the toes of her bare feet as a dammed-up flood of memory breaks and washes over her: Walking in the moonlight; dancing on Navidad Eve, his green-eyed gaze bright on her face; and every moment of those few blessed days and nights they had spent together in the ranchos before everything went sideways. She presses her lips together, trying not to cry, trying to stop the awful mental litany that always follows in happy memory's wake:

What if he's dead? What if my father or Ariana found him again and hurt him? What if it really is eighteen hundred years later and I never see him again? What if it was all for nothing and I'm just stuck here?

Alone. Forever.

The panic rises in waves until her chest is so tight she can barely breathe and she's scrabbling in the pocket of her sleepware. In some backwater of her brain she notes, not for the first time, that her use of transferon has increased markedly in recent months and that that might not be a good thing. But when she gets like this there's nothing else that can soothe her.

It's only medicine. And it's only for now. Just a few more weeks. Once she's home and sees that everything's OK she can start cutting back a little.

Celan pulls out the vial, unscrews the cap, and sits. No fancy zero-G this time. When she gets like this, the fuse is all she needs.

She draws up a full dropper's worth of fluid, pushes up her sleeve and touches tip to flesh, letting the energy build and release as it flows from mind to hand, through the fluid in the dropper and into her bloodstream. As it hits, she relaxes, detaches, and takes the deepest breath she's managed in a week, leaning back in the plush chair and closing her eyes as her mind fills with images.

Mostly, they are pleasant ones: Lang's arms around her, his family's place at Arqueros, the splash of sunlight on an acequia. But darker things also rise – like Ariana, turning

Transway to rubble and threatening the same for the ranchos. Celan frowns, then breaks into a brilliant smile as the vision changes again and she sees herself, quantum band in hand, protecting and defending them all and bringing Ariana to her knees. Turning the tables, forcing her out into the desert. Listening to the woman beg, but refusing to yield. Then turning to where her father stands amazed and telling him that she forgives him. And not to worry. Because she, Celan, is in charge now.

And everything is going to be all right.

5

"So," Brophy says. "Tell him what you told me."

Max Elenas turns from a whispered aside with fellow astral-traveler Valery, his dark eyes scanning Lang uncertainly.

"It's fine," Brophy prompts, leaning back in his chair and propping booted feet up on the heavy wooden tabletop. "He can take it. He needs to know."

The smell of burnt tortillas lingers in the empty dining hall and Lang's stomach churns, the sloppy cooking reinforcing the idea that things still might not be back to normal, Mara-wise.

But maybe someone else made them this morning.

There've been no further meltdowns from Mara this week, most likely due to the fact that Brophy's been spending the majority of his time with her and almost none at all with Lang. He knows it isn't personal, but the absence of his friend's steadying presence has frayed his nerves even more than usual. This meeting, however, with Brophy's astral group, is a necessary one, and as it involves other people it's safe to be seen together.

Max clears his throat. "Well," he says, "the family says her father came around again last week. Asking questions."

Lang groans. Celan's father, Theodore, has apparently decided to start hassling her and Max's childhood guardians Jillyanne and Lena again (along with Max's twin sister Tanny and her daughter Elena). He'd bothered them for a while after Celan vanished – swearing that the Destierra was just for show, that he'd been going to come and get her, that he was never going to let her die. But also that he desperately needed to know if she was still alive, and *where*. She was sick, he'd insisted, and needed help.

The family hadn't known what to think; there were so many conflicting reports about the dismantling of Transway, and no one knew if the ranchos were next on the techs' hit list. They trusted in the elders to keep them safe, but everyone was, understandably, on edge. So they'd told him the truth (at the time): that Celan wasn't there and they didn't know where to find her.

But after Lang and Max became friendly at Rinconada and discovered their common association, they'd set up a meeting with the family and astralled in to explain where Celan was, when she was expected back, and that there was no way to contact her until then. Telling her father that they knew she was alive but not in the ranchos, while the kindest option, would have put the camp in danger, so collectively they'd all decided that the best thing to do was to continue to stonewall him. The truth was so implausible that Theodore would have thought it a lie anyway.

And the tactic worked, at least at first: Celan's father had gone dark for a time. But if he's is actively looking for her again it will only complicate things when she gets back.

If *she does*, Lang thinks, then chides himself, *When*, and refocuses.

"What kind of questions?" he says to Max.

"First he tried tricking them, sabes? Said he'd seen drone pics of her the other week, outside the ranchos, on the road to the city – just to see what they'd say, I guess. Said he had proof positive she was there and was trying to contact him."

"Did they fall for it?"

"Nah," Max grins. "My aunties are too smart for that shit."

"And he still doesn't know about my family?"

"Nay, ese. He thinks you were just some random expro."

"Good."

"But he said some other stuff too. After they still wouldn't talk. That there might be some kind of threat to the ranchos –"

"What?"

" – but that if he knows she's there he can protect them."

A threat. Most likely a bluff. But it could be real, and if it is the person behind it is most likely Ariana Balor. The image of the red-haired woman still makes Lang shiver. Those chilling, crystal-blue eyes, examining him like he was a bug she was about to squash. Celan's father hated him too – had beaten the living shit out of him in fact – but it was an honest, human kind of hate, the kind you have for someone who you believe hurt someone you love. The red-haired woman, though, she didn't hate; she merely extinguished.

"Does anyone know if it's true?"

Max shrugs. "No sé. It's just what he said."

Lang looks to Brophy, who shrugs. The threat might be real – Ariana had vowed to go after the ranchos when Lang and Celan were her prisoners – but it seems like the idea never gained much traction among the rest of the techs. After all, they'd gotten rid of the 'expro threat' outside their walls. The ranchos were on the other side of the mountains. Out of sight, out of mind – that's been the hope anyway.

"You never know with them though," Brophy says. "So we better hope your girl comes back with something great up her sleeve." A smirk. "Other than a few new burns."

Lang shoots him a glare and changes the subject: "Have there been any more drones around here lately? Or don't they bother anymore?"

As the elders protect the ranchos from tech surveillance, Brophy, Max, and Valery guard the camp – the latter two being part of a very meager handful of former Transway residents who grew up in the ranchos and were taught astral travel by the elders; the former is just a natural.

The natural tips his chair back. "Val?" he says, stretching arms up and knitting his fingers together behind his head, biceps flexed.

She shakes her head, short, black hair grazing a sharp jaw. "No. The last one was, like, a month ago."

"And it was shorted out?"

"Of course."

That's a relief, but Lang's knee still jogs anxiously. Maybe he's safe here, but if anyone tries to hurt his family…

"Do you think – " he starts.

"Mira," Max says, like he can read Lang's mind. "Calmaté,

güey. As long as Celan's dad thinks she's in the ranchos he's not gonna let anyone fuck with them."

Brophy and Val nod in agreement and with that, the meeting is adjourned. The four of them rise and make their way out of the dim cavern of the dining hall and into the light of day. Lang squints, taking in a group assembled at the edge of the plaza in the shade of a half-dead cottonwood.

Mara, Zeeb, Jaslene, and Maddy ring a slim, honey-haired girl Lang's never seen before, with two small children in tow: New arrivals, maybe. But that would be a pretty big deal. Most of the Transway refugees that found their way to Rinconada did so within the first few months after the mass Destierra. For this girl to have survived for over a year with two kids to care for would be pretty hardcore.

Still, she doesn't look like the fragile kind of thin – more like a taut wire. She's got some kind of goggles pushed up on her head and a deep frown on her face, directed at Mara. Arms crossed, she grudgingly nudges one of the children, who jams a grubby hand into the pocket of his frayed overalls and produces a small, silvery vial that he holds out like an offering.

Mara plucks it from the boy's palm and quickly inspects it before handing it to Zeeb, who brushes long brown bangs off his round face and appraises it like a jeweler. He grunts once, affirmative, and pockets the transfer.

Lang swallows as the girl's frown deepens, she's definitely unhappy about having to part with the thing. But those are the rules. No one is allowed to hold their own these days. Everyone gets a few drops of medicinal-grade transferon in the morning and that's it. No recreational use.

Unless you're part of the inner circle. And as long as you're not me.

His expression turns as sour as the girl's at the thought.

"...taking care of them yourself?" Mara's voice carries. "What happened to their parents?"

He moves in closer to hear the answer, Brophy at his heels.

"Died. Not sure why. Some kind of poison maybe. Old world shit." The girl's voice is like the quiet scrape of stone on stone.

The hairs on the back of Lang's neck stiffen. There's something familiar about that tone. Something he can't quite place.

"How long ago?" Mara says.

"Couple months, maybe."

"And before that?"

The girl purses her lips. "I told you. We were looking for *this* place. Heard about it from some old guy out by Abiquiu."

"For a year and a half?"

"We got off track. Couldn't keep dragging the kids around everywhere. Too dangerous. So we found a place to stay for a while, went out looking when we could."

"Still – "

"Once their parents were gone, I needed help. Had to find someplace safer. Figured I'd make a big push. Try to find some others."

"Well..."

"Mara," Maddy cuts in, patting her pinned-up braids. "Is the third degree really necessary? These people have obviously been through a lot. Why don't we take the children somewhere they can rest? Give them something to eat and drink."

The newcomer's face registers relief. Both children, the second one a girl, blink big, hopeful eyes. Mara regards Maddy stonily, but finally relents. "Jas, take 'em in the kitchen. Give 'em a snack."

Jaslene nods, reaching out a welcoming hand on either side of Isaac, who's strapped in a sling across her middle. The children latch on eagerly. She tosses shiny brown hair and gives Lang a peremptory glance as she steers them past the astral group and around the side of the building.

Fucking saint you are now, he thinks, watching her go. Still a nice rear view, but her personality has curdled whatever attractions it once held. Ever since she and Gabe got together and had a kid she's been acting like the Virgin of Guadalupe. Pretends she doesn't even know Maddy, though she was once one of her girls, and looks at Lang like he's some pitiful thing. It sets his teeth on edge, especially in light of how hard she'd tried to get back together with him when they first got here. In Celan's absence, she figured it was a lock and got really mad when he turned her down.

But there was no way he was going to start all that up again and he'd made it very clear. Except for that one night – and whatever did or didn't happen (large volumes of whiskey having wiped the slates of memory clean) that was the end of it. After that she'd left him alone. Hooked up with Gabe and was pregnant three months later.

So at least I know the kid isn't mine.

The honey-haired girl clears her throat. "I'm pretty beat too," she says to Mara. "Even if you don't want us to stay, at least let us get some rest before we move on."

"No one said you couldn't stay," Mara says quickly. "We just like to know a little about who we let in here, is all."

"Right. We do get the transfer back though, if we want

to leave?"

Mara's sharp blue eyes narrow.

The girl pushes the goggles further back on her head. "If we like it, we'll stay. If not – "

"Of course," Maddy cuts in again. "It sounds like you've had a bad time – Sonrisa, was it? Why don't you come over to my place? We can make you up a bed – "

Mara snorts.

" – and you can relax."

Sonrisa's eyes dart shrewdly between Maddy and Mara and she cracks the first smile Lang's seen out of her so far.

"Bueno," she says. "Maddy, was it? That'd be great."

Maddy slips an arm through hers, leading her off while Mara watches, fists clenched.

Lang and Brophy share a nervous look.

Then Zeeb slaps a hand across Mara's back. "No worries," he says. "As soon as that girl finds out who else will be sharing that bed she'll run as far away from Maddy as possible."

It takes a second, but Mara laughs. "Yeah," she says. "I guess."

"Hey querida," Brophy says, strolling over to her. "I'm done with the astral stuff. Want to go take a little nap with me?"

Mara smiles at him, and Lang heaves a sigh of relief: Meltdown managed. Maybe this means she'll be in a good enough mood to talk to later.

"NO," MARA SAYS, AVOIDING LANG'S eyes. "Absolutely not." She reaches for the platter of green chile mashed potatoes Sig proffers and scoops out a small amount, nestling it lovingly next to the slivers of dried fish in her wooden trencher.

You knew this was coming, she chides herself. *The minute you offered him that drink you knew it was a mistake. So don't engage. Shut this shit down and move on.*

It had been Lang's turn to help prep dinner tonight and he'd been in one of his charming moods. So much so that she'd relaxed her guard and opened a bottle of Zeeb's prickly pear mead to liven things up. She'd been in a good mood too, even after all the fuss that Sonrisa girl had kicked up, due to Brophy's amorous ministrations this afternoon. After that, clowning with Lang in the kitchen had felt like old times.

She should have known that he would just try to use it to get his way.

"But why?" He presses from across the table, green eyes pleading. "It's not like I'm asking to get all aviados. I just want to go back to where I was at. Where I was comfortable. I was doing fine – "

"This isn't about your comfort. You know the rules."

"Rules." He snorts. "Rules *you* made. None of them are written in stone."

"Because most of us can remember them fine without it."

To her left, Sig snickers. She trains an icy gaze on him until he stifles it.

"Sorry," he mutters, wiry neck bobbing as he bites off a hunk of cornbread.

Mollified, she focuses back on the problem at hand.

"You know I'm not doing this to be mean, Lang. But after everything that happened when we first got here, we all agreed that it was for the best not to keep encouraging that sort of thing. It's not just you. No one's allowed to go crazy anymore. That's why we hold onto all the transfers. And we help Class

Es cut down."

"Cut down doesn't have to mean cut off."

"Yes, it does. It's been over a year and we've been more than patient. Stepped you down by tiny baby steps. You always get like this after a cut." A shrug. "Then you get used to it."

She spoons up a little more potato, lets it melt on her tongue.

Delicious. The chile really makes it.

"It's different with nothing," Lang counters. "It's worse. I can't sleep. I feel like shit all the time."

She rolls her eyes.

"Claro," he says. "You don't understand. You've never had to do it."

There are mutters around the table. Mara shifts uncomfortably; she needs to shut this shit down *now*.

"Yeah, because I'm not dumb enough to catch the CERS," she cracks. "But for those that are, someone needs to be in charge of them. And it needs to be someone responsible. Everyone needs a few drops a day to stay healthy, but no one needs to be constantly aviados. And for the good of everyone they can't be. That's why we do it like this. It works."

Lag puts down his trencher with a clatter, jaw clenched. "Well not for me. And for the record, I don't want to be constantly anything. You know it was only a little while that I was like that. And it was messed up, I know. But I almost *died* Mara, out in that desert. The techs tried to kill me! I just needed to feel good for a while; to get past it. We all needed that back then."

"And *now*?"

"Now, I need it to help…get rid of things. Healing's not as

easy as it looks. Without a little Class E, sometimes things… stick."

He glances around the table, but no one will meet his eyes. Sig looks to Zeeb, who shakes his head.

Bueno, Mara thinks. *Don't feed the bullshit.*

"And I'm not the only one who needs a little help sometimes," Lang says, staring pointedly at her.

Silence. Everyone looks to Mara as she draws herself up on the bench as regally as her small stature will allow.

"Asshole," she hisses. "When I fuse, I don't do it for fun. When I do it, it's D *only* – to give me the fucking energy to supervise every motherfucking thing that goes on in this place. I do it so you have food on your motherfucking plate. Food that no one would've had if I hadn't taken charge when all anyone else wanted to do was party. The shit Zeeb brought in would've lasted us a month, tops. Especially after all those others started trickling in. And then what?"

"We would've starved," Jaslene says.

Excellent.

"Hey," comes a soft voice on her right. Brophy. Mara tenses, antennae up.

Don't you dare *defend him*, she thinks furiously.

But of course he does.

"We all know that's true, Mara," he says carefully. "And we all know how much you've done for everybody. But Lang's done a lot too. He wasn't the only one who was a mess at first, but he realized it. And he agreed do whatever it took to cut down. And he has. There's no reason to make him suffer, or to hold anything against him."

Mara feels herself flush. "Callaté!" she barks, then softens at the hurt-puppy look he gives her.

She takes a deep breath. "I do not hold anything against him. I just feel like letting him get away with his bad little habits sets a bad precedent. He's supposed to be the head healer around here. How does it look if he's a Class E fuser?"

Brophy opens his mouth to reply, but before he can the table rattles as Lang springs to his feet, two spots of color burning high in his tawny cheeks.

"How does it look?" he mocks. "How does it *look*? Who the fuck cares how it looks? Who are you trying to impress? The people I heal aren't fucking *elders*, they're refugees from Transway. It's not like they've never seen a Class E fuser before!"

Mara keeps her seat, raising only her eyes to stare coldly into his.

"Yes," she says, in a voice like she's talking to an especially slow child. "Of course they've seen one, but I doubt they've ever been expected to respect one before."

Lang sucks in a breath and the whole table crackles with static. A hush sweeps over the hall as necks crane to see what all the commotion is about. His jaw works and biceps tense like he might be about to scream or flip the table over. But he does none of these things; in the end he just turns and stalks out into the twilight.

Ugh, Mara thinks. *They never fucking learn.*

Then, clearing her throat, she turns to Sig.

"Please pass the cornbread," she says sweetly.

FUCKMARAFUCKMARAFUCKMARA

Lang stomps across the plaza to the river gate, kicking it open with such force that it slams against the fence and springs back equally hard, whacking him in the hip as he slips through. Cursing, he turns and kicks it again, hard enough for pain to bloom in his toes despite the thick outer layer of boot. He strangles a sob; he will not cry. He will not. She's already reduced him to nothing. She's not going to get that too.

He *knows* how bad he was when they first got here: the village idiot, falling asleep mid-sentence, not even bothering to trans away the burns. He could still heal at will but it was like a bad joke; 'Someone sprained their ankle. Better go wake Lang.' But after what almost happened to Brophy, he'd done his best to mend his ways; so throwing it all back in his face in front of everyone, especially those who came later and didn't see it firsthand, was a low blow.

Blinking fast, he takes deep gulps of air and lets his gaze swing first to the setting sun and then to the just-past-full moon rising over the river valley. Far to the east, a bright star winks in an indigo sky. It makes him think of Celan – Is that the one she's on? Or is she already on her way back home?

And, for the millionth time: *What's going to happen then?*

She won't know where he is, so she'll have to go to the ranchos and find Melia. He astrals to his sister once a week to let her know he's fine and to check in on things with the family. Melia knows the camp's location; she'll tell Celan.

So his girl will be able to find him, but will she still even want him when she does? Maybe she's met someone else, someone better. An alien maybe. He's such a loser; maybe she'd rather be with some tentacle-head thing than him.

The tears threaten again. Angrily, Lang slaps them away. Because the one thing he *does* know about Celan is that she never, ever, *ever* would have put up with this kind of shit. Not for one fucking minute. No way in hell Mara'd be holding *her* transfer She'd have outsmarted them all. She was good like that.

But he's not. And other than breaking into Zeeb's place and stealing one there's nothing he can think of to do. And that would be pointless anyway; they'd all know who did it, he'd get maybe one fuse out of it, and then things would get ugly. Maybe Mara would kick him out of the camp entirely. He could go back to the ranchos, but that's a hundred mile trip; alone, on foot, and without a transfer.

Unless they let him keep it – would they? Or would they make him give it back? At the thought of Zeeb and Sig or Brophy holding him down, hitting him, forcibly taking it, his hands clench into fists and his heart starts to pound. He wants to scream. He wants to cease to exist. He wants to take that gate and slam it into his own face a thousand fucking times.

He needs something. Anything. Right fucking *now*. And if it can't be the fuse it'll have to be whiskey. Which means a visit to Franky.

Lang fumbles for his smoke pouch.

Maddy's houseboy (more like houseman, since he is definitely over forty) is kind of a sketchy character, someone Lang generally tries to avoid. No one knows exactly who Franky is or where he came from; no one remembers him working at Maddy's old establishment on Transway, though all her remaining girls will swear up and down that he's been with them for years. He doesn't go out much; you'll see him at breakfast for his daily dose but that's about it. Among an assortment of functions, however, he is one of only two people (Zeeb being the other) who maintains a still – and there's no way Lang's going to ask Mara's cousin for anything after the scene that just went down. His best bet is to pay Franky a visit now, while everyone is still at dinner. But he'll probably need to bring something to barter.

Like hemp, he thinks, rolling some up in a maize wrapper. That's really the only thing he has to offer unless he lucks out and the man's got a toothache or something. He only has a small amount left over from last year, but maybe it's enough to roll Franky a couple and still have some for himself until harvest.

Lang strikes his flint, and takes a long and shaky draw.

At this point anything's worth a shot.

"THAT WAS BRUTAL," JASLENE SAYS with obvious relish. "Serio. I don't think I've *ever* seen him so pissed."

Mara takes the high five unsmiling, untying her apron and hanging it on a nail. She sweeps one last look around, surveying like a general – Gabe and Danilo on dishwashing detail, Jaslene drying, Lainey sorting and composting – and grunts, satisfied, before pushing open the kitchen door. The sweet air of evening engulfs her as she steps out dodging moths. She lets it thwack shut behind her; done for the night. Free.

But instead of heading for the comfort of an after-dinner drink with Brophy or Zeeb (or even Sig if no one else is around) she leans against the warm wooden wall of the building and sighs, a worm of doubt wriggling fitfully in her gut. Yes, Lang desperately needed to be put in his place, but she's starting to think that maybe she was a tiny bit too harsh. Because there wasn't any applause for her epic takedown after he left, just a long and uncomfortable silence followed by whispers, especially from the direction of Maddy's table.

Not a good look, this kind of challenge to her authority. Not a good look at all. It makes her mad all over again, but also a little bit scared, which makes her even madder.

Because: Is Lang pissed enough to actually try to leave? And: Where would he go – the ranchos?

His family is there, but as far as she understands it he's banned from any permanent return unless he gives Raf's old transfer back to the elders. And that one's long gone.

He could grab another before he left though. Turn that in. Would the elders know the difference? Never having met any, she has no idea. But even if they didn't it wouldn't matter. As upset as he is there's no way he'd be able to make it all the way to the ranchos without using it.

She shakes her head.

No. There's no way he's going there. All his friends are here at Rinconada, and even if he did manage to avoid temptation for a while he's too much of a deep-dyed mess to avoid it forever. If he went home it would be like two days, tops, before he 'borrowed' someone's transfer, fused himself into oblivion, and got his ass kicked out again. And surely he knows it. Fucked up as he is, he can't be completely devoid of self-awareness.

However, there is Maddy to think of: Would he join up with her? Split off?

She doubts it. For all his fusing, Lang can be oddly prudish about certain things. He's never really liked the woman and her girls have always made him uncomfortable. Besides, he's still hopelessly devoted to Celan Mairs, galaxy girl, convinced that she's going to return to Earth from her big mission any day now.

Mara rolls her eyes hard, even though there's no one around to see.

If Maddy had something to offer him though, other than pussy…

But she doesn't. And Mara knows this to be true because after that thinly-veiled threat the other day she'd sent spies; had a guy or two sniff around the girls (and creepy-ass Franky) looking for a fuse. And offering up some pretty tasty perks in return.

Nada.

Still, Maddy might have been expecting that. Maybe she warned the girls. Maybe she *is* hiding a transfer, and waiting for just the right moment to use it to bag the really big game.

Mara shakes her head again. She refuses to let that happen.

Then she sighs, glaring up at the moon like this is all its fault and she's about to jump its ass. She cracks a small, rueful smirk at her own absurdity and pushes off the wall. Time to stop worrying and relax. There's nothing more she can do about any of it tonight anyway. Word is Lang went off on a tear. Maybe he'll get drunk, act a fool, and be too hangdog and hungover in the morning to contemplate further reprisals. Then they can forget about this whole thing.

Meanwhile, a long soak in a cool tub (and maybe little más D) beckons.

Swatting moths out of her face, Mara marches off in the direction of the rambling old adobe she calls home.

BOTTLE WEDGED SECURELY UNDER HIS arm, Lang keeps a sharp eye out for any rocks or roots as he lopes along the river path in the moonlight. Mission accomplished, and it wasn't that bad. Franky had been right where Lang needed him to be and completely accommodating. The man hadn't even asked for any hemp, or anything else tangible, just a short account of Lang and Celan's ill-fated attempt to save the techs from their own failed bot release; a good deed performed in good faith which had resulted in a chain of terrible consequences including the destruction of Transway, Lang's near-death, and he and Celan's long separation.

Lang has no idea why Franky would be interested in the story, or how he'd even known to ask about it (the true story of Transway's demise being a close-kept secret among Rinconada's inner circle). But he doesn't care. It bought him the bottle. And after having to dredge that whole mess up again he's craving its warm embrace more than ever. He's already had a shot or two but he's nowhere near where he wants to be. He'll get there though – and he knows the perfect place to do it.

The path rolls out from under the trees and curves up around some large boulders. At the crest of the small hill a sudden vista opens up with the river spread out below. Then it dips down to circle a little copse right by the water.

You'd pass right by the place if you didn't know: The trees conceal an eroded rock formation, curved in enough to be almost a cave and floored by a flat platform that juts out over the water. It's one of his favorite spots, someplace he used to go to fuse in the camp's early days. He steps lightly over a fallen tree trunk and scrambles up a small rise to the base.

A sudden breeze ruffles Lang's hair as he extracts the cork from the bottle and tips it up for a swig. The air smells of pine and possibility. He takes a step toward the ledge, admiring the light on the water like a raft of diamonds – just as his foot catches on something soft and he stumbles. He nearly rights himself but a scatter of loose pebbles sends him windmilling backwards. There's the brief, horrible sound of smashing glass as he lands hard on his back. For a moment he can only blink in disbelief.

Then: *I fuck up, every last fucking thing. Can't fuse. Can't get drunk. Can't do* anything *right.*

And then the tears do come, bubbling hot and acid with shame, and he can't stop them. He sobs helplessly, convulsively, curling around the black hole in his gut that threatens to strip him of every atom of joy he's ever known until –

"Hey, aren't you the medicine man or something? What happened; you run out of medicine?"

A voice like stone on stone. The soft thing he tripped over. That new girl with the kids.

Sonrisa.

"Fuck you," Lang says, choking the words out as he tries to get hold of himself, and tries to locate her in the dark. From this angle, someone sitting against the concave rock is barely visible. He can see her feet now, though. Too bad he didn't see them a few minutes ago.

"Hey," she says again, offhand. "Don't mean to be rude. Just seems like you're having kind of a bad time."

"Yeah?" he says, sniffling as he sits up cross-legged and checks himself for injury. "What gave it away?"

"Don't be like that. I'm just trying to help."

"By tripping me?"

"I didn't trip you. You fell." She sniffs loudly. "Too much whiskey."

"I'm not *drunk*. I barely got a sip of that. Because you

tripped me."

He knows he's being shitty but he doesn't care. It feels good to argue, to blame someone else for even a tiny corner of his misery.

"Whatever. You're better off not drinking that shit anyway. Smells like fermented ass."

"I am tired," he says through clenched teeth, "of everyone telling me what I'm better off without."

"Like the fuse?"

A stunned beat passes.

"Asshole," he finally hisses, bristling as he gets to his feet. "Seriously. Who the fuck do you think you are?"

"Wait!"

Something in the girl's tone stops him cold. There's a rustle of movement in the shadows, and he turns in time to see a hand reach out past them. The small, silvery vial glints in the moonlight.

"Told you I was trying to help."

Lang's whole body pivots, alive with interest. "Where'd you get that?" he demands. "You turned yours in."

"I turned *one* in," she says, closing her fist triumphantly. "The one the kids had. This one's mine. I'd never be dumb enough to give up my transfer. Especially to some fruity-haired little bitch on a power trip."

"Mara," Lang says. "She didn't used to be like that. She's gotten kind of out of control lately."

"I don't care what her fucking deal is. She's not gonna treat me like some baby that has to be monitored. From what I hear she's a fuser too."

"Class D," Lang confirms.

"So? She's not better than me."

"So you're…"

"Class E," Sonrisa says. "Like you."

Lang is silent for a moment, absorbing this. Then, "Where'd you hear all this stuff anyway? Maddy?"

"Yeah. She's a good old girl. But once she figured out I wasn't up for joining her merry band of putanas she didn't have much use for me. Still," and he can hear the smirk in her voice even if he can't quite see it, "I got a lot of good intel out of her first."

"Oh yeah?"

"Yeah."

"So what do you want out of me?"

"Sientate," she says, patting the spot next to her. "And we can discuss it."

He sits, and it turns out she doesn't want much other than a place to stay that's away from both Maddy and Mara and someone to watch her back. If he lets her stay in the healer's hut and says she's some new protégé she'll give him all the fuses he wants. The kids (Lily and Joaquin) can stay with Taryn and Willa.

"Deal," Lang says.

Sonrisa unscrews the dropper. "How much?"

He pauses. It's been a while since he's had a real dose so he needs to not go too crazy. Still, even a small amount will show in his eyes (to other fusers anyway) so even if he can get up and walk back to camp after it's probably not such a good idea. With his luck, he'd run straight into Mara.

Might as well turn it on a little.

"Sixth," he says finally, pushing up his sleeve. "No…better

make it a quarter."

Wordlessly, she hands it over. The touch of the glass on his arm makes him shiver, little hairs standing up.

Sonrisa chuckles. "Really missed your shit there, huh?"

He tenses, but then an elbow pokes him gently in the ribs. "It's OK."

And at that he exhales, fully for once. Because for the first time in forever he's with someone who understands. Someone like Celan. And who knows if she still feels the same? Maybe she's gotten some supertech alien cura up there. Maybe she'll come back and look at him like he's the piece of shit her father said he was. That everyone says. Maybe she'll –

Cállate, stupid brain!

He sucks in a breath, building momentum, wanting calm, calm, peace and balm, until the energy of the fuse releases – transferred from mind to hand and through the fluid in the dropper as he squeezes the bulb and pushes a surge of Class E into a vein; a surge that races to some secret place inside and hits him like a wave of pure gold joy.

All pain all fear all tears all gone. (Did they ever even really exist?) The night is beautiful; this life is beautiful. Every cell in his body heaves a massive sigh of relief.

Sonrisa leans over to extricate the dropper from his slackened hand and reunite it with the vial. But it's a nice touch, warm and friendly. And the stone against his back is warm too, so warm and soft. And having someone by his side… someone who's not mad at him.

Lang's thoughts drift unhurried as time casts off its moorings and starts a singular slippage. What did Celan call it – a code loop? He grins at the memory then gives himself over to infinity, transfixed by the river's silver bob and shimmer beyond the ends of his outstretched feet. Endless eons (or minutes) later his head jerks up as he comes awake and meets Sonrisa's fuse-bright eyes in the dark.

"Wow," he says.

"I do that shit right, medicine man."

"Yeah…"

She looks him over, chuckling again. "Damn," she says, "lit up like Liberation Day."

"Every last fucking star in the sky."

And with that he and this new girl are both laughing, free and easy, like the best and oldest of friends.

6

The buzz of talk in the crowded plaza hums dully in Shariah's ears. She wraps arms around herself, feeling oddly exposed without anyone to talk to until a tap on the shoulder has her turn to find Kirk's cheerful face, hazel eyes like gentle half-moons, staring down at her. He's grown a few inches over the past year or so. They used to be almost the same height. Now he towers over her.

"Want some company?"

"Sure." She shrugs, feigning nonchalance. But his presence is a huge relief. Today's independent study so she was up in her room alone when her server chimed with a reminder about docking day – all except those at essential posts were required to gather and watch the proceedings communally. It was too late to round anyone up so she'd come down to the plaza by herself. As Bev is with the team in the command center, Kirk must be in a similar situation.

Shariah doesn't need to ask where Bryan is; he and Kirk

were practically inseparable as podmates, but they'd had some sort of mysterious falling out this past spring (neither will say what it was about, though she strongly suspects the Chronie thing had something to do with it) and now they barely speak.

"What's up?" Kirk says casually, running a hand over his close-cropped sandy hair. But she knows he must have heard from Bev that she and Bryan are on the outs now as well.

"Nothing much. Just work. You know."

"Yeah, it's been crazy lately. I don't know how she does it." Kirk tips his chin toward the giant three-sided holoscreen hovering over the fountain, one face each in line with each side of the pyramid's base. The translucent panes above have been temporarily darkened for better viewing. The screen facing them currently shows the team in the command center – Bev's red-gold head is easy to spot among the ranks – but any minute the crew of the Passerine will be (almost) live. (They'll autosplice to smooth over the three-minute delays.)

"I know," Shariah says. "She's amazing."

Engineering programs are tough enough, juggling one in addition to Mars training is pure insanity. But Bev's been determined to go ever since Mr. Timanti first proposed it. Shariah envies her a little; so sure and intent, everything working out for her. No weirdness dogging Bev's steps, no having to endure being 'sorely tested' over and over.

Bev and Kirk knew Lana too; they all (with the addition of Lucas, who none of them see any more since he's not an En trainee) were in the same learning pod from ages twelve to eighteen. During those years the six of them had spent the majority of their time together – learning, playing, and squabbling like the siblings they never had. But somehow Bev and Kirk appear to have emerged from Lana's long shadow unscathed. After the initial shock and horror of her betrayal passed they were able to brush it off and move on, while Shariah, as Lana's former best friend, still has to endure regular rounds of looks and whispers.

At least that's what it feels like.

At a nudge from Kirk and she looks up to see the names and images of the Passerine crew scroll across the screen: Andrea Johnson Chavez (AgEn), Christina Ellin (CompEn), Matthew Feeley (PhysEn), Nigel Gallegos (MedEn), Aubrey Rae Gil (MechEn), Maureen "Mo" Morrison (SanEn), John Nakai (SocEn), L. Solano-Ybarra (EdEn), and Vaughn D. Vogel (GenEn). They must be about to start.

What must it be like? she wonders, gazing at the names in awe. *To do something truly great?*

Shariah has no desire to go into space; it's far too cold and empty and she likes solid ground under her feet – but the idea of doing something special, historic even, holds tremendous appeal. It's what she *should* be doing instead of sitting around worrying about stupid relationships and the ruins of the past.

But at the moment her own research is at a dead end. She can't switch disciplines midstream (and she wouldn't want to give up SocEn anyway), but her area of study – which had been expanded to include ranchos transers in the wake of the demise of Transway – is, quite frankly, boring as hell.

All of the data they have about the ranchos is second-hand, anecdotal, filtered through old expro accounts. And with the expros expunged, there's no new information coming in. She's been sifting through the ruins of Transway for months with little to show for it. Drones over ranchos airspace only provide tantalizing glimpses before shorting out. At this rate they're never going to convince people of the threat the ranchos pose and of the dire need to dismantle them. Her mother's been saying this for years and no one ever listens. Even Mr. Timanti, who you'd think would despise all transers at this point.

But if someone were directly observe them...

An electric shiver runs down her spine. That would be historic. And dangerous. Maybe not going-into-space-dangerous but scary enough in its own right – there are a lot of transers over there. They're not known to be violent but they are unpredictable, what with all the transferon they take. She would have to bring a stun. And wear a disguise, like the SocTechs in the holoshops. But not expro-ish. It'd have to be more subdued. There are definitely enough of them (a few thousand is the best estimate) that everyone wouldn't know everyone else on sight. She could blend in enough to walk around, check things out, maybe even take some images or footage on her server. She could –

"Look," Kirk says. "The Nido!"

Dutifully, Shariah swings her eyes up to the screen, taking in the orbital station's impressive girth as the Passerine's cylindrical form glides towards it against a velvety backdrop sprinkled with stars. Some kind of special sat-cam was launched earlier to record both vessels during their historic join. In the background, a sphinx-like slice of the red planet itself hangs in the sky.

A round, gunmetal-grey aperture like the top of a bottle extrudes from the smooth, white tip of the Passerine, and slowly fits itself into a matching port on the Nido. Rings of metal spin, sliding into place as the screen cuts to Gil and Feeley in the pilots' seats, beaming from ear to ear. At ages twenty-seven and thirty, they are the crew's youngest members and arguably its most photogenic; Feeley especially, with his tousled curls and slow grin, has become quite the favorite.

"It's a lock!" Gil says, blue eyes shining under a fringe of dark bangs. "Perfect!"

She and Feeley hug.

The plaza erupts in cheers, drowning out a short speech explaining the mechanics of what they just witnessed. Then the screen cuts again to an inside shot of the portal to the Nido as the airlock opens and one by one the nine astronauts file through, waving to the folks at home.

Kirk and Shariah whoop and applaud along with everyone else, she with mounting and genuine excitement. She's happy for the astronauts of course, but now she's happy for herself as well. Because she has a plan; a good one. She's going to do something unprecedented.

Now they're not the only ones who are going to make history.

THEODORE BEAMS AS MANY HANDS clap him on the back, the command center's usual air of hushed reserve given over to giddy exuberance. The 'live' feed to the various plazas has been cut off and the crowds are beginning to disperse. But here the work continues with a communications test from the Nido and a full system check nearing completion.

Someone passes him a bottle of something fizzy and he tips it back, savoring the clean bite of alcohol in his throat. It's been a while since he's had a drink – more than a while, over a year. In the wake of the fallout from the Lana fiasco he'd wanted a clear head and a fresh start, and with Transway (and Martinez) gone there wasn't much left in the way of temptation. But today's a special day so he takes another long pull. With what he's just accomplished no one's going to begrudge him a little cheer.

And he could use it. Despite today's public triumph his private visit to Lana's family last week had been an unmitigated failure. He'd thought his new approach so clever – telling them that he'd seen drone footage of her on the road – because unless she's been hiding in the basement for the past eighteen months without ever leaving the house they couldn't be completely sure of whether or not it was true. He thought it would at least make them uneasy; he'd catch a shifty look, a nervous twinge, some tiny tell.

But there was nada. Not one concession or clue. They just sat there shaking their heads, stone-faced. What is he going to have to do, camp out on a ridge with binoculars and wait for her to break cover?

Stupid. There are twelve ranchos, encompassing hundreds of dwellings. She could be staying in any one of them or rotating between several – who knows how many hidey holes she has? So unless he's willing to play hardball it seems that he's reached an impasse. Because if he's still hoping to win his daughter over, threatening her ranchos relatives is not exactly going to do him any favors.

He takes another brooding pull at the bottle as the screen crackles to life, a grinning Nigel flanked by a pale but cheerful-looking Andrea Johnson Chavez and the dark, solemn countenance of Vaughn D. Vogel. They have a bottle too, and as Nigel raises it in a toast Theodore brightens up his own face and follows suit.

"One down, two to go," Nigel says. "Small steps for man and all that. Everything's up and running here, all systems go. Though I have to admit I'm anxious to get some real ground under my feet. Even if it's full of perchlorates. Ready to do this again in ten days, Theodore?"

The room erupts anew and Theodore chuckles. In a weird way, this docking felt like the more difficult maneuver. Though everything has been engineered to the hilt to prevent error and run through simulation after endless simulation, until the Passerine actually docked no one knew with one hundred percent certainty that it would work. Any number of things could have gone wrong, either during the flight or during docking: a surprise meteoroid, a wobble in gravitation, an infinitesimal misalignment. But it seems like the ghosts of Luna Sigma have finally been laid to rest. With the Passerine in good shape and the Nido occupied and fully operational, the two lander trips down to the surface seem like small potatoes. Though in truth he knows they are not.

'Six minutes of terror,' is how the final descent to Mars was described by the old-world NASA agency. The thin atmosphere is notoriously short on friction with which to slow the descent of approaching spacecraft.

But they have ten days to worry about that. Right now, brave faces and celebration are the order of the day.

"Can't wait," Theodore answers. "But you've all earned a break. Enjoy it. Let us know if there's anything you need."

They virtual-toast again and the screen goes dark. Theodore drains the rest of the bottle and heaves a sigh, albeit one

81

that, due to his ongoing personal conundrums, is only partially of relief.

AS SOON AS THE HOLOSCREENS wink off, the interior panes of the pyramid brighten, throwing a lambent wash over the plaza that makes Shariah squint and nearly trip over a couple seated on a bench by the fountain.

"Sorry," she mutters as she hastens towards the elevator, a torrent of ideas rushing through her brain:

It would be best to schedule her first visit to the ranchos during some kind of festival, when lots of people will be milling around. Too bad their annual 'Liberation Day' has already passed, that would have been ideal. But maybe there's another one, some kind of harvest thing. Or trade days; they have those too.

Aside from the stun and a good disguise she'll also need an imagecard. Bringing her server is too risky – someone could easily ping it and find out her location. Plus it's far too noticeable. She has clearance to do her Transway surveys so there's no issue there; she can check a roller out. And it's less than an hour's drive so she can definitely get there, do some reconnaissance, and get back again without anyone knowing she was gone (unless they look at her georecs, but hopefully no one will).

But she can't drive the whole distance; someone might see the roller and blow her cover. She'll have to hide it somewhere on the outskirts and walk the rest of the way. There's excellent drone coverage of the terrain almost all the way to the borders of the nearest two ranchos (Pescados and de la Virgen, respectively) so she shouldn't have any trouble finding a good spot.

There's almost no traffic on the old road anymore, but to be safe she can hook up a drone feed and keep an eye out to avoid any untimely encounters.

It's a little bit dangerous, not telling anyone else about her plans, but she can't risk being denied permission. This is too important.

Better to beg for forgiveness.

Though she probably won't have to; all the amazing intel she'll gather should more than make up for any liberties taken. Her mother will be so impressed with her daughter's initiative that she probably won't even care.

Shariah whips out her server and starts to search the recs for information about ranchos festival dates, not looking where she's going until –

"Hey! What's your problem? Couldn't even break up with me without your mother's help?"

Bryan – big as life with a fresh sneer curdling his handsome face. She never even saw him coming.

But she holds her ground.

"My mother?" she says, matching his condescending tone. "My mother had nothing to do with it. We broke up because you couldn't be serious and act normal for one night, even when you knew it was important to me."

"Yeah. Right. Just couldn't leave it alone, could you? Had to twist the knife. Had to go and sicc her on me and my friends. Shut us all up."

"Shut you – what? What are you even talking about?"

"Do I even have to say it? The *Chronies,*" he draws the word out mockingly. "You told your mother about us, made her shut us down."

Shariah raises her chin, offering him a look of complete and utter contempt. "I did no such thing. I mean, I may have *mentioned* it to her, but it was only in conversation, to explain why we broke up, not as some evil plot of revenge. She thought it was just as stupid as I did."

"Apparently not," Bryan says crisply. "Because she's seized all of our data and frozen our investigation indefinitely. Any further work on this and I'll be kicked out of the En program."

She blinks at him, nonplussed. Then: "You're investi – that's ridiculous! You didn't have an investigation, you had a *delusion*. It was all a bunch of bullshit."

She's close to yelling now.

"Really?" Bryan says, smirking. "If it was such bullshit then why did she even bother? If it wasn't as a favor to you, maybe there really was something behind it. Something important. Makes you think, doesn't it?"

"All I think," she says evenly, "is that you're even more of an idiot than I ever suspected. By a full order of magnitude."

A shrug. "You can think whatever you want, but you know there's something there; something weird. And it's not just the angles in the plaza. We've been outside, with instruments, measuring daylight. No matter how you slice it we're still off by three days. Something happened, Shariah, between summer solstice '16 and summer solstice '17, and I bet I know when it was. Right around Ord 63. Right about the time when Lana – "

"Don't you *dare* say that name!" Shariah says with such vehemence that several onlookers' heads swivel in their direction. "Don't you dare throw her in my face. That has nothing to do with anything."

Bryan retreats a pace, palms up, real regret in his eyes.

"Sorry. I wasn't trying to – "

"I don't care what you were trying to do. Just go away, Bryan. Take your stupid angles and go away and leave me alone!"

But it's she who turns and walks away, almost runs, chased by a maelstrom of confusion that pushes her past the elevators and down the first available corridor, searching for a restroom or an empty lab; anywhere dark and cool where she can sit and collect herself.

He's an idiot, she thinks. *A complete and total –*

But Bryan is highly intelligent and always has been. And there *was* no real reason for her mother to have gotten involved in the Chronie mess; Lead SocEns have far more important things to do than crack down on a few MechEn crackpots. Her mother has always put such a premium on independence. She'd never embarrass her daughter; never get involved in Shariah's personal affairs.

'Any further work on this and I'll be kicked out of the En program.'

Unless, of course, he's telling the truth; unless something *did* happen, and Ariana Balor was involved. Shariah ducks into a restroom, shuts the stall door behind her, and sits, frantically scrolling on her server until the words blur, looking for something, anything, to drive these extremely unsettling thoughts out of her head.

7

Deep in concentration, Celan presses her lips together and leans over the holo, using the combined anti-gravity fields of five simulated Convention ships to nudge the simulated rogue planet toward the edge of a simulated wormhole.

Just a little closer...

And it's in!

Quickly she sets the countdown for thirteen hours and 45 minutes Madren time and switches views to the Oro-fuchans, who are busy assembling another team of simulated ships at the other end. They give her a wing-dip, their equivalent of a thumbs up.

Now all they have to do is wait.

She exhales, reclining in her chair. Maybe some lunch would be a good idea. But before she can get to her feet there's a chime from the capsule's sensors. A docking request, which can only mean –

"Ree!" she says aloud as the Plejaran's face appears in a sidebar on her holo. "I didn't expect you all so soon!"

"My Madren friend," Ree says, "so good to see you."

"You too!" She taps the blinking light on the holo to approve the request and rises, a little lightheaded before gaining purchase in reality and crossing the room to the oval door of the airlock.

She taps her foot impatiently as the Plejaran ship runs through the docking protocols, then steps forward as the airlock hisses open to greet the tall, pale, humanoid form of one of the first non-Madrens she'd ever met. When Ree appears, Celan is happy enough to hug the woman, but Plejarans aren't physically demonstrative outside of their triunes so she settles for a slight bow instead.

Ree looks her up and down thoughtfully.

"What?" Celan says, suddenly self-conscious.

"Your hair," Ree says. "I thought only very old Madrens had their hair turn that color."

Celan shrugs. "Space effects." She knows very well that white hair is a symptom of heavy fusing, but the Plejarans, thankfully, do not. (She's been debating whether or not to try and dye it somehow before she goes home.)

"Ah," Ree says. "Well, it is very becoming."

"Thanks."

"And you have lost weight as well."

"Probably. I've been busy."

"So we hear," says a new voice, and Celan glances behind Ree to see Chan, followed by Ness, stepping though the airlock and joining the Plejaran woman in her chamber. All three are very similar in appearance, though the two men have blue eyes instead of Ree's green. All are hairless, save for the slight silvery fuzz atop the crown of their heads, and all are dressed in the same white, shapeless garments they were wearing the first time Celan saw them, what feels like millennia ago, on a faraway mesa.

"Leading an inquiry!" Chan says, beaming like a proud papa. If he had suspenders, his thumbs would be hooked right through. "Well done."

"Thanks."

"And such an original idea too," Ness notes.

Celan preens.

"Are you sure you aren't working yourself too hard, though?" Ree asks. "We know it can be difficult at first to sync up with those who operate on different time scales. But everyone respects that. You don't have to push youself."

"I guess," Celan sighs. "But if I'm leading the inquiry I have to actually be there, you know? As much as possbile."

"There are many ways to lead," Ness says sagely.

Celan nods as if she understands him (although she's not sure she does), and almost hugs herself with joy – not at the advice itself but just because it's such a *Ness* thing to say. Of the three, Ness and Ree have always been the more serious personalities where Chan is the ever-jovial bright star. As far as she can tell, Chan also functions as the emotional linchpin of the group; the one the other two mutually adore while loving each other in a more subdued way. Because they're all partners, not only in work but in life, the triune (almost always in the form of two men and one woman or two women and a man) being the primary Plejaran romantic/domestic grouping.

This had been made clear to her on the second night of their trip to Va'anak when, after a delicious meal and a few drinks, Chan and Ness had gone off together with obvious amorous intent and she'd made a comment to Ree about nice couples. Ree kindly corrected her, explaining that while young Plejarans had relations in all types of groupings, at the age of ninety or so (about the equivalent of thirty in Madren years) they partnered into triunes. She, Chan, and Ness were all together, although they didn't always all have sexual relations at the same time.

Celan had been fascinated by this, though reluctant to pry, but Ree was open to discussion: In the Plejaran woman's opinion, the sharing of cultural differences and similarities was part of what the Convention was all about. So she'd described how the three of them would eventually settle back on their home world to have children, of which, since Plejarans reproduce very similarly to humans, the usual number was two – one for each pairing within the triune. But they weren't ready for that yet; they were still too young and too involved in their work with the Convention. But someday, she'd added happily, it would be a wonderful experience.

Celan remembers wondering if some day that would be true for her and Lang too.

"So," Chan says, snapping her back into the present. "We've got an idea. How about getting out of this capsule for a while?"

"Can we go to Va'anak?"

"Unfortunately, no," Ness says. "The wormholes aren't conducive to travel there right now. We'd have to take too many detours."

She frowns, disappointed.

"We were thinking, though," says Ree, with a glance at her two partners, "of a trip to XǐNeru."

"What's that?"

"A tidally-locked planet in the Evvútu system. It's one of the most beautiful worlds out there."

"And one of the most historic," adds Chan. "Filled with relics and fascinating exhibits!"

"So this is an educational trip?" Celan says, eyeing him with suspicion.

"Everything is educational," Ness says primly. "But aside from its beauty, XǐNeru also has great K'Shiran cultural significance. A visit is required for all Convention members before they are allowed more than basic use of the quantum band. We've tarried a bit, I'm afraid, in taking you there."

So that's it! Celan thinks, partially relieved that her being kept in the dark hasn't necessarily been personal so much an oversight on the Plejarans' part. Though they could have been sent away on purpose for that very reason: To keep her from learning while maintaining plausible deniability.

But why would the Convention do that? For the millionth time she wonders if they aren't secretly observing her; taking notes, finding her lacking somehow. Do they have enough background data on Madrens to find her transferon use problematic?

When she first got here, she'd had no knowledge about the construction of Dyson cells and wouldn't have known the first thing about how to block a view. Plus, she figured that any attempt to do so would look far worse than just going about business as usual. Once she found out there definitely were views of a sort she'd made it a point not to alter her behavior in any way, hoping they'd decide that fusing was normal for her species and leave it at that.

And it seemed to have worked. Chan saw her fuse on Va'anak and hadn't argued with her medical explanation. And truly, it *is* medicine. After all that's happened, without it there's no way she'd still be even partially sane.

So maybe this new trip is legit, proof that she's done everything right.

"What's so special about XɪNeru?" she asks.

"XɪNeru is breathtaking," Ree says. "You won't be sorry to see it. But it's also sad – a reminder of what can happen, even to transentient species and advanced civilizations, when they are not at peace with themselves. When they use the gifts the Convention has given them for selfish, power-seeking ends."

Celan twists the band on her finger, a bit chagrined as she recalls her daydream about besting Ariana the other day.

But I wasn't really going to do anything that bad. Just kind of put her in her place. I mean, after everything she did –

"The XɪNeruans developed two very distinct types of civilizations," Ree continues. "Ones that vacillated between war and reconciliation throughout their history. During the time when they first made contact with the Convention, they were in a period of peace. But this eventually fell apart and they ended up using the quantum bands to destroy each other."

"That's terrible," Celan says.

"Yes," says Ness. "You have no idea."

She must look as pained as she feels because Chan gurgles out a laugh. "Don't worry," he says. "It isn't all depressing. Xɪ

Neru also has some of the finest recreational facilities in the Orion-Cygnus arm."

"Really?"

"Really."

Ness and Ree nod.

Privately, Celan thinks it more than a little strange that the powers that be would stick some kind of galactic wayvern next to a memorial to a lost civilization. But who knows? Maybe when they're done touring the ruins she'll finally get that gargleblaster, as well as a chance to level up with the quantum band. After all, if they're taking her there then they must have decided that she's trustworthy. And *normal*.

"Alright," she says. "I'm in."

"Excellent," says Ree. "Tomorrow morning?"

"Can it be afternoon?" And in answer to their quizzical looks adds: "We have two more simulations to go in this series. So I just need to finish up a few more things."

8

"No." Mara sighs in mild exasperation. "You have to make it even. Here, let me show you."

She nudges Jae aside and leans over the clay pot on the table, expertly patting and smoothing until all sides are the same thickness.

"There," she says. "Mira? Así. Otherwise it won't fire right."

Jae nods her sleek, dark head in acknowledgment and Mara gives her an encouraging pat on the back. "You're doing a good job though," she says. "Just fifty more pots to go!"

Jae laughs, slumping her willowy form in mock-weariness, as Mara exits the small workshop and strides past the dining hall. The last of the breakfasters are straggling in, and she gives them a sharp eye before pressing up a steep rise to a newly-cleared area, brushing a film of drying clay from her hands as she goes. This new field is farther from the river and, being a bit uphill, not as well-suited to ditch irrigation as the others, so they're going to try some clay pot irrigation here next spring and see how it works out. They've managed to scavenge a good number of bricks and the remains of an old woodstove, out of which Alex and Sig have constructed a makeshift kiln.

She can't wait to try it out.

It may take a while to get the firing temperatures correct but they have all winter to perfect their technique, and plenty of clay from some digs upstream. She's hoping that once it's all up and running they can start making some good plates and bowls to replace those nasty trenchers too. It's hard to keep wood clean and carving new ones all the time is a pain in the ass.

Mara bounces a few steps happily then stops, checking to make sure no one's seen her. It wouldn't do for the camp leader to be seen skipping like a little girl. But she *is* happy. Everything's falling into place: Lang, Maddy, everything.

She powers up the last few feet and halts at the edge of the clearing, watching as Brophy and a few of the other burlier guys attempt to extract a large tree stump. After a few minutes more wrangling it suddenly gives free. She claps and whistles and Brophy turns and waves, sculpted torso gleaming. He strides over and lifts her easily, spinning her around.

"Ew!" she says. "Put me down. You're all sweaty!"

"You love it," he says, but sets her down as directed.

She slips an arm around his waist to show him that really he's right, and together they walk back to the group in the field.

Mara almost skips again, but forces herself to refrain. This is how it should be: Brophy sweet on her again, Lang off with his new girl – happy and healthy and no más fuss. She never

should have doubted herself for being too hard on him. Sometimes people need a firm hand; sometimes, they actually *like* it.

It's a strange turn that for all the hours she'd spent bitching back in the day about the techs' heavy-handedness towards
Transway, she's now starting to feel a grudging sort of respect
for them. They were in charge of a population that kept refusing to do things their way. So of course they were frustrated,
and sometimes they had to be harsh. It's just what you have
to do when you're the one(s) in charge...if you want to *stay* in
charge, that is.

And this applies to the Maddy situation as well. Though
Mara still suspects the woman of running a few girls, she's
been far less blatant about it lately and, most importantly, has
refrained from any more challenges to Mara's authority. Even
if she *had* been holding a transfer in reserve to try and snare
Lang, she'd missed her chance. He's Class E-free and perfectly
content with Sonrisa.

When they reach the group at the stump she disengages
from Brophy and surveys the excavation, running a hand along
a smooth section of exposed bark. Good grain in the wood;
they'll get a quite a few trenchers and platters out of this.

"Split this thing up into chunks," she orders. "And try not
to splinter it too much. This should tide us over 'til that kiln
gets going."

"Yes, ma'am," says Gabe. There's a bit of cheek to his tone,
but Mara laughs. Jaslene's man is close enough to the inner
circle to get away with it. Plus, it's always good to show a sense
of humor.

"But first you all look like you could use a little break," she
adds. "Come down to the kitchen and we'll see if we can find

you a snack."

This is met with vigorous approval; they've all already burned off their first meal of the day and won't get another until evening. Most people squirrel away a small midday snack from their breakfast leftovers but there are no official between-meal offerings to be had.

When you're the one in charge though you can do whatever you like, so Mara leads the way to the dining hall – Brophy in tow, camp spread out below, and feeling like the queen of it all.

STRETCHING LONG ARMS UP OVER his head, Lang strolls out of the dining hall and into the morning sun. Light pours over his face like warm syrup, and the earth beneath his feet is velvet-smooth. He breathes deep, taking in the sweet late-summer air and the faint mineral tang of the river. In the wake of his return to the fuse the tensile stress that exists between him and the rest of the world has receded and what remains is an easy peace. For now, at least.

"So," says Danilo, beside him. They start off across the plaza with the short, stocky man taking pains to match his long strides. "Looks like things are finally going all right for you, güey."

"Kind of, yeah."

"More than kind of. I mean, everyone's noticed."

"They have?" Lang's pulse quickens.

We've been careful. They can't possibly know.

"Yeah. Having a girl around does good things to a man." A knowing grin apples Danilo's round cheeks, punctuated by a merry wink.

"Sure," Lang mutters.

"Just don't let her run you too much, man. Once they get those claws in…" He makes a sound like an angry cat.

Lang snorts, but smooths it out into a convivial chuckle.

There's nothing going on between him and Sonrisa. Even if he had been interested (which he's not) she'd made it clear the first night that she wasn't into any of 'that messy shit.' The official story is that she's a healing prodigy who needs extra attention to help get her up to speed. But all the time they spend together, his doing special favors for her (like the burrito he's currently bringing her for breakfast), and the fact that they both sleep in the hut together says otherwise to most people. Rumor has it he's smitten, and he's been careful neither to confirm nor deny. Let people think whatever they want.

As long as it's not the truth:

The reason he's bringing Sonrisa breakfast is that she can't go herself; she needs some E in her first thing in the morning and there's no way to be certain that Mara, Sig, and/or Brophy (the only three still actively fusing) won't notice the telltale shine in her eyes. As Lang's only just started up again his evening dose is enough to hold him for twenty-four hours, and the shine doesn't last that long.

But Sonrisa still needs to at least pretend to take a few medicinal-grade drops of transferon in the morning; to refuse them would be strange.

So they've worked out a system where her special morning meditations keep her in the healer's hut during breakfast, requiring someone to bring her drops there. Lang, of course, isn't to be trusted with a transfer, but Danilo, as the outermost member of the inner circle, is; and he's the one with the most time on his hands and the least propensity for asking difficult questions. And, most importantly, he's not a fuser. Her eyes could be practically on fire and he'd never know the difference.

It's a good system, albeit one that will only work until Lang starts needing a morning cura again too. Then he's not sure what they'll do. Sonrisa will think of something though. She's good like that. Like Celan was.

Is.

He sighs sourly, wishing that all this deception wasn't necessary. That he could be honest. It's obvious that he's better off like this. Apparently, *everyone's* noticed. So why does Mara have to be so shitty about it? She needs what she needs and he needs what he needs.

Why am I always the fucking problem?

Lang rolls his shoulders, shrugging off aggravation as they approach the hut. There are shouts from the clearing out back – Willa and Taryn tossing a ball with the kids. His other two apprentices had been happy to house Lily and Joaquin due to the pressing needs of Sonrisa's accelerated program. Neither woman seemed to mind, even though it meant putting their own training on hold.

Another thing to add to the guilt list, but he quickly shuts it down. Sonrisa's right – this is all Mara's fault. If she wasn't so unreasonable (not to mention hypocritical) Sonrisa would have her own rooms somewhere and be able to care for the kids herself. There's just not enough space in the healer's hut for all four of them.

He gives the group a quick half-wave before rapping a warning tattoo on the front door. He waits a moment, then swings it open to reveal Sonrisa – folded into a half-lotus on a crude cushion on the floor. Sunlight streams through the window haloing her honeyed hair. At the sound of their footsteps she opens her eyes and smiles, the picture of beatific bliss.

Lang bites back a laugh.

"Mornin'," Danilo says, jocularity quickly sobering in her most serene presence. "Ready for your drops?"

"Bueno," she says, rising with all the grace of a fairy queen. "I really appreciate you taking the time to come by special for me. I know you must have lots of other things to do."

Danilo shuffles aw-shucks-style as he takes out the transfer, unscrews the dropper, and draws up a small amount. He hands it to Sonrisa, who decorously places one, two, three drops under her tongue before she passes it back, gently brushing his forearm with her other hand as she does so.

"Gracias," she says, "I feel better already."

The man actually blushes as she gives him a quick hug. Then Danilo ducks out the door; his footsteps receding towards the plaza.

She and Lang share a smirk.

"Laying it on thick today, are we?"

"There ain't no such thing."

"Hungry?" He proffers the burrito.

But she waves it away. "Maybe later."

He puts it down on the bench, shaking his head. "How can you eat everything cold like that?"

"Tastes better."

"Crazy girl."

"Fuser bitch."

"Chingate."

"You wish."

"I already got a girl."

"Right. Your imaginary friend who lives in space. Is that where you go when you vamos aviados? Freak," she adds, rolling her eyes to complete the Mara impersonation.

They both crack up.

"What's so funny?" says a voice from the doorway. Danilo didn't close it behind him and now Willa's standing there.

Lang straightens his face.

"Nada," Sonrisa says. "Just a little prana humor."

Willa gives her a strange look but doesn't press it. "Well if you're all done in here the kids were asking for you. Maybe you want to come play with them?"

"Oh sure. But Lang just brought me breakfast. Maybe later?"

"OK," Willa says, shrugging off.

Lang shifts his weigh uneasily, scratching the back of his neck.

Sonrisa punches him lightly in the arm. "Hey. Fuser bitch. Don't freak out. She can't tell, right?"

"No, only Mara and Sig, and sometimes Brophy. But he's Class S now; he doesn't do it much anymore. We just don't want anyone getting suspicious and saying anything or one of them might come sniffing around."

"Well, if they do I'll just close my eyes and pretend to be holy."

She reprises her beatific smile and he chuckles appreciatively.

"So what's the deal today?" she says, pirouetting as she twists her hair up into a bun. "Any appointments? Anything interesting?"

"Not much. Couple toothaches. Someone who keeps puking after breakfast."

"Pregnant."

"It's a guy."

She laughs. "Nice."

"I'm sure you can handle it."

Sonrisa shrugs, noncommittal, and bends to unwrap the burrito, avoiding his eyes.

Lang watches her, wondering for the millionth time what's really going on here. Because the weird thing is, Sonrisa actually *can* handle almost any injury or illness entirely on her own. Her whole fake-healing-prodigy thing is...fake.

He'd suspected as much, knowing how long she'd been taking care of the kids on her own – there was no other way short of being insanely lucky or insanely tough that they all could've survived. An infected cut, a flu, a bad sting or bite... the odds were too great. So he'd tested his hypothesis (as Celan would say). Two days later, when his prodigy was supposed to be helping him with a particularly nasty infection, he'd cut his own prana off and watched her unwittingly finish the job. He'd repeated the same ruse a couple more times to be sure and then asked her about it point blank.

She acted like she had no idea what he was talking about.

Which made no sense whatsoever, because there's no doubt the girl can heal. So either she doesn't know, doesn't want to know, or she knows damn well what she can do.

But if that's the case, Lang thinks, watching her poke at the food like it might bite her, *why won't she just admit it?*

9

"Theodore," says the sharp-faced, steel-haired woman who's all but materialized in the corridor in front of him. "I realize you've been busy getting us to Mars, but you are a *very* hard man to track down. It almost feels like you're avoiding me."

The woman smiles, but her grey eyes narrow, regarding him shrewdly.

Miller. Shit. What does she want?

Roberta Miller (who's communications he *has* been assiduously avoiding) is the newest addition to the triumvirate of Lead SocEns that governs the city; he and Ariana Balor being the other two well-established parts. Miller had been chosen by a convocation of emeriti late last year to replace Frank Martinez, finally declared dead after his mysterious disappearance around the time of the demise of Transway. Sometimes, Theodore likes to think his friend went down with the ship; he can't imagine Martinez living in a world without Maddy's. He almost smirks at the thought but catches himself; nothing but the soberest countenance will do in front of Miller.

Even Ariana is afraid of her.

"My apologies," he says, quickly. "Things have been crazy lately. Once boots are on the ground, so to speak, I'll have more time."

But it's what she wants the time for that worries him.

Because part of Miller's mandate upon assuming office was to launch a formal investigation into the events surrounding Ord 63 (the official moniker of the Lana fiasco). She's taken her time – out of respect maybe, or just getting up to speed on everything – but for the past few months she's been increasingly intent on gathering intel.

Although Theodore had been rendered unconscious along with nearly everyone else that day, and (unlike Ariana) did not have a large part in the action, there are still things about that general time period that he'd rather no one knew: The fact that he was aware of Lana's fusing and had been planning to handle it quietly; the fact that she'd been able to trans tech; and, especially, that he'd provided his daughter with the means to survive her immediate banishment in the desert, leading to her (presumedly) successful concealment in the ranchos. He thinks he covered his tracks, but with all the data floating around out there you never know.

Miller's eyeing him like she can read his mind.

Theodore swallows.

"Come," she says. "Walk with me."

He paces her in silence as the corridor turns to the left and one wall opens out into a bank of windows with a view of dun-colored flats stretching endlessly away under a shock of blue sky. Miller stops, gazing out. Theodore halts alongside.

"Honestly," she tsks, after a minute. "You and Balor. Acting like this is some kind of witch hunt."

"I'm not – "

"You are," she says sternly. But then her face softens. "*You* I understand though. You lost your daughter. I imagine that time is quite painful for you to speak about."

He clears his throat, surprised. "Uh, yes. It is. I appreciate your understanding."

"It is important, however," she continues, "that in order to prevent anything similar from ever happening again, we discover the exact nature of what occurred. There are some discrepancies, inconsistencies. My predecessor, for example – Mr. Martinez's last bot recs place him on Transway the night before the incident, but after that he went permanently offline. He was declared deceased for expediency's sake, but if he'd really been killed by the expros shouldn't we have been able to track the body? While alive, they could have temporarily disabled his bots with transferon, but that would have worn off fairly quickly after death. Unless they somehow knew that geolocation persists until cremation."

She takes a deep breath. "So with all of that…do you think he could have had a role in Ord 63?"

Theodore balks, taken aback. "I doubt it. He was completely against tearing down Transway. I don't think he would have ever done anything to make that end seem necessary."

"True. But weren't you *both* against it right up until the resource vote?"

"Yes," Theodore says, pursing his lips. "That's a matter of

record. But I'm afraid I can't see what that has to do with anything. I reversed my position. Surely you don't think I had anything to do with his disappearance?"

"No," she says. "Of course not."

He takes a half step backwards, as if to go. "Well, if that's all then – "

"However," Miller says, and he freezes, grimacing. "There's also the matter of Lana's recs, which I'm hoping you *can* shed some light on. There are georecs that place her in her bunk during many of the same time periods when the reader in the transer lab places her there instead. They must have been hacked, but there's zero evidence of anyone getting into the system."

"There seems to be no accounting for it."

"And why would she cover up being in the transer lab in the first place? Was that where she was meeting her expro contact?"

"No. That person was not a subject of my former lab and there are no views of him ever setting foot there prior to Ord 63. Believe me, I've checked."

"Yes. But then how do we account for her georecs? Highly irregular."

Theodore shrugs. He meets Miller's gaze, willing himself not to flinch.

"Do you think," she says slowly, as if testing out an idea, "that it's possible Mr. Martinez might have had something to do with it? I mean, as a known Transway sympathizer who had clearance to all manner of things?"

Theodore's eyes widen in surprise. This he didn't expect. But it's an easy way to tie up some loose ends.

"Anything's possible, I guess."

"And do you think," Miller continues, lowering her voice although there's no one in the immediate vicinity to overhear them, "that he might still be alive? In hiding maybe? With… them?" Her eyes flick out the window, as if the man might be crouched behind a tumbleweed.

"I don't think – "Theodore starts, but then he checks himself; this could cover a multitude of sins " – that that's totally unfounded. Confidentially, I have quietly been pursuing this line of inquiry for a while. Frank Martinez was a friend as well as a colleague and I have a personal interest in discovering what happened to him."

He pauses, then follows her lead and lowers his voice as well. "You see, I have some contacts in the ranchos from my transer lab days to whom I have paid the occasional visit. Made inquiries. I've had the occasional lead, but so far, nothing definite's turned up."

"The *ranchos*?" Miller says. "You mean you've been out there? Isn't it dangerous?"

"Not really. They're not some kind of city-state, just a bunch of farms and old houses. Not exactly the rampant threat our third party would make them out to be."

Two birds, one stone, he thinks.

Ariana's been making noise about a preemptive strike against the ranchos for some time. This maneuver should give Miller pause in supporting her while also giving him official sanction to be in the ranchos so he can continue his search for Lana. Privately, he believes Martinez to be dead, but to keep things on the level the next time he's out there he can always ask around.

Miller sighs. "Ariana is a bit…overzealous in my opinion, at least where the ranchos are concerned. I did agree with the eradication of Transway but frankly, I think at this point we have quite enough blood on our hands. She does have a point, though, that some of the refugees from Transway who have settled there could be stirring up resentment."

"They're not."

"Really? How can you be so sure?"

"Because, as I just said, I've been out there. I've looked and I've listened. There's nothing. No threat at all. And even if they were of a mind to take against us, they have no weapons and no way to gain access to the city."

"True," Miller says. "But you never know. Without drone footage it's hard to say what goes on."

"I can get you all the footage you want," Theodore says, confident now. "Firsthand."

Miller raises a brow. "All right then, Theodore. Tell me what you have in mind."

THE ROLLER SKIDS TO A stop, kicking up a cloud of dust. Cautiously, Shariah edges it forward through the wide, bashed-in doorway of a boxy, concrete structure she found on a geosurvey map two days ago. Inside, it is goosepimple-chill and creepy with cobwebs, but it's the perfect cover. And it's only about a mile from here to the nearest rancho.

She breaks and parks, clicking open the little half-door and sliding out of the driver's seat, dragging her pack with her. She drops it in the back seat within easy reach and steps lightly to the threshold of the bashed-in door, lifting the binoculars around her neck to her eyes. She does a thorough search of the immediate area but sees nothing save a few birds.

Excellent.

Satisfied that she hasn't been observed or followed, she returns to the roller and flips open the top flap of the pack to reveal her disguise: a yellow-and-white striped dress, maybe a touch too garish (not wanting to generate a rec of having printed out any expro-style clothes she'd ended up borrowing it from a holoshop server), but as it's the annual Chile Fest at ranchos Pescados/de la Virgen hopefully she won't stand out too much in the crowd. She drapes the dress over the side of the roller then removes the binocs and her light, tan jacket and slips the unfamiliar garment on over her head. A decent fit, not too tight or suggestive, to avoid attracting any of that kind of attention she'd made sure to borrow it from a larger girl. She smooths it down then opens the backseat door and sits, tugging off her boots and shimmying out of her pants.

So far, everything's gone according to plan: She'd declared her destination to be a survey area on Transway – as far away from Albakirk and as close to the old road as possible. There she'd hidden her server, counting on its static location not to give her absence away. But this meant she couldn't hook up a drone feed and has had to rely solely on the binocs to scout out dangers on the road.

Luckily, she hasn't encountered any.

There's nothing she can do about the georecs in her internal bots, but as it's far more involved to search those than to just ping her server, hopefully no one will. It was also risky not to tell anyone about her plan, but after much deliberation she'd decided that it was the best option, at least for this first run. Because if she comes back with enough good intel she may be able to garner support for future missions. A preemptive ban would've left her dead in the water.

Besides, she thinks, shoring herself up, *I've got a stun. I'll be fine.*

She stows her tech clothes under the seat and slips her feet into brown huaraches that feel unsettlingly flimsy for all the walking she'll be doing. Technically, she could put the boots back on – decades' worth of documented trade between Transway and the ranchos means that many transers own items of tech-made clothing, but she wants to look as authentic as possible.

And so, for the finishing touch, she extricates a long, white scarf and wraps it into a sort of makeshift turban to hide her hair. Though there are fair-haired transers, she fears that her white-blonde shade might be a bit too noticeable.

She ducks her head to take one last look in the roller's rearview mirror and pats the headscarf, satisfied. Then she exits the vehicle, neatly shuts the door, and inspects her pack once more – *stun, check; water and snacks, check; imagecard, check* – before shouldering it and setting forth into the unknown.

TWENTY-FIVE MINUTES OF HIKING OVER rough terrain and she's limping badly.

How do they walk in these things? Shariah thinks, poking at a blister, furious that such a small detail could end up stymieing such an important investigation.

There had been a first aid kit in the roller and she curses herself for not bringing it. She's sure that none of the Passerine crew has had to deal with any pesky problems of this nature. But there's nothing else to do, so she grits her teeth and soldiers on, thinking how strange it is that she's run into absolutely no one on this crumbling road. Judging by the tumbledown houses strung out along the verge she's definitely reached the outskirts of the ranchos.

They're probably all at the fiesta.

She palms the imagecard and takes a few quick snaps, trying to take her mind off the pain. But after another five minutes her right heel is raw and bleeding.

Disheartened, Shariah plunks down on a large rock and inspects the wound. Her bots will take care of any infection but it looks awful and feels worse. A little water might help clean and soothe it. Then she could wrap it in something; she's loathe to give up the headscarf but she still has her bra, a slight thing made of soft jersey. Maybe she can use that.

She's just about to try and find a safe place to wriggle out of it under her dress when hears an odd creaking sound and looks up to see a strange contraption barreling down on her – a bicycle tugging a small laden cart on some kind of wobbly tether. She jumps to her feet, tensing to run in case it should break loose.

But it doesn't. Instead, the driver – a scrawny old woman, grey hair tangled like frayed rope – skids the whole contraption to a halt and peers at her curiously.

"Esta bien, mijita?"

Shariah freezes, frantically trying to recall the few words of ranchos speech – a patois of Spanish and English – that she's been studying just for this occasion. Many techs speak it to some degree as well, like Mr. Timanti, but her immediate family never did.

"Bueno," she says finally. "It's just my foot." She tips back the heel of her shoe to show the wound.

The old woman cackles. "Never wear new sandals on a fiesta day, no matter how pretty they may be."

Shariah shrugs ruefully.

"De donde vienes?"

Donde...donde...Where! Maybe she wants to know where I'm from?

"Rancho Leones," she says, naming the farthest one.

"A little lost then aren't you?"

"I – I was just – " Shariah swallows. "My cousins live here. But no one was at the house. So I figured they were all at the fiesta."

"Who are they?"

"My cousins," she repeats, realizing her mistake at once and feigning to sway on her feet, hoping fatigue and confusion will cover any lack of exact specification. She has no idea what names it would be safe to use.

"And you are?"

This she has prepared. "Shari Arianas," she says, worrying as she says it out loud that it's not convincingly 'ranchos' enough.

But the woman just nods and jerks her head to indicate the cart. "Pues, mijita. You don't look like you weigh much. Get in. Give those pretty feet a rest."

Shariah hesitates for a moment, but not wanting to arouse suspicion by refusing she steels her nerve and climbs in, positioning herself amidst some soft sacks and making sure her weight is distributed as evenly as possible. Then, with a bone-rattling lurch, the old woman pushes off and they go jouncing down the road to the fiesta.

ATRAVESAR – TO GO THROUGH THIS

THE SOUNDS OF FESTIVITY GROW from a soft murmur to a roar as they roll over a little bridge and out into a large field packed with booths and banners. The sight and smell of hundreds of people is overwhelming and Shariah concentrates on taking more surreptitious images in order to ignore the queasiness in her gut. Finally, they come to a halt and she heaves a sigh of relief, preparing to vanish into the crowd. But the old woman appears at the foot of the cart before she can exit.

"Feeling better, mijita?"

"Mucho. Bueno," Shariah says, scrambling to the edge. She throws her legs over the side and her pack over her shoulder. "Muchos gracias."

But an ominous cackle from the old woman stops her cold.

"Gonna run off just like that? All fine and fancy up at Leones…don't they teach you any respect?" She points to the bundles in the cart.

Horrified, Shariah eyes them – they look heavy and she's already injured. But she doesn't want to incite any ire.

Maybe she can tell I'm not really from here. Maybe this is some sort of test.

"Can I help?" she says grudgingly.

The old woman grunts and tugs the nearest bundle forward until it hangs over the edge of the cart. Then she crouches, slinging it across her back, and stands.

"Allí," she says, pointing with her chin towards a booth cattycorner to their current position, arrayed with a selection of sheets and blankets. Then she clomps off, clearly expecting to be followed.

Sighing, Shariah sets her pack on the ground and attempts to imitate the old woman's actions: she tugs out a sack and crouches, shifting it awkwardly onto her shoulders. But when she tries to stand, she can't find her balance – the burden tips back and forth precariously until the whole load slides off and pitches into the dust, taking her headscarf with it. Everyone in the immediate vicinity seems to stop and stare at her dazzling halo of hair. She bites her lip, trying to decide whether to just cut and run when –

"Necesita ayuda?" says a voice and she turns, breath catching as her gaze falls upon the most beautiful man she's ever seen.

Tall, blue-eyed and black-haired, with impossibly broad shoulders, a tapered waist, and tawny skin that shines in the sun, he smiles down at her like a young god. He moves closer and instinctively, she inhales; deliciously crisp and clean.

Shariah's legs loosen. Gently but firmly, the man catches her elbow as if to steady her against a faint. The touch sends a bolt of current through her and she has the sudden, insane urge to mash herself against his chest.

"Are you OK?"

"Uh. Y – yes," Shariah stammers, forcibly mastering herself. "Bueno. It's just that I walked really far before this old lady picked me up and I hurt my foot." She shows him her bleeding heel and bows her head, then looks up again through a fringe of long lashes. "I was trying to help her unload, but I don't think I'm very good at it."

Lush lips split in a wide grin. She wonders briefly what they taste like and feels her cheeks flush. Mercifully, he doesn't seem to notice.

"Don't worry, cielo," he says. "This isn't a job for a pretty little thing like you. Why don't you sit down and rest and let me handle these." He gestures at the sacks. "Then we can go fix up your foot and you can enjoy yourself."

"Gracias," she murmurs.

He's not a normal man; he's one of *them*, Shariah tells herself, as she scoots her butt up on a makeshift bench. But this council is lost in a ripple of muscles as he picks up a sack and hefts it effortlessly. She could watch him all day.

What is this? Some kind of spell?

But that's ridiculous. There's no such thing as spells, only science. This man is very attractive and she's tired and disoriented. She'll rest for a minute, get her foot bandaged, and then proceed with her original plan. Circle the fairgrounds. Make full use of the imagecard. Then she'll head home.

She's already had more than enough ranchos for one day.

But the man (whose name turns out to be Alonzo) appears to have other plans. After making quick work of the sacks (and politely ignoring the old woman's insinuating smirk), he helps Shariah back to his family's booth – a large, fancy one selling sandals very much like the evil pair on her own poor feet – and brings her an ice-cold mug of beer to sip while his two sisters cluck and fuss; peppering their first aid with some salt for the shoemaker responsible for what they clearly think are complete abominations in footwear.

Shariah experiences a fleeting moment of panic – what if they can tell the shoes aren't handmade, that they came out of a printer in Albakirk? But the two women never seem to entertain any such possibility. They unceremoniously toss the offending items and, after the application of a bit of prana (which Shariah desperately wants to refuse but doesn't dare) as well as a soothing salve and a clean bandage, slip her feet

117

into a brand new pair of their clearly superior brand. She balks at the gift, claiming she has nothing to give in return, until Alonzo cuts in, saying that that she can make it up by having lunch with him.

The beer must have gone to her head, because she finds herself happily accepting. And so, as his sisters (she never does catch their names) titter and wink, Shariah strikes off into the crowd on the arm of the most beautiful man she's even seen, not quite believing that what's happening is entirely real.

A LIGHT BREEZE RUFFLES THEODORE'S hair as the roller's fat tires crunch along the crumbling road. He keeps one eye on the drone feed, scouting ahead to ensure avoidance of any encounters with hostile or curious ranchitos. But it's a fiesta day, so he's unlikely to encounter anyone.

Anyone sober enough to challenge me, that is.

He chuckles.

He'll park in his secret spot and hike up to Rancho Pescados from there. He's not planning to try to talk to Lana's family, though. Hopefully, they are all at the fiesta and he can do some nosing around. Not that he would break into their house per se, but if they've left the door or a window unlocked, well, he wouldn't entirely rule out a quick look-see.

If that's not possible, he has backup in the form of a set of imagecards – half the size of his palm and each containing an image of a chessboard with the words 'Your move' printed below – that he plans to leave around in some likely locales. He and Lana had maintained a running chess game for all the years she lived with him. If she sees one of these, she'll know immediately who it's from, and understand that he means her no harm. Maybe it will remind her of better times, whet her appetite for a return to civilization.

He steers the roller carefully over a large buckled section of road until, with a tooth-rattling bang, it comes down flat again.

We can go to Mars, he thinks ruefully, *yet still not have any kind of hovercraft down here.*

But living in an enclosed city-state there's never been a real need for that kind of thing. Rollers may be clumsy and bulky but they're sturdy beasts, well-suited to the work he's doing now – officially-sanctioned work, thanks to Miller's endorsement. Now he doesn't have to worry about sneaking around, which is why he was able to leave the city fully kitted-out in ranchos-wear with a server and a stun in his pack. It makes things so much easier.

It also means that he'll have to do some real recon later to justify this little jaunt, but that won't be so bad – he'll go down to the fiesta and take a whole slew of images of shiny, happy ranchitos selling blankets and sandals and looking as non-threatening as so many colorful butterflies. If he's clever he might even be able to get a few of them talking, and covertly record some footage of them saying that they have no interest in the techs and are willing to live and let live. And maybe (if he's really lucky) even saying they're glad Transway is gone, that it was a bad influence on the youth or something. That would be a coup – one vid of an actual transer saying something like that would top a thousand words of Ariana-fueled hysteria.

As he turns onto the rutted dirt track leading to his make-shift garage, he glances down at his dusty clothes and swallows. It's hot today; by the time he gets to the fiesta he'll be authentically sweaty. And thirsty. Maybe they'll have some kind of beer tent – that would be a perfect place to get people talking. The thought of a cold beer makes his throat constrict; it'd be a nice treat after all his work is done.

He pulls up to the boxy, concrete structure and brakes, pausing to take a few slugs from his water bag before he maneuvers the vehicle through the bashed-in door. But as he wipes his mouth on his sleeve he spies a flash of white inside and cranes his neck, blinking in disbelief – another roller's already parked there.

He gapes at it. Who else could be out here – Ariana? Never. But she could have sent someone.

Or it might not be a tech at all. Plenty of rollers went missing from Transway after the mass Destierra. He slips a hand into his pack, pulling out the stun. There's a simple enough way to find out.

Quietly, he slides out of the driver's seat, sidling up to the gap and peering inside, all alertness. No one seems to be in evidence though, so he enters the enclosure with stun at the ready and circles around to the front passenger side of the unknown vehicle. Leaning in over the door, he can see its serial number printed on the dash. He takes a quick shot of it with his server and then, feeling confident that the roller's driver is currently elsewhere, does a quick search of the interior. There's a tech uniform neatly tucked under the rear seat.

He nods, satisfied, and exits, getting back into his own vehicle and retreating a ways down the track before stopping to look up the serial number in the Bank. As he assumed from the presence of the uniform, the roller is definitely in current service and not a rogue, which means there should be a record of it being checked out to –

A double take.

Shariah Balor? *Did her mother put her up to this?*

But as he digs through the relevant recs a different picture emerges: It looks like Shariah went out alone early this morning, allegedly to do survey work at a location in the ruins of Transway, where, it seems, her server still resides. That was one of Lana's old tricks, so it's possible that whatever Ms. Balor is up to is something she hasn't told her mother about, though he doubts it's anything similar to what Lana was doing. The thought of Shariah Balor fusing makes him bark out a wholly inappropriate laugh. She *is* studying transers though, so maybe she got bored sifting through garbage and decided to liven things up with a taste of the real thing. He can't say he'd blame her.

Still, this presents a dilemma – should he let her be or try to find her? The ranchos aren't especially dangerous, and once within the perimeter it will be increasingly difficult to geolocate her bots. Besides, whatever work she's doing here is more than likely at cross-purposes to his own.

Shariah's a big girl, and undoubtedly well-prepared.

He grunts, shoving the server in his pack. He'll proceed as planned. Leave Ms. Balor to her own devices, but make sure to keep an eye out for her at the fiesta.

For now, the main issue is finding another place to park.

SHARIAH COLLAPSES PANTING IN THE back seat of the roller, mind on fire as she blinks up at the underside of the silver solar canopy.

What. the fuck. did I just do? And why?

Surrounded by the familiar trappings of tech it seems almost impossible to believe that she's just run all the way back from the house near the fairgrounds where she'd spent the better part of the afternoon in the amorous embrace of Alonzo, whose exceptional endowments turned out not to be limited to those immediately visible.

Did he trans me? she thinks, searching her mind for some kind of simple explanation. *Is that why I did it?*

He *had* brought her that beer (and a second one at lunch); he could easily have spiked it with transferon. But why would he do that to a presumed ranchita? They were all used to that stuff. Unless he suspected –

Shariah frowns, shaking her head. There's no way he could have known she was a tech; she'd showed up in the back of a *cart* for fuck's sake. For all he knew that old lady was her grandmother.

She'll find out soon enough though, because even after Transway was razed her mother (and some others) had insisted on leaving the scanners at the city gate intact while the ranchos remained in existence. If there's any transferon in her system they'll detect it.

But deep down she doesn't really think there is. Because the mortifying truth is that she'd wanted Alonzo from the very first moment she saw him. So she'd let him take her to lunch, and had another beer, and when he'd suggested a little postprandial 'nap' at his cousin's house (no one would be home, he said; they were all at the fiesta) she'd practically knocked the table over in her haste.

But why?

Up until a few hours ago, she, Shariah Balor, SocEn trainee and daughter of two Leads, had never so much as touched a transer in her life. She could barely even stomach Transway; so how the hell could she have so enthusiastically agreed to have sexual relations with one of its (at least tangentially related) creatures? Admittedly exceptional relations, but that's no excuse. This is not the kind of thing she does, or has ever considered doing, even in her wildest dreams.

So why did she do it? Is she going crazy? And then, with growing horror: Is this how it started with Lana?

Shariah sits bolt upright and shakes her head. No. The expro Lana was with was creepy and mangy, nothing like the divinely healthy Alonzo. And Lana hadn't just slept with the man, she'd fused with him too. She, Shariah Balor, is not like Lana. Sex, unlike fusing, is perfectly healthy and normal. She'd just gotten so used to doing it with Bryan that she didn't realize how much she was missing it. And there was Alonzo, looking like sex itself.

It was perfectly healthy and normal. And, most importantly, it was an anomaly. A once-in-a-lifetime deviation. Pheromones! – maybe transers have more of them or something? Maybe that's what happened. She'll look it up when she gets her server back.

She blows out a breath, groping under the seat for her tech clothes.

Experiments often turn up anomalies; she just wasn't prepared. The heat and the noise and the bleeding foot and the crazy old lady had all unbalanced her and left her open to them. And then Alonzo had swooped in. And he wasn't some nasty, dirty expro; if she's totally honest he smelled a bit like

Bryan. Psychologically speaking, what she did makes perfect sense.

It could happen to anyone.

Comforted by this rationalization, Shariah finds herself humming a tune as she changes clothes, one played by a roving band of musicians while she and Alonzo had lunch. She grins, remembering how he had pulled her up out of her seat and danced her around the dining area to the cheers and whistles of the other patrons. Then she shivers, recalling the exquisite feel of his body on hers.

It seems kind of silly now, how she ran off without even saying goodbye. But when she'd ventured upstairs at his cousin's house to freshen up after a few rounds on the couch in the basement, she'd heard someone at the back door and dashed out the front. Good thing she'd had her pack with her; she'd planned to use the imagecard to get a few quick snaps of the interior.

Now she extracts the slim device and scrolls – *there's some good stuff on here* – before setting it on the seat while she pulls on her boots. The uniform feels strange without undergarments on, but those had been, of necessity, sacrificed in the name of a hasty exit. Fully clothed, Shariah balls up the yellow dress and tosses it into a shadowy corner of the shelter. At this point, it's definitely worse for wear. She flushes, imagining Alonzo's deft fingers tugging at it all over again.

What must he think of me?

But it doesn't matter. It's not like she's ever going to see the man again. He probably doesn't even care that she disappeared. Probably went out and found another woman in five seconds flat. Maybe he thought some boyfriend came looking for her and that's why she ran.

She *is* coming back though. Of that she's sure. She's not going to let this little anomaly ruin some very promising research. Next time she'll be more accountable. Next time she'll say where she's going; maybe even take someone with her. Next time she'll make sure not to get too close to any of the males.

Decided, Shariah tucks the sandals into her pack (she is definitely keeping those) and climbs over into the driver's seat. She smooths her hair in the roller's rearview mirror and looks herself hard in the eyes, silently vowing to take the events of this day to the grave. Then she starts the engine and backs out of the shelter into the late-afternoon sun, no longer thinking about Alonzo but of plausible explanations in the unlikely case the scanners do pick up something.

A broken transfer among the rubble and a scratch on the hand should cover her.

10

Cool night air brushes Lang's face with soft fingers as he stretches out on his cot, crickets chirruping a small symphony-in-the-round. He looks up through the hut's window, watching darkened leaves and branches shift against patches of starry sky. Sonrisa took off a little while ago to spend the night with the kids, but she'd given him a good hit of Class E first.

He crosses ankle over ankle and laces hands beneath his head, mentally running a tally of the last few days' work: Two bad burns, one near-drowning, three abscessed teeth, and a snakebite; lots of pain and stress but not one bit of it clinging to him. Part of this is due to having such excellent help (though Sonrisa still won't own up to her considerable talents, a mystery he has decided to let remain unsolved for now) but the larger share is a product of his nightly doses of stress relief. He feels like he could float up through the roof and out into the firmament.

Visit Celan…

He grins at the thought, wondering if it's possible to astral into space. (He doesn't see why not, you'd just have to make sure you could find your way back to Earth somehow.) Then the sound of footsteps on the path outside makes him cringe. He sucks in a breath, trying to hold as still as possible. But the shape illuminated by solar torchlight that looms up by the door is one he recognizes instantly.

Shit.

There's a knock and then: "Lang? You in there?"

Brophy's tone holds no urgency so he makes no reply. He can see his friend through the window, but from this angle his friend can't see him.

"Lang?" Brophy's voice comes again, followed by the awful sound of the door creaking open.

He shuts his eyes tight; nothing to do now but feign sleep and hope for the best.

"There you are." More footsteps as Brophy enters the room. "We need to talk."

He feels his friend closing in, shining the light on him. Any second now the jig will be up. But there's one thing he can still try. "Fine," he says. "Just get that thing out of my face."

Brophy points the torch away as Lang presses fingers to his eyelids, rubbing vigorously. If he can just catch a glimpse of his friend's eyes without exposing his own – *Yes!*

A fraction of a second's glance and he confirms it: Brophy's not fused up, so he won't be able to see that Lang is. Now, at least, there's a chance at pretense.

He swings his legs over the side of the cot and sits up, offering a silent plea to Madre that this 'talk' has nothing to do with any suspicions about his current condition.

"Hey," he says with a big fake yawn. "Que pas'? Anything wrong?"

"No. No one's sick or anything." Brophy shifts his weight uncomfortably. "I just feel like maybe we should talk. You alone?"

"Yeah."

His friend drags a chair over and straddles it, then lays the torch sideways between his legs and clears his throat.

"What's going on?" Lang presses. "Is Mara mad again?"

"No, no es eso…"

He girds himself for a salvo, but only silence follows. In its wake he feels his eyes start to close and bites the inside of his cheek to try to stop it. That was a pretty hefty dose; he needs to stay alert. Fumbling for his smoke pouch, he concentrates on rolling one.

Finally, Brophy says, "Mira, OK? I know this isn't really my business, but what exactly is going on with you and this Sonrisa girl? I mean, what about Celan? When she comes back are you just gonna like, drop her?"

"Sonrisa?" Lang says, at once relieved and confused.

"Her, Celan – either one. I mean, you do have your charms, but I doubt they'll be enough to get them to just up and agree to share."

Lang chuckles, striking his flint and dragging on the smoke. He offers it to Brophy, who declines with a flick of his wrist.

"Serio. It's not funny, güey. I thought you loved Celan. That you were, like, waiting for her. She's gonna be back any day now and what's gonna happen then? How's she gonna feel when she finds you with somebody else?"

"How's she – what? No! 'Scúchame. Of course I love Celan. I think about her all the time." He props his lids open as wide as possible and meets his friend's gaze guilelessly. "Sonrisa's not – I mean, I know maybe it looks like we are – but we're not, OK?"

"You're not together?"

Lang shakes his head no. "Never even kissed."

"Well then why in the last living fuck are you acting like it?"

"We're not – " he starts.

"You *are*. You're like, joined at the hip. Giggling, whispering, giving each other secret looks."

"We're healers," Lang says defensively. "It can get intense. We joke around sometimes; blow off steam."

"Riiight."

"I swear, that's all it is."

"Does this girl even know about Celan? Or is there gonna be another Jaslene situation here in a minute?"

"Hey!" Lang says, stung. "It's not like that. And that wasn't even my fault; I broke up with Jaslene fair and square but she wouldn't take no for an answer. Yes, Sonrisa knows all about Celan and no, she's not jealous. She doesn't care! She's not into any of that stuff anyway." He pauses, then adds pointedly, "But we do *like* each other. As friends. And it's nice to have a friend, sabes?"

Brophy stiffens. "What's *that* supposed to mean?"

"It's just – I never see you anymore," he mutters, the words leaving a backwash of guilt as soon as they're out of his mouth. Because ever since Sonrisa (and her transfer) showed up he hasn't missed his friend's presence much at all; it's actually been a huge boon that Brophy's been off making up with Mara and not hanging around making trouble.

But this bit of emotional judo has the desired effect – Brophy's shoulders slump, his face softens. Lang offers him the smoke again. This time he takes it.

"Aww," he says, dragging deep. "I'm sorry. But you know I gotta do right by Mara."

"I know," Lang says. "And I'm not mad. But you shouldn't be either. I'm not doing anything that would hurt Celan."

"I didn't really think you would. I just didn't understand why you'd let people think it."

"I can't control what people think, or what they say. And I have way too much shit to do without running around chasing down rumors. You know how people gossip around here. Before this they had me and you together."

Brophy laughs, sheepish, exhaling twin jets through his nose. "Yeah. True."

"And when Celan gets back I'll explain everything to her upfront."

As long as she does come back, he amends silently. *And as long as she still wants me.*

He shudders, thinking on tentacle-head things and scratching his chin absently until his friend passes back the smoke, squinting hard at him.

"You OK, güey?"

"Yeah," Lang says. "Just tired. Been a long week."

"Well, I'll let you rest up then…unless you want to come have a drink?"

"Nah. Just wanna sleep."

Chair legs scrape the floor as Brophy gets to his feet. "See you at the fiesta?"

"Quizás," Lang says, swinging his legs back up on the cot; he stretches out again as the door opens and shuts. As Brophy's footsteps recede, he takes a long drag of smoldering hemp and runs a hand over his face with the intense relief of one barely scraped by disaster. He's pulled it off.

They don't know. *We're safe.*

But his earlier peace is still broken; and he really wishes Brophy hadn't gone and brought up Jaslene. Because the closer Celan's return date gets the more nagging certain unresolved issues become – like what really happened with Jaslene that one night when he'd gotten drunk instead of fusing? He can't remember much of the party itself, but he recalls waking up around dawn in the storage barn with CERS coming on and Jaslene asleep on a sack next to him. She had been fully dressed, but his pants were undone. Not off or down, just undone.

He didn't know and didn't want to know what had happened, so he'd up and left – stumbling around until he found a safe place to fuse himself into oblivion. By the time he came back (and down) she was acting like he didn't exist and there was no way to ever bring it up again.

So the case is closed.

But what if something *did* happen: Should he tell Celan, or should he forget the whole thing? Because what if it was nothing? What if they both just passed out and that was it? Maybe he'd gone for a piss and was too drunk to button up afterwards. Besides, it was almost a year and a half ago; Jaslene is with Gabe now and they have a fucking *kid*. If he tells Celan and she gets mad and doesn't want him anymore, and then it turns out nothing ever really happened, that would be the worst.

So it's back to square one – forget about it.

Lang exhales, staring up at the shadowy ceiling and fervently praying that Brophy is satisfied – that they've cleared things up and all's right with the world. Hopefully, his friend will go back to kissing up to Mara and leave Lang and Sonrisa to do their thing. Hopefully, there'll be no more talks like this one to stir shit up. Hopefully, Celan's return will involve far more important matters than who might have possibly hooked up with who.

As he stubs out the smoke and closes his eyes, Lang makes a mental note: *That door needs a lock. Ahora.* He'll talk to Sonrisa about it first thing tomorrow and see what they can rig up.

"ÓRALE!" MARA CROWS, POINTING HER nearly-empty glass at Sig as he drops his last three chits into the pot. "You're out, ese! Loser pours the next round."

Sig bobs a scraggly head of pale hair before pushing away from the scarred, wooden table and shuffling over to the makeshift cooler to procure more beer. They're taste-testing Zeeb's new yarrow brew, set to make its debut at this week's harvest fiesta, and it has been unanimously declared 'some good shit.'

Gleeful, Mara rattles the dice in preparation for her next throw. Only she, Brophy, and Zeeb remain in the latest round of Veinte Uno. Gabe had been the first one out, and had wandered off to have a smoke and check that everyone on dinner cleanup duty finished their chores. Mara shakes the dice again, impatient, but refrains from her next toss. Better to wait until they're all topped off.

The light of one algalamp salvaged from Transway plus

a couple of solar lanterns lend a cozy glow to their main living space. Aside from the large oval table and chairs, there are benches along the walls and even a couch of sorts topped with cushions stuffed with cattail fluff. The dun-colored walls are hung with scavenged oddities and the flat, carved cutouts Brophy likes to make when he's bored. If Mara squints, she could almost be back at Alamora, though this house, while similar in construction and layout, is smaller and lacks a second story. It had been in a state of considerable disrepair when they'd first claimed it – the cleaning alone took weeks – but she's done her best to make it a home.

Across the table, Brophy and Zeeb are in a huddle; they seem to be in disagreement about something. She's about to break it up – *this is funtime, no serious talk allowed* – when she hears Lang's name floated around. She puts down the dice and perks up her ears.

"Something's off," Brophy is saying. "It's like he's at it again."

"There's no way," Zeeb says.

"How can you be so sure?"

"Venga ya, Brophy," Mara says, butting in. "Knock it off. Your boy is fine; he's happy because of that Sonrisa girl. Two little healers – like peas in a freaky little pod." She downs the rest of her beer and thunks the glass on the table like it's an official decree. "Give it up already."

"I don't really think that's what's – "

"Serio?" she says. "He finally stops bitching and moping and starts acting right and you gotta go borrow trouble? He's getting laid. Leave him alone."

Brophy gives her a pointed look. "He is *not* getting laid.

Or at least he wasn't tonight. I went over to see him and he was alone. And acting weird."

"This is Lang we're talking about," Zeeb notes dryly, lacing fingers over his still-convex but much diminished middle.

Mara chuckles.

"Seriously, you know how he gets. Kind of…" Brophy makes a noncommittal gesture. "But trying to be normal?"

"Again – Lang," Zeeb says.

Now they're all laughing, even Sig as he returns bearing several bottles.

All except Brophy.

"Oh come on," Mara says, cajoling. "Cálmate. Está bien." She rises and circles around behind his chair, clucking sympathetically as she reaches to massage his neck. "Were you not feeling well, querido? Is that why you went to see him?"

Brophy tenses at the touch. "I'm fine," he says tersely. "We had some things to discuss."

Mara snatches her hands away and plants them firmly on her hips. "What *things*?"

"Just…things."

"*What* things?" Her voice takes on a sardonic edge. "Like how jealous you are of his new girl?"

"I'm not jealous." Brophy snaps, whipping around to face her. "I just had some questions. I didn't get why he'd hook up with Sonrisa. Especially now. Why he'd risk hurting Celan."

"Celan?" she says, eyes widening in incredulity. "Are you fucking kidding me? He's not going to hurt *Celan*. Celan was a trick, a bait. A little honeypot whose pinche ass isn't up in space; it's parked in Albakirk as we speak, on the pile of medals they gave her for helping to destroy Transway."

135

"That's not true!" Brophy protests. "You know it's not. You saw her fuse. You saw her Destierra'd."

Mara juts out her chin. "A setup," she says. "All for show. I bet daddy came and got her five minutes after they dropped her off."

"No. She went with the Plejarans. I saw her. I saw *them*."

"A tech trick. A fake. Some kind of holo."

"No! That's not what – "

"'Stante!" Zeeb cuts in, raising his arms like a referee. Both Mara and Brophy's heads swivel in his direction. "Enough already. Though I am inclined to agree with mi prima on the matter of Celan Mairs and the Alien Visitation, I would actually like to enjoy the rest of my evening. So." He reaches for the glass Sig refilled and takes a decorous sip before continuing, "Let's cut the crap, shall we? Brophy, you are never going to convince anyone that this Plejaran shit is real so just stop trying it. And Mara, just because Brophy goes to see Lang it doesn't mean they're having some secret affair. It's good to have eyes on Lang sometimes; lo necesitamos."

"So *you* told Brophy to go over there?" Mara says, looking between the two of them.

"I may have suggested…" Zeeb says.

Brophy sighs.

"…or I may not have. But the point is that there's no way he's getting any E. I've got all the transfers on lockdown. I'd know if one was going missing."

"Yeah," Sig says. Everyone's drinks topped up, he sits down with a glass of his own, wiry shoulders hunched forward earnestly. "Zeeb's mama's got 'em all. She barely leaves the house. And he has me count 'em twice a day. There's no way."

"See?" Mara says to Brophy. "You're imagining things."

Brophy is silent for a moment. Then: "I offered him a drink. He turned it down."

All four eye each other, suddenly uneasy.

"Well, how bad was he?" Mara says. "Was he like – " She lolls her head to one side, jaw slack and tongue out.

"No." Brophy sighs. "He was just...off. I don't know. Maybe you're right. Maybe nothing's really wrong after all."

"Oh no you don't," Mara says firmly. "You brought this up in the first place and you can't just walk away and leave it there. If Lang's turning down drinks, maybe he is getting E somewhere. And if he is, I bet I know who's giving it to him."

She and Zeeb share a look.

"Maddy," he says grimly.

Mara grunts, returning to her seat. She picks up her glass, examining the contents meditatively. "I suspected that bitch of planning something like this for a while. But when I sent out spies – nada."

"So?" Zeeb says. "Whatever else Maddy is, she's not stupid. She got over on high-level techs for years. She knows what she's about."

"And I don't?"

"Hey," says Sig. "This is easy enough to work out." He tips his chin at Brophy. "Fuse up, ese. Go back over there and check for the shine."

Brophy takes a long sip of his drink then coughs nervously. "It would be weird if I went back tonight," he says. "He's probably asleep."

"So wake him up," Mara says. "Or better yet, I will. I can tell if he's been into anything." She starts to rise.

"I think," Zeeb says slowly, motioning for her to sit, "that we should wait. Not do anything tonight. If Brophy's wrong then there's no harm done and we avoid a weird scene. Maybe Lang's girl is there now. Maybe they're in the middle of it. I don't know about you but I wouldn't want to walk in on that shit."

"True that," Sig says, with a mock-shudder. He and Mara clink glasses in solidarity.

Zeeb rests thick, hairy forearms on the table and takes on an instructional tone. "We need to play it smart," he says. "Not be hasty. Because if Lang is fusing up and we catch him at it, then what? We yell at him? Kick him out? If Maddy is supplying him then that's playing right into her hands." He lifts his own hands, palms up. "She gets our healer and we get fucked. So we have to catch her at it too. Sabes?"

"Ah," says Sig. "My man's a smart one."

Zeeb blows Sig a kiss before continuing his address: "So first things first. Before we say anything to Maddy we need to know if Lang is really fusing. And you three," he indicates Brophy, Mara, and Sig in turn, "are the only ones who can tell."

Brophy clears his throat. "Uh, I actually haven't been fusing much lately." Though at a sharp look from Mara adds, "But I can take one for the team."

"Good," she says. "Because it's mostly gonna be you and Sig on that. I have way too much other shit to do to be chasing Mr. Shays, especially when there might not even be good reason."

"Me and Lang and Sig?" Brophy cracks. "That'll be one hell of a threesome."

Mara opens her mouth to retort but Zeeb heads her off.

"Fiesta's the day after tomorrow. We're all free then. We stick close, ply him with drinks. See what we can see. Just friends wanting to spend time together; he won't suspect a thing."

"He said he's not sure he's even gonna go," Brophy mutters, running the edge of one thumbnail along a groove in the tabletop.

"Well then your first job is to get his ass there."

"Go sweet-talk his girl," Sig says. "Say they're such a cute couple and we're all dying to get to know her."

"Say whatever you gotta say," Zeeb says.

Brophy nods, but without much enthusiasm. He doesn't raise his eyes from the scarred wood.

Mara scoffs: What the fuck is his problem? Why talk smack at all if you're just going to weasel out of actually doing anything about it? She's revving up to call him out when the front door swings open and Gabe's big, bluff form stomps into the room, followed by Jaslene, sans Isaac.

"Que pas'?" Jaslene says brightly. "Effie's babysitting, so it's my night to *roll*, and Gabe says that yarrow brew's a-ma-zing!" She does a little shimmy of celebration.

There's a split-second's pause and a few shared looks around the table, but then that's it: by mutual agreement the subject of Lang has been officially dropped for the night.

"Yeah girl," Mara says, switching up her tone. "Come out and play! Mama needs a night off."

Jaslene whoops and they all raise their glasses as Sig scurries off to get her one too; Mara kicks out a chair and gives her a high five as she sits.

Might as well let the good times roll.

There'll be plenty of time to deal with that other shit later.

⊏► 11 ◄⊐

Celan's breath catches at the view beneath her feet as she steps out onto the transparent tube-bridge spanning InDrenÏ Gorge. Carved by endless torrents of glacial outflow from XÏNeru's iceside, the sunside vista is a kaleidoscope of rainbows glittering in spray that falls in stomach-dropping vaults to the river-veined plains below. The bridge crosses the deluge right at the divide between the tidally-locked planet's day and night sides. Built by the XÏNeruans themselves, in better times it was a symbol of mending the divide between them.

Too bad it didn't work, she thinks, moving aside to let a few fellow tourists pass. She shrugs deeper into her jacket and closes her eyes, letting the soothing shush of the rushing water envelop her. By all rights the sound should be deafening; the bridge materials must provide some sort noise-dampening effect.

InDrenÏ Gorge is the final stop on a tour that started

three Madren days ago, when she and the Plejarans had kicked off a series of guided visits to the former dwellings of the vanished inhabitants; a deep dive into the long and fascinating history of this singular place.

The XïNeruans had been BCOs like Madrens and Plejarans, though ones with horn-like growths on their heads and a common ram-ish ancestor, who'd wandered freely through the habitable zones before splitting off into iceside and sunside subtypes. Therein lay the trouble: due to the height of the divide and the unnavigable nature of the water-ways between them the two races then developed separately for untold generations (whatever knowledge of cave-ways their ancestors must have known having been summarily lost). The sunsiders spread out onto vast estates in the warm river valleys, while on the other side, the iceside denizens built starlit castles of frozen rock. There were always rumors, of course – tales of demons and fairies to scare the children into obedience – but it wasn't until the end of the first XïNeruan millennium that these had been proven true by the confluence of two lost parties of explorers that came upon each other right here at InDrenï.

And then the wars started, Celan thinks wryly. *Of course.*

To be fair, the icesiders and sunsiders did look quite a bit different by then; the sunsiders were darker of skin, longer of limb, and sparser of hair than their iceside counterparts (as well as having far smaller eyes). Both were still recognizably XïNeruan (to a non-XïNeruan that is), but it was a long time before the two civilizations could acknowledge each other as belonging to the same species. Even during times of future peace, the sunsiders ever thought the icesiders somewhat crude and brutish while the icesiders dismissed the sunsiders as both ignorant and arrogant.

When she'd first arrived, Celan had expected to see some kind of nuked landscape or bombed-out ruins, but it's nothing like that. What's eerie about XïNeru is that all the old structures are mostly intact. All of their works are still here – the cities and towns, the massive hydro-electric constructs, the schools, the art. They didn't destroy their world or its environment. In the final conflict, the XïNeruans simply figured out a way to use the quantum bands to erase each other on a subatomic level.

Celan shudders. *Creepy as fuck.*

"Quite a view," says a voice beside her, and she jumps a little in her skin.

But it's only Ness, contemplative as always.

"Yeah," she says, for lack of a better response, and shivers anew – not so much in response to the evil fate of the Xï Neruans but from the downshift of her system from well to slightly-in-need-of-Class-E.

"Really makes one think," Ness continues, "about all the potential lost in hostility."

All three Plejarans have been laying the don't-destroy-those-different-from-you stuff on thick all day and she's officially sick of it.

It's ridiculous. All these lectures. I'm not the one trying to destroy anybody. It's the techs doing that.

But in lieu of going another round Celan merely nods.

"This has been a great experience," she adds, trying to jolly him. "I really appreciate you all bringing me here."

And she means that. For in addition to the rounds of

sightseeing, Chan, Ness, and Ree finally deigned to show her more about the workings of the quantum band. Turns out it's not much harder than transing tech back home. There are limits, of course, but only those of imagination. The trick Chan did with the thermos when they first met had been a product of water vapor in the air filling a vessel from his ship's Suster, which could be calibrated to send its products to locations within a small, defined radius. Once he demonstrated the technique, it was easy for her to imitate. And easy to expand the concept to other things – like all the tech in Albakirk.

She sighs.

That was her mistake; one tossed-off comment about 'showing them who's boss' had sent the Plejarans into instant red-flag mode. She'd been forced to explain something of the tech vs. transer issue – something she'd glossed over previously. They knew nothing of the Destierra, only that she'd been "separated from her party" (Brophy and Lang's astral search and rescue having made that little retcon seem legit). She still hasn't told them everything, but she'd apologized profusely for her joke, swearing that she would never even think of using the band for any less-than-peaceful purpose.

After seeing XïNeru she can forgive them a bit of hypervigilance on that count.

She presses palms against the smooth inner curve of the tube and leans forward, so it's almost like she's standing on air.

If my father could see this he'd give up on Mars in a minute.

But this world is a K'Shiran Heritage site (which means no resettlement), and one webbed with sunside rivers filled with a species of tiny fish that, while apparently having had no taste for the leathery XïNeruans, could team up to chew a

144

soft, Madren-like limb off in less than a minute. Celan winces, eyeing the lovely valleys with unease and pitying whoever found this out the hard way.

"So where are we meeting for dinner?" she asks Ness.

He gives her what appears to be a rueful grin, like he knows it's time to dial down the sermons and relax. It's their last night here; time for some fun. Chan and Ree certainly seem to think so – they'd disappeared right after the final tour with a promise to reconvene later at one of the many eateries dotting the slopes around InDreni.

"Ree said to meet them at DaRacai at 19:00, your time."

Using the band, Celan conjures a chronholo – 19:00 is in half an hour and it'll take at least that long to reach their destination. No time to go back to her room; she'll have to find somewhere else to mitigate the oncoming CERS. There should be some sort of restroom at the wayvern; hopefully one with doors.

Different species have radically different notions of privacy. On Va'anak all quarters were completely open, even the bathrooms, and she'd had no choice but to risk fusing in view of the Plejarans. When, inevitably, one of them walked in on her she'd explained that she had a condition that caused deregulation of her endorphin system, and that the transfer contained medicine to mitigate it. They never questioned this, just suggested that she consult one of the Convention's MedAIs for an evaluation and (hopefully) a more permanent remedy.

Celan had promised to do so, but of course she never did. So she doesn't want them catching her still at it.

She clears her throat. "DaRacai is what – 10,000 meters?"

"Yes," says Ness. "Remember to adjust your band for the

altitude."

"I will."

Then, as if on some silent signal, they both turn one hundred eighty degrees, taking in the vast expanse of turquoise ice fading to black in the permanent twilight of XɪNeru's night side. If they'd had more time, Celan would've liked to go on an extended sled-trek; there are no critters dangerous to Madrens in the frozen lands. And that immutable sun is freaky after a while – on the iceside at least the stars (and the system's several outer planets) appear to move in the sky as XɪNeru makes its solar orbit.

"They marked their days by the moon of a distant star," she says, quoting a scrap of old Transway poetry.

Ness gurgles Plejaran amusement.

"You Madrens," he says. "Such bards."

"That's not mine," she clarifies. "And it's not even true, scientifically speaking."

"Yes," says Ness. "They marked time by the stars, but not 'days' such as we know them." (The Plejarans' home world rotates much like Terra Madre, albeit more slowly.)

"No wonder the icesiders developed advanced technology before the sunsiders," she says. "They had constant observation of the cosmos. Astronomy and questioning their place in the universe would have come naturally to them."

"Their observatories are quite extraordinary," Ness agrees. "We only saw one of the minor ones this time. Next time, make sure to go to SaNăc."

Celan files this away as another place to take Lang.

"Do you think," she says, taking refuge in the purely theoretical, "that this is why they couldn't get along?" She gestures to indicate both sun and ice sides. "That they came from such different physical worlds that they could never really understand each other's point of view?"

"Well," Ness says, motioning for them to walk, "there's a branch of pan-morphology that posits something similar. It's well-known that bilateral species like ourselves, while very good and building and creating things, are also prone to getting caught up in binary thought patterns. When both sides are in harmony, bilateralism works very well. When they're not, the results can be very us-against-them. You don't see that kind of thing in radials so much."

"Like the WDM,K*DU," Celan says, almost colliding with a po-faced, pelican-beaked Heliote, fully encased in some sort of elaborate breathing apparatus. She mutters a hasty apology and falls back into step with Ness. "They're very one-for-all and all-for-one."

"Exactly."

"But you're bilaterals and you've all always gotten along."

"Our home world is fairly homogenous and so are we. That always helps," Ness says modestly, though she can detect a hint of justifiable Plejaran pride in the millennia of peace and prosperity his species has enjoyed. "But there are also our triunes. I think that's a big factor."

"Huh," Celan says, hoping this isn't going to take a turn for the squick. With Ree it's one thing, but she's not interested in discussing intimate matters with Ness.

"Think about it," he continues. "From earliest memory our children have the benefit of a three-fold perspective on everything. Nothing's ever just one way or the other. They see us cooperating, trying to find a middle ground."

"True," she says, relieved. "I guess it's harder for us with just two."

"And you've also had some pretty significant geographic boundaries to overcome," Ness allows. "All those oceans and continents made for some large divides. But you'll always find a third option helpful in resolving binary disputes of any kind."

Briefly, Celan wonders if the expros represented that third option back home. One that, thanks to Ariana, is now destroyed. But maybe not; Lang had said that he was going north with Mara and Brophy. They were planning to start a new settlement of some kind. So maybe that third option still exists.

She'll find out soon enough.

Two more weeks, she thinks, and shivers.

At the far end of the bridge they step out onto rocky ground, then breeze through a short line before boarding a bubble-shaped elepod to DaRacaï, soaring so high above In-Drenï Gorge that the line between light and dark becomes infinitesimal. The dip-and-swoop of the lift causes her stomach to do likewise and she grits her teeth, hand brushing the outline of the transfer in her pocket.

As soon as they get where they're going she's going to need it.

12

"Shariah Balor," a deep voice intones, snapping her out of an internal debate over whether tomato or pesto sauce would go best with her noodles and veg. Shariah chooses pesto and picks up her tray, reluctantly turning to acknowledge the presence of Theodore Timanti. It's been a long time since she's spoken more than a few brief, stilted words to him – mainly on those inevitable occasions when their SocEn spheres overlap.

Despite his frequent policy clashes with her mother over the years, she used to secretly sort of like Lana's father. He could be very entertaining under the right circumstances. But ever since he chose to let his daughter die instead of trying to help her Shariah hasn't wanted much to do with him. She respects his work with Mars and the Passerine (from a safe distance), and she understands that helping Lana would have been a major breach of tech policy.

But every time she has to meet him in person it sets her

teeth on edge.

"Yes?" she says now, forcing her expression into one of blank neutrality.

"May I have a word?"

"About what?"

Timanti's lips twitch with amusement, he too is holding a tray and they are holding up the line. "Why don't we get our drinks and sit over there?" He points with his chin to two seats at the end of a long table by the windows. "And I'll explain."

Shariah's stomach sinks – what could he possibly want with her? She does not, under any circumstances, want to discuss Lana. But he's chosen his moment well: She's by herself this evening and there's no one in the immediate vicinity to latch onto. Plus, Mr. Timanti is still a Lead SocEn, one of her mother's closest colleagues and, most important for an En trainee, her own superior. There is no way to bow out gracefully.

So she trails him over to the drink station, stopping to check her server for messages and letting people go ahead of her, all the while searching the caf for someone who might come to her rescue. The pickings are slim to nonexistent though, and so, glass of iced tea added to her tray, she advances grimly towards the appointed table.

He regards her placidly as she slides onto the seat opposite and Shariah tries to mirror his mien – no point in antagonizing him. After a few minutes of strained pleasantries, she shifts focus to twirling up a large forkful of noodles and cramming it into her mouth. When she looks up again, still chewing, he's eyeing her wolfishly. She swallows.

"So," he says. "I'm curious…what exactly were you doing

in the ranchos the other day?"

Shariah half-gasps, choking on a bit of broccoli and cursing herself for being so obviously taken off guard. She hacks into a napkin as he waits for her response, fingers steepled above his plate.

She could kill him.

"Mr. Timanti —" she starts, when she finally stops coughing.

"Please, call me Theodore. You're not a little girl anymore."

"OK, *Theodore*," she says, with an acerbic bite. "If you must know, I was doing some research for my transer study."

No use denying it. Keeping things short and sweet is her best bet.

"Unauthorized research," he notes, arching a brow. "In the recs your 'purpose and destination' was declared as a socio-archeological study of the ruins of Transway, which is where, incidentally, you also left your server unattended for several hours."

Shariah puts down the napkin and sighs. "OK fine. You got me. Put me on Notice if you have to."

"This isn't about Notice," he says. "More like simple curiosity."

"Well, that's what it was for me too," she says, taking a steadying sip of tea. "There's not much left to study on Transway at this point so I went to the ranchos to see if I could find anything more interesting. They were having some kind of festival and I decided to take a chance. I left the server because it's much easier to ping it than to track bots. I set up the autoreply to say I was busy, so as long as it was located where I said I was going to be anyone looking for me probably wouldn't bother to look any further."

"Fair enough. But I still don't understand; if you were doing work for your mother wouldn't she insist you take your server in case of emergency? I can't imagine she would – "

"She didn't know, OK? Is that what you're getting at? I didn't tell her, or anyone else. Are you planning tell her? Or have you already?"

Theodore's expression shifts from smugness to mild surprise. "No," he says. "I haven't. Nor am I planning to. But I *am* curious as to the evolving nature of your research."

Shariah thinks fleetingly of Alonzo's lush lips and feels her cheeks flush. But she quickly recovers. "You already know," she says, suppressing an eye roll. "Or you can probably guess. I want to find out what all those ex-Transway types are doing over there. Whether they're stirring up trouble, and what kind of threat they might potentially pose."

"Ah," he says, frowning. "I had hoped that the fact that you'd done this on your own might mean you were taking a different tack than your mother on this issue. Being a bit more lenient towards those who have never done you any harm." He looks almost disappointed.

She flushes again, but this time in anger. "Never done *harm*?" she says, incredulous. "I cannot believe that you of all people, who lost a daughter to those… ingrates, can sit here and tell me with a straight face that they've never done any harm. They harmed you. They harmed me. They as good as murdered my best friend. And *you* let them." She bites her lip like she might have gone too far and braces for an angry backlash.

But Theodore merely nods.

"True," he says, breaking off a hunk of bread and chewing

thoughtfully. "It was a terrible loss. But the rules were clear and I did what I had to do. Publicly excusing my daughter would have sown disunity. Left the Lead SocEns open to accusations of favoritism. Nepotism. It was simply impossible." He pauses, hesitant, then seems to decide something.

"However," he continues, locking eyes on hers, "what is lost may occasionally be found. If you know where to look, that is."

It takes a moment for the implication to become clear. Then her jaw drops in shock.

"Found? You don't mean – "

"I do."

"Is that why you were in the ranchos?" she says, pulse quickening. "Have you found…something?"

Nonchalant, he stabs a bite of salad like they're discussing the weather. "Most likely, yes."

Sharia gulps at her tea.

Lana…alive!

It's almost too crazy to believe.

But how did she survive the Destierra? And why would she be in the ranchos? How long has she been there? And: How long has he known?

"I'm sure you have a lot of questions," he says, putting down his fork and regarding her calmly. "And I'm prepared to answer all of them. Just not here, obviously."

"Yes," Shariah says. This is far too confidential a subject to be spoken about freely inside the city; too many open channels both human and mechanical.

"So I have a proposal. The next time you go out to the ranchos I will accompany you. I can give you a hand with your research and we can talk. Would that be acceptable?" He dabs his lips with a napkin then drops it onto his tray. "Maybe sometime after the Mars landing. I'll be happy to work with your schedule."

"Tomorrow," Shariah says. He can't drop a bomb like this and just walk away. If Lana is alive then she needs to know details.

Right. Fucking. Now.

"Tomorrow?" he says, taken aback. "I won't have time to go to out to the ranchos then. Why don't we – "

"Tomorrow," she repeats, looking him hard in the eye. "On Transway."

He sighs. "Very well. But it will have to be early."

"Fine with me."

"And I can only give you half an hour."

"OK."

"Well then. How about 06:00? You can meet me just outside the gate." He gets to his feet and picks up his tray. "I'll check out a roller."

"Great. See you then."

Shariah watches him go, then turns to stare numbly out the window, twisting her napkin into bits as she takes in the sunset glow of the mountains against a violet sky. Unbidden, a flash of memory fills her mind's eye – she and Lana, age eleven, walking arm and arm through the indoor gardens the first day they met, laughing at the antic flights of bee-bots. Though she would never admit it out loud, it was the first time she had ever felt truly comfortable with one of her peers. Most of the others were intimidated by her. But Lana had been sweet and kind, in addition to brilliantly intelligent, and, as the only other child of a Lead SocEn, she was the only one who could understand the unique pressures Shariah felt.

They'd been inseparable after that. Endless sleepovers and whispers and secrets and crushes and private jokes. Seven years of them. It couldn't all have been a lie.

Is she sorry for what she did? Does she wish she could come home? And, most important: *Does she still hate me?*

Shariah's stomach tightens as her eyes flick down to her still-laden plate. She pushes it away. Notice or no, she knows she won't be eating another bite.

IN THE PALE HOUR BEFORE sunrise the next morning, Theodore takes a careful sip of hot beverage from a small travel mug and leans back in the driver's seat of the roller with a groan. He closes his eyes, trying to shut out the onset of a headache. In hindsight, that third generous pour of Scotch last night might not have been the best idea. But he'd been anxious. Concerned about the wisdom of his strategy with Ms. Balor.

He hadn't planned on telling the girl about Lana, only on trying to flush some intel out of her concerning her mother's ranchos plans. But the fact that she hadn't been operating under Ariana's aegis, combined with that passionate little speech of hers about losing her best friend, had spurred him into taking a risk.

A risk, yes, but a calculated one.

And one that, judging by her reaction, may well prove beneficial to his cause. Because it's obvious that the girl still has unfinished emotional business with Lana, so she's not going to do anything that would jeopardize her chances of seeing her friend again – which, he assumes, includes passing damning information about the place where said friend currently resides along to her mother.

He takes another sip and passes a tired hand over his eyes, shivering in the desert night-chill as he mentally scrolls through all possible versions of the truth he's promised Shariah today. There are several ways he could play this; he's just not sure which one would be best.

Should he tell her that he has contacts in the ranchos, plants that pretended to be expro refugees but in reality infiltrated the community and have been reporting to him ever since? Maybe they also took Lana there after the Destierra and have been keeping her safe. Or maybe she made her own way there and ran into one of them later?

He grimaces. It all sounds so farfetched, like some old world spy novel. But the real story isn't that much more believable.

The crunch of boots on gravel jolts him into alertness and he opens his eyes to find Shariah approaching – right on time, lips set in a grim line. When she reaches the roller she says nothing, just gets in the passenger side and nods as if to say, 'Let's go.'

Theodore slots the mug into a cupholder and keys the engine, pressing the pedal and turning the wheel in the direction of the area where Transway used to be.

AFTER TEN MINUTES OF HIDEOUSLY uncomfortable silence, Shariah climbs down from the roller, rubbing her arms in the brisk air. Her thin jacket is made for climate-controlled indoor spaces; she'd forgotten how cold it could get outside overnight, even in summertime. It makes her uneasy, this feeling of exposure, even as she tells herself that there's no real threat.

Shutting the half-door behind her, she lets her gaze grope over crumbling hulks of ruined buildings before meeting Theodore's eyes across the roller. Following his lead she removes her server from her pocket and places it on the seat. Then, at some unspoken signal, they both turn and begin to walk abreast down the dead street.

At fifty paces Theodore halts, clearing his throat.

"So," he says mildly, "what would you like to know?"

Shariah crosses arms over her chest and glares at him, but keeps her voice even.

Best cut to the chase.

"Is Lana alive?"

"Yes," he says. "I think so."

"You think so? You haven't seen her?"

"Not since the Destierra, no."

"Then why do you think she's alive?"

Theodore sighs. "When she was dropped off, I left her with the means to survive for a few days. None of those items were ever recovered, except for the server, which she purposefully left where she knew I would find it. I was going to come get her and take her to Winnipeg. But when I came for her she was gone."

"And you never bothered to tell me any this? You knew how upset I was."

"I was afraid you'd tell your mother."

Shariah sucks her teeth; she wants to be angry at him for heartlessly leaving her to mourn, but she has to admit that that's a fair assumption.

"What about her bots?" she says instead. "Couldn't you track them?"

He shakes his head. "She shut them off."

"How?"

A shrug.

Shariah shifts uneasily. "So you think someone else came and got her?"

A nod.

"Expros?"

"Probably."

"So then why do you think she's in the ranchos now? I thought they didn't allow any Transway refugees to resettle there unless they had family connections."

Theodore has the breathless look of a man about to jump from a great height. Behind him, the first sliver of sun appears over the top of the mountains.

"She does," he says softly.

"She – what?" Shariah says, completely thrown. "This isn't the time for jokes, *Theodore*. You said you would tell me what happened. I want to know the truth."

"And that's what I'm telling you."

"No," she says. "You're not. You're trying to tell me that Lana was a transer – "

"She was."

" – who came from the *ranchos*?"

"She did."

Shariah glowers at him, convinced that this is some kind of desperate attempt to throw her off base, to cover up... something by means of the most audacious lie possible.

"I don't believe you."

He shrugs again.

"So what was she then? A science experiment? Some urchin you picked up and raised as your own to prove the existence of transer intelligence?"

The ghost of a wince flits across his face. "Lana was my daughter." A pause. "*Is.* She is the child of myself and a woman from Rancho Pescados who was living on Transway during the time that Lana was conceived. I was unaware of this conception, and so Lana was born and raised in the ranchos until, after her mother died, she came to live with me."

"So what about Winnipeg?"

"That was a lie."

She looks down, biting her lip as if trying to process this information. But inside she's stewing: Now she *knows* it's bullshit. Lana hadn't come down from Winnipeg to live in Albakirk until she was eleven, and even then she'd needed several months of private tutoring before she was ready to start Ed with the rest of them. There is no possible way that some snot-faced ranchos brat who grew up planting potatoes and chanting nonsense could have caught up with years' worth of advanced tech knowledge in that space of time. And not just caught up – performed brilliantly, from the first day she walked into class.

He's definitely lying.

But why? And can she gain anything by playing along?

She raises her chin and meets his gaze steadily.

"I want to see her," she says. "Talk to her."

"So do I."

"So what do we do? Go and see her family? I thought you said her mother was dead."

"She is," Theodore says, raking a hand through his hair. "But there are other relatives still around. So far, all of my attempts to get information out of them have failed. But you, as her best friend, may have more luck."

So that's it, she thinks. *Lana won't talk to him so he's trying to use me to get to her. Maybe she's still mad that he killed that psycho she took up with.*

Or maybe it's all a bunch of bullshit. Maybe Lana's not really alive at all. Maybe he's trying to distract her from her research. Or give her a reason to try and convince her mother to preserve the ranchos!

That must be it. Shariah grimaces, ninety-nine point nine percent ready to throttle him with her bare hands. But she doesn't want to flat-out accuse him of anything, not yet at any rate, so she just tosses her white-blonde hair and says, "Maybe."

THEODORE GULPS, TAKING IN THE furious girl before him with alarm. He'd launched what could have amounted to the greatest weapon in his arsenal – the honest truth – but it seems to have failed completely. He can tell she doesn't believe a word. And, worse yet, now suspects some treachery.

"If you'd just come and meet them," he tries, "you'll see."

"Sure!" Shariah says with false brightness as she turns back towards the roller. "I'd love to meet Lana's transer family. Maybe I'll bring some Chronies along for the ride. They live for this kind of thing."

She stalks off, shaking her head.

"Chronies?" he says, trailing at her heels, desperate to keep her engaged. "What are those?"

A snort. "Oh, you know. The ones who think the calendar's off."

He stops, stock still.

"Who *what*?"

She halts, annoyed. "Bryan and his friends," she says. "They had some solstice thing where a crystal didn't shine in a fountain and then it did, but three days off when it was supposed to. It was dumb. It's not really a thing anymore."

But Theodore is not quite listening to the full explanation; his mind is alive with echoes:

'She set the calendar back! To cover the fact that the bot release failed. You'd all been unconscious for three days!'

Lana's words, when she'd been questioned after Ariana thwarted the expro plot against the city; not a confession but a desperate plea for credence. Words that, due to her transferon-addled state, he'd dismissed out of hand.

He breaks, running for the roller and snatching up his server, searching madly for a little-used application, half praying it will prove true and half hoping it will not. He holds the server up to capture an image of the sun, now fully risen above the horizon.

"What are you doing?" Shariah says, breathless at his elbow. Her expression is keen, his genuine agitation having banished her show of distrust.

"What day is today?" he asks her.

"Ord 243," she says warily.

"Yes," he says, swiping and tapping. "And on Ord 243 at 06:35 at this geolocation the solar declination ought to be 8.25 degrees, the azimuth 87.37, and the elevation 10.78. So, if we compare these calculations with those of the image I just took we can see that we are indeed…"

He hushes, waiting for the calculations to complete. Then he stops; his heart, his blood, the entire world seems to freeze on its axis. He holds up the server so Shariah can see the indisputable results and says, very quietly:

"Three days off."

▭► 13 ◄▭

Lang's hands go slack as the warm prickle of prana begins to subside and the last of the red, blistered flesh on Effie's arm returns to a smooth, unblemished state; he sighs, satisfied with his work, and shakes them out. The girl had burned the entire length from wrist to elbow when she slipped on some spilled sauce in the kitchen and fell into the stove. Effie makes a small sound of approval as he releases her. She holds her skinny arm out, marveling.

"I always heard you had talent," she says. "But this is the first time I've seen it for myself. You're some kind of miracle man."

"Not really," Lang says, ducking his head. "It's just prana. And I'm just the channel, not the source."

"Damn good channel though."

"Gracias."

"See you later?" Effie flutters long eyelashes at him, tossing her curls winsomely. "We made green chile potato salad. And there's a new yarrow brew. I heard it's *delicious*."

He forces a smile. "Can't wait."

With a last flirtatious wink, Effie jumps up and smoothes down her stained work-shirt.

"Better go change into something pretty."

"Take it easy this afternoon," Lang tells her. "And be sure to drink lots of water."

"Drink lots; got it!" she says as she sashays to the door. "Doctor's orders."

"I'm serious."

"So'm I. It's fiesta day."

She yanks the door open to make her exit, but her eyes are still on Lang, so when she turns to go she walks straight into an uncharacteristically flustered Sonrisa. His apprentice has been at large all morning but he's been far too busy to wonder what she's been up to.

Probably off with the kids somewhere.

Sonrisa recovers quickly though, trading 'excuse mes' and a few pleasantries with Effie. But when his patient finally takes leave she groans.

"It's crazy out there. Everyone running around getting shit ready."

"Yeah," he says tightly.

"What, you aren't ready to fiesta?" She does a few goofy dance steps, trying to jolly him.

"Looks like it's not gonna be much of a party. For me anyway."

"Huh? Why?"

Lang frowns. He hates to spoil the day for her, but she needs to know what's happening. He takes a quick glance out the window; Effie's gone and no one else is approaching.

"Brophy stopped by earlier to let me know that my presence at the fiesta is now required," he says. "And that I better make sure I'm not fused up."

Sonrisa's eyes harden. "He *said* that?"

"Not in so many words. But I know Brophy, and he said enough for me to get the message." Lang rinses his hands in a small bucket on the bench, then dries them with a scrap of cloth hanging on the wall. "Looks like they're on to us. Or me anyway. He didn't say anything about you."

"But what are they planning to do? Take turns spot-checking your eyes all night?"

"That's what I'm guessing."

"That's bullshit," she says, crossing arms in front of her chest. "In fact, that is the most almighty bullshit I have ever heard in all my life. These people are supposed to be your friends? That is not what friends do."

Lang shrugs. "At least Brophy warned me. He didn't have to."

"Threatened you more like. Probably on the orders of his little – "

"Whatever," he says, cutting her off. "There's not much I can do about it, other than show up and try to be a good boy."

"Yes there is," Sonrisa says. "You could find a way to show them how much they need you. And remind them that you don't have to put up with any of this shit at all if you don't want to."

"What do you mean?"

"I mean, give them something to think about."

"Like what?"

"Like that you could just…refuse. To heal anyone else. Until they stop fucking around and give you your transfer back. Bet that would bring them around quick." There's a cold, alien tone to her voice that he's never heard before.

Lang shudders. Of all the sins he's committed, through ranchos' eyes that would be by far the most unforgivable.

"I – can't do that," he stammers. "I could never do that. What if someone was really sick? Or hurt bad? They could die – "

"And it would all be your fault," she finishes wryly.

"No! I mean, yes, but that's not why – "

"Never mind," she says, with a quick quirk of her lips. "I was just kidding."

He struggles for a few seconds more until this sinks in. "Oh," he says, dredging up a laugh.

Stupid. Of course. No healer would ever do something like that.

"Gotcha," she says, swinging her arms and bouncing like a boxer warming up for the ring.

"Hilarious."

"You can at least show them they don't have a *total* hold on you, though," she says, still bouncing. "That they can't force you to come to their stupid party just to see if you pass inspection."

"Oh yeah?"

"Yeah. Show 'em they can't treat you like their little lap-dog. 'Good boy!' 'Sit boy!' 'Put that transfer down boy!'" She orders, mimicking Mara.

Lang starts to laugh, for real this time.

"So what do you suggest we do instead?" he says. "If we stay here they're gonna come looking for us. Or at least Brophy will."

"Fuck Brophy!" she says. "Fuck 'em all! Let's go out to the cave. Have our own fiesta. They can't make you go to theirs. Maybe you just don't want to. Maybe you're too holy now for all that drinking and carousing. Maybe you need to meditate upon the Will of the Universe instead."

Sonrisa stops bouncing and reprises her beatific look, honeyed hair haloed in the morning sun.

Lang chuckles again, then hesitates. His evening dose is not optional; with his long history of fusing as soon as he started up again he was immediately back in CERS mode. Still, he could put it off long enough to make an appearance, have a couple of drinks, and prove to everyone that he's fine.

But why should I?

And what are the chances that those couple drinks multiply into an insane amount and he wakes up hungover, CERS-ado, and next to Madre-knows-who? Celan's due back any day now. Nothing ever came of that unsettling night with Jaslene but he can't afford another slip-up.

This last decides it.

"All right," he says. "Fuck it. Let's go."

AND IT'S SUCH A FINE *romance now*
When you don't stand half a chance now
Face the music and you'll dance
They want to see they want to see
All of that proverbial incongruity!

Mara shouts out the final verse of the old Fused Up! song along with the rest of their small circle as Zeeb adds a final wild guitar flourish and Brophy winds down the bass line. Her man looks faintly embarrassed, which is beyond stupid in her opinion. Fused Up! was his old band back in Transway's glory days – when music had poured out of every open doorway and Arlo's was *the* place to be. She hadn't known him well then, he was a Big Deal and she was just a random dishwasher; they got together only after he quit the band. But it was a lucky thing he had, in more ways than one; it meant he'd escaped the fire that killed so many of his friends and former bandmates. With the passing of Tomás last spring, he's now the sole surviving member of Fused Up!.

Still, she thinks, as he and Zeeb nod and begin a more subdued tune, *he's a part of* history. *He should be proud of it.*

She swigs her brew and taps her foot impatiently, peering out past the perimeter of their little group to where the orange sun is beginning to merge with the dark line of the horizon.

Where the fuck *is* he?

The fiesta's been in full swing for hours, everyone enjoying the food and drink and the freedom from chores. Now the bonfires are being lit, but there's still no sign of Lang. Or Sonrisa. Mara tsks, humming along half-heartedly until Zeeb and Brophy finish to a scatter of applause. They lay aside their instruments and fist bump.

"Break time," Zeeb says.

"You had one job," she says, scowling at Brophy as he approaches. "You said you were going to get him here. So where is he?"

A shrug.

"Off in lala-land," Jaslene says, smirking as she rearranges a mewling baby Isaac in her arms. "Drooling on himself." She shakes her head. "Same as it ever was."

Zeeb and Sig laugh, but Brophy's face is grave. "I doubt

that," he says.

"Why?" Mara says. "Did you say something to him?"

"I said some things. But not every thing. Just...things."

She gnaws her lower lip in frustration. It's been a while since she's spent much time with her man when he's under the influence and, as annoying as the lean-and-dream Class E shtick used to be, at the present moment this cryptic Class S shit bugs worse. Her eyes tick across the field to where Maddy's group is gathered; a few of her girls shaking their hips to the syncopations of a cluster of hand drummers – to widespread, enthusiastic appreciation.

Ugh.

"Claro," she says, chugging the last of her drink and getting to her feet. "If no one else is gonna do anything then I will."

She thunks her mug down on the makeshift bench. "Save my spot," she orders Zeeb, then tugs at Brophy's sleeve. "Vámanos."

Brophy escorts her obediently down the slope from the cleared field to the plaza, followed by a clucking Jaslene; Isaac's starting to wail and she bounces him on her hip, cooing. In front of the dining hall, they all halt.

"I gotta go take this one in the kitchen and feed him before he freaks," Jaslene says, with a nod at the baby. "But I'll check the buffet too, see if we're running low on anything."

"Bueno," Mara says. "And keep an eye out for Lang. Just in case."

"Oh I will," she says, sardonic. "But I doubt he's got much of an appetite."

She ducks into the hall as Mara, Brophy in tow, marches

over to the healers' hut. All is dark and quiet and, when she sticks her head in to confirm, totally deserted.

Where the fuck is *he?*

She slams the door shut, cursing, and makes to return to the plaza, but a movement in the dying light catches her eye – someone drawing quickly back around the corner of the house. She springs forward in time to catch Sonrisa's wiry form making for the shadows under the trees.

"Hey!" Mara shouts.

The girl freezes. She's too close to pretend not to have heard.

"Hey," Mara says again.

Slowly, Sonrisa turns. Her face is very pale and she's sweating, as with some recent effort. "What?" she says.

"Nada," Mara says, eyes narrowing. "Just wondering why you seem to be avoiding us. It's fiesta day. Do healers have some kind of problem being social these days?"

"No. Willa and Taryn are there, right?"

"That's not what I mean."

"I don't know what you mean," Sonrisa says, sticking her lower lip out, truculent. But then, seeming to reconsider, she morphs her pinched expression into something approaching friendliness. "But I really kind of do. You're looking for Lang, right?"

Mara says nothing.

"He said he had to do something earlier," the girl continues. "That he was going to meet me. But he's not here. So I thought maybe – there's this…cave where he hangs out sometimes. Meditates."

Of course, Mara thinks grimly. She knows the spot; it's

where Lang had been holed up when Brophy got injured way back when. *Aviados as fuck, too.*

Her jaw clenches. "Well let's just go pay mister holy man a little visit. And I hope you two parted on good terms this morning. Because when we find him, I'm going to kill him."

"Actually," Sonrisa says. "I think he's probably at the party now. Let's check there first." And before Mara can say anything else the girl tears off in the direction of the fiesta.

"Hey!" Mara yells again, but this time Sonrisa doesn't stop. She wheels on Brophy. "What the hell is going on?"

But he doesn't respond; he's standing silent in the setting sun, eyes far away and face twisted in a terrible grimace.

"Brophy!" she says, alarmed.

"Something's wrong."

"What?"

"Something's *wrong*." He groans. "At the party."

Normally, she would dismiss this as Class S superstition. But something in his terrified tone pings a deep fear in Mara's gut. She grabs his hand, pulling him forward.

"Come on," she says. "We can deal with Lang later."

This snaps Brophy out of whatever trance he's in and together they break into a run.

LANG STARTS AWAKE AT THE sound of a twig-snap somewhere close by. He gropes out a hand; it's full dark now – where is Sonrisa? She was right next to him...when? It was still light when that first fuse wore off, hours ago, so they took another hit and –

Maybe she woke up first and had to pee or something.

Another twig-snap. That must be it. Any second now her

head will pop up above the edge and –

"Lang?"

Brophy's voice.

His bones go cold; even if there was anywhere to hide, he's not sure he could get to his feet right now to find it. He can only watch helplessly as Brophy's fuse-bright eyes materialize up the rise to where he's seated against the concave rock. He blinks up at his friend with a one-shouldered shrug as if to say, 'Fine, you got me.'

But as Brophy's features resolve it's clear that he's neither angry nor accusatory. He looks scared. And, even stranger, he's holding a transfer. He crouches at Lang's side, grasps his arm, and suddenly it's clear he's about to –

"Wait!" Lang says. "I don't need – "

"This isn't E, it's D," Brophy says, and before Lang can protest further the shot hits his system. Suddenly, like someone threw a bucket of cold water on his heart, he's wide awake.

"What the – ?" he sputters.

"No time," Brophy says, hauling him to his feet. "We gotta get the fuck out of here."

"But what – what happened? Is someone hurt?"

"*Move,*" is the only answer.

So Lang shuts up and stumbles after him, out onto the river path to Rinconada. But Brophy turns right instead of left, heading in the other direction.

"Hey!" he says. "Brophy, wait! Where are you going? At least tell me what's going on."

But he doesn't turn around and Lang, with a last, confused look towards camp, chases after his fast-receding form. They follow the path for a bit under soughing, night-black boughs until it crossroads with another, wider, one. Brophy turns left onto this wider path, which runs steeply up from the river in the direction of the old Taos road. Now they can walk abreast instead of single-file. Lang trots along at his friend's side in the light of an almost-full moon, throwing questioning glances, but Brophy doesn't say a word; not until they reach the old road does he finally stop and address him.

"Who was it?" he says bluntly.

Lang knows exactly what is being asked, but not wanting to rat out Sonrisa is reluctant to answer.

"Uh," he says. "Well…"

"Because Mara's about to tear Maddy's throat out," Brophy continues. "She's convinced she must have had a transfer hidden somewhere – "

"It wasn't Maddy."

"Then who? Your little friend?"

Lang hangs his head, sheepish.

"Of course it was."

"But don't blame Sonrisa – "

"Oh, I haven't even *started* blaming Sonrisa," Brophy says through clenched teeth. "It was her, right? It's been her – she's been giving you E for weeks. You've got CERS again, don't you?"

Lang rakes a hand through his hair. "Just a little."

"And today she convinced you to blow off the party and go vamos aviados, didn't she? But you know where she was when you were nodding the fuck out? Not sitting there next to you – she was out doing the devil's work."

"What?"

"Finding a nest of hornets. Bringing it into camp. And

setting it loose at the fiesta," Brophy finishes, face full of thunder. Lang has rarely, if ever, seen him this angry.

There has to be some mistake.

"That's crazy," he says. "I know her. She would never do a thing like that."

"She did," Brophy says, with absolute conviction.

"But we've found nests before. There are lots of them around. Maybe – "

"As of this morning there were none within a mile of camp. And certainly not any near the dining hall. Max and Val and me spent all day yesterday astralling all over to make sure. With how many shitfaced people were gonna be staggering around tonight we didn't want to take any chances."

"But couldn't you have missed – "

"No," he says. "We didn't."

"Well – but, I mean – everyone's all right?"

Brophy draws a long breath. "Once the swarm started, your little friend put on quite a demonstration of her healing abilities. You definitely taught her well."

"She's always been good at it," Lang admits. "I really haven't taught her much at all."

His friend shuts his eyes and shakes his head like this, somehow, is the final straw.

"So everyone's all right?" he presses, anxious.

"Jaslene's dead."

The words are a shockwave and an explosion; his body lifted up and punched by an invisible hand. Lang's lungs try for air and fail to find it as his gut lurches and he leans over and retches into the dust. When the meager contents of his stomach have been ejected he straightens, and the tears start –

not wrenching sobs, he's still too aviados for that – but a silent stream accompanied by the feeling that he must be, has to be, dreaming.

That can't be real.

Brophy watches him for a moment, but only for a moment, before wrapping arms around him and pulling him close. Lang leans into his friend, sniffling.

"Is Isaac – "

"He's OK. She got on top of him. Protected him. That's how she got stung so bad. The main swarm was mostly in the hall, but the nest was by the kitchen and that's where they were. Your little friend didn't get to them until it was too late."

"You're *sure* it was Sonrisa that did it?" Lang pleads.

"That nest didn't move itself and it sure as fuck wasn't there this morning. Only a powerful healer could've kept it quiet enough to move it. And we know that wasn't you."

"It wasn't!" Lang says. "I swear on – on Celan. But I still don't – " And then he's taken back to earlier today, to his conversation with Sonrisa, to the things she'd said with that cold tone in her voice: 'You could show them how much they need you....That you don't have to put up with any of this shit at all.'

And suddenly it's clear; she wasn't kidding. She had a plan. A demonstration. So of course she hadn't refused to heal anyone *this* time; she had to show them what she could do. Next time, however –

He groans. "How could I be so fucking *stupid?*"

Brophy grips Lang's shoulders and spins him around, looking him hard in the eye. "I'm not gonna say that it's not your fault because it kind of is. But it's not just your fault. You were played, ese. Big time. And by someone who knows how.

Someone who played Maddy and Mara too, who, by the way, definitely should've done us all a favor and listened to you when you said that last cut was no bueno."

"But – "

"And far as that goes, it's my fault too. I knew how miserable you were; I've been there. I should have forced the issue instead of trying to keep the peace. But what's done is done. We can't fix it. What we gotta do now is get the fuck out of here until everyone cools down."

"But I want to go back and explain," Lang says, jerking free of Brophy's grasp. "Try to help. We can't leave them all here with Sonrisa."

"Yes we can. And we will, for a little while at least. You don't get it: Everyone's out of their fucking *minds* right now. Gabe swore he was going to murder you and I could tell he wasn't playing. That's why I came and got you. 'Cause when it all went down your little friend made sure we knew exactly where you could be found."

Lang's stomach twists again, but there's no lunch left to lose.

"She played it off all innocent. No shine in her eyes; must have skipped her evening dose the way she was sweating. But she passed that off as stress; said she had to go lie down after."

"So everyone thinks she's – "

"The hero," Brophy finishes. "So the last thing you want to do is show your face again until they've figured out what that girl's about." A pause. "She's Class E, obviously."

"Yeah."

"Enough that she won't be able to hide it for long?"

"No. Not without my help," Lang says bitterly.

"And she has a transfer."

He nods. "She came in with two; only turned in one."

"So we lay low for a bit," Brophy says. "Let them see for themselves. But we gotta be quick about it. There's a posse out for your head as we speak."

Lang glances over his shoulder. *Nada.* But he can hear shouts now, down by the river.

He shudders. "Let's go."

Brophy slings an arm around his shoulders, drawing him into the shadows on the far side of the road. But they're not heading away; it looks like he's steering them back towards Rinconada. Alarmed, Lang digs in his heels in to bring them up short.

"I thought we weren't going back to camp."

"We're not. Not all the way. We just need to get to the shed where the rollers are. It's right by the road. We have to be careful, but it sounds like they're searching the river first. If we hurry, no one should be around."

"And then?"

"Then," Brophy says, "we're going to the ranchos."

"But what – "

But he's stopped by the surprising, although not unpleasant, press of Brophy's lips on his. The kiss only lasts a few seconds, and then they're moving again, jogging forward side by side.

"What was that for?" he whispers.

In the dark beside him, his friend shrugs.

"You know," he says. "For luck."

▭▸ 14 ◂▭

Celan breaks into in a brilliant smile as Convention-standard blue stars of approval fall in a shimmering rain around her and her WDM,K*DU, Orofuchan, and X'z'x'z colleagues' holos. They've just wrapped up the presentation of their initial inquiry findings, demonstrating that there exists a feasible path for knocking the rogue planet threatening the 'DU (as she's come to call them) down a series of four wormholes and letting it out near the Orion terminus where there is nothing for it to smash into. Of course, the alignment of the holes won't perfect for another 394 years, which is cutting it uncomfortably close for the 'DU, but it *is* an option.

Whether it's the solution they eventually choose or not isn't the point.

I did something, she thinks. *Something important. Made us Madrens look good, and* smart. *Next time we come back they'll really respect us.*

Even Ech'unu Wehoo seems impressed.

When she finally disconnects from her holo she feels like dancing; some taunting, shimmying butt-shake of childish glee. If only Shariah could see her now, or her father. Or Ariana. Or any tech at all who looked down their noses and said that fusers were useless. At this point she's proven beyond a shadow of a doubt that even the (admittedly large) amounts of E she's been taking don't have any negative effect on her mental capacity. Still, she knows she needs to cut down, and she's going to do it. Soon.

But maybe one last zero-G for old time's sake...

Free as air she falls into her favored chair and snuggles down, savoring the knowledge that she has done the unimaginable. She, against all odds, made first contact. She, previously lowest of the low, is now the highest representative of her species. She, herself, will determine the course of human history.

And there's nothing any of them can do about it.

She's reaching into her pocket for the transfer when the tell-tale chime of docking sends a sour note to the pit of her stomach.

Ugh.

But it's not like she can pretend to not be at home.

Still, she had hoped that Chan, Ness, and Ree would stick to communicating their congratulations in the holo hall and not make any personal appearances tonight. Over the past few days, after what she's come to think of as 'The Incident at In-Drenï,' they've become a constant nagging presence.

They just don't get it though. She doesn't need a MedAI. She was just in a hurry and forgot to adjust her band for the altitude, and then when they'd had to wait in the bar at Da-

Racaí for a table that stupid gargleblaster – combined with the dose of Class E she'd take in the restroom and her empty stomach – had caused her to faint.

It could've happened to anyone, but from the way they've been acting you'd think it was some kind of five-alarm fire.

Celan rolls her eyes: 'Incident at InDrení' sounds like the title of one of the vintage sci-fi novels she used to borrow from her father's library. In her mind's eye she can even picture the cover – little green men in bubble helmets standing over her prone (but artfully arranged and scantily-clad) form.

She smothers a laugh as the door depressurizes and schools her face into pleasant blankness.

"Well done," Chan says, as he steps into her cell, but his usually effulgent manner is subdued. Behind him, Ness and Ree are silent.

"Thanks," Celan chirps, trying to seem as perky as possible.

"So are you all ready for your trip home?"

"Guess so. Everything's all wrapped up here for now. Think I'm gonna go to bed early tonight. Get a good night's sleep. Want to be fresh and ready for tomorrow."

She pastes on a grin, hoping they'll take the hint.

But no such luck; Ness and Ree share a look and then Ness steps forward, saying, "There's a MedAI ready in our capsule. I know you said you didn't need one – "

"I don't."

"But we can't allow you to make the trip home until we figure out what happened to you at DaRacaí You could have died, Celan."

"I fainted."

"Your skin turned blue," Ree says. "For your species, that is an indication of severe respiratory distress."

"I told you. It was the altitude. And that stupid drink."

But Ness is grim. "It was more than that. After comparing the baseline readings of the bodily functions stored in your band with the readings at the time of the incident, the AI said that the increased altitude and the alcohol alone could not have accounted for such a rapid and steep descent into hypoxia. There was a third factor, which it couldn't immediately identify. Until we know what that is we can't be responsible for transporting you anywhere else."

"But you brought me back here."

"To finish your inquiry," Ree says. "And to allow you to access a better class of MedAI. Which, for some reason, you refuse to make use of."

She says this kindly, with an air of gentle puzzlement, but Celan's pulse rises and she grits her teeth. This reminds her too much of her father, and his trick with the bots when he found all that Class E in her system. But that had been a lesson: Lying and getting upset are bad tactics when dealing with this kind of situation. Transparency is her best option. And this isn't like it was with her father. The Plejarans don't know a Class E fuser from a hole in the wall.

With effort, she masters herself and when she looks up again, it's with determined candor.

"I'm sorry," she says, meeting each set of eyes in turn. "I made a mistake and I didn't want you to know. I just – " and here she lets her breath hitch " – just wanted everything to be perfect. Remember back on Va'anak? When you said I should have my medication looked at? Well, I kept meaning to but I

got so busy I never got around to it. And then at InDrenï…
we were having so much fun. I forgot it's not supposed to be
taken with alcohol."

She dips her head for an added show of chagrin.

"Ah," Chan says, tipping his head back in a Plejaran gesture of understanding. The others follow suit.

Mentally, Celan pumps a fist.

"But why didn't you just say this at DaRacaï?" Ness says.

"I – I didn't want to look incompetent. I was just about to
do the inquiry presentation. I didn't want anyone to think – "
and now the hitch in her voice is real.

*That I'm a useless fuser. A waste of space. The loser freak that
everyone in Albakirk thinks I am.*

When she reaches up, it's to brush away a genuine tear.

And this settles it. Plejarans don't cry, but they can recognize Madren distress. All three close in, each in turn pausing
in front of her for a short bow and a pat on the shoulder. From
them, it's basically a group hug.

Celan heaves a deep sigh. "So you don't have to worry
about taking me tomorrow. I'll be fine on the ship. When I get
back home I'll see a Madren med and get the dosage adjusted.
Then I'll have it entered into my band so when I come back it
can work with the Convention's AI."

She blinks up at them. "Please. I really need to go home."

There's a breath of a pause and then: "Of course!" Chan
booms, his normal cheer restored.

Celan almost faints from sheer relief. If they wouldn't take
her back, if they'd insisted on endless scans from the MedAI,
maybe they would have found something amiss. And that
would have ruined everything.

"Don't ever feel like you can't tell the truth," adds Ree. "It's very important. But maybe we forgot how intimidating this all can be at first. You just seemed to have taken to it so well."

"Oh, I did," Celan says, giddy now. "This has been the most amazing experience of my life! I can't wait to come back. Just maybe with a few other Madrens next time."

"Every species has its flaws," says Ness. "But you'll find that energy is always better put into resolving them than in trying to hide them. Honesty is a mark of sanity among the transentient."

"Claro," Celan says, confident enough in her success to risk a little sass. "That's something, coming from a species with no flaws at all."

"Well," he says. "We have been around for a billion years. Anything can perfect, if given enough time."

"Even us?"

Chan pats her shoulder again, with what feels like encouragement. "It's good to have goals," he says, followed by what sounds suspiciously like a snicker.

Celan chuckles too, though she's fairly certain that this last is more on the order of Plejaran shade than an actual vote of confidence. But in light of her close call she's more than willing to let it go. After all, she's going home with a quantum band and a major success under her belt, and no one left thinking she's defective. If that's not a win, she doesn't know what is.

And she *is* going to cut down. She swears on the whole of Terra Madre.

Next time there won't be any incidents at all.

◻▸ 15 ◂◻

The buzz of her server is like that of an irritating insect, but Shariah ignores it, knees drawn tight against her chest as she stares out her bedroom window at a late-summer storm settling in over the Manzanos. Today's the big day: the Mars landing. She's supposed to be watching it in the plaza with everyone else. But she couldn't care less.

Let them put me on permanent Notice, she thinks viciously. *Like it matters.*

For the past twenty-four hours she's been holed up here, stomach churning and lungs tight, torn between an unthinkable confrontation and a desperate need to know:

How could she have done this – not just to me, or to Lana, but to everyone?

Her mother, the best and brightest, the shining example of the perfect tech that she's looked up to her entire life: A liar, a cheat, and a murderer. Or maybe not murderer, not exactly – maybe Lana is still alive out there somewhere. But even if she is, even if she can be found and brought home, the person Lana was is most likely dead and gone.

Shariah digs fingernails into her palms so hard they leave marks.

Theodore had promised that she could stay out of this. That she wouldn't have to go openly against her mother if she didn't want to. That, after the Mars landing, when he made a formal report of his findings to Roberta Miller, he would say that an anonymous source brought the date/sun discrepancy to his attention. Unspoken was his request that Shariah not warn her mother in advance. But that's really beside the point.

Because what could she even do? Knock us all unconscious again while she fixes it?

Maybe her mother could have come up with some plausible excuse, though – feigned surprise and said that the date reset was an accidental anomaly that must have occurred when the system went down on Ord 63. And maybe, if she hadn't deliberately shut down Bryan's investigation, Shariah would have been able to drum up enough reasonable doubt to let her do it. But it's obvious that she's still trying to cover it up.

And facts are facts: Two Lead SocEns together had to print the reader to approve a reset of the whole system. Martinez was AWOL and, according to Theodore, it was already reset when he woke up. So Lana's version has to be true – Shariah's mother took Theodore's unconscious hand and used it, along with her own, to fix the failed bot release and make Lana look like a liar.

That was the worst part, when Theodore revealed all that his daughter had told him; that she and that expro man weren't trying to kill them all, but to save them. He said he'd thought it all a desperate lie at the time, but now it was looking like it was true. It's insane to think that two fusers, the absolute lowest of the low, the kind of people devoid of any real conscious thought or concern for others, would have risked their lives to help people who didn't even like them. Who'd have left them for dead. But it seems they had. And as much as a part of Shariah is relieved to know that her best friend never actually tried to kill her, the knowledge is supremely unsettling as well.

A tap at the door brings her head up as, seconds later, it whooshes open to reveal public enemy number one: Ariana Balor in all her shit and glory. Something shrivels in Shariah and she nearly bares her teeth, but with supreme effort manages a neutral tone.

"What do you want?"

Her mother purses her lips, hands on hips. "Since you seem to be ignoring my messages, daughter dear, I thought I'd come to inform you personally: we successfully landed on *Mars* several hours ago. Your presence, however, was suspiciously absent from the viewing. I can't imagine you're still upset about that idiot boy so I'd like to know why exactly you are here in your room instead of joining the celebration. The second lander is due down in half an hour and I expect you down as well – on the plaza. Where you belong."

What if I don't give a shit? Shariah thinks. *What if I tell you to go fuck yourself?*

Using crude expro language, even in her head, emboldens her to the point that she's about to actually say something to that effect. But she brings herself up short, knowing she has no logical explanation for her rage.

Don't want to tip her off.

187

So instead she pockets her server and meets her mother's eyes coolly.

"Sorry," she says. "I'm not really in a celebrating mood."

"Not everything is about you and your *mood*, Shariah. This is one of the biggest events we may ever witness in our life-times and we are all supposed to be witnessing it together. Need I remind you that Unity is the first social precedent?"

"Fine," she says, but takes her time getting to her feet.

"And I want to see some enthusiasm," her mother orders. "You can mope all you want later, but when we get to the plaza this attitude needs to be gone. You are the daughter of a Lead SocEn and on track to be one yourself. You need to start acting like it."

"OK," Shariah says, letting a sliver of irony infuse her tone. "Lead on."

THE MOOD IN THE COMMAND center is cautiously jubilant as the tiny dot that is the lander bearing Nigel Gallegos, L. Solano-Ybarra, and Mo Morrison rushes toward the rust-red surface of Mars. It will be out of sight of the Nido's sat-cam momentarily but it won't be long before the ground-cam near the landing site picks it up. At least, that was how it worked with the first round and there's no indication that anything will be different this time. They are safely inside Phobos' or-bit and there are no dust storms or any other special hazards waiting for them on the planet's surface. Just the descent itself, which is hazardous enough.

Once again, Theodore wishes for a landing like one from some old world screener, an effortless glide with a spaceship coming to rest like a cloud touching the tip of a mountain.

But for all the impressive technology involved in travelling to another planet, actually landing safely on the surface of one has been the most difficult obstacle to overcome.

'Six minutes of terror' was no lie.

Hands clasped behind his back, he stands center-stage in front of the main viewscreen, face impassive. But there's a tender ridge of flesh on the inside of his right cheek from how hard he bit into it the first time. Watching the first lander come screaming in only to break seemingly in midair and hit the ground in a series of heart-stopping bounces had been one of the most terrifying moments of his life. The nano-foam body sleeves had worked beautifully though, and Gil, Chavez, and Vogel had all emerged shaken, but triumphant. They'd picked up one of two small, bot-built rollers stashed (to avoid being accidentally crushed by a pogoing lander) in a cave nearby and made the half-hour journey to the habitats unscathed, beaming back reams of stunning footage for the folks at home.

So now it's time for the repeat performance.

His shoulders stiffen as the ground-cam picks up a dot against the orange sky, a dot fast enlarging like some great carrion bird out of an ancient tale. It hurtles toward the ground until its enormous shadow almost blots out the light and then... A massive hit, clouds of dust, and the lander bounces – one, two, three times – before coming to rest, teetering, rocking side to side like the first one did.

There's a collective exhale as it stabilizes: They're down. They're safe.

A cheer goes up behind him and Theodore beams, poised for the final affirmation. After several minutes Mo Morrison

189

emerges from a hatch on the craft's underside, followed by Solano-Ybarra. But when the ground-cam closes in on them, the faces behind their masks look distraught, not exultant.

What happened? Theodore thinks. And then, with a shock of horror: *Where's Nigel?*

When the answer comes it is staticky, like a transmission (which of course it is) from another world:

'Sleeve malfunction.' Morrison croaks out. 'Snapped his neck. Nigel's dead.'

A STUNNED HUSH FALLS OVER the plaza as the words sink in. Shariah gasps and, before she can remember how angry she is, turns to share a shocked look with her mother.

"How awful," Ariana says, hand to throat. "I always liked Nigel."

"Wasn't he one of Mr. Timanti's friends?"

"Yes. One of the more sensible ones." Her mouth draws into a moue. "Poor Theodore. He really didn't need something like this, especially after all that other unpleasantness."

That you *caused*, Shariah thinks, momentary solidarity fading. But her scowl is lost on her mother, who's been accosted by a pair of CompEns eager to share their reactions to the news. She turns away, not wanting to be drawn into the conversation, and takes a few steps in the opposite direction, scanning the murmuring crowd. She spies Lynette and Kyle, two GenEn trainees she knows vaguely through Kirk, and moves towards them, only to be brought up short by the sudden materialization of Bryan.

"Hey," he says quickly, eyes lowered, and moves to duck past her. Obviously, he hadn't meant to seek her out.

But she grabs his arm. "Hey," she says.

He looks down at her hand on his sleeve and then back at her as if to say, 'What?'

Shariah bites her lip. "I just wanted to say…I'm sorry. You were right."

"About what?"

Not wanting to risk being overheard, she points up at the translucent panes, then at the fountain.

Bryan's eyes widen. "Seriously?" he says.

"Yes."

"But what – ?"

Shariah shakes her head, cutting her eyes in her mother's direction.

"Later," she says. "I'll explain. We can go for a walk – *outside*."

Bryan looks like he wants to say more, but settles for a nod. His face is so sweetly serious that on impulse, she throws her arms around him and pulls him in for a hug which, to her immense relief, he returns. When they pull apart they're both smiling, but recalling the tragic circumstances, sober their expressions immediately.

"See you," Bryan says, but like it's a question.

Shariah pats the server in her breast pocket to promise a forthcoming message. He nods again and they share one last, meaningful glance before she turns and walks back over to her mother, who, mercifully, doesn't seem to have noticed the exchange. Her bright red head is in a hushed huddle with the dark, wiry one of Alton White, former manager of the transer lab and currently the lead on bot-testing. In the absence of expro subjects Alton has been an integral part of Ariana's attempt to avoid a return to the lottery by moving all tests into a strictly virtual environment.

Shariah halts at a polite distance, so as not to interrupt. High above, the holoscreens are showing footage of Nigel's body being borne in a Martian roller by his weeping colleagues, to be laid in state, perhaps, in the habs. The three astronauts already there have been informed and there is a wrenching cut to their reactions. But her mother's eyes are bright, and Shariah thinks she detects a ghost of a smile as she pats Alton's arm with what looks like encouragement before he melts back into the grieving crowd.

Just how crazy is she?

"Mom?" she says, approaching warily. "Is everything all right?"

"Of course," her mother says briskly. "It's terrible, obviously, what happened to Nigel. But at least he was the only one harmed. I was just thinking of something else again – an opportunity that may emerge from this tragedy. You know the old saying? 'From ashes grow roses'... or something like that."

"Yes."

"Well," her mother says. "That's what I mean."

"Oh."

Something, maybe a genuine note of confused despair in her tone, makes her mother cock her head sympathetically.

"I know you've been having a rough time of it lately, dear. So I'll give you a hint." She leans in and tucks a lock of hair behind her daughter's ear as she extracts the server from Shariah's pocket, placing it next to her own on a ledge near the rushing fountain before murmuring, "It involves our friends across the mountains."

The ranchos.

Shariah goes very still, at once frightened and determined to muster every bit of faux-enthusiasm she possibly can.

"Really?" she says.

Her mother nods, smiling.

"I thought you said there wasn't enough support for any action right now."

"There's not. So I'm certainly not going to take any," she says, with a hideous wink.

"So…?"

Her mother leans in again, whispering like they're girl-friends discussing a crush. "So I have it on good authority that, while everyone is focused on Mars, some sort of natural disaster may take place that will rid us of our transer problem once and for all."

"What? When?" she says, with what seems like breathless delight.

"I can't really say *what*," her mother says. "These sorts of things are highly unpredictable. But my expert now estimates that sometime tomorrow night might be a good *when*. When everyone's sleeping, safe in their beds."

She almost croons this last and Shariah's stomach twists. But she says, 'Wow!', bouncing on her heels like it's Navidad morning. Then she stops, thinking that maybe this is just a touch too much. But one look at her mother's beaming face shows it's not.

Never enough enthusiasm for some good old-fashioned genocide.

"Strictly top secret information of course," her mother orders. "But I know I can trust you."

"Of course," Shariah says, adding one of her famous eye

rolls for good measure, even as, without a trace of guilt, she calculates how she's going to relay this news to Theodore.

After what just happened to Nigel Gallegos, he's probably not going to be in the best frame of mind, but he needs to be informed about this turn of events as soon as possible.

A SLOW SUN SLIPPING BEHIND the western mesa bathes the Sandia Mountains in a pink-orange glow as Theodore swirls the ice in his latest glass of Scotch and takes a long, meditative sip.

If it had been anyone other than Nigel.

Not that he actively wishes one of the others had died in his friend's place. He just wishes, fervently, that it hadn't happened at all. Or at least not in so cruel a fashion; not after two hair-raising landings and one collective sigh of relief. It seemed they'd pulled it off, and then…

The shock of it, the strain of being the strong one; mouthing platitudes, staying dignified.

He tosses back the rest of his drink, then turns to pour another, eyes catching on the chessboard still sitting on the ancient, polished surface of the heavy desk. The pieces are frozen in the last move he made in his last game with Lana, as if she's about to walk in the door at any moment and make another. As always, his first impulse is to gather them all up and lock the whole thing away somewhere. But something always checks it, so instead he swivels his chair and trains his gaze on the vista displayed like a work of art outside his private library window.

He sips again, inviting sweet relief or simple numbness.

Time was this long summer dusk would have been punctuated by the lights of Transway, each a pinpoint promise of joy to be had, of release. He wouldn't have been holed up in here, surrounded by ancient books and alone with his grief. Martinez would have burst in and dragged him out to Maddy's. And he would have protested, of course, saying that it was an unfit place to mourn such a solemn occasion. But Martinez would have said that the only way to deal with death was to live life – as well as you possibly could, enjoying every last thing it had to offer.

But Martinez – like Nigel, like Lana – is gone.

He swirls the ice again, thinking on the day he first met the man. Ancient history now it seems, back when Theodore Timanti was a newly-minted minor SocEn engaged in earnest volunteer work on Transway. In the wake of his parents' deaths he'd grown restless running endless simulations of potential space-colony societal trajectories and had fallen in with Francis Campana, a staunch advocate for the rights of the expros. Campana was fascinating, a charismatic former Lead who maintained that expros had just as much inherent intelligence as techs, and could be brought around to full participation in society with a certain amount of specialized assistance. But you had to meet them where they were, he said. Not where you wanted them to be.

Prior to this association, Theodore had never paid Transway much mind. Like many others, he'd shrugged off its existence as a convenient experimental tester pool and not much more. An avowed non-carouser like his own father, in his youth he had only ever gone out there a small handful of grudging times. But under Campana's tutelage he began to explore the place – just official interviews at first, communing with its denizens to try to facilitate bot acceptance and integration. It was in this guise that he'd met Mair Tyras, proprietress of Arlo's and Lana's eventual, erstwhile mother. That affair had led him to an awareness of some of Transway's other, more fun-loving, functions, and upon Mair's desertion, he'd sought solace at the occasional wayern and, on one especially dark night, at Maddy's.

Enter Frank Martinez – who, like Campana, took a keen interest in Transway, but unlike that of Theodore's original mentor, an interest with a decidedly libertine air. Theodore remembers fighting his way through the crowd, ill-at-ease in the ribald tumult, with his only intention being to find the nearest exit, when he'd attempted to squeeze past a laughing man perched on the edge of one of Maddy's myriad stages. Obviously a tech and even more obviously inebriated, the man was in the midst of some sort of game that involved flipping chits into the cleavage of one of Maddy's more generously endowed girls. Theodore had paused, equal parts intrigued and appalled, for one fateful moment in which the laughing man hooked an arm through his and corralled him into joining in. He'd been mortified at first, until several shots of whiskey saw him flipping like a pro. After that, he and Martinez were fast friends.

But Theodore soon discovered that for all his jollity, Martinez was smart and ambitious and laser-focused on becoming a Lead SocEn. In retrospect, he can see that he had been groomed in a way: to be his friend's lieutenant, to help temper the man's slightly seedy image with his own reputation as an earnest crusader, and to make a run for Lead in the same year as Martinez and his arch-nemesis (one Ariana Balor).

And it had *worked*: That first year as Lead was one of the best of Theodore's life. In his mind's eye he can see himself, young and strong, with a wry grin and a ready quip, amazed at having had the good fortune and good sense to get out from under the long shadow of his parents' tragic legacy and become something grand in his own right. The young man adrift had found a stable harbor, and become a pirate king.

Theodore chuckles at the thought, taking another soothing sip as the sky turns lavender and the ephemeral glow of the mountains darkens with the onset of night. The drink covers him like a blanket and he wants nothing more than to sink, down and down, into its warm embrace. He sighs, leaning back and closing his eyes, until all at once they fly open to the sound of a jangling chime. Someone's at the bunk's outer corridor door.

This is highly unusual. Any of his Mars colleagues would know better than to bother him tonight unless it were a serious emergency. And they'd message him first.

He groans, rising from his chair and thunking his empty glass down on the desktop. Not wishing to be disturbed, he'd left his server in the kitchenette. If he retrieves it, maybe he can deal with whoever-it-is without actually having to see them face to face. After what transpired today, no one could begrudge him a little liquid solace, but it's not really a good look.

He shuffles down the hall and swipes the server off the table, blinking blearily at the small screen as he scrolls through messages. *Nada.* Nothing that looks important. But the door chimes again, insistent, so he pops up the hall view to see –

Shariah Balor? What the fuck does she want?

197

But he knows the answer before he can finish the question – Ariana. This must be something to do with her mother.

Girding himself, he crosses the small space to the corridor door and presses the panel to open it. It whooshes aside to reveal a slight, white-blonde form practically vibrating with the force of some crucial news.

"Mr. Timanti!" the girl says, breathless. "We *really* need to talk."

⊏▸ 16 ◂⊐

Lang jolts awake with the afterimage of Jaslene's hideously swollen face burned into his brain. A dead, blue face, but open-eyed with a crawling, insectoid blackness. And those *teeth*. He gasps for air, blankets strangling him as he struggles, skin slick with sweat. Only after a full minute does he remember where he is: in his old bedroom at home in the ranchos.

After an all-night ride over dead roads and rough terrain, he and Brophy had arrived at the Shays' early this morning, saying that they were planning to wait for Celan here. This had been accepted by the family without comment and followed by a round of hugs and introductions, along with stern orders from his mother for them to go and get some sleep.

Weak with relief, Lang sinks back down into the mattress as he takes in the room – all soft, pretty touches; Melia's really made it her own. From the angle of light in the lace-curtained window it appears to be close to sunset. He takes a deep breath, and the smell of chili almost makes him gag. *Fuck*. He's right on the leading edge of CERS.

But Brophy has a transfer.

He sits up and throws his legs over the side of the bed, causing his gut to lurch violently. He needs to find Brophy *now*. Grimacing, he stumbles out into the hall; gritting his teeth against a rising tide of bile. As he approaches the kitchen his mother comes into view, dark hair tucked into a neat bun at the nape of her neck as she stirs a steaming pot on the solar-cell stove. Another step and he can see the long, pine-wood table, and (thank Madre) Brophy, chatting with Lang's sisters like it's an everyday thing.

He halts, shivering, on the threshold, and coughs softly. No one looks his way. Melia's busy wiping the table while Cass chops something on the counter. There's something achingly familiar about the whole scene, one like so many lost evenings of his youth – back when everything was normal and he was still good. He sniffles, then coughs for real. This time Brophy looks up, and he must have been ready for something like this because he comes right over, broad form blocking Lang from the family's eyes as he passes him the vial.

"Hey, güey," Brophy says in jovial tones. "Get enough sleep? 'Cause you still look like shit. Go wash up; we're about to have dinner." But he serves this with a hefty side of hard eyeball, as if to say, 'This is for get-well purposes only; do not subject me to your fuckery.'

Lang retreats into the bedroom and takes a minimal dose. He'd like nothing more than to knock himself into next week, but knows that if he does so his friend will find him there and cheerfully stomp his ass; there was no mistaking that look. He transes the burn and sits very still for a minute as the balm spreads through his system. Then he tucks the vial away and gets up to check himself in the mirror – a little tired and pale maybe, but not too bad. The worst is the hair; what were once subtle threads of white are now full-on streaks, lending him an odd, incongruous air. There's nothing he can do about it though, so he finger-combs it as best he can before splashing his face and neck with water from a pitcher on the dresser.

Then he tries a smile: Not great, but it'll have to do.

Out in the hall, dinner's starting to smell good. He's not usually hungry right after a fuse, but as he drops into the chair across from Brophy his stomach rumbles and he realizes he hasn't eaten since yesterday morning.

"You're looking thin, mijito," his mother fusses, concern creasing her kind face. She half-turns to hand Cass a small stack of something on a plate. "Have you not been feeling well?"

There's a hiss as Cass drops the first doughy sopapilla square into a pan of hot oil, and the scowl she gives Lang is equally furious; her disdain for the family fuck-up is ongoing.

"I'm OK," he says, avoiding both her eyes and those of his mother. Instead, he grins hopefully at Melia.

"He's feeling much better now," Melia says, smacking him swiftly upside the head with one hand as she sets a spoon down in front of him with the other. "Aren't you?"

She's the only one in the family who knows the truth about his fusing and must have a good idea of what just transpired in the bedroom.

"Yeah," he mutters.

"See?" she says. "He's fine."

She turns to grab more place settings as he feels a kick under the table; Brophy's palm is outstretched and his expression pointed. Reluctantly, Lang relinquishes the transfer. Then the pump at the sink cranks to life and he realizes he's dying of thirst. But before he can get to his feet Melia hands him a full mug; he sighs his thanks and gulps at it. Unlike Cass, his youngest sister generally only pretends to be mad at him.

"So Cass," she says casually, setting down cups. "How's Isaiah?"

Cass gives her a vicious look.

"Who's Isaiah?" Lang says, sipping more water.

Melia smirks. "Cass's ma-an."

"Really?"

"Don't act so surprised," Cass says.

"I'm not," he says quickly, though in truth he is a little. It's strange to think of his younger sisters being old enough to have *men*. But Cass is nineteen now. A woman grown.

"Isaiah Caras, from Carneros," Cass says, a touch haughtily. "He's a carpenter."

"Very nice family," their mother adds.

"Well," Lang says. "That's really great. Hope I can meet him someday."

There's an awkward pause.

"And that's not all," Melia swoops in. "I just was telling your friend here that you all came at the right time. No more boring old ranchos; things are finally getting *interesting* around here."

"Huh?" he says. "How?"

His sister grips the back of the chair next to Brophy and leans in, honey-brown hair spilling over slim shoulders.

"There's all kinds of crazy talk going around…" she trails off, building suspense.

"Like what?"

"Like that the techs are going to attack us; and that Celan Mairs is going to come with helpers from the sky and fight them off!" Her smile widens at Lang's stunned expression. "But no one knows what's really going on."

"Serio, Melia," chides Cass. "That is *not* what they said. All you do anymore is run around spreading stupid rumors."

"So it's not true?" Lang says, cutting off a retort from Melia. He shoots Brophy an anxious glance.

Cass tsks, poking at the sizzling sopas with a long-tined fork. Her face sours as her floury fingers tuck a stray lock of long, dark hair behind one ear. "What they *said* was that the techs may be planning to do something to the ranchos. They don't know exactly what. But they're setting watches at night, just in case."

"Well I heard what I heard," Melia insists. "About Celan."

"Probably from some expro."

"Paz said it," Melia counters. "Isn't she, like, your idol or something?"

"She's not my *idol*. She's just usually very level-headed is all."

"Girls." One word and a frown from their mother is enough to quell the bickering.

"Anyway," Melia continues, crossing long arms over her chest. "It's not just Paz; the elegidos are saying stuff like that too. That's where Paz heard it, from Carlos. One of the elders had a vision about it."

"And?" Lang says.

A shrug. "No sé. I told you – no one knows what's really going on. Anything could happen." She tries to make this sound ominous, but Lang can tell she's elated by the drama in the way only a sixteen-and-a-half-year-old can be. If he wasn't aware of how badly something like this could play out it would almost make him smile.

He sucks down the last of the water and is about to get up for a refill when, behind him, the creak-and-slam of the screen door is followed by footsteps, and the ominous rumble of his father's voice.

"Langton. Someone wants to talk to you."

Melia plucks twice at the left collar of her blouse. An old sibling sign meaning 'blue-robe.' Elegido.

Wincing, he turns in his seat to face whoever it is.

"Carlos," he says, by way of greeting.

The elegido nods, peering down the length of his thin nose with his face squinched up like he smells something bad. Lang's father stalks past them and plants himself at the head of the table; Cass puts a couple of freshly-made sopas down in front of him and he picks one up and takes a bite, staring straight ahead and chewing like there's nothing unusual going on. But everyone else is staring at Carlos, who, clearly relishing his role, sweeps the room with imperious eyes before informing Lang: "The elders want to talk to you."

Lang pales. He just fused up. Carlos can't tell but the elders might be able to. According to rumor, they only transfuse in emergencies, and while catching him out doesn't exactly qualify as one in his mind it may well in theirs. If a fused-up elder gets a good look at him within the next few hours the game is up.

"Uh, OK," he says, playing for time. "But we're just about to eat. How 'bout I go by there after dinner?"

"No," Carlos says. "They want to talk to you *now*. I'm supposed to walk you over. So you don't get *lost*."

Cass titters, but everyone else is silent.

And then there's nothing else to do.

Lang stands, head hung like he's going to his doom. "All right," he says. "Let's get this over with."

GLASS PANES GLINT IN THE light of the setting sun as the domed structure of Pranascuela rises in splendor above the trees, looking completely unchanged since the last time he saw it, three-and-a-half years and a lifetime ago. Lang stops for a moment at the edge of the clearing, regarding it mutely, until Carlos pokes him between the shoulders. Neither had said a word on the walk over, but the elegido's disdain had been palpable all the same.

I deserve it, Lang thinks miserably. *Whatever they do, whatever they say. Maybe they should just kill me and get it over with.*

But despite the conspiracy theories he used to hear floated around on Transway, he doesn't think the elders really go in for that sort of thing. Even so, he mounts the broad steps up to the entrance with dread. In all the long months spent back in the ranchos after Raf died the elders had never once summoned him – not to chastise or instruct or anything else. They'd let him be.

So why now?

The only reason he can think of is that they want to formally shame or banish him. Tell him he's a piece of shit and that he should get out and never come back. Turn in his trans-

205

fer. But seeing as he no longer has one, in that at least they'll remain unsatisfied.

At the top of the wide stone steps, one of the heavy double doors is propped open. When they reach it, Carlos stops and cocks his head, motioning him inside.

"You're on your own, *Langton*. This is as far as I was instructed to escort your sorry ass."

Lang takes one last, longing look at the freedom of the forest before crossing the threshold into the hushed hall. To his right the entrance to the domed instruction area arches, immaculate white mats empty of pupils at this hour. On his left is a series of closed doors leading to various smaller rooms.

Seeing no one, he shuffles forward a few cautious steps. He strains his ears but hears nothing; not a murmur, not a footfall. Then a sudden raspy skritch makes him jump a little in his skin. He's brushed against a large banner on the wall – The Precepts, the list of the elders' commandments for right living. He shudders. At this point, he must have broken every last one.

He turns quickly away, only to find that he is no longer alone; twenty feet from him three white-robed elders now stand. His throat catches at the sight of ancient Caron; she was always one of his favorite teachers. Flanking her are iron-haired, doughty Owen and the slighter, yet no less intimidating form of Cruz. Lang meets each of their gazes in turn and, sure enough, in Cruz's mild grey eyes he finds the shine.

He braces himself.

Here we go...

But the man makes no acknowledgment. And Lang is shocked to find no trace of Carlos' earlier enmity reflected in any of their faces. No pity either; they look kind, friendly.

"Langton Shays," Caron says. "Welcome home."

"Uh, gracias," he mumbles.

"Beautiful evening, isn't it?"

"Yeah."

"Como estas?" says Cruz. "It's been a while since we've seen you."

"Uh, yeah...I'm fine. How are you?"

Would you please just yell at me already?

But instead, Caron smiles and beckons him. "Please, come sit and talk with us."

There is no way to refuse. Cruz and Owen close ranks around him as Caron leads the way past the stairwell that descends to the bathing pools. Lang's gaze lingers on it, he wishes they were heading down there right now. He remembers floating, drifting in the hot water then emerging clean and dry into the bright light under the dome; the prana energy thrumming in him, equal parts ecstatic and terrifying. He recalls a lesson at the age of fifteen – right after he'd been allowed his first official drops of transferon – when it first seemed that some sort of bright light had been turned on in him as well.

Each student in the class was given a sickly plant in a pot and instructed to attempt to heal it by applying a half hour of prana energy each day for seven days. But at the end of the first half hour Lang had opened his eyes to find the surface of the soil roiling with little yellow worms, peacefully separated from the plant they'd been infesting, while the plant itself was now healthy and green. Confused, he'd shown it to Caron, thinking it a fluke, a one-time accident of fate. After all, they'd been doing similar lessons at 'scuela since they were kids and nothing like it had ever happened to him before.

But it was no accident. He'd advanced quickly after that. So much so that sometimes, in lieu of a lesson, Caron would turn him loose in the elders' garden plots and have him trans the plants until the waves of prana flowing through him subsided. He'd been sure it would eventually run itself out, that the Universe would realize it had made a mistake and seek out someone more worthy. He knew he wasn't special.

But it hadn't. His fifteenth summer had brought a record harvest. And even now, after everything that's happened and every awful thing he's done, that power, like a jealous lover, still refuses to leave.

Caron halts in front of a nondescript door marked with a single painted red poppy. His dread intensifies a hundredfold: La Sala, strictly off-limits to 'scuela students and most elegidos other than those who serve it. It's not a place of discipline, but rather someplace for the elders to relax, meditate, eat, and do whatever else they do when unobserved by their charges and free to be 'themselves.' So the fact that they would invite him in – the most unworthy, the prodigal – is downright terrifying.

But Caron makes no comment, just turns the knob and ushers him inside. Lang draws a breath and enters.

The room is clean and pleasant, with wide, open windows and long, diaphanous white curtains shifting in the evening breeze. The stone floor is covered in a colorful array of woven mats and rugs and the far wall is floor-to-ceiling books slotted neatly onto burnishes shelves. Some of them look ancient. Candles glow at intervals, giving off a faint, sweet scent of honey, though the appetizing smell of posole is even stronger.

The table in the center of the room is set for four and laden with bowls of simple fare: aside from the posole there's a green salad, a dish of calabacitas, and a jug of cider.

"We know it's dinnertime," Caron says, pale blue eyes almost apologetic. "We thought you might be hungry. Have you eaten?"

Lang shakes his head no. If he tries to speak, he's afraid he might burst into tears. Then, either Owen or Cruz rests a comforting hand on his shoulder and he does anyway.

BACK AND FORTH MARA PACES, through the living room and in and out of the bedrooms and the pump room (the old house's former kitchen, now a place to get water, do the wash, and attend to bodily functions) dodging bodies and half listening to the talking and crying, whispers and shouts of the makeshift wake taking place around her.

They'd buried Jaslene this morning, in the late summer heat it had to be done as soon as possible. Gabe has been inconsolable, raging one minute, sobbing brokenly the next; Taryn and Willa temporarily tasked with care of Isaac.

Forty-eight hours straight now she's been up, ever since her happy harvest fiesta turned into a horrorshow, going over and over and over events in her mind, trying to figure out the answer to the question of the day: What really happened?

She snatches a mug of beer off the table and downs it, plunking it down empty at the other end without breaking stride.

Sonrisa is a Class E fuser – that much is fact. Immediately following the discovery of Lang's absence from the cave they'd gone to search the healer's hut again and found the girl there instead, with eyes practically on fire. And she'd admitted it right away, though she refused to give up the transfer, claiming that it was hers and that she was too traumatized to heal anyone else without it. Zeeb had confirmed that there were no transfers missing from his cache other than the one he'd lent Brophy for the night. So either the girl was telling the truth about having smuggled the transfer into camp or Maddy had slipped it to her on the sly. But the older woman steadfastly denied any responsibility.

Then Max and Val chimed in, insisting that there had been no hornet nests in the camp before the fiesta and especially not any in or near the dining hall. They'd checked for them they said, as part of their routine astral sweeps: The swarm could not have been a natural occurrence. Somebody must have set it up.

So it was back to Sonrisa, who at first denied everything and then, under duress, admitted that it was all Lang's idea – a preemptive plan to get people to accept their fusing through a public demonstration of their healing abilities. They'd set the nest up early that morning, she said, and then he took off to 'meditate' while she kept it quiet until the party was in full swing. He was supposed to meet her to release it, she said, but he never showed up. So she got worried and went looking for him, thinking that the nest would be fine for a little while without her monitoring it. She was really sorry that anybody got hurt.

It's a good story, but no matter how furious Mara is with Lang (and she is *livid*) she has to admit that the idea of him planning something like this is ridiculous. While he's certainly not above flirting to try to get his way, this kind of evil scheme is way out of his wheelhouse. More likely Sonrisa came up with the idea herself and got him to go along with it. Then at the last minute he had an attack of conscience or fear and bailed the only way he knew how. Of course, without bothering to alert anyone else to the possible danger.

Maybe he thought the girl wouldn't go through with it without him.

But that leads to the other big question: Where the fuck is he?

Wherever it is, it involves a roller and, most infuriating of all, Brophy – who in the aftermath seems to have gone AWOL with him and left her with this mess. Sighing, Mara rests her throbbing forehead against the cool, stained-glass pane of the pump room's back-door window. A dark blue sky studded with silver-white stars and a round moon, it's a lovely relic of old-world craftsmanship. Something about it had made her hopeful when they'd first claimed this place for their own; that despite the years and untold strings of calamities, some things of beauty were strong and could – *would* – endure.

But now…

"Uh, Mara?" comes a tentative voice behind her.

Sig.

She whirls. "What?"

"Hey, uh." His Adam's apple bobs as he gulps nervously. "Do you know if there's any more of that salsa? In the walk-in, maybe? We're almost out here."

"Do I look," she says, in calm-but-deadly tones, "like I give one last raggedy fuck about the current location of *salsa*?" She yells this last and Sig scatters.

Unbelievable.

211

She presses palms against her eyes; so tired but there's no hope of sleep. All the beer in the world won't touch the amount of D chugging through her system. Speaking of which, maybe it's time for another little pick-me-up: She's reaching into her pocket for the vial when the sound of footsteps makes her grimace.

Ahora no, she thinks. *Not unless you want the beatdown of your life.*

But as she raises her eyes to shoot death rays at whoever else dares approach her with some bullshit in this time of crisis, she's astonished to see a shimmering image of Brophy, trailed by Max and Val's solid forms, emerge through the pump room's swinging door.

What the – ?

She normally can't see astral forms (as that's undoubtedly what this apparition must be). Most people can't, except for those specially attuned to that sort of thing.

But maybe all the D...

"Oye," Max says. "We know you're busy, but this can't wait. Brophy 'sta aqui. On the astral. He needs to talk to you."

"I know," she says.

"You can see me?" Brophy says.

"Hear you too."

All three faces register shock.

"So," Mara says, with what she feels is a supreme effort of self-control. "No offense to either of you," she indicates Max and Val, "but can you kindly get the fuck out of here so I can speak to this asshole alone."

They make a fast exit, leaving her and Brophy standing opposite each other, face-off style. She crosses arms over her chest.

"Lo siento," he says immediately.

She gives him the barest of nods, 'Go on…'

"But I was worried something even worse would happen if I didn't get him out of here and give everyone a chance to calm down. It wasn't Lang's fault. It was Sonrisa. She had a second transfer. She's been fusing him up for weeks. She set the hornets loose. She's a fuser too. Class E."

"We know," Mara says.

"You do?"

"It took all of two hours to catch her at."

"Oh wow," he says, looking supremely relieved. "So we can come back now?"

"Sure," Mara says, with sarcastic cheer. "Now that Jas is in the ground everything's fucking fabulous. You'll be heroes of the day!"

"That's not what I meant."

"Except," she continues, "for the small fact that Sonrisa is saying that the world's worst piñata was not actually her idea. That it was all your boy's. That he meant it as some kind of demonstration of their healing abilities but then chickened out, got aviados, and fucked everything up, leaving her to do it all on her own. That's why Jaslene died. Because of him, not her."

Brophy looks stunned. "But that's – I mean, you don't really believe that Lang would – "

"I don't know what to believe."

"He didn't know anything about it," Brophy argues, panicky. "She got him out to the cave with a bunch of lies. He thought they were just going to hang out and fuse up. He had no idea what she was planning to do."

"So that's what he's saying, that he had nothing to do with it? Just an innocent victim?"

"Venga ya. You know Lang. Fucker's got issues a mile long but he would never deliberately put anyone in harm's way. And everyone else knows it too. Even Jaslene, as much as she hated his ass, knew it. After all the bad blood they had, that time with Isaac's fever he was there inside of a minute."

"That was before."

"Before what?"

"Before he started fusing again. Before he got desperate."

"Mara, no. It's not like that. It was all Sonrisa's idea. She planned it herself and never told him anything. And yeah, if he hadn't started up again and if he'd been at the fiesta, the whole thing never would have happened. He knows that. He blames himself. He feels terrible."

"Seguro." A pause. "And I'm sure you do too."

"Why?" Brophy says cautiously. "I mean, I said I was sorry and I am, for taking off without telling you. But it looks like I did the right thing." A pause. "I was just trying to help."

"Help him, you mean."

"Help *us*. I didn't want anyone to do or say anything they'd regret. You heard Gabe – shit was gonna get ugly. And Lang's been our friend a long time."

"Our friend." Mara sneers. "What friend? More like your little cariño. How's that working out, by the way? How grateful was he for the big rescue? Did he melt into your arms?"

Brophy's shaking his head. "It's not like that."

"Then what is it like? And whatever you do, do not drag Celan, the fake-ass space-beard, into this. Not this time."

Brophy's image seems to waver for a moment until he's nearly transparent in the half-light. But then he shores himself back up. "Claro," he says. "I won't tell you the truth then."

"The truth?" Mara says bitterly. "You wouldn't know the fucking truth if it walked up and bit you in the nalgas. Though actually, maybe you'd like that."

"Mara, stop – "

"No!" She stamps her foot. "No me mientas! Stop trying to shit me. Stop telling me you're not in love with him."

Their eyes meet, and in the darkness and silence stay locked on each for a long time.

"I don't know," Brophy finally says. "Maybe it's just that I've been him. But there's nothing going on between us, and that's not why I helped him. I helped him because – "

"He's our friend," Mara finishes acidly. "Who bitches and pouts and whines and acts like he has it so tough when any one of us has been through ten times worse shit than he's ever even heard of."

"He does, sometimes," Brophy says. "I know that. But you can't stand there and tell me that he hasn't had a really bad time over the last few years."

Her eyes roll skyward and she tsks, annoyed.

Then: "What did we do," he says, very softly, "back in the day, when Raf gave him that first shot? You remember – that night at Alamora? We stood there and we watched. And we laughed, 'Oralé! Fused up little brother!' He was just a dumb ranchos kid; didn't know a goddamn thing."

"So? That wasn't our fault. He chose to do it of his own free will. Nobody forced it on him."

"True. But he had no possible idea that you could be one-

and-done like that. That that's how it is with some people: One fuse and they can never stay away from it again for long. And then after Raf died he went a whole *year*? You saw him when he came back; he was losing his fucking mind. That's the thing. You don't know until it's too late."

"It doesn't matter," she says flatly. "We didn't make him like he is."

"But he made himself like us. And he's done the best he can ever since."

Mara says nothing, an unpleasant sensation crawling up the back of her spine. There is a measure of truth in Brophy's words, but –

'Maybe it's just that I've been him.'

"Or maybe not," she says out loud.

"What?"

"All this care, all this wonderful understanding – all for him, not for me." She moves in close, finger pointed in accusation. "Where were you today, when we buried one of our best fucking friends? Not here with *me*. Not helping *me*. You were with *him*. Drying his tears. Holding his hand. While I was here all alone!"

"You weren't alone, Mara. There were plenty of other people – "

"That's not what I mean and you know it!" she shouts.

"But we – "

"You know what? I don't care what you do! Run off with him for all I care. I don't care if I ever see you or Langton fucking Shays ever again for as long as I live."

"But Mara – "

"Vete a la chingada!"

Brophy cringes like a kicked dog. "You know I love – "

"Fuck! You!"

And with that his shimmering form vanishes and she's alone. Breathing hard, her whole body screaming with rage, Mara whips her head around, searching, searching...

"Ha!" Her fingers close around the cold iron of a pipe wrench, most recently used by Brophy in his ongoing war with the house's ancient plumbing.

The stained glass window shatters with the first blow, but she keeps on hitting until every last piece is ground to dust.

"SO WHAT HAPPENED?" MELIA ASKS, breathless. "What did they say? Did they kick you out?"

"Don't sound so thrilled."

She punch-taps Lang's arm. "You know I'm not."

"I know," he says. "But I'm sure *he'll* be pissed I wasn't run out on a rail." He nods toward the house to indicate their father.

"Never mind him," Melia says, with a dismissive wave. "If they said you can stay he can't do a thing about it."

"I mean they didn't, like, *decree* it." Lang finishes rolling a smoke and strikes his flint, taking a deep, soothing drag. "Not in so many words..."

"Well what did they say? Dinos."

Lang shifts his weight on the crude wooden chair by the fire pit and takes a sip of cider. One of the yard dogs snuffles over and he pats its head absently. When he returned from dinner he'd found Melia and Brophy sitting out in the front yard around a small blaze, no doubt having positioned themselves in a prime spot to get the first scoop.

"OK, so," he says. "The first thing that happened was they took me in La Sala."

Melia's eyes widen. "No!"

Brophy starts to laugh. "Sweet Madre," he says. "Not la sala! Anything but thaaat!"

"Shush," Melia orders. Then to Lang, "So what was it like?"

He shrugs. "It was just a room. I mean, it's nice and everything. There were books and candles and – "

"Venga ya!" Brophy cuts him off. "We don't want to hear about the décor. Did they mind-meld you? Beat you with a stick?" He's laughing harder now and Lang realizes that his friend is a little drunk.

Wonder what that's about.

"Actually," Lang tells his sister. "They gave me dinner."

"Shut. Up."

"Hand to Madre." He places the other, still holding the mug, over his heart. "They were really nice."

"Could they tell you were fused up?"

"Cruz could. But they didn't say anything about it until the very end. Mostly, they wanted to talk about Celan."

He takes another drag as Melia, impatient, motions for him to go on. He exhales a cloud and continues, "They wanted to know who she is; if she was really one of Mair Tyras' daughters. They thought all those girls died years ago."

"Couldn't kill 'em all," Brophy says, raising his glass, presumably in a toast to the Mairs sisters.

Lang and Melia ignore him.

"So I told them, you know?" Lang says. "What she told me – about Arlo's and the fire and how she lived as a tech and all of that. And they also wanted to know about the Plejarans. Like, did she really go into space? I told them she did. I mean, we," he indicates himself and Brophy, "saw the Plejarans too. We talked to them. I don't care what anybody says, they were not some holo. They were real."

This sobers Brophy a smidge. "I touched their ship," he says. "I was in astral at the time, but still. You know; you can tell."

"True," Melia says. "I believe you."

"So," Lang says. "That's about it, I guess. Oh, and I told them that Celan was supposed to be back soon. Like any day now. Tomorrow is exactly eighteen months."

"Hmmm," Melia says, like she's considering something. Then, "So what did they say about the fusing?"

Lang clears his throat, wishing he'd been smarter and not given away that they'd said anything about it at all.

"Um, well," he starts, tapping ash nervously. "They said they knew about it, obviously."

"Obviously."

"And they said they could, uh, help me. Maybe."

"That's great!" His sister enthuses.

"Yeah," he says. "It is. They said that maybe I could help be an example or something. For others. I guess they've been having a lot more problems with fusers these days?"

"A lot of expros came back," Melia says. "After Transway was destroyed. They didn't take all of them, but if people had family…"

"So I said I'd do it –"

Melia gasps, then cheers.

" – as soon as I take care of a few things."

She opens her mouth to protest.

"They said I'd have to stay with them for a few months at least," he hastens to explain. "And I don't have a few months right now. I can't just drop everything; not with Celan coming back and with what's going on at Rinconada – "

Brophy cuts in. "About that – " as Melia says, "What's going on at Rinconada?"

Lang doesn't answer her. "Que pas'?" he says to Brophy. "Did Max or Val – "

"No," Brophy says. "After dinner I astralled up there myself. I had to apologize to Mara for taking off like that, talk to her, find out what was going on."

"And?"

"No bueno."

"What?"

"Seems like your little friend is saying it was all *your* idea, that the nest was supposed to be some kind of healing demonstration, but at the last minute you bailed and left her to do it all alone."

Lang's heart jolts. "Are you fucking kidding me? What a liar! How is it even possible that someone that twisted could be a healer?"

"No sé. Maybe you should ask the elders."

"Ha," he says, stomach roiling with the remnants of recent posole. "No one believes her though, right? I mean, even Mara must know I would never – "

"Mara's *insane* right now, güey. Fused up out of her mind. I don't think she's seeing things very clearly at the moment."

"Fuck." Suddenly, all he can think about is going another round with the transfer. Maybe he can convince Brophy to let him hold it for a while. He takes a final draw on the smoke then stubs it out in the dirt.

"Hey," Melia cuts in. "Would one of you kindly explain what all this is about? I thought you said you were here to wait for Celan."

"We are," Lang says. "Or at least I am."

And he knows, deep down, that that's the real reason he didn't jump at the elders' offer, why he said he had to wait: He needs to be here when Celan gets back and he needs to show her that he hasn't changed. Because for all the endless agonizing over whether or not she'll still want him when she returns, in the darkest part of his heart he knows she will. And she'll want him exactly like he was before – because she won't have changed either.

Celan's fusing was the one thing he'd left out of his account to the elders; they didn't seem aware of it and it hadn't seemed fair to her to bring it up. And, somehow, he knew it would disturb them more than anything else he'd shared. Surely, it isn't that big of a deal though. Celan is smart and (mostly) level-headed. And she wasn't taking that much before she left.

She'll be fine, he thinks. *She'll be fine, and I'll be fine and we'll be –*

Melia nudges him with the toe of her sandal and he realizes she's still waiting for clarification on Rinconada. But he can't, or won't, speak of that with her.

Brophy clears his throat. "There was an accident," he says. "And someone set your brother up to take the fall."

Lang eyes him gratefully; not the whole truth but enough for their purposes. "So we have to go back and clear things up," he tells his sister.

"What – " Melia starts, but Brophy jumps in again.

"If we're gonna go though, we gotta go soon."

"One more day," Lang says. "Tomorrow's eighteen months exactly. And then there's the techs too. They could attack. If anything happens I want to be with my family."

"Is that shit even real though?"

"I asked the elders about it. They didn't tell me everything, but yeah, they think something might be going on with the techs. Tomorrow night they said. Everyone has to be on alert."

"Told you," Melia says.

"I don't know," Brophy says, scratching the back of his head. "If we wait on this it could be too late."

"So go then," Lang says. "Take the roller. Work things out with Mara. I'll follow as soon as I can."

"That's way too far to walk."

"I could astral in."

Brophy gives him a long look and then shakes his head. "If you really want to straighten things out then everyone needs to be able to see and hear you. We'll go together. The day after mañana."

"OK," Lang says.

But his eyes shift sideways, and he doesn't sound too sure.

▭▸ 17 ◂▭

S hariah flinches as the stone-faced, fair-haired young woman shuts the door of the primitive (but undeniably tidy) little house where Lana allegedly grew up firmly behind her and Theodore. It's not quite a slam, but there's definitely a strong whiff of 'and don't come back' in it. Not that the family had been uncooperative. The young woman (Tanny), in tandem with a grizzled older lady named Jillyanne (who claimed to be Lana's mother's cousin) had told them quite a few things before turning them out.

All of which seem patently absurd.

"So what do you think?" she says, squinting up at Theodore as they make their way down the rocky path past the fish ponds at Rancho Pescados.

The morning is bright and hot and her companion wipes his brow, looking queasy. That must be one serious hangover he's working on after the condition he was in last night. One look (and whiff) of him at the door of his bunk and she'd known he was in no fit state to go anywhere more appropriate to discuss her mother's ranchos-destroying plans. Though he'd assured her that his library was free from all surveillance, in the end they'd ended up standing by the window in Lana's old bedroom with both their servers sitting several rooms away and their plan formulated in tense whispers.

There was no way to stop Shariah's mother beforehand – that they'd both agreed. Without knowing the details of her plot they'd have had a very hard time proving anything. What they needed to do was to go out to the ranchos themselves, try to get Lana out of there, warn as many people as possible, and stay to witness (and take plenty of vids of) whatever happened. Then they'd have a leg to stand on.

It's amazing he can stand at all today, she thinks sourly.

Theodore heaves a sigh. "I don't know," he says slowly. "I mean, obviously they're lying about the space part – "

"But they believe the ranchos are threatened. That much is clear."

A nod.

"So why lie then? Why stonewall you forever and then, when it could actually help them, make up some ridiculous story about aliens? It doesn't make any sense." She kicks at a rock with the toe of her boot, feeling a momentary satisfaction as it plops into the nearest pond with a sploosh, sleek forms of fish scattering in its wake. They'd worn their tech uniforms to try to look as official as possible for this visit; there's some ranchos gear stowed in the roller for later.

"Sure it does," he says, jaw set grimly. "It makes perfect sense...if my daughter is dead."

A chill goes through Shariah but she shakes it off, shaking her head for good measure. "No. They were certain of it: Lana's alive."

Theodore stops to regard her directly. Reluctantly, Shariah halts and faces him. "Think about it," he says. "They didn't say anything before because they *had* nothing to say. Maybe they knew she was dead; maybe they really didn't know anything. But they knew that as long as I thought she was here they'd be protected. Now though, with the ranchos immediately threatened, the jig is up. She's not here, and they can't magically produce her, so of course they're going to make up some story to try to stall."

"It didn't sound like something they made up, though. It wasn't rehearsed. It was..." She searches for the right word. "Hesitant. The way people talk when they're saying something they were told but aren't quite sure of. And that they don't think you're going to believe."

She knows the tone; it was the way some of the less-fervent Chronies used to speak.

"So they don't think she's in space?"

"I don't think they know the whole story. They say they heard it from some 'astral emissary' – "

Theodore snorts.

" – so maybe Lana's been hiding somewhere else, one of the refugee camps maybe, and they were told the alien story to protect her and whatever expros she's with. Maybe now they'll contact this 'emissary' and have them go get her. They did say that she was supposed to return tonight. They just weren't sure exactly where she'd be."

Theodore sighs again, passing a hand over his wan face. A flight of birds lifts off from a nearby tree with a great flapping and cawing. He flinches like the noise hurts his head.

"You can't really believe she's dead," Shariah says bluntly. "Not after all you did to convince me she was alive."

"Maybe she's not," he admits. "Maybe you're right. But Shariah, if Lana really has been hiding with expros all this time and hasn't been here, sheltering amongst her family, the person we knew her as may as well be. Even if we somehow could find her and see her again it might not be an experience either of us would relish."

His expression is full of careful regret, like he's doing her a big favor by offering her an out. 'Let's just give up and go home,' it says, 'rather than deal with any unpleasantness.' Anger surges through Shariah then, so swift and deep that she has to clench her teeth to keep from screaming.

"You know what I don't *relish*?" she says, quiet but fierce. "I don't relish knowing that my mother is a genocidal psychopath. I don't relish the fact that she tried to murder my best friend to cover up her own mistakes. And I don't *relish* that in the last few days my entire worldview has fallen apart to the point that I'm actually siding with transers." She huffs out a breath. "But all those things are true and I have no choice but to face them. And if Lana is alive, and if she does come back tonight, then I'm going to face her too."

She bores her gaze deep into his as she lands the clincher. "You want to be a coward? Fine, be one. Go. But I'm putting on my ranchos clothes and I'm going to keep looking. And I'm going to warn as many people as possible about what might happen tonight. You can do whatever you like."

And with that she turns and stalks off towards the gravel road and the roller, not looking back. There's silence for a moment, then the sound of chastened footsteps, following.

Shariah grunts, satisfied, and marches on.

"GOOD MORNING, MISS MARA." MADDY'S voice trills from outside the screened kitchen door. "And how are we today?"

Mara shrugs, scraping the last of a batch of fried potatoes from a pan onto a big serving platter. She knew this was coming after all the accusations thrown the night of the fiesta. It was inevitable that once word got around about Sonrisa being a fuser who'd snuck a transfer into camp that she'd have to eat crow. Mara's still not one hundred percent convinced that Maddy had no hand in it all, but in light of there being no evidence to the contrary there's not much she can do. May as well get it over with.

She'd been hoping to put it off until later this afternoon though – when, just possibly, she might have had a chance to get some sleep first. In the wake of the terrible fight with Brophy none had come last night, so as much as she loathes the stuff, she's actually considering taking a hit of Class E to knock herself out for a few hours. Zeeb and Sig had begged her to do it and let someone else manage breakfast for once, but she'd resisted. After all the shit that's gone down she had to show her bones.

She finishes scraping and motions for Danilo to take the platter out into the dining hall.

"What do you want, Maddy?" she says, without turning around.

"Just a word, if you don't mind. About our mutual friend."

"Who?"

A tinkling laugh, like shaking nails in a jar. "Why, our

friend Sonrisa, of course."

A muscle twitches in Mara's jaw. "She's not our friend."

"Maybe not yours, dear. But I have a feeling she may soon be mine."

At this, she bangs the pan down on the sideboard and storms over to the door, finding a moment's joy in the sight of Maddy scurrying out of the way as she slams it open and stomps outside. The sun stabs her eyes like a knife but she forces herself not to wince.

"Really, Maddy?" she says. "You're going to hook up with a piece-of-shit fuser that played us both, lied to everyone, fucked up our healer, and killed Jaslene? That's who you're doing business with these days? Well, you can have her. Take her and get the fuck out!"

"Now, now," Maddy says. "There's no need to be hostile. I haven't done any business with anyone. Yet."

"So what do you want? An apology? Fine. Here it is: I'm sorry I accused you of giving Sonrisa a transfer. OK? Like I said, she played us both. And the sooner Lang gets back the sooner we can get rid of her and move the fuck on."

If *Lang comes back*, she silently amends.

But he has to. Just because she yelled at Brophy a little surely they're not really going to abandon the whole camp forever. Max said they were in the ranchos – they won't be able to stay there very long with Lang's Class E habit back in effect. They *have* to come back; there's really nowhere else for them to go.

"Lang?" Maddy says, screwing up her face in mock-confusion. "Sonrisa says this whole thing was his fault. That the nest was his idea."

"Bullshit," Mara says flatly. "You know he'd never do a thing like that. It was her idea. She tricked him. She never told him a thing."

"Yes. She's quite a tricksy little thing, isn't she?" Maddy's tone is almost admiring.

"So you *don't* believe her."

"I believe she knows what she's about. That's all that matters."

Mara sighs. "Mira, Maddy. I don't have time for games today. I have work to do. You want to hook up with Sonrisa? Make her your healer? Good luck with that."

She turns to go back inside as Maddy says, "Wait! You want the truth? Well, here it is." She drops her voice conspiratorially. "I do have a transfer."

Mara stops, fingers on the door handle. "What?"

"But I never gave it to Sonrisa, or your boy. I have it for a different reason."

Mara pivots, arching a brow. "Which is?"

"I need it," Maddy says. "Not for me, though." A breathless pause, like she's about to divulge something momentous. "I need it to keep Franky's bots offline."

Mara gapes at her, completely thrown. "Franky's...whats? What are you even talking about?"

Maddy's grin widens, like she knows she's scored a point. "Back when you were stirring soup at Tosh's, I don't suppose you ever heard of Frank Martinez?"

"Claro. The Lead SocEn."

"Yes." Maddy waits a beat for the implication to sink in.

Mara's eyes widen. "You mean Franky is – he's *here*? At Rinconada?"

"He's been here this whole time, dear."

"But –"

"We had a deal, he and I, regarding Transway," Maddy says. "About how he was going to keep that Balor woman from ruining things for everybody. She had some bot plug-in she was going to release to try and put the techs off us for good. So we agreed, he and I: He would sabotage her effort; tweak the thing to knock everyone out for a few hours. Meanwhile, he'd be with me, the lone holdout, transed up a bit to take his bots offline so he wouldn't be affected. But we'd say he passed out too and I'd managed to bring him around with a nice dose of transferon. Then he'd wake them all up, and voila! – Balor's an idiot and Transway saves the day. Win-win."

She stops, obviously enjoying whatever expression she sees on Mara's face. Mara's brain feels peeled like an onion, layer upon layer of shit to process, but she manages to ask, "So what happened with that?"

"Well," Maddy continues. "I decided a few hours wasn't quite enough. To be really convincing, they had to be out for a few days. Because we needed Timanti for any permanent block on Balor and he'd turned on us, you see. We needed to get him back in the fold. So it couldn't just be a small matter; it had to be life-or-death. At first Frank protested though, said that three days was too long a time and he didn't want to take the chance of any permanent damage to anybody. But he was unused to transferon, and my girls can be very persuasive." A smirk. "Eventually, he came around."

"It was a perfect plan, until your boy went and ruined it."

It takes Mara a minute to put this together. "My boy – you mean, *Lang*?"

"Him and that tech girl. Fusers, trying to be heroes." She scoffs.

A wave of dizziness washes over Mara. This is too much to take in, too much information. But a still, small portion of her mind cautions her not to completely take the bait, if that's what's being offered here. It's a good story, but there's no proof that it's actually true.

"So," she says, forcing an offhand tone. "What would you have done otherwise? I mean, what if the techs didn't believe you either? That you'd saved the day, I mean. What if they Destierra'd you and wrecked Transway anyway?"

Maddy's eyes harden. "If they had been so...ungracious, it would not have ended well for them."

"Really? What were you going to do?"

"Some things, my dear, are better left unsaid."

"OK," Mara says. "But I'm curious. Why did you keep Franky around then after everything went to shit? Why didn't you just dispose of him instead of dragging him all the way up here?"

A tiny flicker of doubt flits across Maddy's face, but it vanishes just as quickly. "As long as he's alive I can be sure keep his bots offline. If he's dead...I don't know. They might not shut down right away. They could send out some signal to track his body."

Mara chuckles. "Is that what he told you?"

Maddy says nothing.

"So what's stopping Franky now," she continues, "from running back to the techs and spilling the beans? You can't tell me he's staying here just 'cause he loves you."

"Oh, he does," Maddy says, and the smirk is back. "In a

manner of speaking anyway. You see, the transferon I use on him is pure Class E."

Of course, Mara thinks. *That'd be the way to do it.* Then: *Is there a chance this crazy chizz is actually* real?

"You'd think he'd've put up some kind of fuss."

Maddy pats her braids. "Oh, I don't think he really minds anymore."

"Well," Mara says. "That's a really good story, but I don't see what it has to do with the healer situation."

"It doesn't really," Maddy admits. "Except for it being yet another instance of your boy Lang being an unmitigated fuck-up. But then, that's really sort of worked out for you, hasn't it? Jumped up quite a bit since the old days; you're quite the leader now."

"What's your point?"

"My point, my dear, is that your hold over this place has reached it's inevitable conclusion. Maybe you're too pure to make a deal with Sonrisa, but I'm certainly not."

Mara shrugs. "So make a deal. Dig your own grave, Maddy. Maybe you'll have a healer but you still have to eat. And *I'm* in charge of that. And when Lang gets back – "

A nasty laugh. "*If*, you mean. And even if he does bother to turn up, by this time tomorrow I'll have him buried in dirt so deep that he'll never be able to show his face here again. Half the camp already thinks it was his fault and the other half is open to suggestion. I'll get Sonrisa to publically apologize and beg for forgiveness. Say he put her up to it. And if I know her she'll be quite convincing. After that, the more you support him the worse it'll be for you. Once I have the numbers on my side that's it."

Mara shakes her head. "People know Lang. They won't believe you."

"You'll be surprised what people will believe."

"I can spread rumors too – "

"You go right ahead then. This time tomorrow, we'll see who's been more effective."

Mara swallows. *Can she really do it? Do that many people trust her?*

Then Maddy's tone softens. "But you do have some useful knowledge, and a certain amount of leadership skills. So I'll make you a deal – you let me lead from now on, forget about your idiot healer and let him live happily ever after with your man, and I won't totally destroy you. I'll let you stay on here and look after the kitchen. It'll be just like old times. How does that sound?"

Mara's jaw clenches as a wave of hot rage slams her heart into high gear. She wants nothing more than to grab this bitch by her stupid braids and pound her face into the wall until it's nothing but bloody pulp.

"I'll give you until this time tomorrow to think it over."

With one last, haughty glance, Maddy turns and sashays away, not bothering to wait for a reply and not looking back. This turns out to be a mercy though, because the moment the woman rounds the corner of the building Mara only manages one step toward the kitchen door before she's falling, end-lessly down into the endless dark, and for a long time knows no more.

18

"Órale." Theodore tips his mug at the short, stocky man by the cask in a show of thanks before taking a sip of beer.

Daniel. Or is it Samuel?

The two men responsible for this hospitality have similar names and, being brothers, look very similar too. Their wives, Junie and Clarisse, are much easier to tell apart.

Daniel (or Samuel) grins, even white teeth in a round, dark face, as he refills his own mug and they walk back over to the group sprawled out on an assortment of chairs and benches in the family's yard. A few neighbors joined them a little while ago and it's shaping up to be a bit of a party.

Settling down on the end of a bench at a rough-hewn picnic table, Theodore catches Shariah's eye; a grey-haired neighbor woman seems to have cornered her in what he gathers is a not-very-interesting conversation. The girl shoots him an irate look.

He sighs. *What more does she fucking want?*

He's the one who's been doing the heavy lifting all day, literally, because for all her high-toned speech this morning Shariah's proven oddly reluctant to actually talk to any ranchos people. She'd refused outright to go into the Pescados/de la Virgen casagrand and when the few people she did warn about the tech attack merely shrugged, she'd fallen into total sullenness. When they came across Daniel and Samuel attempting to fix a broken cart on the road, he'd stepped in to provide the extra muscle while she did nothing but stand around looking bored. His efforts had earned them an offer of refreshment, served with quite a bit of interesting ranchos' gossip.

You'd think she'd be grateful.

A few well-chosen words in the ears of Clarisse and Junie and he's already confirmed almost every word of Jillyanne and Tanny's earlier assertions – that Lana (or Celan as they all call her) is at something called the K'Shiran Convention, and that her return is imminently (and eagerly) expected. And, moreover, that she will use her newfound galactic knowledge to ward off a tech attack and singlehandedly save the ranchos from doom!

Theodore chuckles. He has no idea if they really believe any of this or if it just makes for a good story, but it's good to know that the tale is in general circulation and not just something Lana's family cooked up. To this group he and Shariah are Frank Jos and Shari Anas, a father and daughter from Rancho Leones who there would be no reason to lie to.

He sips at his drink and stretches stiff legs – a little hair of the dog is the perfect thing right now. Maybe that's what

Shariah is mad about, but that's just too bad. It's been a long day and it's shaping up to be an even longer night. He's not going to make it without some fortification.

A burst of laughter perks up his ears: Junie's joined in an argument with Clarisse and a few of the men. It seems the topic of Celan Mairs' return has been revived.

"Wherever she goes, it's not like she's gonna come here to Cabras," Junie is saying, dark eyes sharp. "Her people were from Pesacdos. That's where she'll be."

But Clarisse disagrees. "Nay," she says, drawing herself up to her full, impressive height. "When Celan Mairs comes back she's going straight to Arqueros. That's where her *man* is."

She plants a decisive smack on Samuel's cheek as punctuation.

"The Shays boy?" a burly neighbor-man says. "He's long gone. If he's even still alive, he sure as shit ain't living at Arqueros."

"He's there right now," Clarisse says.

The men laugh, shaking their heads.

"Serio! 'Sta aqui!" she insists. "You know my sister's best friend Nala? La gordita? Well, her prima Ursalita is from Arqueros and she swears on her life that she and her brother saw Langton Shays walking down the road with Carlos the elegido yesterday evening."

"Chale!"

"Yes, güey. And he looked a mess, too. She said Carlos was taking him to see the elders."

"No lo creo."

"Believe what you want," Clarisse says, with a toss of her comely head. "But they saw him. And I think if Celan Mairs

237

is gonna come back she's gonna go wherever he is."

That seems to settle things. No one else argues the point and they all return to whatever conversations they were having before the outburst. All except Shariah, who's managed to free herself from the grey-haired woman. She scoots over and drops onto the bench next to Theodore, hissing 'Lang Shays?' in his ear and gnawing her lower lip anxiously.

"It's just talk," he tells her, taking another sip of beer. "Rumors, like the space stuff. Don't let it bother you."

"Well it does." Then: "You're *sure* he's dead?"

"He was Destierra'd," Theodore says, as if that settles the matter.

"So was Lana."

"OK," he says. "I'll be frank with you. The truth is that the body was never recovered. Only some clothes."

"I never knew that!" Shariah says, scandalized.

"Well, now you do."

"But does that mean he could really still be out there?" She looks tentatively over her shoulder, like the expro man might be poised to jump out from behind a tree.

"No. He was almost two hundred miles from the ranchos when they left him and deep into CERS. There's no way he made it all that way on foot in that condition. He probably got eaten by mountain lions."

That's what Theodore's always told himself and in the absence of an actual body the thought has been an immense comfort.

"But what if the expros – " Shariah starts.

"What? Tracked him?" He shakes his head. "Impossible. They don't have the technology."

She quiets, brooding, and Theodore uses the opportunity to take a long pull of beer. He has to hand it to them, despite the lack of technology ranchos' brewing skills are on point.

He downs the rest and peers around the yard. The sun is starting to dip towards the mountains, throwing out long golden rays that make the rustic house (and it's equally rustic folk) glow like something out of an old fairy tale. Maybe if he plays his cards right and humors them, the family will let them stay the night. Even if they have to bed down in the yard, it's not that chilly yet and if it is there's a fire pit. A nice bonfire, sleeping under the stars…

Maybe there'll even be a moon out.

He casts his eyes skyward, bathing in the rich azure hue. Then a nudge at his elbow makes him turn to see Shariah, staring pointedly at his empty mug.

"What was that, your third or your fourth?"

"It's just beer," he says witheringly.

"Strong beer. You need to eat something."

"Well we can't just demand food out of these people. And it's not like there's a caf around the corner."

This earns him an eyeroll. "Obviously."

But moments later – as if on cue – Junie and Clarisse appear with an assortment of bowls and platters, laying out chips, bread and tortillas, and several different kinds of toppings and dips on the picnic table.

"Need a little something in the stomach before we all get too drunk," Junie says with a wink.

He winks back. "Gracias."

"See?" he says to Shariah as the women walk away. "All good. Dig in."

239

She eyes the food dubiously as he gets to his feet. In answer to her questioning look he raises his mug, as if in salute.

"Need something to wash it down," he says, and before she can reply he turns on his heel and makes for the cask, deftly avoiding whatever sour note she was about to strike.

If the girl is going to leave him to glad-hand everybody, she's just going to have to put up with whatever is needed to make that possible.

SUNLIGHT SIFTS DOWN THROUGH THE apple tree boughs, dappling Lang's face and hands with shifting shadows. He reaches up, plucks a fragrant ripe fruit, and tucks it in the sack slung against his hip, nestling it in with those already harvested. He squints up at the crackling blue sky and sighs. Wishes it was old times; and that Raf was here.

Perched atop a ladder in the orchard that marks the heart of Rancho Arqueros, he could almost be fourteen again, young and carefree, before anything crazy had happened. On a day like today he and Raf would've been sneaking hard ciders, plunging sticky hands into the cool waters of the acequia, groping for hidden bottles filched from the root cellar. He swallows, thinking of the flood of cold sweetness in his throat; the subtle lift, dancing him out beyond the reach of the black clouds of fear and regret that threaten to smother him like a rotten blanket.

He grimaces, snaps off another apple.

Cállate, stupid brain!

Though after the day he's had no one could really blame him for wanting a drink.

Everyone's mad now.

Brophy was at him all morning about Rinconada, hammering on about how it was Lang's responsibility to return as soon as possible and straighten things out; and Lang repeatedly promised that they would leave first thing tomorrow morning. But when he also suggested that if he were to accept the elders' offer at some later date maybe they could send an elegido to tend to the healing needs of the camp in his absence, Brophy had blown up, accusing him of desertion, cowardice, and any number of unpleasant things.

"I brought you here to save your ass," he'd said through clenched teeth. "Not so you could give up playing expro and run home to mama. You fucked up and now you need to make it right!"

Then he'd stalked off, refusing all entreaties and leaving Lang with a gnawing anxiety that only grew as the day wore on. Because part of him wonders just how much of Brophy's anger is really about Rinconada and how much might be a touch more personal. Nothing has been said about that kiss; they'd both been pretty fused up and Lang wasn't about to make things awkward by mentioning it. Brophy knows he loves Celan. That's not going to change.

But if she doesn't come back...

He can't even finish the thought.

She will. She has to.

He plucks another apple, polishing it on his tunic before tucking it in the sack. At least Brophy's surly presence has been removed for the afternoon; his friend was press-ganged after lunch by Lang's father and some other Arqueros men into helping with a ditch repair. But as soon as he left Melia'd started in – all about how Lang had to do the right thing for the family and stay in the ranchos – and Lang, to his infinite chagrin, had told her in no uncertain terms to leave him the fuck alone. And so she had. She hasn't so much as looked his way all afternoon.

Without any conscious decision, he finds his arms and legs moving, climbing to the ground. A cider might hit the spot after all.

At the bottom of the ladder he pauses, checking to see if anyone has eyes on him. But all of the Arqueros pickers are busy. And it's just as well; no whispers, no stares brimful of that bitter brew of curiosity, pity, and disgust he's gotten to know so well over the past few years. Best of all, Melia and Cass are nowhere to be found.

He slips off the sack and rests it at the foot of the trunk. Here at the northern edge of the orchard he's close enough to home to hopefully avoid anyone who might waylay his purpose. Once clear of the trees, he hastens across the yard, breathing in the rich, spicy scent of chile wafting through the screened kitchen door. His mother must be back from the annual roasting and apple-pressing at the Perditas. Later, when the party really gets going over there and the hard stuff starts to flow, a more family-friendly crowd will gather at the Shays like they always do. But for now, all is quiet.

He circles left around the cottonwoods in the front yard, a sense of imminent relief growing with every step. He'll grab a couple few bottles from the cellar and find a nice, private place to get pleasant. If only he had a transfer everything would be perfect, but for now, cider is better than nada. Cheered, he whistles a jaunty tune as he rounds the corner of the house, but it freezes on his lips when a familiar voice calls his name.

Melia.

Slowly, he turns, trying to look as bored as possible.

"What?" he says, as his sister sidles over, a knowing look on her face.

"Qué haces, hermanito, creeping back here?"

"Not creeping," he says. "Just walking."

"Walking where – down to the cellar maybe?"

"None of your business," Lang retorts. "Where are *you* walking?"

"I had to use the bathroom."

"Oh," Lang says, wishing he'd thought of that.

"I don't care if you have a cider," Melia says airily. "Just be careful is all."

'Don't get too fucked up,' is all. Lang's jaw clenches.

"I mean, I get it," she continues. "Brophy has your transfer so you need a little something to tide you over 'til he gets back."

"That's not – " he starts.

But it is. His cheeks flush; he hates how easily she can read him.

"Mira," he says. "You don't understand. I just – it's – "

"Lang," she says softly, reaching for his hand. "This is exactly what the elders want to help you with. You don't have to be like this anymore. You can be normal again. You can be… my brother."

She gives him a tiny squeeze and just like that the sting of tears is in his eyes. He snatches his hand away to dash at them.

"You don't understand," he says again.

She obviously thinks he's stalling. If she knew the truth she'd know that's not the case. But the shame of what happened to Jaslene and his role in it is not something he can discuss with her. What respect she still has for him he wants to keep.

"I want to do it," he says. "And I will. But I have other things I have to do first. I have responsibilities."

He does like the idea of it, though: Coming home. The way the elders put it – like he wasn't some asshole loser but someone they genuinely cared about, someone whose existence mattered – had made it impossible to say no.

But he needs to face the mess at Rinconada first; he owes Brophy that much. And before he got so pissed off this morning, his friend had brought up a few good points: Chiefly, that the elders had never offered to help anyone in Lang's situation before; they'd let Raf die of fusing, and Celan's mother before that. And what about that whole year Lang was home after his initial disastrous time on Transway? There'd been no mention of a miracle cure then.

Maybe, Brophy posited, the elders didn't really care about Lang at all; maybe he just hadn't been useful enough before. And maybe now they're only using him as bait to land a much bigger fish. Because when Celan Mairs returns from whatever galactic conference she's been attending, they'll need some kind of lure to override any tech loyalties she may have and convince her to bring whatever knowledge she's gained to the ranchos instead of to Albakirk.

All of which, as much as Lang is loath to admit it, makes a certain kind of hideous sense.

But he can't say any of this to Melia; he doesn't want to rile her further. Especially now, as green eyes so like his own regard him, plaintive.

"You don't *have* to do anything," his sister says fiercely. "Those people up at that camp – they aren't family. And from what I can tell, they aren't even really your friends. They don't care about you, only what you can do for them."

Lang's lips twist. "Yeah," he says. "There's a lot of that going around."

Melia's scowls.

"You know I don't mean you," he says, resting an appeasing hand on her shoulder. "I know you love me, and I love you too. And I'm sorry about the way I am, but there's nothing I can do about it right now. I told you I was doing fine up there and I was, for a long time; they were helping me cut down, almost to nothing. But then some really shitty things happened and it got all out of hand again. But that's why I need to go back. I need to make things right. Then I can go stay with the elders.

"So," he continues, turning his back on the root cellar. "As a token of good faith, I'll be good tonight, OK? No cider."

Melia opens her mouth like she's about to launch another argument. But then she just sighs and grabs his hand, tugging him back towards the orchard.

"Oh, you can have your cider, you old caraculo. Just not here all by yourself. You have to be social about it."

Lang starts to protest but she cuts him off, saying, "The Perditas have some really good shit this year, I hear."

"But you know those people; they're all gonna look at me weird."

"Not if you're with me," she says, hooking an arm through his. "And then only if you act a fool."

She's wrong, though. People will stare, and whisper, and

245

make him feel like a freak. But at least there'll be cider, and maybe he can track Brophy down too. Even if he's still mad, there's no way his friend will let him be sick without a transfer. So Lang lets himself be led through the lengthening shadows, nursing a tentative hope that whether or not Celan returns tonight, or the techs attack, or any other form of general insanity goes down, at least the evening will have gotten off to a decent start.

▭▸ 19 ◂▭

"Entering orbit, Terra Madre," Chan's voice crackles through the speaker in Celan's helmet. She cuts her eyes to the window in the floor in front of her seat to find a blue-green sphere glowing bright against the black matte of space. Then she lets the breath she's been holding for what feels like the entire journey go in a rush. It hasn't been charred to ash or smashed into a thousand pieces or sucked into a black hole or pulled out of orbit by a passing rogue.

First fears unrealized; she'll have to wait and see about everything else.

She shifts in her seat, marveling at the sheer luminosity of it, the swirl of colors like blown glass. In that moment her world is indescribably beautiful. And getting rapidly larger. Chan has the geolocation, and once they get in low enough he'll set down slightly north of the ranchos. Celan doesn't want any fancy flyover and fanfare. She wants to slip in quietly. From the drop point to Rancho Arqueros is only a few miles. She needs to get her legs under her, suss things out a bit and, as her fluttering stomach reminds her, administer some Class E. Local time will be a little after 19:00, close to sunset. She can make it to the Shays' on foot before full dark.

As the wormhole cycle is currently on the wax, Chan, Ness, and Ree have plenty of time to wait for official word from her before they leave, so she won't risk being stranded in a hostile situation. If need be, they can be called in to back up any and all claims as to her recent doings and whereabouts. And formally introduce themselves, of course.

This last makes her crack a tiny grin: The thought of the Plejarans marching up to the gates of Albakirk and knocking on the door.

Ariana would lose her shit for sure.

She closes her eyes as they enter the atmosphere, but the descent is smooth – the star-shaped vessel is a remarkable feat of fluidonic engineering – and it's not long before they cease to go down and start to move forward. She lifts her lids to a blur of brown and green in the floor-window. There's a slowing, and then a final, shuddering stop.

They're back.

Home.

She whips off the helmet and unbuckles her harness, swiveling her chair around to watch as the Plejarans make final adjustments from their stations at three equidistant points of the ship's interior. The stations are static, but the number and placement of passenger seats in the center of the space can be adjusted to accomodate up to six humanoids. At the moment, though, hers is the only one.

"Happy?" Ree says.

"Yes!"

"Don't stand up too fast. You'll need a minute to adjust."

"Sure."

The window beneath her feet now offers a view of weeds and dirt, so Celan leans back in her chair and gazes through the wide strip of transparent material that bands the ship. Emblazoned there is a stunning view of pine trees, dark silhouettes against a hot-orange sky. A thrill runs through her.

"Ready?" Chan says.

Slowly, she gets to her feet. There's a slight wave of lightheadedness, so she grips the seat-back to steady herself, but it quickly passes. Leaving the helmet on the chair, she smooths down the front of the blue shift she printed out for the occasion (a product of nostalgia for the last time she was in the ranchos). When she feels stable enough she tests out her land legs, walking over to a low cabinet set into the wall near Ness's station.

She crouches, sliding open a small door and removing a belt-pack containing a bit of food and water and a few other necessary items, which she fastens around her waist. Then she reaches in again for the pièce de résistance – a hooded cloak printed from environment-sensing nanotech material that can create shifting patterns of camouflage, which will allow her to pass along the old road unseen. She straightens, fanning it across her shoulders and clasping it neatly at the throat. The silver clasp is dual-function and can be activated as a commlink for immediate assistance if need be, though she can also use her band to signal the ship.

She gives the clasp a pat, satisfied, and turns to find Chan, Ness, and Ree quietly watching her.

"No one should come back from space without a cape."

But they don't seem to get the joke. She grins anyway and offers a slight bow, which they return.

"Be careful," Ree says.

"Call if you need us." This from Ness.

"I will."

"And let us know when we can meet more of you!" Chan beams.

Celan nods, and Chan waggles his fingers, activating his band. There's a hiss as the ship's outer door depressurizes and lifts up. A ramp descends and extends to meet the earth. A waft of fresh air hits Celan and she breathes deep. Then she walks to the door, squares her shoulders, and steps outside.

A GUST OF NIGHT-BREEZE SCATTERS dust and debris along the cracked old road. Shariah shivers. The sun has gone down behind the mountains and evening is fast encroaching. She shares none of the joy of the pack of revellers she's trailing, joined in raucous song on their way to crash a cider party over at Rancho Arqueros. After bolstering themselves with snacks and endless mugs of beer, a group from Daniel and Samuel's decided it was high time to seek out further adventures, and Theodore had insisted they go along.

'In case Lana shows up,' he'd said, but Shariah knows that's bullshit. He just wants to drink and carouse some more, which he could have done perfectly well back at Rancho Cabras. There seemed to be no end to the supply.

It'd serve them all right if my mother does attack tonight, she thinks viciously, then immediately regrets it. Junie and Clarisse are too nice to wish ill upon, and completely understanding of her plight in having to deal with a drunken 'parent'. They'd let her know that she (and her father, if he was mobile enough) were welcome to come back later and sleep in their barn if in need of a safe place to crash.

She hitches her pack up on her shoulder, knowing that she's safe pretty much anywhere with the stun inside, but still wishing to be tucked in her own bed, dreaming away this whole fruitless day. Because she's certain now – wherever Lana is, it's nowhere near here and the likelihood of ever seeing her friend again is almost nil. Maybe Theodore was right, maybe she is dead. Or maybe she's at one of the refugee camps. She's obviously become some sort of folk hero to these people, but the tall tales they've been hearing all day don't amount to any real-world information.

She should have gone and gotten the roller hours ago. Parked it somewhere nearby so they could make a fast escape. But it's all the way over by Pescados and at this point, stun or no, she doesn't want to go wandering around by herself in the near-dark. And there's no guarantee of finding Theodore again without her server. He still has his, since his visits to the ranchos are officially sanctioned, but she'd left her own back in Albakirk, with Bryan.

What if my mother does *attack? How are we going to get out of here?*

If worst comes to worst maybe she can get Theodore alone somewhere, stun him, and then wait until he comes around – (hopefully) more sober and ready to listen to reason.

He'd be mad, sure, but once I explained –

The rollicking group makes a sharp left and her calculations are cut short as she hurries to catch up. A wide dirt track

251

winds up into the feet of the mountains – well-trodden and lined with thick stands of evergreens and the occasional house. After only a few minutes' walk, sounds of revelry and glints of light begin to filter in. The group lurches right almost at random and Shariah draws up close behind Theodore as they wind through the trees.

When they come out into a field lit by three big bonfires, she scans the scene: It's pretty crowded, which hopefully will make it harder for Theodore to access the keg. To the left is a large house with a wide patio, where dancers throng around a bunch of musicians. It's obvious that is where the drink is flowing too, and the group immediately gets in line.

Shariah falls in with them, people-watching for lack of anything better to do. A bunch of young women are play-ing some kind of sing-song drinking game, which she tries to follow, curious, until one of them gives her a hard look and she turns hastily away. She's searching for something else to focus on when her eyes fall on two men at the edge of the closest fire circle. They appear to be making up after some kind of argument. Idly, she studies the two – one is tall and broad-shouldered, classically handsome (and eerily reminis-cent of Alonzo). The other is also tall but lankier, with an angular face framed by white-shot dark hair that lends him a fey sort of otherworldliness. He's clad in some sort of dress-thing over long pants and there's something about him that is unsettlingly familiar.

Shariah realizes she's staring and turns away before the men notice, only to find Theodore glowering openly in their direction. Confused, she takes a half-step toward him, just as he yells, 'You!' and lunges. Both men look up and the lanky one starts in alarm, stumbling backwards over a big log in his panic. His drink goes flying but he lands well, rolling and letting the momentum carry him to his feet.

Theodore is not so lucky – he must have meant to barrel into the man and knock him flat, but the log arrests his flight and as he attempts to clear it the lanky man has enough time to regain his balance, draw back a fist, and punch him square in the face. Theodore hits the ground hard, blood pouring from his nose.

"Crap," Shariah mutters, rushing into the fray.

"Chingao!" the broad-shouldered guy is saying. "You know this guy, Lang?"

Lang...Shays?

Her breath catches.

So Clarisse's sister's friend's cousin really did see him?

But maybe she was wrong. Maybe it isn't really him. Maybe it's just someone who looks like him. But as she crouches, struggling with Theodore's prone form (he's knocked out but breathing) she hears the man say softly, "It's Celan's father. Last time I saw him he tried to kill me."

"Oh shit," the broad guy says. "Looks like maybe he's trying again."

Lang Shays makes a sound that tries to be a laugh but doesn't quite make it.

Suddenly furious, Shariah glares up at them. "He wasn't trying to kill anybody. He was looking for his daughter. Trying to find out if she's even still alive. If she is though, I'm sure it's no thanks to either of *you*."

Both double take; the broad guy recovers first. "And who are you?" He sneers. "Another tech bitch who destroys people's lives over nothing? If it wasn't for this guy," he gestures at Lang, "neither you or this *payaso*," he indicates Theodore, "would even still be here. Serio, Lang. You should've let 'em all die when you had the chance."

"I was Lana's best friend," Shariah says, ignoring this last, "before you all got a hold of her. *Celan*, I mean," she amends acidly.

Lang looks to his friend. "He's bleeding bad, Brophy. Maybe I should – "

"Oh no, you don't. Don't tell me you're gonna *heal* this asshole. Are you fucking crazy?"

"But he's her father – "

"And the minute he gets conscious again he's gonna kill you dead." Brophy pauses, bemused. "Nice punch, by the way."

"Thanks."

"Sometimes I forget you're not a total wuss."

"Ha. *Ha*."

"Please," she cuts in. "I don't expect you to help him. But can you please just help me? I can't lift him. Help me get him out of here and we can forget we ever saw each other."

The two men share another look.

"Claro que…no fucking way," says Brophy.

"Then what?" Shariah says, struggling to hang on to her composure as she realizes her only protection is now out of reach. Her pack is sitting more than an arm's length away; it slid off her shoulder when she reached for Theodore. She can feel Brophy's eyes on her; no way to grab it subtly. She takes a deep breath. "If you're going to kill us just get it over with."

"Whoa, hey," Lang says, raising his hands palms up. "No one's killing anyone here. Brophy, can you help me lift him?"

"What? Do you have any idea how fucked up – "

"I'm not gonna heal him, at least not while his hands are free," Lang says wryly, squatting down near Theodore's body and feeling for his pulse. "We can take him up to the house. There's a cellar we can put him in. Then we can figure out what to do."

"You really think that's a good – "

"I don't know what else to do," Lang says, a frayed edge to his tone which she notes sets Brophy into action immediately: With a grunt that sends her scrambling to her feet, he swings an arm down and snatches up her pack, opening it and pawing around inside before slinging it over his shoulder next to what looks like some kind of water bag. Then he steps forward to help Lang hoist Theodore between them.

"Got your stuff, got your stun, so whatever you were planning, don't even think about it," Brophy says. "Better come with us…" He trails off, leaving room for a name.

"Shariah," she says resignedly.

There's no choice now except to follow them and hope for the best, but for some strange reason she isn't really scared, even now that her cover has been blown. And despite everything she has to admit she's also a little bit intrigued. Because the evil-fuser version of Lang Shays that she remembers from the Destierra screener had seemed much older, harder, and enveloped by an almost palpable air of menace. She and Bev had held hands that day as he was loaded into the roller – both sobbing, glued to the screen as Bryan stared stonily and Kirk made stupid jokes until they all told him to shut up. (Lucas had been a no-show for that particular event). But this Lang, despite the white in his hair, seems close to her own age and certainly not any kind of a threat. Definitely not like someone who, whatever his personal feelings towards them, would ever try to murder a city full of people.

CELAN INHALES ANOTHER DRAUGHT OF sun-soaked, dusty-pine, mountain-dusk scented air and grins. Real air! And real ground under her feet. She stamps at the surface of the road for good measure, then stops, feeling foolish, and re-sumes her pace. She's already passed Cantaros and Leones and is just level with the turnoff to Rancho Balanzas. She hadn't spent much time in these 'upper ranchos' as a child. Occupied as they are by artists and craftspeople instead of farmers and fishers they've long had a reputation for a kind of snootiness. But even their unfamiliar lights are welcoming tonight.

Here and there bonfires glint through the darkling trees, and there are faint sounds of music and laughter. It seems like there's some sort of celebration going on. To come home to a fiesta: Solid timing! Her grin widens as she entertains the (admittedly silly) notion that the festivities are in her honor.

Enter the conquering heroine...

She draws her cloak close and dances a few steps happily. Her blood is singing, humming. Every stir of breeze makes her shiver deliciously; and the smell of the cookfires...she can almost taste the air. Some of this is due to the hit of E (mixed with a little D for alertness) that she'd administered behind an old stone wall as soon as she was well away from the Plejaran ship, but a larger share is due to the overwhelming sensation of *home*.

Everything about this place is wonderful.

At the sight of a screaming flock of children she'd laughed

aloud; a mother chiding a small boy had almost made her weep; and seeing a young couple holding hands had infused her with a deep pang of longing, chased by fear.

What if –

But she'd quickly shut it down.

Everything's going to be fine.

When she gets to Arqueros, the first thing to do is find Melia. Surely, Lang's favorite sister will know his whereabouts. Then she'll ask Chan, Ness, and Ree to take her wherever he is. Most likely he's still with the expros, and wherever they are is where she needs to be.

Because they're the ones who have most earned a place at the K'Shiran Convention.

She's thought about this a lot, ever since her time on XïNeru. Now that she knows the ranchos are safe, as long as Albakirk has let what remains of the expros be she has no further beef with the city. Let Ariana strut and fret, let her father go to Mars or whatever else it is he wants to do. Same with the ranchos – for as much love as she has for the common folk of her former home she has very little to spare for the elders. They let her mother, Lang's cousin Raf, and so many others die of fusing, even though it was something they themselves invented then denied all responsibility for, pretending it was some kind of Transway scourge.

In her opinion, neither they nor the techs deserve contact.

But the expros are a different story. With all their transferon use, she's betting they're all transentient, and after all the shit they've had to put up with from techs and elders alike, they're the ones most deserving of a chance at something better. Lang, Brophy, Mara, Zeeb and Sig, even

Jaslene – they're the ones who belong to the great Madren galactic future. Everyone else is simply irrelevant.

Celan stretches her arms wide, like an old-world queen in a gesture of magnanimity, basking in the sheer rightness of it all.

The expros, the third option, the balance.

Then a sudden rustle in the brush makes her whirl. A large dog bounds out, grey and white and eerily reminiscent of Oso, Jillyanne's old wolfhound. Unlike the humans she encountered earlier, it appears he can see, or at least smell her. He snuffles around the hem of her cloak then plops down in front of her, panting.

"Hey, there," she says, revealing herself.

The dog barks once, but then merely grins; Celan reaches out to pat him on the head. He rolls over for a belly rub and she obliges, grinning at the absurdity of her own first re-contact. After a thorough mussing, complete with wild leg-kicks and much licking of the hand, she straightens and draws the cloak back around her.

"Well, I'm kind of in a hurry," she says, half-joking. "Wanna go for a walk, boy?"

She expects him to bound away again but the dog, apparently delighted with the hide-and-seek game, jumps up and trots beside her for quite a while. She finds a good stick to entertain him with and they make their way, tossing and fetching, down the road to Rancho Arqueros.

SHARIAH TRAILS BROPHY AND LANG (and Theodore) away from the lights of the party and down a shallow incline. They cross a tiny bridge over a stream, which leads into a space marked by long rows of overhanging trees – too regularly spaced to be a forest, must be some kind of orchard. On the far side a clutch of dun buildings comes into view, very like the place they just left. There's a bonfire here too, but just one, ringed by what looks like several families with children. This relaxes her a fraction. It looks pretty wholesome. As long as they stay here she should be safe. Though from what exactly, she's not totally sure.

What are they going to do, burn me at the stake?

The men give the group by the fire a very wide berth as they make their way around the side of what must be the main house. They're halfway to the back corner when the sound of running feet brings them to a halt. A girl appears – tall and slender, maybe a few years younger than Shariah – who bears a very strong resemblance to Lang.

Funny to think of him having a family.

"Que pas'?" the girl says, motioning to Theodore; his nose has stopped bleeding, but his shirt is a red mess.

"It's Celan's father," Lang tells her. He shifts his weight and Theodore moans softly. "He's out here looking for her. Supposedly. But he found me instead."

"And you hit him?"

"He attacked me first."

The girl snorts.

"And he's really drunk."

"Well, now we know where she gets it."

Brophy chuckles, but Lang rolls his eyes.

"Melia, please. No jokes. Can you go open the cellar door? We're going to keep him down there for the night. If he's part of whatever the techs are planning maybe they won't go ahead with it without him."

259

"He's not," Shariah says without thinking.

Lang, Brophy, and Melia all turn to look at her.

"How do you know that?" Brophy demands.

"Well, uh..."

"Are you a tech, too?" Melia says, eyeing Shariah's ranchos attire.

What will they do to me if I tell them the truth? But then: *Maybe if they know they can stop it somehow.*

"Yes," she says, decided. "And it's not some official plan. It's only one person. She was the one behind destroying Transway and now she wants to get rid of the ranchos too. She said there's going to be some kind of 'natural disaster,' but I don't know what exactly. It's supposed to happen sometime tonight."

"Ariana Balor! Holy fuck." Lang's face contorts like he's about to be sick. Theodore's weight starts to sag on his end until Melia steps in and helps prop the Lead SocEn up. The girl may be skinny, but she's obviously tough.

"But how do you know all this?" she says to Shariah, frowning. "You don't look much older than me. I doubt you're some big jefe over there."

Shariah looks at the toes of her sandals and says, very softly. "She told me. She's my – m - mentor. But I don't agree with her. I want to stop it."

Close enough.

"I'll go open the door," she offers. "Just tell me where it is."

Brophy smirks. "Nice try. But there's no way we're letting you out of our sight."

"Don't worry," Melia tells him. "If she tries to run I'll chase her down and beat her ass." Then, to Lang. "You know how fast I am."

Shariah doesn't doubt it.

"Around the corner." Melia cocks her head. "And hurry. This vato's getting heavy."

Shariah nods and circles briskly around the corner of the house. She does, briefly, consider making a break for it, but she can hear the others not far behind and has no desire to end up in the same state as Theodore. If she's going to be locked in some filthy hole all night she might as well endure it sans broken nose. Unconsciously, she rubs hers as she scans the thick adobe wall, finding windows but no door.

She shrugs helplessly as the group bearing Theodore appears.

Melia laughs. "Mira," she says to Lang and Brophy. "Guess they don't have cellars over in tech town." She waves a long arm at two broad flat slats of wood that sit an angle abutting the wall of the house. "Doors," she says. "Allá."

Shariah's eyes had skimmed right over them, the bulk of the house shadowing out the light of the rising moon. Still, she feels incredibly dumb as she yanks them open to reveal the top of a stone staircase flanked on one side by a wooden ramp. Below yawns blackness.

"There's a lantern down there," Melia says. "I know where it is."

She shifts Theodore back over to Lang and vanishes down the steps. Light wells up from the depths as, grunting, he and Brophy lower the man onto the ramp; at the bottom, Melia pulls on his ankles until he's resting on the floor. Brophy gestures for Shariah to descend next. Sighing, she does.

She braces for mustiness, but is greeted by a pleasant,

nutty smell. The floor is earth-packed, but surprisingly tidy. Crates stuffed with potatoes and other vegetables are stacked neatly against the walls, along with sacks of (grain?) and barrels that might be wine or beer of some kind. The low ceiling is cobweb-free.

She moves away from the bottom of the stairs to make room for Brophy and Lang, then they all stop and stare down at Theodore. His eyes blink open, attempt to focus, and flutter closed.

"There's some rope over there." Melia indicates a coil atop a barrel. "We need to tie him before he wakes up."

Between the three of them, Theodore is propped to a sitting position and roped against a barrel, his feet stretched out and bound in front of him (but not too tightly, Shariah notes, just enough to keep him from using them in any way). When they're finished, the trio regards their captive solemnly until Lang breaks out in a fit of sneezes, sniffling and wiping his nose on his sleeve like a little kid.

"Hey, uh, I'm gonna need a minute here," he says, nudging Brophy. "Can you…?"

"Yeah," Brophy mutters, digging into a pouch on his belt. He presses some small object into Lang's outstretched hand.

"Thanks," Lang says, pocketing it. "Be right back." He crosses the room in two long strides and disappears up the steps.

Brophy and Melia share a look.

"Should I – ?" she says, sweeping an arm out after him.

"Yeah," says Brophy. "Just make sure we know what his condition is. And *where* he is…in case it's more than 'a minute.'"

She nods and starts forward, but stops to hook Shariah's

arm through hers.

"What?" Shariah says, surprised.

Melia grins. "My brother told me you used to be his girl's best friend. So tonight you're going to be mine."

"But I thought – "

"Can't leave you down here alone with Brophy; if anyone comes along that could be a real bad scene. You're coming with me, but if you do one fucked-up thing or make one false move, I will make sure your pretty face ends up worse than his." She chin-points at Theodore. "Entiendes?"

Shariah nods mutely.

"Bueno." Melia releases her and trots lightly up the steps and Shariah, with one last backward glance at Theodore, follows her obediently out into the night.

As soon as she emerges from the cellar Melia slams the doors shut and hooks Shariah's arm again, yanking her around towards the front of the house.

"You don't have to drag me," Shariah protests.

Melia ignores this, craning her neck as she scans the area.

Shariah spots a tall form near the orchard. "There!" she says, pointing.

Melia blows out a breath. "OK," she says. "We're going to follow him and you're going be quiet. No questions. No comments. This isn't your business."

"OK. But...he's your brother?"

"Yes. And no *more* questions." She elbows Shariah hard in the ribs.

"Ow."

They keep to the shadows, once again avoiding the group in the front yard, and when they enter the orchard they stay close under the trees. But it doesn't seem to matter. Lang is completely focused on whatever task he's about and doesn't turn around, even when Shariah steps on a branch that cracks like a whip. Back near the little bridge he finally stops, slumping onto a crude wooden bench and running a hand over his eyes like he's sad or tired. Moonlight filters through a gap in the branches above, enough so that Shariah can see him reach into his pocket and push up his sleeve. He makes a motion like twisting off a cap and before she can fully register what she's witnessing he's already done with the fuse. He tucks the transfer away, briefly presses a palm against his arm, and rolls his sleeve down.

He does all this casually, like brushing his teeth, and when he's done he doesn't fall to the ground or foam at the mouth or any of the other reactions she used to see in old screeners of the transer lab. He merely stretches his arms out across the back of the bench, crosses ankle over knee, and closes his eyes like a man savoring a good meal.

And just like that she's furious; wants to smack that goony smirk off his face. Tell him that even if he's not a mass murderer he's still sick and wrong and he should never have even thought about touching someone like Lana. He messed her up. Told her lies. Made her think fusing was no big deal and that it couldn't hurt her.

She never actually liked *it*.

Shariah grits her teeth; she's going to slap the truth into him, whatever the consequences from Melia. She takes a step forward, determined to do just that when –

"Lang?"

A voice – soft, but familiar as breathing.

Lang's eyes fly open and he looks around like he thinks he might be hearing things. Then he flattens against the bench, terror on his face as two small hands appear in front of him and reach up to push back what must be a hood, revealing a shock of hair like new snow and a face pale and drawn, but radiant.

Lana.

But not the one Shariah knows.

"Celan?" he says, utter awe in his voice. "Are you…real? Am I seeing things?"

The cloak swishes open to show a body very much solid and alive. Celan cocks one hip, saying, "Not unless you turned Class S while I was gone."

He gapes for a second more and then laughs, relieved.

"Couldn't if I tried."

She grins like this is something delightful as he gets to his feet, smoothly lifting her off hers and kissing her fierce and deep. Her arms wrap around him and hold on tight as she returns the kiss like she wants to swallow him whole. Stunned, Shariah turns to Melia, who's also staring, open-mouthed with shock. They both take one, two stumbling steps backward before they turn and run, tearing through the trees, not caring how much noise they make in the effort.

There's no way either of those two will hear.

◻► 20 ◄◻

Lang must be dreaming; he has to be. He can't believe the woman in his arms is real. But she is – warm and close and smelling like sun-warmed sand and clover and something else, faintly metallic.

The scent of stars, maybe.

She looks like a star too, with that shining hair and glittering eyes. Like some kind of goddess. But not a cold, remote one – one that, like a star, gives warmth and light; one you can touch. He rests his cheek against the top of her head and breathes deep, a delicious shiver running the length of his spine as her lips brush his neck.

"Celan," he murmurs.

He can feel her giggle, though the sound of it is muffled against his chest.

"What's so funny?" he says.

"Nothing." She pulls back, beaming up at him. "It's just so crazy. I can't believe I found you like this. I thought – "

"I know," he says, gently tucking a lock of hair behind her ear. "All the ways I pictured this and none of them even came close. It's like – "

"A dream," she finishes. "The best one ever."

"But real," he adds, tentative though, like he's still not quite sure.

"Claro," she says. Then, teasingly, twining her fingers through his. "One hundred percent. Let's go to your room and I'll show you."

"Uh…" Lang says, as a wave of recollection of everything that's happened so far tonight crashes in. They definitely can't use the house for any amorous purposes at the moment. In fact, he should tell her –

But a divot of frown appears between Celan's eyes at the hesitation and he can't abide it. He can't let reality in. Not yet. Not when there's *this*.

"There's too many people around up there," he says, swallowing. "Too much going on. We won't get a chance to be alone."

"Oh," she says, brightening. "Then how about here?"

"On the bench?"

She wrinkles her nose. "It doesn't look too comfortable."

"Splinters."

They both chuckle. Lang's eyes scan the dark, searching. Then he leans in and unhooks the clasp of her cloak, whisking it off her shoulders. His breath hitches at the sight of the same blue dress from their last trip to the ranchos, the one he's pictured her in a thousand times since. Not taking his eyes off her, like she might really disappear if he does, he steps around behind the bench to a spot near the acequia where a soft bunch of sweet grass grows and lays the cloak down over it. Then he holds out a hand, beckoning, and she takes it. The press of her body on his is dizzying.

"This work?" he whispers.

She nods as they sink to the ground, tumbling down together like the earth is an ocean and it's going to be a very long time before they come up for air.

MIND RACING AS FAST AS her feet, Shariah chases Melia through the orchard, across the edge of the yard, and around the back of the house to the cellar. Before she can catch her breath Lang's sister has the doors flung open and is barreling down the steps exclaiming, "Celan's back. 'Sta aqui!"

Shariah follows close behind, hearing Brophy snap, "Don't fuck around."

"Serio," Melia says. "I'm not kidding. She's here. We just saw her. Her hair is totally white now, too."

They both turn to Shariah for confirmation; solemnly, she nods.

"Oh shit," Brophy says. "Really?"

"Can someone please tell me what the fuck is going on?" Theodore's voice, still slightly thick, but cognizant. They all look at him.

"Oh yeah," Brophy says to Melia. "This one's awake; I was gonna gag him but I don't think he can breathe through that nose."

It does look bad, Shariah notes, sort of bent and mashed and hugely swollen at the same time.

"Honestly," Melia says. "You know how to astral but couldn't deal with this?"

"I'm not your brother."

Tsking with annoyance, Melia crouches next to Theodore. "OK, I'm going to touch you, very softly, but if you try to bite me or anything I will hurt you."

Theodore glares, but doesn't protest. Shariah watches as Melia closes her eyes and reaches up to rest light fingers on either side of his face. A minute ticks by and nothing seems to be happening, but when Lang's sister lets out a breath and straightens Shariah can see – the nose is still a little crooked, but it is several sizes smaller and much less pulpy-looking.

She gapes back and forth between Melia and Theodore; in her studies she's read accounts of transers who supposedly could do this sort of thing, but she always dismissed them as exaggerations or outright nonsense. Alonzo's sisters had 'transed' her blistered foot that day and it hadn't magically healed on the spot. But maybe, as with anything, some are far more talented than others.

Melia arches a brow. "Never seen healing before?"

Brophy's words rebound: *Not your brother.*

"Can Lang do this too?"

"My brother can heal anything," Melia says, with obvious pride.

And suddenly, it all starts to make a tiny bit of sense – why Brophy and Melia have been treating him like some special thing to be coddled and fussed over instead of like public nuisance number one. Maybe that's what Lana saw in him too. If she really was from around here she probably grew up thinking the same way.

Maybe he used it to influence her.

"Thank you." Theodore, addressing Melia, cuts into her

thoughts. He twitches his nose, but doesn't seem particularly shocked at its semi-repaired state. "Did I hear someone say they just saw my daughter?"

"Yeah," Melia says. "We did."

"Well, she's what I'm here for. So if you'll kindly untie me, I'll go and get her and then we'll both," he chin-points to include Shariah, "be on our way."

Melia smirks. "She's with Lang right now, and they're, uh, *reunioning*. So I think we better wait on that." She plops down on a barrel.

At the mention of Lang's name, Theodore's veneer of civility cracks.

"Mira, you pinche little shits," he hisses. "Untie me now! I don't want that piece of garbage touching my daughter! He's done enough damage already."

Melia nudges Brophy with the tip of her sandal and makes a 'shut him up' gesture. Brophy reaches for the knife at his belt, causing Shariah a severe jolt of panic until he reaches down further and slices a strip of cloth off the top edge of a sack. Theodore's still spewing invective as Brophy gags him.

"Thank Madre," Melia says.

They're all silent for minute: Shariah still reeling, Brophy making a show of polishing his knife before re-sheathing it, and Melia brooding. Then Lang's sister gets to her feet, positioning herself directly in front of Theodore and putting hands on hips.

"'Scuchame," she says. "That 'piece of garbage' you're talking about is my brother, and I want you to know he's worth a hundred of you. *Any* of you. What can you all do? Can you heal? Can you help anything? No! You sit inside and play with your fucking machines. The sun could go out and you'd never even notice. No wonder you're all so useless! No wonder all you know how to do is destroy whatever you can't understand."

Shariah winces, thinking on the sun angle and the three lost days.

"And for your information," Melia continues, "your precious daughter's no saint. She's just as big a fuser as Lang is, maybe even worse. He wasn't the one who started her on it. She did that to herself, and when she did she dragged him back down with her. Made him a thousand times worse. Now he's been offered a chance to get better and because of her he's probably going to fuck it up!"

She chokes on this last but refuses to let tears fall, gritting her teeth and glowering like some kind of avenging angel.

"And who raised her?" she demands. "Who made her like she is? If you want to blame someone for the *damage* try looking in a mirror."

Theodore's eyes narrow, angry and defiant; he's obviously not been swayed.

But a sickly sort of realization trickles into Shariah's gut. The way Lana looked just now, the way she acted – like fusing was some kind of silly joke. If she's been away from Lang for a year and a half, then it's not him making her that way. Or not just him anyway. Not anymore. Part of it has to be *her*.

She gnaws her lower lip, disconcerted.

Done with Theodore, Melia turns to Brophy: "They're in the orchard, back by the bridge. Someone needs to keep an eye out."

"I'll go," he says.

"Stay by the front."

"Right."

He vanishes up the steps. The doors thud into place. Melia seats herself once more on the barrel and leans back against the wall, sighing. "Well," she says. "This is turning out to be quite the night."

Shariah swallows. After all the exertion and fear of the past couple hours her throat is bone dry.

"Do you have anything to drink?"

Melia shakes her head no, but then adds: "Wait. Brophy left his water." She reaches out a long arm and snags the bag from the edge of a shelf, tossing it to Shariah.

She catches it easily, there's not much left and it's pretty light. She finds the spout and pops off the cap, sniffing gingerly at the contents.

Melia's lips twist wryly. "It's just water."

Shamed, she takes a slug; it's a little warm, and unlike the super-purified stuff she's used to in Albakirk it has a rich, earthy taste. But does the trick. She takes another pull and sighs with relief. She offers the bag to Melia, but Lang's sister waves it away. Shrugging, Shariah recaps it and settles down on a stack of sacks, curiously examining an array of crude tools hung on the far wall. She can only guess at their uses.

"We'd notice if it went out," she says after a minute.

"Huh?"

"The sun, I mean," Shariah says, feeling stupid; the look Melia gives her does nothing to mitigate this.

"I just mean – " she starts, then stops. She's not sure what she means. Just that for some strange reason she wants this ranchos girl to like her; to see that she's different, not like the other techs. So she changes tack, "Do you really think Celan came from space just now? There wasn't a ship or anything. If there were aliens wouldn't they have come with her?"

Melia shrugs. "Who knows?"

"She looked like she'd been somewhere though. Somewhere else, you know?"

"Yeah." Melia gives a short, mirthless laugh. "Planet Fusemore."

"They seemed happy to see each other."

Melia says nothing.

Shariah bites her lip again, scuffs the dirt floor with her heel. Then, in a rush: "Do you think they're going to be alright?"

Melia meets her eyes levelly.

"Honestly?" she says. "I have no idea."

CELAN PRESSES HER CHEEK TO Lang's chest, marveling at the marriage of their shared pulse, the plushness of flesh on flesh. The soft plash of the acequia is like a lullaby; the grass beneath her cloak a featherbed. This is better than Lang's room. This is better than anything. She doesn't ever want to move from this spot.

All that worry for nothing! she thinks. *Everything worked out perfect.*

After introducing them to the expros, she can send the Plejarans on their way with grateful thanks and then she and Lang can spend a few days having fun. Or more than a few days, maybe a week. Maybe a month. She's earned it.

She props her chin up, taking in the planes of his face – gorgeous eyes closed and a small smile playing on his lips.

"Lang?"

"Mmmm?"

"I love you."

"I love you too."

He drags slow fingertips down her back and she shivers. She wants to stay out here all night, sleep under the stars. But his eyes blink open like he's just thought of something alarming.

"Hey." He raises his head a fraction, tugging on a lock of her hair. "This is like, space effects or something, right? I mean you're not…"

Walking out into the snow? She thinks wryly. *Fused up beyond all recognition?*

"Of course not." She grins. "Space effects."

"Good."

"Speaking of which, you've got a lot of white going on there too."

"Yeah. I was pretty bad for a while back when –" He halts, as if checking himself. "Then I got better. Now…well, you can see my eyes."

"They're beautiful." She gazes deep into sparkling green like sunlight on a mossy pond.

"So are yours."

"This whole *world* is beautiful," Celan says dreamily, resting her cheek back against his chest. "Really, you have no idea."

Strong arms pull her tight. "I do."

"But there are so many other beautiful places too. I can't wait to show you it all! Va'anak has the most amazing sunsets, and oceans like you wouldn't believe."

"Sounds great."

"It is."

"But lonely sometimes," she finally adds.

"Did you have anyone you could talk to?"

"Well yeah, sure. I mean, that's what transentience is – when you speak in your own language and another species speaks in theirs, but you still understand each other."

Lang lifts his head, surprised. "You mean back on the mesa, those aliens we met – "

"The Plejarans."

" – were speaking a different *language*?"

"Uh-huh."

"Whoa," he says. Then: "We should have come with you."

"But you couldn't've. There wasn't time. And I had to – "

"I know," Lang says. "I'm just glad you're here now. I was afraid – "

"Me too," she whispers.

They fall silent, bathing in the slight chill of the evening air and listening to the soft chirr of crickets. Minutes pass, and Celan feels herself start to drift. She's almost asleep when Lang clears his throat.

"Celan?" He says, nudging her. "We can't stay out here all night. We're gonna need to get up soon. We have to go back to the house."

"What?" she says. "Why?"

"There's a lot going on at the moment. A lot of stuff I have to tell you. But it's hard. I just – "

"Want to lay here forever?"

"Yeah." He sighs. "Pretty much."

Gently, he shifts her over and sits up, brushing grass seeds from his hair. She follows suit. They face each other, cross-legged.

"Now don't be mad," he starts, in placating tones. "But

your father – "

"Is dead?"

"No."

"Is *here*?"

"Um, yeah." Lang scratches the back of his head, sheepish. "He's kind of like, tied up in my cellar right now."

"What?" she says, incredulous. Then she bursts out laughing at the absurdity.

"I'm serious," he says, with a nervous chuckle. "Celan!"

But this only makes her laugh harder, rolling around and hugging herself as she convulses, helpless. She tries to stop, tries to get herself under control, but each time the mental picture of Theodore Timanti trussed like a chicken in Lang's basement makes her lose it all over again.

Eventually though, the waves begin to subside and she can breathe again. She sits up, wiping her eyes.

"I'm sorry," she says. "It's just – "

"I know it sounds crazy," Lang says. "But it's true. He came out here looking for you with some friend of yours from Albakirk…Sariah?"

This finally sobers her. "*Shariah's* here?"

"They came together; showed up at the Perditas cider party. He tried to hit me – "

"What?"

" – but I knocked him out."

"Good for you," Celan says, delighted.

"Yeah, well," Lang says grimly. "I did what I had to do. But we couldn't let them go because there's some rumor that the techs are going to attack the ranchos tonight and we thought that if we had them – "

"Wait, *what?*"

" – then they might not go through with it."

"OK," Celan says, mind racing as she struggles to process all this information.

So much for everything's perfect, she thinks sourly. *Fucking Ariana.*

"Who said the techs were going to attack?"

"The elders," Lang says. "Someone had a vision or something. But then your friend Shariah confirmed it. She said that her mentor, Ariana Balor, was behind it. That some kind of natural disaster was going to happen tonight."

"Mentor?" she says, shaking her head. "Ariana's her *mother.*"

His jaw slackens. "Holy shit."

"Is she there?" Celan says, clambering up and pulling her shift on over her head. "With my father?"

"Yes," Lang says, scrambling up and hurriedly dressing too. "They're with Brophy and Melia."

"Melia's involved?"

A shrug. "She involved herself."

"All right then," she says, snatching her cloak off the ground and throwing it across her shoulders. "Let's go get to the bottom of this."

☐► 21 ◄☐

L ang trails Celan through the orchard, stumbling over
untied boots. His eyes are well-adjusted to the dark, but
a stray root nearly sends him sprawling.

"Hey!" he says. "Celan, hold up."

She freezes, then pivots on one heel and traces her steps
back to him. He kneels to tighten his laces like a man grac-
ing a queen.

"Rise!" she mock-commands when he's done, and he
does, planting a kiss on her lips for good measure.

"You may kiss me again, sir," she says loftily..

He smirks, warming to the game. "I can do lots of things."

"I know." She laughs. "But we have to be serious now.
We can do more things later."

"Promise?"

"Swear."

"As you wish," he says, and releases her.

"I just wish…" Celan says as they start to walk again.

"What?"

"That we could just have one night, you know? Tonight! To be happy. Without all this – ugh!" She waves her hands to indicate the whole general clusterfuck.

Lang rests a reassuring arm around her shoulders. "Don't worry. We will."

But inwardly he winces.

Is anything ever *going to be all right?*

Between the horror at Rinconada and Ariana's renewed viciousness he's not so sure. But of one thing he's certain – he's not going to act on the elders' offer unless the girl by his side is part of it too. He's never going to leave her on her own again.

Together they stride under swaying boughs and moon shadows until at the thinning edge of the trees a black shape rears up, tall and broad, blocking their path.

Brophy.

A bit guiltily, though he can't quite say why, Lang lets his arm drop.

"Hey," Brophy says, giving Celan a quick appraisal. "Wow. It's really you."

"Hey, Brophy," she says. "Que pas'?"

"A whole lotta shit," he says. "Sure you're ready?" He nods pointedly at her hair.

"Space effects."

"Yeah, OK."

"Brophy," she says, with a wearisome air, "do not start with me. Seriously. Now is not the time."

"Ah, but when is it ever?"

His tone isn't mocking, not exactly, but Lang can sense something roiling below the surface: Jealousy, maybe?

280

Celan snorts. "If you keep giving me crap you're not getting a ride on the spaceship."

At this, all traces of snark flee. "The Plejarans?" Brophy says eagerly. "They're here?" He cranes his neck to look past Celan and Lang.

"They're *near*," she corrects him. "And they'll come if we need them. And, I have this."

She holds up her right hand, palm outwards, displaying a thick silvery band that circles her index finger. It glints in the moonlight.

"What's that?" Brophy says.

Lang peers at it, curious as well. He'd noticed it earlier, but was too distracted by other things to focus on such trifles as jewelry.

"A quantum band," she says, with obvious pride.

Brophy leans in closer, squinting. "What does it do?"

"Lots of things. Like maybe stop that bitch from destroying the ranchos."

"Really?"

"Well, the Plejarans might have to help."

"Where are they?"

"A little north of Leones. But they can get here fast."

"Bueno." Brophy nods succinctly, then turns, motioning for them to follow.

He falls in on Lang's right as they make a wide circle around the continuing festivities in the Shays' front yard. Lang has the sudden urge to grab both of their hands, one on each side, but he quickly dismisses it.

"Did she say anymore," he asks Brophy instead. "Shariah, I mean. About what her mother has planned?"

"Her mother?" Brophy whistles through his teeth.

"Yes," Celan confirms. "Whatever else she told you is bullshit. Ariana Balor is her mother. And they both hate all transers and expros. If she's here, it's not for any good purpose."

"That might actually help us, though," Brophy says. "There's no way that bitch is gonna do anything to the ranchos while her kid is here."

"Did you search them? Do they have servers? Stuns? Some kind of signaling device?"

"Shariah had a stun, but I have it now." Brophy pats the pack slung over his shoulder. "We didn't search your father."

"OK," Celan says. "But he's tied up, right?"

"Yeah."

"What about Shariah?"

"Melia's got her."

"Are you sure – "

"Don't worry. Melia's tough."

"Yeah," Lang adds, just to say something.

He's feeling a little left out of the conversation, so to make up for it he takes Celan's hand. She gives him a squeeze and he can feel the cold metal of the band press against his palm. It makes him shiver.

STILL PERCHED ATOP THE SACKS, Shariah starts at the sound of the doors, followed by many feet upon the stairs. She and Melia both jump up as Brophy appears, followed by Lang and Celan. The lantern light throws shadows across Celan's face, highlighting the gauntness in her cheeks even as it dazzles her hair with diamonds.

Shariah sucks in a breath. No matter where it is she's actually been all this time Lana – *Celan* – looks alien enough to have walked straight off an alternate plane in some galaxy far away. But she smiles at everyone, and this warms her several degrees closer to human.

Theodore grunts against his gag; his daughter spares him a swift glance, then hones in on Shariah.

"So," she says dryly. "Still doing your mother's work, I see."

Sharish stutters, surprised to be addressed first, and so familiarly. "N-no," she says. "I'm not – "

"What is it with you two anyway, that you can't just live and let live? No one here poses any kind of threat to you or the city. These are families, farms. Not big, bad expros." She shakes her head, as though incapable of fathoming the depths of such stupidity.

Shariah bristles. This is too much. "For your information," she says. "I am *not* here to help my mother. I disagree with her, if you can wrap your head around that. He and I," she flicks a hand at Theodore, "came here to warn people. And also, we came to find *you*. To try to help you."

"It's obviously not me that needs help right now."

"Her hair," Lang puts in. "It's space effects."

"Oh for fuck's sake." Melia snorts.

"Please," Celan says, with what Shariah must admit is an extremely well-executed eye roll. "You can all see me, right? Standing here in front of you, fully functional? The person who's just spent the past eighteen months as the first and only Madren representative to the K'Shiran Convention? So can we stop with the stank faces and focus on the problem at hand: What kind of 'natural disaster' is going to happen to the ranchos tonight and what is the best way to stop it?"

Shariah tilts her head thoughtfully, no matter what her old friend has been up to there is no mistaking the brisk note of confidence in her voice.

She can't be that *bad off.*

"I don't know," she confesses. "That's the problem. Something's going to happen but I'm not sure what exactly. Whatever it is though, she said it would be late tonight, when everyone's asleep."

Safe in their beds, she thinks, recalling her mother's gloating tone with a shudder.

"And you all believe this?" Celan says to the general room.

Melia nods. "Yes," she says simply. "Something is going to happen, but I really don't think either of them are a part of it. Your father showed up ripped to the tits. Your friend here was just trying to deal with him."

"Could've been a ruse."

"It wasn't a *ruse*." Shariah says, voice straining on the last word. "I swear! We came out here this morning. Went to see Jillyanne and Tanny."

Celan's face registers shock.

"Then we walked around talking to people. We helped these people from Rancho Cabras with their cart and they invited us over for drinks, and then we went for *more* drinks at Rancho Arqueros, which obviously didn't end well."

Theodore grunts again, louder this time. They all ignore him.

"You saw Jillyanne and Tanny?" Celan asks wonderingly. "How are they?"

"They're fine," Shariah says. Her eyes meet Celan's and hold a moment.

There's definitely something still human in there.

"OK," Celan says, as if making up her mind. "Take that gag off my father. Let's see what he has to say about all this."

FURIOUS, THEODORE SPITS OUT BITS of burlap, fervently wishing he could get his hands free, and tight around Shays' neck. The utter helplessness of his position, far from chastening, only serves to make him angrier. It should be that piece of shit tied up on the floor, not a Lead SocEn who's only crime was having had a little too much to drink and (rightfully) defending his daughter's honor.

"You bastard!" he yells. "Let her go!"

Shays ducks his head, all faux-innocence. "I'm not doing anything bad to her. I love her."

Lana gives the piece of shit an adoring look, then adds haughtily. "And I love him too. And now that *that's* established, if we're going to talk like adults here we need to get one thing straight: Lang has never forced, coerced, or otherwise inveigled me in any way. Ever. He's only done right by me."

"He destroyed you!" Theodore thunders. "With that poison. You look –" Rage chokes off the rest. This is bullshit. This is not his Lana. That girl was tractable, sensible, and above all grateful. This bizarre apparition looks at him like she's not quite sure he's from the same species.

"I look like someone who's been in space for eighteen months," she finishes evenly. "Because that's where I have been. Exposed to radiation, cosmic rays, and what-have-you.... you know about these things, right? Because of the Mars project? Or did that not work out?"

This solicitiousness is like oxygen to a blaze; the nerve of her to spout science at him at a time like this.

"You're deluded! Insane! You have NOT been in space. That's just what he's convinced you is true. You've probably been locked in some basement, talking to the wall the whole time." He shakes his head sadly. "I just want to help you, Lana."

But his daughter is unmoved. She makes an odd hand motion, and there's a flash of silver in the half-light. She presses a palm to her chest and murmurs a few quick words.

"What is *that*?" Shariah says.

Theodore tries to catch the girl's eye; maybe *she* can get through to Lana.

"I called the Plejarans," Lana says, matter-of-fact. "We're going to need their help with whatever your mother has planned, and it's obvious that without them we have no hope of convincing him," she inclines her head toward Theodore, "that I'm not stark raving mad."

"You really – ?" Shariah starts.

"Yes," Lana says, with a great show of forebearance. "I've really been in space. On an orbital station in 60QR system, about ninety light years from here. It's the current location of the K'Shiran Convention, which is like a galactic version of what the old world United Nations used to be, except with more actual power.

"But they only accept transentient species and when I ran into the Plejarans on a mesa after my Destierra it turned out I was. So I went with them, to get us joined up."

"Ridiculous," Theodore says, trying once more to get Shariah's attention.

But she's still focused on Lana.

"What were they doing there, though?" the girl says slowly. "The Plejarans, I mean, on the mesa?"

"Shariah!" he hisses, scandalized.

His daughter shrugs. "Gathering data. They keep tabs on sentient worlds, just in case they happen to turn transentient."

"You *talked* to them?"

"So did we." The big man called Brophy, silent thusfar, now speaks up. "Me and Lang did. Before Celan left. I touched their ship. It was definitely real."

Shariah shifts her weight uneasily.

"Stop encouraging this," Theodore commands her.

But it's Lana who replies. "What?" she says. "Reality? The thing that when you stop believing in it, doesn't go away?"

"Don't you dare quote Dick at me!"

"Why not? You taught me everything I know. Well," she adds, "almost."

With this, she dismisses him and addresses Shays and Brophy: "Come on. We've got to go meet them."

"The Plejarans?" Shays says, with a nervous look.

"Who else?"

And, turning neatly on one heel, she starts up the steps; the two men follow, and the doors slam unceremoniously shut behind them.

There's a moment's silence, then Theodore orders Shariah, "Untie me. Now."

But she looks past him to the skinny ranchos girl who fixed his nose; Shays' sister apparently, not the person to be taking cues from in his opinion.

"Should we go too?" she says.

"Why are you asking *her*?" Theodore demands. "I am your superior, Shariah. Untie me."

287

"Let's wait here," the ranchos girl says. "If anyone comes by we don't want him getting loose."

"Getting loose?" Theodore sneers. "I am not some kind of animal! You heard me, Shariah. Untie me. Now. That is a direct order."

But she makes no move until Shays' sister holds up the strip of burlap recently removed from around his mouth.

"And I recommend reusing this," the girl says, passing it over grimly. "Unless you like listening to him bitch."

To his extreme consternation, Shariah actually takes the thing, but merely pockets it before sinking down cross-legged on the floor. She regards him steadily for a long moment.

Then: "I'm sorry, Mr. Timanti. But I can't untie you until I'm sure you're not going to start any more fights."

"With who?" he retorts, indignant. "Shays? A few hours ago all you wanted was reassurance that he was dead. Now he's your *friend*?" He injects as much contempt as possible into this last.

Shariah sighs. "No, of course not. I just think there are bigger things going on right now than some personal vendetta. You hate him, we get it. But I don't think he's actually a danger to anyone."

"Except Lana."

"No," she says, "not even that."

Theodore scowls, so she continues: "Look, me and Melia," she indicates Shays' sister, "were there, OK? When she came back. It was like she appeared out of thin air, and Lang was completely shocked. And then they, like, *leapt* on each other, like they'd been apart forever. And it wasn't an act; they didn't know we were there. So wherever she's been it wasn't with him. He hasn't been holding her hostage."

"So where *do* you think she's been?" he says huffily. "In space?"

Shariah looks to Melia again.

"I don't think she's lying about that," Melia says grudgingly. "That hair though..." She scoffs. "Space effects my ass."

"She seemed so sharp though," Shariah says. "Cognizant. I doubt she's really been fusing that much."

"You don't know fusers then. Even Class Es, they don't always act a mess. They can seem almost normal a lot of the time. Believe me," Shay's sister adds darkly. "I know."

Theodore gloats: *Finally someone talking sense.*

"You see?" he says, triumphant. "He *is* a danger, Shariah; he *is* influencing her!"

Melia trains her gaze back on him. "I thought we went over this already, tech man. My brother may have problems, but he is not *the* problem, not where Celan Mairs is concerned."

"Give me that gag back," she orders Shariah.

Shariah's hand moves towards her pocket.

"Wait!" Theodore says.

He does not want to be gagged, or to continue to be bound in this ludicrous truss. The more he sobers up the more the hot waves of rage recede, replaced by cool cunning. No matter how it pains him, if he wants to be free he's going to have to at least pretend to play along. He can settle with Shays later.

"You won't," he says, pleadingly. "Hear any more, OK? I don't want to argue. You've made your point and we can agree to disagree. Quietly."

Best not lay it on too thick.

But Melia's brows knit; she seems to regard even this

stingy admission suspiciously. Still, she lets the matter of the re-gagging drop.

Shariah's hand returns to her lap and she gives Theodore a appreciative look.

Good.

He quirks his lips ruefully, and dips his head in a show of chagrin. As far as getting untied goes, getting back in Ms. Balor's good graces looks as if it will be a necessary start.

⊏◦ 22 ◦⊐

Celan speeds up double time as she and Brophy chase Lang's long strides down a twisting path through the woods behind his house. She'd asked him to show her the best place for a Plejaran rendevouz that did not involve landing their craft in his yard and he'd obliged – there's a clearing about a half-mile in, well away from any houses or prying eyes.

It's very dark, though. Overhead pine boughs shift, releasing a sharp, resinous scent and blocking out any light. She stumbles on a tree root and curses. Brophy grabs her elbow before she can fall.

"Thanks," she says.

"No problem."

It's only in the pause before she starts moving again that she remembers the quantum band.

Duh.

"Hey!" she calls after Lang; he stops and jogs back over

to them.

"I thought you – "

"Shh!" she says, concentrating.

There's light around, even if it's hidden. And it isn't entirely; between black boughs glows a strip of starlight. She stretches up a hand to transfer a bit of it to her band, and in her palm a small cool ball of light begins to grow.

"Whoa," says Brophy.

Lang stares in unabashed awe.

Celan grins. "No big," she says, rounding the light out to the size of a child's ball. She gives it a quick toss and catches it. "Come on."

She takes the lead, phosphorescence lending the trees an eerie gleam. It calls to mind the fairy tales she used to borrow from her father's library; a taste for fantasy was something they both shared.

My father, she thinks. *In the ranchos. Tonight of all nights...*

She hadn't formulated much of a plan for dealing with him, and secretly hoped she wouldn't have to. As long as all was well with Lang, and the ranchos, she could have avoided that awkwardness. Maybe just sent a message to let him know she was alive and well and left it at that.

At this point, what more do they really have to say?

But now, with him here and still treating her like some kind of mental deficient, even though he's the one drunk and tied up on the floor, it's obvious that he's in need of a little lesson in humility. If he likes the fantastic so much, he'd best get ready to deal with a wallop of it.

An owl hoots nearby; reminding her of Wehoo. Celan laughs.

"Hey," Lang says softly, nudging her arm as he falls in beside her.

But he's not really asking anything, so she doesn't answer. It's just an acknowledgment, of the wonders she can do.

He knows now, she thinks. *How we'll never be helpless again. How we'll never ever again be at their command. This time, they'll be at ours.*

Then she checks herself, remembering XĩNeru and the Plejarans' alarm over her talk of tech vs. transer. Whatever happens, she has to be just and merciful. Cool and collected. She can't afford to lose her shit and risk their place at the Convention.

Gratefully, she nudges Lang back.

Another five minutes' hike and the path opens out into a meadow ringed by a fringe of dark trees. Long tufted grass lies silvered in the moonlight and Celan is reminded once more of a fairy tale: A magic glade, where a flight of winged sprites could appear at any moment and dance them all down under the hill. She activates the band to send exact coordinates to Chan, Ness, and Ree.

They might not be pixies, but for now they'll have to do.

"On the way," she confirms.

They all scan the sky, expectant.

Then Brophy coughs softly. "So like, what's the plan?" he asks. "I mean, when they get here. Do we know what we're going to do?"

"Well," she says. "I've been thinking – there's only so many things that a 'natural disaster' can be: there's floods and storms, fires, tornados, earthquakes."

"The four elements," Lang notes. "Like we learned in

'scuela."

"Exactly. And there'll be four of us with bands. So if we each concentrate on one we should be able to cover everything. Monitor small changes in weather, atmosphere, whatever."

"Your band can do that?" Brophy says.

"The band can do almost anything. But it has to work with what's around."

"So it's like a transfigurational superconductor?"

She turns and grins at him, pleasantly surprised, until she recalls that for all his expro-ness, Brophy also used to work for the techs and probably knows a lot of scientific lingo.

"Yes," she says. "That's precisely what it is."

"And you know how to use it? To stop an earthquake?"

"One of the Plejarans can take that one. I'll go for something simpler, like fire. Once we know which it is, everyone else can join in."

Brophy chuckles. "What could go wrong?"

Celan opens her mouth to retort just as Lang says, "Hey! Shut up. I think they're here."

She whips her head up to see the star-shaped ship hovering silently just above the treeline. When in motion, it's uncanny how much it resembles a classic flying saucer. They must have used some kind of cloaking device if they flew this low over the ranchos. Either that or there'll be a lot of seriously freaked out folks up at Leones tonight.

The sleek craft lands with a whisper on the grass about fifty feet away. All is still as it powers down, then there's the distinct hiss of decompression as the ramp descends, followed by the pad of soft feet.

Here we go, she thinks, stepping forward to meet them.

LANG'S KNEES TREMBLE AS THE tall, pale forms of the Ple-jarans emerge into the earthly night. He's not scared of them, not exactly, but the first (and only) time he met them he was both in astral form and aviados as fuck; so although he knows it occurred it's always seemed a little bit like something out of a dream.

This time though, there's no mistaking: The aliens have landed. This is real.

For Celan there's obviously no issue at all. She marches right up to them like they're anybody, diving right in and outlining the situation. Their expressions don't appear to change, but then, they aren't human. A frown could be a smile to them; a laugh, a declaration of war. This isn't just tech vs. transer stuff. Or even another city-state on Earth (and he can hardly even imagine *that*, never having been anywhere outside a hundred mile radius of Albakirk).

They're from another planet.

He tries to catch Brophy's eye, hoping to find a mirror of his own awe. But his friend doesn't seem at all perturbed, he's watching the scene unfold with an expression equal parts eagerness and amusement.

'Nothing like a few aliens to make things interesting,' it implies.

Lang sighs.

Then Celan motions them over and things get even more surreal. He's going to have to *talk* to them. He keeps his head down until he's alongside her; Brophy draws up on her other side.

"Well," says a clear, pleasant voice. "What a lovely triune you have my dear! And here I was under the impression you were all romantically binary."

Celan chuckles, and Lang looks up, surprised, into the face of the middle member of the group. He (as Lang guesses) is well over six feet tall, with bright blue eyes in a smooth face topped by a tuft of silvery hair.

Those eyes seem to be able to read right into his soul.

"Uh, hi," Lang says, shuffling nervously. He's not exactly sure what a triune is but from the context he has a pretty good idea.

Can they tell? he thinks. *About me and Brophy?*

But there is no him-and-Brophy, not really. It was just one kiss.

At least Celan doesn't seem to mind the implication. But she probably thinks they're joking. If they even can joke, in terms a human would understand.

"You," the Plejaran says, snapping him back to attention, "of course, are Lang. We did meet briefly, but I recall it was rather...insubstantial. In the interim I've heard so much about you. You are apparently quite proficient in the energetic healing arts."

"Uh, yeah," he stammers. "I – uh – "

"And you," the Plejaran continues, ticking his head right, "are the astral master known as Brophy."

"Claro que sí. That'd be me."

"Splendid! I, as you may or may not recall, am called Chan, and my companions here are Ness and Ree." He gestures left and right to indicate each in turn.

"Great to see you all again." Brophy chuckles. "Really. It's been too long."

Lang has a swift urge to smack him upside the head.

"Now I understand there's a bit of trouble going on," Chan says seriously. "And we will be happy to help you sort it all out."

"They're going to follow us," Celan says. "Not in the ship, but on foot. We'll go back to the house so everyone can meet them and see that I wasn't bluffing. Then we can find a secure place to prepare for the attack. Someplace quiet, where we won't be interrupted."

Aliens in the basement, Lang thinks faintly.

But there's nothing he can do now except go along for the ride.

"Sure," he says, showing them all his best brave face. "That sounds like a great idea."

◻▪ 23 ▪◻

"What's taking them so long?" Shariah says, knee jogging impatiently. She jumps up from the sack of stacks she's perched on (long having finished her business with Theodore on the floor) and starts to pace the small square at the bottom of the stairs.

Melia shrugs. "Who knows? Maybe they had to make a pit stop on the Moon."

"I thought you said you believed – "

"I do. I was kidding. Relax."

"I don't know how you can be so – " she starts, but is hushed by the sound of creaking doors.

She squints up the stairs, heart hammering in expectation of the alien, fantastic, and exotic, only to see a very ordinary-looking girl about her own age staring back at her.

"Who are you?" the girl says. "And what are you doing in our cellar?"

Behind Shariah, Melia swears, "Shit! My sister!" There's

the sound of a wild scramble followed by the swish of something being whisked off a shelf.

Some kind of cloth maybe, to hide Mr. Timanti.

Shariah gulps.

"Just a friend of Melia's," she calls up. "We were just, uh, getting something." Then adds brightly, "Is there anything we can bring up for you?"

"Is Melia down there? She's supposed to be helping me." Without waiting for an answer, the girl stomps down the steps, dark hair brushing thick shoulders.

"Wait!" Shariah says. "She said she wasn't – "

But the girl pushes past her, saying, "So this is where you've been all night; I've been looking all over! Is Lang down here? Is he mucho borracho?"

Shariah turns, braced for the worst, only to see Melia planted firmly in front of Theodore and the barrel. As she'd guessed, there's some kind of tarp covering him now. From the looks of it though it won't stand much scrutiny, so as added distraction she hurries to position herself between the two sisters.

"What do you want, Cass?" Melia says casually. "Lang isn't here. I think he's still with his friend over at the Perditas."

"So he's still *getting* wasted then," Cass says. "Lovely."

"Callaté. He hasn't been drunk in ages. He just went over there to be social."

"Right. And I'm sure we'll hear all about it in the morning: How he knocked over the keg, faceplanted in the bonfire, and embarrassed the whole family for the thousand-and-first time. He should've never have come back here. If he loves those expros so much he should just go up to their camp and stay there!"

300

Melia bristles, but visibly masters herself and takes a deep, slow breath. "He's fine," she says. "You don't know what you're talking about."

"Fine?" Cass says. "Are you kidding me? He hasn't been fine since – "

But she never finishes the thought, interrupted as it is by a series of violent sneezes that clearly did not originate with any of the three girls.

"What was that?" Cass says. Then, as her eyes hone in on the source – the barrel, and what is at close range very obviously a tarp-covered body – continues: "Oh, I get it. Fine my ass! I knew it!"

And, shoving Melia aside, in one fluid motion she yanks the tarp off. "Why you still bother to cover up his bullshit I'll never – Wait," she says, confusion dawning as Theodore is revealed, "who's this?"

Shariah looks to Melia, who for once seems to be at a total loss.

"What the fuck is going on?" Cass demands.

When neither one of them says anything, Theodore clears his throat. But before he can utter a word, there's a sound of feet on the stairs. Shariah and Melia register mutual horror.

Then Lang's voice calls out: "Everything OK down here? Why were the doors open?"

"Lang!" Melia says. "Cass is here looking for you. Better get back to the Perditas right now if you don't want to do a shit-ton of dishes!"

The feet spin and make for the surface. But Cass is faster than she looks. She drops the tarp and pounds up after him.

"Fuck!" Melia yells, before taking off in her siblings' wake.

Shariah is left blinking blankly up the stairs, unsure of whether or not to follow. Are the aliens with Lang? What happens if Cass sees them? Maybe they look human enough that in the dark she wouldn't be able to tell. Then Theodore clears his throat again, and she cuts her eyes to him.

"If you don't mind," he says mildly. "I think at this point I would be much more of an asset to you all mobile than I am restrained."

A thought occurs. "Did you sneeze on *purpose*?"

"It was a very dusty tarp," he says. "And, need I remind you, I don't have use of my hands. It's not like I moved my legs or something."

Shariah regards him carefully. He seems far more reasonable than he did a few hours ago. And it's true, they may need to move quickly now. And, if he should try anything funny, Brophy does have the stun...

"OK," she says. "Let me find something sharp to cut with."

LANG TEARS TOWARD THE TREES, panting not so much from exertion as with fear: at all costs he's got to lead Cass away from the old barn. Because everyone (Plejarans included) is *in* the barn right now, waiting for the all-clear. Its big, wooden bulk had blocked a clear view of the back of the house from the woods, so when they'd all emerged they hadn't immediately noticed the open cellar door. Once they had, he'd been sent ahead to reconnoiter.

He risks a quick glance over his shoulder, only to find no Cass. He skids to a stop, hope rising: Has she given up already? Gone back to the party to bitch about her shitty brother? He starts to retrace his steps. Then he hears her scream.

Shit.

He breaks into another run; and when he reaches the front of the barn his worst fears are confirmed. Cass is on the ground, struggling mightily against the force that is Melia, while Celan and Brophy stand several feet away, hurriedly conferring. Melia has one hand clamped over Cass's mouth, but she's obviously desperate enough to bite, because Melia suddenly shrieks, waving that hand frantically in the air as Cass yells:

"What the fuck *are* those things? What is going on? Get the fuck off me, Melia! *Now!*"

With a final buck she throws her sister off and scrambles to her feet. But she only gains a few yards before Brophy springs, stun in hand, and drops her in the dirt.

"What the fuck?" Lang says. "You stunned my sister!"

"She was gonna bring the whole house down on us," he says. "What was I supposed to do?"

Lang rushes over to Cass and crouches. "Will she be OK?" he says, feeling for a pulse; it's there and beating strong. She seems to be breathing normally as well.

Thank Madre.

"We'll put her in the cellar," Brophy says. "She'll wake up fine in about fifteen minutes."

"What about Theodore, and Shariah? We can't – "

"No," Celan cuts in. "We have to get them out of there. As soon as possible. Someone might have heard her scream." Her eyes dart side-to-side. "Someone might come."

"But then where do *we* go?" Lang says, stepping around to hoist Cass under the shoulders. He gestures at Brophy to grab her legs.

"Back to the ship," Celan says, as if it's the obvious choice.

"And then?" Lang says, as they haul Cass up.

"Don't worry. I know the perfect place."

WHEN THEY EMERGE FROM THE depths, it's with Theodore in tow, hands bound in front and the stun at his back. Shariah had been busy freeing the man's feet when they got down there with Cass, claiming she'd heard screams and thought a hasty move was in order. True enough, but Brophy gave her a hard look just the same.

Lang had refused to let them use the leftover rope to tie Cass, however, pointing out that she could always astral for assistance. They did make sure to close and bar the doors, this last at the insistence of Melia.

"It'll slow her down. She'll yell for awhile now before she thinks to astral."

Sensible, but his heart still sinks as they make their way through the woods. Cass was already mad before, after this she'll definitely hate him forever.

We had to stop her though, he tells himself. *She would have gone straight to an elegido or elder and it would have been impossible to explain everything in time for the attack.*

But when she's found, and she tells their parents what happened, things will probably get ugly. Melia's confident that as long as they stick to the story of accidentally locking her in the basement no one will believe the rest; they'll think she tripped on the stairs and hit her head. Even if this works though, it's still a nasty trick.

A pointy elbow pokes his ribs, followed by a hiss:

"Stop stressing!" his sister says, like she can read his mind.

In front of them, Shariah turns slightly, as if to comment, but then seems to think better of it and returns to pacing Brophy and Theodore in silence, solar torch light swinging an arc out in front of her. When they'd brought Cass down to the cellar, Celan had gone ahead with the Plejarans to prepare their escape.

"Where do you think we're going?" Lang says, trying to set his mind on other things.

"Who knows? I can't wait to see these aliens though." Melia rubs her hands together in gleeful anticipation; she'd caught Cass running out of the barn and never actually got a glimpse of them.

"Yeah, well. They're nice enough I guess."

"*Nice?*" his sister mocks. "I *guess?*"

"I haven't really talked to them that much."

"But you can – talk to them, I mean? There's some form of communication?"

"Oh, yeah," he says, realizing an explanation is in order. "That's what transentience is. We can understand them, and they can understand us, even if we're speaking different languages."

"*Really?*" Melia says, clearly thrilled. "And you've done this?"

Lang nods. "I didn't even know I was at first. It just kind of happened."

"So you think I can do it too?"

"I don't see why not."

"But how does it work?" Melia presses. "I mean, how do you become transentient? Is everyone?"

"I don't know." Lang says. "You'd have to ask Celan about

that."

At the name, Melia makes a *pfft* noise.

Annoyance flares. "What, you have a problem with Celan now? What's she ever done to you?"

"Not me. It's what she's done to you."

"She hasn't done anything to me. She's my girl. I love her."

"She *encourages* you."

"To do what?" Lang says, but even as he feigns ignorance he knows exactly what she's referring to. And it's true, maybe. But that doesn't change how he feels.

"You know," he says, chuckling a bit for effect. "It's kind of funny..."

"What is?"

"You talking about her like it's all her fault. It's the same way her father talks about me."

Melia rounds on him. "I do NOT!" she shouts.

Lang halts alongside her, palms up. "I was just kidding. Bájale."

But instead of calming, Melia takes this as a cue to really lay into him, causing the three people in front to turn and observe them with unconcealed aggravation.

"Hey!" Brophy calls. "Save the slap fights for later, alright? We're in some serious shit here. And don't forget," he adds. "I have a stun, and I have no problem using it."

This has the intended effect: Melia hushes. But when they start walking again she darts ahead and catches up with Shariah, hooking an arm through the tech girl's like they're the best of friends.

Lang bites his lip, trying shake off the vertiginous sense of things spiralling out of control. Maybe this is all too much to handle. Maybe they *should* find an elder and tell them what's going on. But he knows that if he suggests it he'll be shouted down instantly. And then everyone, especially Celan, will be mad.

He shakes his head, and resigns himself to bringing up the rear in silence.

⊂► 24 ◄⊃

As the path opens out into a good-sized clearing Theodore stops stock-still, blinking in disbelief – of all the things he had expected to see, the sight of his daughter flanked by two towering, uncanny figures in white in front of an oddly-shaped, unidentifiable silver-grey vehicle, is just about the very last thing he could have imagined.

Brophy pokes him with the stun. "Move," he orders.

But he's frozen to the spot.

This has to be some kind of illusion. A holo. Maybe instead of being taken by the expros she was captured by another city-state. Maybe they learned about the Mars settlement and this is part of some elaborate plan to thwart it.

It simply cannot be what it looks like.

It *cannot*.

Behind him, Brophy makes an exasperated noise and grabs his arm, frog-marching him closer as his daughter steps forward, smiling, to meet them.

"Occam's razor, dad," she says lightly. "And it looks like you could really use a shave."

Shariah lets out a loud cackle, though there's a note of hysteria in it; then Melia murmurs something and she quiets. The two girls, joined by Shays, brush past him and Brophy to stand by Lana.

"Sorry there's no time for long introductions," she tells them. "Ness and Ree are waiting. Chan's already on board."

"But where are we *going*?" pipes up Shays, a little petulantly in Theodore's opinion.

Lana gives him an indulgent look.

"Not far," she says. "Just over to Pescados, to my old house where I grew up. Remember what Tanny and Jillyanne said when we visited last? It's abandoned; people actively avoid it. No one will bother us there."

"But what about Jillyanne and Tanny?" Shays says. "Won't they – ?"

"It's far enough away from their house and the ship has a cloaking device. No one will see."

Shays grunts, apparently satisfied. Everyone starts toward the ship and Theodore is forced along with them, regarding the tall, white figures with trepidation. They certainly don't look human. Could they be the result of some kind of genetic experimentation? He scrolls through the list of city-states in his head, trying to think of the least-known one.

Maybe Canberra; who knows what they get up to down there?

But then one of the figures opens its mouth and releases a stream of gibberish and Theodore digs in his heels. "W – what was that?" he gabbles, panicked. "What is it doing?"

Everyone turns to look, puzzled. Even Shariah, who says,

"They just said, 'Welcome,' and to take a seat in the middle when we get inside."

"Wait," Lana stops her. "You understood that?"

Shariah nods.

"But my father didn't....Huh. Interesting. You got it too?" his daughter asks Melia.

"Uh-huh."

"Well, that's really interesting. I figured all of *us* would, but I wasn't sure about techs."

"Wait," Shariah says. "You mean they aren't speaking *English*?" She looks faintly horrified.

The white thing gibbers again.

"But they *are*," she insists. "She just said she's a Plejaran named Ree and not to worry about it right now!"

"And she's right," Lana says smoothly. "We need to get a move on. Let's get on board and I'll explain on the way."

And with that she disappears up the ramp to the ship. Melia, Shariah, and Shays follow, and the white thing directs more yammering at Brophy, who replies conversationally, "Yeah, I guess all of us aren't transentient yet. Is that normal?"

More noises.

"Well, that's good to know."

He takes Theodore's arm, as if to guide him up the ramp, but Theodore balks again.

Is this some kind of practical joke?

But why would Shariah be in on it? There's no way she's had contact with Lana all this time; it's only been a few days since she learned her former best friend was alive. Maybe Melia got to her though. They were gone for a while when they went after Shays; maybe his sister threatened her, forced her

311

into some kind of collusion. Maybe she –

"Do you want me to stun you?" Brophy says, but not in a threatening way, more like he's offering a favor.

And for a brief, painful moment, Theodore considers it: sweet unconsciousness, no more confusion. Maybe when he wakes up all of this will make sense, or even, by some blessed chance, be *over*. He might wake up in his bed in Albakirk, or at the very least in Daniel and Samuel's barn; a little hungover but firmly footed in reality.

Then pride stiffens his spine and he shakes his head no. He's not going to let these ingrates cow him, and especially not his daughter. He can just imagine the look of smug satifaction that the knowledge of him taking an easy out would bring to her face. And not only hers, but Shays' as well. And that, more than anything else, is intolerable.

"All right." Brophy sighs. "Let's do this."

He starts to steer Theodore forward once more, but the Lead SocEn shrugs him off and strides – body erect and head held high – up the ramp to meet whatever waits inside.

SHARIAH FINDS SHE'S HOLDING HER breath as she settles into her seat and straps the harness down. She's still stunned by the fact that a few minutes ago she was apparently conversing with an alien *from another planet* in a completely different language without even realizing it. And she's worried about Theodore, too. As obnoxious as he was earlier she's starting to feel a tiny bit sorry for him; he's looking pretty peaky right about now.

She shoots a swift, worried glance at Melia (for whom she's certain concern for Mr. Timanti remains at a minimum), and Melia pats her hand soothingly. She envies the girl's composure.

How is she not freaking out?

And: Is it possible that this is all some kind of elaborate fake? But that seems unlikely. These ranchos people are dirt farmers. After all the time she's spent among them she can say with certainty that there's no way they could have built a craft like this. Let alone fly one.

She peers around, assessing: all passengers are seated in the center of what appears to be a large, flattened hexagram, while the Plejarans man three equidistant control stations located at three of the interior angles. At least, that's what she assumes their positions represent. There isn't much of the kind of instrumentation that one would expect aboard such a vessel – nothing like the complex mechanisms displayed in the screeners of the Passerine. And nothing's labelled either; there isn't anything that could pass for writing anywhere, even over the doors or on the ship-encompassing transparent band that serves as a window. Everything's very bare.

Still, it all has a distinctly high-tech feel. Even the chair she's sitting on has a slick, almost nanotech-ish sheen. Definitely not something that could have been built by ranchos or expros. But another city-state...

Courtesy of her mother, she's heard plenty about them over the years: What they're up to, where they've been. A few have made it to the Moon, one to Mars (though they never established a colony), and one other (Hafar, she thinks) is supposedly engaged in a bot exploration of Titan. Certainly any one of them has the technology to create a convincing-enough fake alien craft. Somehow though, she feels like anything they would have come up with would be more Passerine-ish, more elaborate, and far less Linear A than this.

And why go to all the trouble? Or, more to the fine point: How? How could some random city-state have put all of this together in advance to show up here, in the ranchos, at the exact right moment to capture her and Theodore, when prior to yesterday evening they themselves had no idea they'd even be out here? Even as late as this afternoon, they hadn't known for sure that they'd be here all night.

Celan could be working with them, true. Or her relatives maybe. But that doesn't explain the fact that she, Shariah, can communicate with them and Mr. Timanti can't. That makes no sense at all. And Celan had seemed genuinely puzzled by it too. There are just too many moving parts for this to all have been planned out in advance.

Occam's razor, Shariah thinks, but this time doesn't laugh.

A vague whir stirs the air and there's a soft press like a palm against her chest. She looks down through the floor-window in time to see the craft lift silently off the ground and, once clear of the treeline, make a perfect right-angle turn and skim forward. Another point in the real-alien theory column: This ship is obviously light-years' more advanced than any-thing possessed by any city-state she's ever heard of.

Shariah licks dry lips, taking comfort in the knowledge that it won't be long until she finds out what's really going on. Because of all the things another city-state might do with them, taking them all to Celan's old house for a nostalgia tour has to be at the absolute bottom of that list. If they're off this ship in less than ten minutes and still in the ranchos when they disembark it will go a long way towards convincing her

314

that, unbelievable as it may be, things are exactly what they seem. These are real aliens, there's a real galactic federation somewhere, and, most mind-bending of all, her troubled former best friend is clearly on good terms with it.

My mother, she thinks, with a touch of real fear, *had better watch out.*

▭ 25 ▭

Celan steps carefully down the ramp and out into the darkness, a little nervous, though the Plejarans' scanners had found nothing human in the near vicinity. There shouldn't be any more interruptions. Still, she's glad she told everyone to wait inside while she made sure the coast was clear. Now that she's actually here, she wants a few minutes alone.

She whisks up another light and points it, solar-torch style, in a slow arc – taking in the rutted dirt track leading up a small rise to the house. They'd set down just below, where the cover was thicker. To be sure no one loses the ship's location, the Plejarans had turned cloaking off after landing. All the ship's outer lights are off though, and the translucent panes let no interior light escape, so as the ramp closes behind her it's rendered practically invisible.

Dirt crunches under her boots as she starts to climb; the track is weedy and eroded in places but easy enough to follow. In her youth she must have walked it a million times.

At the top she pauses, and surveys the yard. It's not as overgrown as she would have expected; though that makes sense seeing as it's mostly composed of sand and rock. A few gnarled trees bow around the perimeter. She stalks past them, noting the ancient fire pit partially filled with trash.

Then, finally, she stops and looks up at the house. The old adobe still stands, though a portion of the left front corner lies in ruins. There are a few marks of graffiti, proving (along with the fire pit trash) that the place has not been completely avoided in the interim years.

The front door yawns open.

Celan shivers. It's been hours since her last fuse; right around sundown and it's getting close to midnight now. While not completely in need she is alone, maybe for the last time until after whatever Ariana has planned happens. Best have a booster now to avoid getting ill at some crucial moment.

She steps up to the threshold and shines the light around inside; the place has been thoroughly looted, even the clunky old woodstove is gone, but it's as good as any for her purpose. She sits down cross-legged, setting the light on her knee, and takes out the transfer. Not *too* much, she doesn't want to appear off to anyone. Mostly E, mixed with some D for energy and alertness, and a tiny pinch of S to help with visualization.

There, she thinks as it hits. *Perfect.*

She sits very still for a few moments, then moves to get to her feet. But a sudden wave of memory fixes her in place: her mother, sweet and lovely, chestnut hair and warm brown eyes, standing in the sunlit kitchen mixing batter in a big red bowl; her stunning sister, Cyrinda, yellow hair flying as she pirouettes around the table, laughing while Taegh, prickly-pear hair falling in his eyes, picks out a tune on his guitar.

Chasing Tanny and Max around the yard, Oso nipping at their heels; listening to her mother and Jillyanne direct the sewing of banners for their booth on fiesta day; sitting at the kitchen table, eating apples and jam and dreaming out the window about how it would be when she was older and could wear a blue robe, and heal all the lost world it seemed.

She couldn't do it then, but as she twists the band on her finger, thinks: *But now I can.*

Maybe not heal the whole world, not entirely, but she can at least defend this corner of it. Protect and defend it from anyone seeking its wanton destruction.

Celan's hand closes fast around the band and now she does stand, stalwart, in the ruined kitchen, holding it to her heart in a silent vow of fealty to the ranchos, the expros, and all those who have been hurt by the malice of one evil woman. For as soon as Ariana Balor attacks, it will all be over; after tonight, no one ever need fear that malice again.

She's going to make sure of that.

LANG'S LONG LEGS CREST THE small hill easily, eyes taking in the dark, empty yard. The moon is almost set but there's still enough light to make out vague shapes of trees, and a house.

Celan's house, he thinks, almost reverently.

And in such an out-of-the way place. It makes sense, though, that the elders would have wanted to keep her mother, the failed elegida expro, as far away from others as possible. His own home in Arqueros was always a hub ‒ neighbors stopping by for this or that, or just to chat.

It must have been lonely here.

True, she'd had her sisters (or one at least, Nola having run off by the time Celan was three). And Jillyanne and her mother; but still...

Lang squints, marking a faint luminesence inside the hulking house. That's where she must be – remembering. Concerns sated, he hunkers down on a large, flat rock. When Celan had asked everyone to wait on the ship he was pretty sure that this was why, so she could have a moment to herself with no one to see if she got upset. But after more than a few moments passed he'd figured it would be wise to get out and make sure she was safe.

But it seems she is.

He tilts his head back to a clear night sky with the wide swath of Milky Way shining like a crown. Funny to think he's spent the last couple hours hanging out with people who just came from there. But the Plejarans are so casual about everything that it feels kind of silly to treat them like gods. When he left they'd been in the middle of giving their passengers an introductory holo presentation about the K'Shiran Convention, with Shariah translating for a still-rattled-looking Theodore.

It *is* weird that a tech girl can understand them. But maybe it's her age that accounts for it, rather than her tech-ness. No one else save Celan's father is over thirty.

That could be it.

The crunch of boots makes him sit up in time to see a shadowy form approaching. Celan still has her witch-light in hand, but it's brightness is nothing compared to that of her eyes.

"Hey," he calls softly, getting to his feet. If she's too fused up maybe he can hold her here for a while; keep her from going back to the ship until she's chilled out a little.

"Lang." She halts a few feet from him, then says, in a normal-sounding tone. "Weren't you all going to wait on the ship?"

"Everyone's still there. But you were gone a while and I got worried."

"Oh."

He clears his throat. "Hey," he says again, "wanna come sit a minute?" He motions towards the rock.

She seems to contemplate this, but whether she's actually considering it or trying to work out his motive for asking he's not sure. Either way, she shakes her head no.

"Not now," she says. "We have work to do."

He shifts his weight. She *seems* fine, but the twin torches that are her eyes tell a different story. That must have been one serious dose she just took. Maybe the fact that she seems so normal is the scariest part.

She moves closer, burning that gaze into his, as if daring him to comment.

He swallows. "If you're sure."

"I am."

"Órale," he says lightly. "Let's go then."

The familiar expression takes the charge out of the air.

Celan grins. "Vamos," she says. "But not aviados. Or at least, not until this is all over."

Lang chuckles weakly and takes her hand; together they head back down the path to the ship.

It's OK, he thinks, giving her what he hopes is a reassuring squeeze, even though right now he's the one who could probably use it more.

It's all OK, he tells himself. *Even when it's not.*

26

"This is really where you grew up," Shariah murmurs, eyes roaming out past their small spur of Pescados to the mountains rising blackly beyond. Beside her, Celan makes a small noise of affirmation. It's deep night now, but as yet all is still save for the rustle of brush and the soft hoots of night birds. Shariah rubs her bare arms against the chill and shakes her head wonderingly. For of all the impossible things she's been fed today this is somehow the most difficult to swallow: That her friend, her *best* friend, the straight-laced, sensible tech girl that she'd known all those years had, in fact, been a chimera. A cuckoo in the nest.

But not of her own choosing.

Because, apparently, it had all been Theodore's design. He'd wanted to use his daughter as an *example*. Shariah rubs more vigorously, hunching her shoulders up almost to her ears.

Across the yard, the rest of their crew is ringed around

323

the fire pit. Due to the screen of trees and hump of hill that hide the yard from prying eyes, a small blaze had been deemed safe to light. It had given them something to do as well – clearing the pit and gathering up deadfall – something to ward off the growing sense of unease that's cast a pall over them all.

"And you really had no contact with the city?"

"No," Celan says. "I told you. I came there when I was eleven. My father found me, wandering around in the ruins after the old Arlo's burned down."

Shariah winces. She remembers it now, or remembers hearing about it: the tragedy at the original Arlo's wayvern – seventy-nine tech lives lost, along with countless expros. Her mother had been grim but stoic on the subject, hoping that it would serve as a wake-up call to everyone about the dangers of Transway. Her mother –

A horrible thought occurs, but she pushes it away.

"Did you know anyone?" she asks instead. "Anyone who died?"

"My sister," Celan says shortly. "Well, not immediately but it wasn't long after. Her man Taegh died too, in the fire; him and most of their friends."

Shariah scuffs a sandal in the dirt, hoping the same horrible thought hasn't occurred to the girl beside her.

"I'm sorry," she says.

Celan nods again; but her face is shut like a door. It's impossible to tell what she's thinking. Then: "You look cold," she says. "Go sit by the fire."

Shariah knows when she's being dismissed. She scuttles toward the warmth equal parts scared and relieved. Scared because she's afraid of what Celan might do if she suspected,

324

if she knew...but there's no proof that Ariana Balor had anything to do with a wayvern that burned down almost a decade ago. The fire had been investigated and declared an accident. And all those techs died too. She would never –

But she did, a small voice insists, *or at least she was* willing *to; she put us all in danger with what she did after the bot release failed.*

Shariah plunks down next to Melia on one of the big logs serving as benches and stares mutely into the flames.

"Is fire the same color on your planet?" Brophy is saying to the Plejarans. "Or do you even have it there?"

She rolls her eyes. He's been asking question after question since the presentation earlier, like a five-year-old: 'Dad, why is the sky blue?' It was cute at first, but now it's starting to grate.

But the Plejarans don't seem to mind. Ness nods pleasantly from his place on the far side of the firepit, where he and the other two stand in a small huddle.

"Yes," he says pleasantly. "We're BCOs like yourselves; our home world has plenty of free oxygen. A bit more than yours, actually. Our fires tend to run a bit blue."

"Huh," Brophy says. "So it's probably good Celan's doing that one. You've got wind, and water, and earthquakes and all that though?"

"Not so much of earthquakes," Ness says. "But we've studied the mechanics."

"And we have *plenty* of wind and rain," adds Ree.

All three gurgle-laugh, like this is some kind of running weather joke on wherever-it-is-they're-from.

Shariah casts a swift glance at Theodore. He still looks

perturbed, but better for being back on solid ground. He still claims that everything they say sounds like someone about to be sick.

No wonder he's so stressed out.

Well, that and the fact that his hands are still tied. But there's no way she can release him with everyone else around, and after all she's learned in the past few hours she's not really sure she wants to.

In a way, he's as bad as her mother. Both talking a good game about Unity and Clarity and the rest of the social precedents, all the while sneaking around behind everyone's backs with private schemes and experiments, not caring who gets in the way or how anyone else might be affected.

'Absolute power corrupts absolutely,' the old saw says. But the Lead SocEns aren't supposed to have absolute power; that's why there are three of them. That's why all the Leads from all disciplines vote on all major decisions. That's why there are recs and views – people aren't supposed to get away with these kinds of things!

Her fists clench in righteous indignation, until a new, more insidious thought occurs: The fact that she's sitting here in the ranchos instead of home in bed means that when it came down to it she was willing to sneak and scheme with the best of them.

But I'm trying to save people's lives.

Which is probably, in one way or another, how Theodore and her mother saw their actions as well.

She bows her head and covers her face with her hands, too confused to cry. Then Melia pats her gently between the shoulders and a few stubborn tears do manage to squeak out.

Angrily, she wipes them away. But before she can sink any further into despair a shout from across the yard brings her head up fast.

Lang and Brophy are already on their feet, and everyone else is craning their necks in the direction of what are clearly voices – Celan's and someone else's – arguing. The voices get louder and closer, and the two men rush forward as Celan appears out the darkness, harried by a wiry, ginger-haired woman with whom she appears to be on somewhat familiar terms.

"You see?" Celan is telling her. "There's no need to alert anyone. We have everything under control."

The woman takes them in, Plejarans and all, looking completely unruffled. She's clad in well-worn homespun pants and a vest, with a large bow strapped across her back; and seems older than everyone except maybe Theodore, with a hard-bitten edge to her.

"You the aliens?" she barks at Chan, Ness, and Ree.

"Yes," Chan says politely. "And you are?"

"Lena. This one," the woman jerks her chin at Celan, "says you're here to help stop the attack."

"We are."

"Well then you're going to have to come with me."

"You don't have to – " Celan starts, but Lena bowls right over her.

"There's an elder and a couple elegidos down by the ponds," she says, "who need to be informed immediately of any unusual activity tonight." There's a quick flash of humor in her eyes. "And I'd say this qualifies as such."

"We don't have time!" Celan counters. "It could all go down any minute. We need to stay here."

Lena shrugs. "Stay if you want to; it's your house. But the rest of you still have to come with me."

She's clearly used to being obeyed, but it seems that where their group is concerned, Celan's authority holds sway. A few uneasy moments pass and nobody moves.

Lena takes a step backwards. "Fine. I'll bring them here."

"No!" Celan yells, as Brophy brings the stun up.

He aims and fires, but the ginger woman is faster - with preternatural reflex she yanks Lang in front of her and he drops like a sack of bricks. With that as a distraction, she vanishes into the night. Brophy lunges after her as Celan kneels beside the fallen, checking for injury.

"He's OK," she says finally, pillowing her cape under his head. "He'll be fine."

She straightens, meeting everyone's eyes as if to dare them to claim otherwise. But for the first time that evening, Shariah sees a flicker of uncertainty flit across her former best friend's face. She makes a soft, attention-getting sound.

"What?" Celan snaps.

"Just curious," Shariah says. "Why you don't want any of them to help."

Celan shifts her weigh to one hip and crosses arms in front of her chest. "Well, they don't have quantum bands, for one," she says. "And they're just going to complicate things. There's not enough time to explain."

"So what do we do? Find another place to wait?"

"It's too late. If we move now we might miss the attack."

"So what –"

Brophy returns then, huffing. "She's gone," he tells Celan. "Couldn't find her anywhere." He looks down at Lang. "Sorry about that."

"It's not your fault," she says. "You tried."

"How long before – "

"It's about ten minutes from here to the ponds, but Lena's fast. Depending on who the other three are it could be twenty or thirty until they get here."

"Do you *know* her? Lena, I mean," Brophy asks.

Celan nods. "She used to be my guardian, sort of – she and Jillyanne have been together for years. She must have been on watch or something."

"Let's go back to the ship," Brophy suggests. "Put on the cloaking."

This sounds entirely reasonable to Shariah, but to her surprise, Celan shakes her head no.

"I think...." she says slowly. "That it's better to be outside."

"So we just *wait*?" Brophy says.

"Why not?" Celan says, voice carefully light. "At this point, we're getting pretty good at it."

But the grin she gives them looks grim, and in her tone Shariah thinks she can detect a distinct and worrying note of strain.

▭▸ 27 ◂▭

Celan's ears are alert for the sound of footsteps as she licks her lips, willing herself to calm. Chan, Ness, and Ree are in formation around her, and Brophy's crouched behind a boulder, stun at the ready in case anyone tries to crash the party. But the fire's been smothered and their group has deserted the yard for the trees. Hopefully, that will be enough to convince Lena and company to look elsewhere. She just wishes Lang would wake up; he's been dragged out of sight and propped against a nearby tree.

It must be fifteen minutes at least, she tells herself. *He'll wake up soon.*

She should be concentrating, meditating like she was earlier, stretching out her senses to perceive even the slightest hint of disturbance. Of flame. Because she's positive that that's how Ariana's going to do it: What could be easier, in the late-summer dryness? What could be sure to leave no trace? And, as long as it poses no threat to them, who in

Albakirk will ever bother to investigate?

A muscles twitches in her left cheek. She's not sure she can take much more of this: Knowing something is coming, but not knowing exactly where or when. But then a new thought occurs, and she smothers a laugh at its perfect absurdity:

Maybe, after all of this, nothing's even going to happen.

Maybe Ariana realized her daughter had gone missing; maybe she tracked her here. Maybe she's called the whole thing off. They'll wait up all night like idiots, like little kids on some twisted Navidad Eve.

She rolls her shoulders, smiling in the dark.

Then a whoosh in the air, like the draft of a thunderstorm, makes the hairs on the back of her neck stand up. Maybe she was wrong; maybe it will be a flood instead.

Then Brophy yells, "Fire!"

One minute she's staring into blackness, and the next the whole world is ablaze.

Celan closes her eyes, reaching out, feeling the element; it's everywhere, hungry, seeking to devour everything and everyone she loves. She tries tamping it, cutting off oxygen, and finds she's gasping for air as well.

She senses the Plejarans around her, following her lead, lending the strength of their bands to hers.

If the XïNeruans could erase *each other,* she thinks grimly, *We can surely put out a fire.*

There are voices, shouting, and sounds of running feet – and a jolt of memory, swift and strong, of being young and helpless, of running and screaming, heart pounding as she searched the crowd on Transway for Cyrinda and Taegh; the litany in her brain:

They'll be out here; they'll be out here. I know they'll be out here.
Fire. Arlo's. *Ariana.*

And suddenly it all comes together, in a rush of rage so vast and visceral she feels like she could set fire to the entire world. Then it's easy: She's one with it, herself a flame. It's hers to command, and she can do whatever she wants with it. Her vision is a wall of red, but instinctually she knows which way to turn – towards the city, towards Ariana Balor.

Slowly, she turns. Slowly, she raises her arms and spreads them wide.

But louder than the roar there's a voice, urgent.

Lang's voice, like a shock of cold water.

"Celan, *don't.*"

And she can see now, the city burned to the ground, glass pyramids twisted and melted, bodies charred and blackened... and beyond that the Plejaran ship leaving, never to return.

The fire goes out.

She sways for a moment, ringed by stunned faces – the group, the Plejarans, and a flash of ginger hair, swirls of white robe and blue – in a rain of ash, before her legs give way and it all fades to black.

THERE'S A MOMENT OF UTTER silence, then everyone starts yelling at once. Darkness has again descended and all is confusion until the Plejarans each conjure up a light. Then Theodore can see – Shays is on the ground, huddled over a smoking form. He stumbles forward until he's at the man's side.

"Is she...?" he says, voice a horrified croak. Every inch of his daughter's skin is livid with red weals and blisters, white hair blackened and burned, save for a small ring at the crown of her head. In that moment she looks absolutely alien.

Shays says nothing.

"Is she...?" Theodore says again. He can't say the word, can't even think it.

After all of this, she cannot be gone.

She *cannot*.

But Shays doesn't answer, he appears to be in some sort of trance. Carefully, he places one large hand over Celan's heart and lifts his chin up, eyes closed. He draws a deep, deep breath and holds it for what seems like an age of the world. When he exhales, the horrible burns are beginning to fade: blisters evaporating like morning dew, the redness soothing back to smooth, unblemished skin.

Finally, Theodore sees his daughter's chest rise – rise and fall, rise and fall – several miraculous times.

"She's alive," Shays rasps. Then he crumples, draping himself over her unconscious form, shoulders hitched with big, wracking sobs like he might tear himself to pieces.

Theodore reaches out his still-bound hands and places them atop the man's head, like a benediction.

"Thank you," he says.

☞ 28 ☜

Mara wakes to motes of sunlight and shadows of leaves dancing on the far wall. She watches them, uncomprehending, for what seems like a long time before it hits her: She's in an unfamiliar bed, in an unfamiliar room, and she has no idea what day or time it is.

Maddy, she thinks, with a stomach-drop of shock, *that bitch was gonna take over!*

She tries to sit up, but the room tilts dangerously and she falls back against the pillows, heart hammering and head throbbing dully. She opens her mouth to yell, to alert somebody, but her throat is too dry. Only a faint croak comes out. And it may be too late anyway: Maddy had given her twenty-four hours to make a decision and that would have been the next morning. From the angle of the sun through the window it looks like late afternoon. Unless it's only been a few hours, she's sunk. And she suspects it's been a lot longer than that.

Stupid, stupid, she chides herself. *Now everything's ruined.*

And the bitterest part is that she'd tried so hard to make this place a good place, not some skanky ghost of Transway. But it'll be Maddy's show now, hers and that horrible psycho-healer's.

She can't do it. She *won't.* Won't cook and clean and kow-tow to those motherfuckers. She'll take whoever's willing to risk it and start over, make a new camp somewhere else. And Maddy can't stop her.

Jaw clenched, she throws the covers off and swings her legs over the side of the bed where she teeters for a moment, fighting another wave of dizzyness, as the door creaks open and a short, plump woman bustles in with a tray. When she sees Mara, she lets out a startled squeak and parks her burden atop a dresser.

"Mijita!"the woman says, rushing over to her, "don't try to get up. You need to rest."

And suddenly the pieces snap together: The woman is Lavinia, Zeeb's mother. This must be her bedroom.

"Vinni!" Mara says. "Que pas'? What day is it? What's happening?"

"No te molestes," Lavinia says soothingly, soft hands eas-ing her back into bed.

"But Maddy!" Mara pleads. "What happened with *Maddy*?"

"Maddy?" Lavinia sniffs. "Que nada. Same as always. No better than she should be."

"You mean she hasn't...taken over," Mara whispers this last.

Dark brows knit. "Taken over what? The camp? Of course not! She made some noise for a minute, but when Langton came back they chased out that Sonrisa girl and set it all to right. Did you know that that house boy of hers was actually a tech in disguise? Imagine!" She shakes her head, clucking.

Mara nods. She did know that. Maddy had told her. But then how does Vinni know? And if Franky really is Frank Martinez, how long before the techs swoop in here and –

She halts that train of thought: there are more important matters at stake. Because if Lang is back then it means that someone else probably is too.

"So is...?" she trails off, picking at the coverlet.

Lavinia smiles. "Brophy's here. And they brought some others along: That girl who was in space, and her tech father, and some strange pale folk, but decent enough I guess."

Mara considers this: Celan must be the space girl. And if her father is here that would explain how Franky was recognized.

But pale folk? Could she mean white robes from the ranchos? Elders?

"How long have I been out?"

"A couple days. Not long."

A couple *days*. Thank Madre she'd had backup, albeit unlooked for.

There comes a soft knock on the door, and a voice: "Vin? Está bien?"

Brophy. Mara sucks in a breath.

"Everything's fine," Lavinia calls. Then, to Mara with a small grin: "I'll leave you two alone."

The woman exits, though not before depositing the contents of the tray on the nightstand. There's a pitcher of water, a stack of tortillas, and a small pot of honey. One whiff and Mara realizes she's famished. And *thirsty* – she chugs down half the pitcher and is spreading honey on a tortilla with a spoon when a heavy tread echoes on the wooden floor.

"Mara," Brophy says, closing the door behind him.

But she waits a few more seconds, rolling her snack into a long cylinder, before looking up.

"Hey," she says casually, "que pas'?"

She takes a big bite, chews, and swallows, watching his face.

His solemn mien cracks into a tentative smile. "Looks like you're feeling better."

She gives him a quick, one-shouldered shrug. "You know me."

"Yeah," he says. "I do. Scooch over."

She does, and the bed creaks as he sits down on the edge. Close enough to touch, but she doesn't reach for him. Instead, she puts her snack down on the plate beside its unhoneyed fellows and brushes off her hands.

"I'm sorry," she says briskly. "OK? For *some* of the things I said. But between Jas and Maddy and everything, I just – "

"It's OK," Brophy says quickly. "It's not your fault. I should have – "

But he falters, like he can't quite finish the thought. Instead he wraps strong arms around her and pulls her close. She stiffens, resisting, until his familiar resiny scent envelops her and she sinks fully into the embrace, closing her eyes and feeling small and safe for the first time in a while. Eons pass as they breathe each other in, then Mara's stomach pangs and she pulls away, reaching for more food.

Brophy watches happily as she chews.

"So what happened?" she says around a mouthful. "Vinni

338

said Celan's back? And she brought elders with her?"

He chuckles. "Not exactly."

And then he tells her the whole story: About the trip to the ranchos, and the Plejarans, and the attack, and Celan nearly burning herself to death. And how after it was all over the Plejarans flew him and Lang up here immediately to straighten out the whole Sonrisa thing. But no one was ready to split up just yet, so Celan's father, her tech friend, Shariah, and Lang's sister came along too. And then Franky turned out to be a Lead SocEn in hiding, who, in exchange for a guaranteed return trip to Rinconada, had promised to divulge information that would clear Celan and Lang's names once and for all. So now the techs are on their way back to Albakirk (along with video testimony from Celan and Lang about the events of Ord 66) to take down Ariana Balor once and for all.

"Wow," Mara says faintly, when he finally pauses for breath. "That's...a lot."

"No shit."

"And there are really aliens here? Right now? At Rinconada?"

"Uh-huh. Chan, Ness, and Ree are gonna stick around for a little while. For as long as the wormholes are stable."

"Claro," she says, hitting a note so wry that Brophy guffaws.

She laughs a little too, then their eyes meet and they both sigh.

"You know, I really do love – " he starts.

She holds up a hand. "But you love *him* too."

Brophy's handsome face falls and his gold-brown eyes flick to the play of light and shadow on the wall. "Not like it matters," he finally says.

"It does though."

"Nothing's ever going to happen."

"That's not the point."

A pause. "I know."

She swallows. "So where does that leave us?"

"Anywhere you want I guess."

She gives him a narrow look. It's not fair to make her be the one to have to choose. But then, she's always been the one in charge before. Maybe she doesn't have make up her mind this second though. Maybe, for once, she can drift a little first. So she reaches to embrace Brophy, but instead of sinking deep she keeps her eyes open, looking past him and out through the open window.

We shall see, she thinks.

29

"**M**s. Balor? They're ready for you now."

"Affirmative," she replies, "On the way."

The clipped voice on her server cuts out and she rises from the bench by the fountain, wincing internally. Beside her, Bryan rises too.

"Want me to walk you over?"

Shariah shakes her head. Part of her wants to grasp at every last shred of comfort before this final curtain falls. But it's better to have a few minutes alone. In the end, that is how she will have to face it.

It's the final day of the tribunal held by the council of Lead SocEn emeritii, where the matter of the events of Ord 63 (now 66) and the more recent "unsanctioned and unconscionable" acts of Ariana Balor will be formally resolved.

They've been watching the public testimony all morning. Mr. Martinez admitted to intentionally botching the

Pollomax release in a calculated attempt to subvert the out-
come of the resource vote of Ord 60, 2217 and prevent the
destruction of Transway. But exactly how he did it remains
a mystery; he refuses to disclose that information or name
any of his co-conspirators (though surely he must have had
some). For his crimes, he will be formally Destierra'd, but in
truth that's just a formality. Shariah knows that Rinconada's
astral team will secretly track the rollers and return him there
after he's dropped off. Say what you like about expros; they
take care of their own.

Part of Shariah wishes she was headed back with him. It's
peaceful by the river, plus there's the added bonus of being able
to fully relax among those who know the whole story – the
real one. Because as much chaos as her and Theodore's return
(with Martinez in tow) had caused, it would have been orders
of magnitude worse if they'd revealed everything. The official
story is that Shariah got wind of her mother's plot to destroy
the ranchos, became alarmed at the senseless loss of life, and
enlisted the help of Mr. Timanti. Then they'd personally alert-
ed the ranchos population and thwarted the attack.

In the process, they'd had a surprise run-in with Lana Timanti and Langton Shays, who were in the ranchos for a visit.
The pair had miraculously survived their individual Destierras
and were living in various refugee camps, one of which had
also been home to a certain former Lead SocEn, whom they'd
begged to come forward and absolve them. They desperately
wanted to prove their innocence, but had no recourse to do so,
being cut off from the city and terrified of anyone discovering
their continued existance. But the unprovoked attack on the
ranchos, witnessed by Theodore and Shariah, and the addition
of Martinez's testimony, had finally given them the means to

tell their side of the story.

Their vid had been played earlier today, to universal shock and awe.

Seriously, Shariah thinks, with a swift glance around the packed plaza, *you could have heard a stylus drop in here.*

Everywhere her eye falls though, people actively avoid it. Irony of ironies, but she really should be used to it by now. What could anyone possibly have to say to the ex-best friend of ex-evil rogue Lana turned daughter of a soon-to-be-deposed Lead SocEn?

Her mother's words: 'Don't ever blame yourself for whatever idiocies those around you fall into.'

Thanks, mom. I'll keep that in mind.

At the last moment before she turns to go, Shariah hooks her arm through Bryan's. Maybe she could use a little moral support after all. This will be the first time since her return that she's going to see her mother in person.

She has spoken speak briefly to her father, who, when faced with a preponderance of evidence had admitted his role in the cover up and the three-day reset. In some ways, that was almost worse than having to testify against her mother – to see Nathan Balor so diminished and know that he will remain on house arrest for the rest of his life.

She's still not sure what they're going to do with her mother. That the Pollomax plug-in turned out to have been viable after all is now far beside the fact. But maybe the knowledge will be a comfort to her when she's being sentenced for fraud, attempted murder, and genocide.

Shariah sighs.

The crowd parts silently as she and Bryan make their way across the plaza. He's been a rock throughout this whole ordeal; safe in his arms at night she can drop the dignified veneer and just fall apart. Even he doesn't know the whole story, but he's the only one she's told about the Plejarans, guessing that if anyone could appreciate that particular bit of insanity it'd be him.

She had not been disappointed.

He's dying to talk to Lana, and to Lang (with whom he's oddly fascinated), and he's made her swear that when the Plejarans return she'll bring him along to meet them. They have to be careful, though, inside the city, so they've developed bywords to make these discussions sound like they're talking about some obscure old-world screener. No one's going to find their sudden mutual obsession with *The Chronicles of Astrum* suspicious in the least. Not for a former Chronie and his freakshow girlfriend.

Emerging from a sea of faces, they enter a hushed hallway, burnished almost painfully white. Two SocTechs stand at the far end, stuns in hand, flanking a closed door. There's really no reason for them to be there, no one's going to make any mad dashes in or out of the chamber, but she supposes it lends a bit of theater to the proceedings, which is all any of this is anyway.

Shariah bites her lip, momentarily ashamed of her newborn cynicism, but the fact is that for such a grand and formal inquiry designed to expose the truth, so much of what she's going to say will be a lie. Not about her mother's role in things, Ariana Balor needs no help damning herself with her own actions. But there are other things that will never be fully revealed. Not necessarily the big things, like the existance of the Plejarans and the K'Shiran Convention – she and Theodore (and Martinez) had agreed to leave that entire matter out for now on the grounds that it would only sow fear and confusion in the city.

It's the little lies, and especially the lies of omission, that prick at her conscience. In the private testimony leading up to today's, she'd said nothing about Celan growing up as an expro and Mr. Timanti's role in bringing her to the city; and, more recently, of his role in his daughter's survival of the Destierra.

He hadn't tried to bully her or swear her to secrecy, she could have said all that and more. And it seems like he almost expected it. Every time she's seen him lately, his shoulders have been hunched in the posture of a man braced for a blow. In the end it had been her decision, and hers alone, to leave him out of it, to let him live out his term as Lead SocEn, and even, a little bit, to let him play the hero.

And she's not exactly sure why.

Maybe it's a way to help the city heal, to preserve continuity and allow at least one of that ill-fated triumvirate to emerge untainted. Maybe it's in silent acknowledgment of all the man's lost in life.

Maybe it's just a final fuck-you to her mother.

But she is aware, very accutely so, that by choosing this she is acting akin: Making unilateral decisions, sneaking and scheming behind the scenes, covering things up. All for the greater good, of course. But that's what they all say.

It's the best she can do though; the best that she has to offer. So it will have to be enough.

She and Bryan halt in front of the two ridiculous guards and he releases her, though not without a steadying hug and

345

a soft, sweet kiss.

"I'll be here when you're done," he says.

"I know," Shariah says, and turns, giving the guards a brief nod. Then the door whooshes open, and she steps through it.

⊃► 30 ◄⊂

There's the faintest tint of gold on the cottonwood leaves. Not quite autumn yet, but moving in that direction. Lang's arm rests comfortably around Celan's shoulders as they shuffle along the path towards their favorite spot by the river. Not the fuser cave; he'll never set foot in that accursed place again. But there's a nice bench parked right before the path disappears around the big hump of hill. It gets really nice sun this time of morning.

A good place to sit, and just breathe.

They've both been a bit fragile since the attack at Pescados, which luckily didn't spread ranchos-wide. Ariana's fire-starting nanodrones had been positioned at various strategic locations, but their ignition timing was chained somehow, and when the girl in his arms stopped the ones at Pescados she'd stopped them all.

They settle on the bench gratefully; the slatted wood

seat is new but the rest is an ancient iron thing left over from the old world, patched with rust but still intact. As they cuddle up, he forcibly resists the urge to ruffle the silvery fuzz atop her head. While vanity has never been one of Celan's vices, the loss of her hair remains a sore point. But it is slowly growing back; at her request he's been transing it nightly to expedite the process.

"Three more days," she says, picking at a cuticle.

"Yeah."

He knows she doesn't want to go – back to the ranchos, and the elders, and whatever Class E cura they have in store for the two of them. But she'll do it. Despite her distrust of ranchos hierarchy, she'd been shaken enough by the events of the attack that she had agreed to at least give it a try. The fact that the Plejarans weren't going to let her return to the K'Shiran Convention until she "adjusted her medication" had served as a convincer as well.

But no one save he and Celan knows the real truth of the matter: that it is only due to his own actions that day that the Madren race still has a place there at all. Everyone saw her burn, but no one knew what she'd been about to do with the fire. Maybe the Plejarans do, though if so they haven't said a word.

It all happened so fast anyway – he'd come to from the stun just as the world lit up around him. There had been no time to think about the best way to handle things, or whether Celan would be mad; he just knew he had to stop her, to put the fire out. And so he had.

"Maybe it won't be that bad," he says now. "Maybe we'll end up becoming elegidos or something."

A snort. "Yeah. Right."

"Stranger things have happened," he says, which earns him a chuckle at least.

Lang closes his eyes and tips his head back, a small smile blooming on his lips; the press of sun on his face like a warm blanket. Celan's not the only one reluctant to give up the comforts of Class E. They've been taking a bit of advantage of their last days of freedom. Not that they're fused up twenty-four/seven, but there hasn't been much motivation to moderate, other than the occasional hairy eyeball from Melia. She's stuck around Rinconada to guarantee that he won't try to weasel out of anything.

Not that he *would*.

He wants to see Va'anak and XĭNeru and meet Wehoo and the WDM,K*DU and all the other crazy things Celan talks about. And lack of weaseling is a prerequisite to that.

Things will be very different when they return to the Convention, though – the Plejarans have seen to that. After allowing the Madrens some time to "sort things out amongst themselves," as Ness put it, the next wormhole cycle will see a select contingent of Madrens transported there, with representatives from all transentient enclaves. Who exactly that will include remains to be seen, but Chan, Ness, and Ree had made it very clear that they expect Celan to be among that number.

So she can play that card when the time comes, but she will still have to prove herself healthy enough to travel. Hopefully, the elders know what they are doing, and both of them will have a chance to get better.

He shudders then, thinking on Jaslene. It's going to be a long time before the wounds of Rinconada heal. The elegida who's coming to take care of the camp in his stead (*not* Carlos, but a woman called Rosie who was at Pescados and witnessed the attack) should help to facilitate that. Meanwhile, he's been keepng a low profile, staying especially out of Gabe's way.

Still, he wishes –

"It's not your fault," Celan murmurs, like she can read his mind.

She's heard the whole story and has been steadfast in her conviction that Sonrisa was the only real culprit in the tragedy. It's balm to his soul to know how well she champions him, but deep down he still feels that the responsibility for Jaslene's death rests squarely on his shoulders.

Lang swallows hard against the lump in his throat.

"Hey," Celan says, shading her eyes with one hand as she squints up at him. "Is Shariah coming up again before we leave? I really wanted to talk to her."

Nice job changing the subject.

"No sé. Seems like things're pretty heavy in Albakirk right now."

"I feel bad," Celan says. Her hand drops to her lap, where it fidgets with the quantum band. "It's got to be hard on her. She was always so close to her mother."

"Too bad her mother is pure evil."

"Claro," she says. "There's that."

"Imagine that bitch's face if she ever found out her perfect daughter actually took transferon."

"That would probably be worse than anything, even being deposed as Lead SocEn." She frowns. "But it freaked Shariah out. I could tell. She didn't mean to take any; it wasn't her fault."

"Well it wasn't Brophy's either," Lang says, defensive. "It's not like he forced it on her. He had a little in his water bag; he couldn't have known she was going to drink it. And it was barely anything anyway. I doubt she even felt it."

"It made her understand the Plejarans."

"But that was *helpful*."

"Quizás. But I think she's a little scared now. That she could maybe end up like – "

"Us?" he finishes. "Please. There's no way. She needs to calm down."

"It's scary to techs though," Celan counters. "My father wouldn't take any, even once he knew it would it help him communicate with them. And I know he had a million questions."

"He had his buddy Franky to translate."

"Ha," she says. Then: "Martinez was always kind of a closet freak."

"Freakier than us even."

"And *he* doesn't have to go see the elders now."

They both laugh, but there's a catch in it.

"So," she says, pivoting again. "Speaking of Brophy..."

Lang winces. *This again.*

"Can we not?"

"Why?" she says, gaze earnest. "Chan noticed it right away. I thought he was kidding at first but after you told me about you guys it actually started to make sense."

"There is no 'you guys'; it was one kiss," Lang says. "Not a whole big thing."

"But you have feelings for each other. I can tell."

"Sure. I love Brophy. As a *friend*."

She gives him a measuring look out of the corner of her

eye, like she doesn't quite believe him.

"You know I love you," he says.

"I know. But that doesn't mean you can't love Brophy too."

"But it's not – I mean, we're not – " He halts, struggling for words.

Does he love Brophy? Maybe. But not in the same way as he does Celan. She's like a goddess, and Brophy is...Brophy. And after all the drama that went on with Mara the last thing he wants to do is to stir up a similar situation with Celan. Though truth be told he has thought about that kiss. A lot.

But he and Brophy still haven't talked about it. And now that he's back with Mara nothing else will ever –

"Just so you know it's an option," Celan adds.

Lang sighs, and plants a kiss on the top of her head.

A SUDDEN GUST RUSTLES THE leaves on the trees, hinting once more at summer's end. Celan snuggles closer to Lang and grins to herself.

Madrens and their binary relationships.

The last thing any of them needs right now is to be embroiled in some tragic love triangle. A triune would make things so much simpler, but it may take some time for the boys to come around to the idea. They'll probably worry that she'll get jealous or angry; but she won't. She's spent enough time with Chan, Ness, and Ree to believe that such an arrangement is workable. And infinitely preferable to the kind of mess that, from what Lang has told her, occurred between him, Brophy, and Mara and had terrible repercussions for everybody.

Of course, theirs wouldn't be exactly like a Plejaran triune – she has no desire for any intimacy with Brophy and is pretty sure the feeling is mutual – but she's sure they could figure something out.

And it's really just a matter of time. Because although Brophy and Mara are officially back together, it's pretty obvious (to her at least) that it's not going to last. They're both so careful with each other now, almost formal. She's positive that by the time she and Lang return from the ranchos those two will be officially done. And then...

The ranchos.

Celan's jaw clenches at the thought. Putting herself in the clutches of the elders is as distateful an idea as she can imagine. But she promised Lang she'd do it, and she knows he's counting on it. It's silly though, this whole *penance* he wants to do. In her mind, it's clear: He needed medicine. They deprived him of it. So he got it some other way and terrible things happened. It's not his fault.

Yes, they're going to have to cut down on fusing, but there has to be a better way. So, just in case the elders don't actually have the kind of spiritual panacea they claim to, she's been formulating some ideas about what that better way might be:

Some kind of monitoring device that steps us down slowly, while still allowing for the occasional fuse.

A bracelet of some kind, something tasteful, maybe with a stone that changes color when they're free to fuse. Most of the time it could be red, and the device could prevent any kind of exogenous fuses from effecting their systems. It could provide a steady enough dosage to keep them well, stepping them down by nano-increments so there wouldn't be any kind of noticeable side effects.

But once every (week? month? – she still hasn't decided on that part yet) it would give the wearer leave to fuse again, if only for a twenty-four hour period.

That is a good solution – no muss, no fuss, and no endless moaning and rehashing the past. One of the Convention's MedAIs could probably whip something like it up in no time, without any white robes hovering around pretending they actually give a fuck about anything other than keeping her (and Lang) under their thumbs.

She twists the quantum band in growing agitation until Lang clears his throat.

"So they're really not going to do anything?" he says. "The techs, I mean, with the Plejarans? It's so weird that with all their technology they're just going to completely pass on the chance to talk to a whole galactic federation."

This snaps Celan out of her funk. "They can't," she says. "I agree with my father and Shariah on that. They can't say anything, at least for a good long while. The whole transentience thing...it would cause total chaos, especially after all the shakeups they've just had. And it's not like we're going to use the Convention to do anything bad to them." She shrugs. "Besides, I think my father's still set on Mars."

"Mars!" He scoffs. "They could go to Alpha Centauri."

"Maybe they need to do it their own way, in their own time."

"Maybe."

She shifts on the bench, trying to shake the unwelcome intrusion of her father into her thoughts. She's not angry with him, not anymore, and he doesn't seem to be with her either. They've managed to reach a kind of détente; both respectful, cordial even. But the easy familiarity they once enjoyed seems as remote as Va'anak these days. In truth, he seems terrified of her.

She sighs.

All she'd wanted to do was prove herself worthy, show him that she wasn't a complete failure, and teach him a little lesson – not to completely cow the man. But it's not like they're going to be seeing that much of each other anyway.

She sighs again, but then a brighter thought occurs and she laughs aloud.

"What?" Lang says.

"Bryan and his friends," she says, still chuckling. "Shariah's going to give them a whole new conspiracy theory!"

"It's not a theory though," he points out, "if it's true."

She grins up at him. "But that's exactly it: This time they won't be trying to figure out the conspiracy. This time they'll *be* it. Imagine a whole little secret cabal of MechEns sneaking off to the K'Shiran Convention, while everyone else is messing around on Mars."

"But to do that they'd have to take transferon. I thought you said the techs were terrified of it."

"Most of them are. But if there's anyone who'd be willing to try it, my chits are on Bryan and his friends."

Lang snorts. "Perfect. They'll all be trying to start, while we're busy trying to stop."

"Yeah," she says, a knife edge to her tone. "Won't that be something?"

"Well," he says.

She waits, but he adds nothing more.

Celan rests her head on Lang's shoulder and feels his breath in her hair. Above, the blue sky arches, and the wind soughs over the water. They watch the sparks of sunlight, playing patterns on the river.

The Precepts

One Every living thing is imbued with the power of the Universe, which is love

Two The combined sum of that power is greater than the will of any individual person

Three When we face difficulties, we must always search for the answer in love, and in accordance with the Universal will

Four Unless it would do more harm than good, we must always tell the truth

Five We must always take responsibility for our words and actions

Six If we harm another, either intentionally or by accident, we must make amends and realign ourselves with the Universal will

Seven We must seek peace and moderation in all things

Eight We must strive to help others and contribute to the community

Nine We must, above all, be kind

Author's Note

This series has been a long road; never could I have imagined in January 2009 that I would be finishing it in 2021. It's a whole new world, in more ways than one.

To everyone who has aided and abetted along the way, thank you.

Most of all, I thank the state of New Mexico for eighteen years (give or take a few) of being home. Gracias por todo.